SCRIBE

OF

ASTERIA

BY E. M. MEYERS

CELESTIAL PHOENIX PRESS

Book cover by Kim Cavrak at spiritofebullience.com

Illustrations by Anastasia Campo

Editor Heather Hudec at simplyspellboundedits.com

Library of Congress Cataloguing-in-Publication has been applied for.

Copyright registration has been filed for this literary work with the U. S. copyright office

First Edition 2025

Books by E. M. Meyers

<u>Legend of the Serathena Series</u>
Ink of Copper (book 1)
Out now on all major retailers

Quill of Leather (book 2)
Coming May 2025

<u>Standalones in the world of the Serathena</u>
Scribe of Asteria
Out now on all major retailers

Want to purchase signed paperbacks with swag?

Dedication

To every woman who has felt invisible
To the ones who had to hide their feelings, identities, loves....
Who shrank to fit the expectations of others.
Here's to never having to do that again.

Dedication

BEFORE YOU READ

Scribe of Asteria contains adult content meant for the enjoyment of adults. There are many things to love about this story, but before you read it, please note, it might contain content you may not be comfortable with. See below for a short list of content you may take issue with.

Content Warning:
Profanity
On page consensual sex
Dom/subthemes (including: praise, slight degradation, spanking, blind folds, authority)
Mention of alcohol abuse/childhood abuse (physical)

Representation:
Neuro-divergent FMC
Pansexual MMC
Bisexual MMC
Queer normative world

AUTHOR NOTE

Scribe of Asteria is fictional and written by an author that, try as I might, haven't been able to make Olympus real.

Yet.

I have thought about this story, dreamed about these characters, for the last seven years. I have done extensive research, but I get things wrong. There are definitely historical inaccuracies. This is not to be used a history book or a representation of ancient Greek life, rather, it is to be enjoyed as it is. A fun, smutty retelling of the loves of Apollo. It is a standalone in the world of the Serathena, and could be enjoyed more fully if you have read Ink of Copper first, although it is not a requirement. It stands on its own, just like our heroine.

Writing is a labor of love.

There might be mistakes.

There might be misspellings.

There might be stylistic choices that aren't grammatically incorrect, but you may not agree with.

All this proves one thing.

This story is written by a human, edited by a human, for the enjoyment of humans over the age of 18.

Prologue

I never wanted this life.

All those years ago, as I sat alongside my father whilst he calculated the stars, I dreamed of them. The gods. Those mighty beings that lived on Olympus occupied my thoughts. I was a devoted worshipper, an Achaean living amongst the rich array of cultures on a far distant shore.

As a scholar, I was encouraged to think critically, explore all options of the problem at hand, and consider the endless possibilities. My mind was my greatest weapon. But my heart? That was fragile, made of glass, and easily shattered. So, I stayed in the confines of the Library of Alexandria, content to be the only woman amongst my peers who diminished my work. I kept myself as my father instructed: strong, resourceful, and deserving of the position bestowed upon me in teaching the next crop of scholars.

That is until my world collided with theirs. The gods. They brought their endless war to the shores of Alexandria, a place I had always felt safe and secure, long after my father had passed. When the war settled on our lives like a thick blanket of destruction and chaos, I knew the only thing to do was to run.

And I did.

I ran from my burning city and found salvation the night Artemis saved me. But my salvation led me straight into a world that would consume me.

A world that would try to control me. A world I learned to navigate using my wits and mind, just as my father taught me.

I am clever and honest, and both of those traits can get a human like me killed in this realm of myths. Artemis protected me and honed my existence into one that was useful. Athena made me a scribe, giving me status among those who worked for the gods. I began to build a life here on Olympus—a life I was proud of.

I was relatively happy, given the immortality of my existence and the years that stretched before me. Alone, but content. I shrouded myself in mathematics and astronomy, made advancements for Olympus that far surpassed the human realm I had once been a part of. I was an asset to the Tellus Province, specifically Athena's court. I was the only female scribe, tucked away in a dusty portion of an archive we were desperately trying to rebuild. I oversaw the monumental task of cataloging all the artifacts. I took this job seriously. I was proud of it. Had earned it.

I am Hypatia of Alexandria, and I never wanted this life.

Until the day I came to the Cosmis Province, to the Hyperion mountains, and to his court.

I became something I never intended.

Important.

Chapter 1

The Scribe

Artemis and I have been sharing looks for well over fifteen minutes when Athena finally stops talking.

"Anything else that I need to know? Hypatia?"

As is customary in front of the goddess, I stand and bow my head. Nervously, I shuffle scrolls. "I have come across something rather intriguing, My Goddess. I discovered a pattern of stars within the archives that will need further research."

Gently, I touch my hair—a nervous habit. This morning, I opted for the ivory combs that were my mother's and pulled my chestnut hair back into a tight bun. Athena sits back in her large wooden chair as I speak. I had once been so intimidated by her that I shook when I needed to present my findings. But as the centuries stretched on, I became more accustomed to her mannerisms. And her temper.

She taps her finger against the table. This chamber is smaller and cozier—if anything within Athena's palace walls can be considered cozy. She reserves the larger chambers for the calling together of her warriors, men who were once human she made into warrior nymphs. Other rooms she reserves for private audiences. This afternoon, however, we are in her chamber reserved for the Epsilon warriors, an elite group of men who are, for lack of a better term, lords over their perspective provinces. I scan the room, taking notice of only four members. There were always five in number, but several months ago her temper got the better of her, and she sentenced one to the Shadow Realm: a death sentence. I avoid the Epsilon warriors in most situations. They are unusually arrogant, and in a world surrounded by arrogant men training for a coming war, that says something.

"What's the finding?" Athena tilts her head thoughtfully.

"I'm unwilling to state it fully, as I haven't had time to properly research."

Artemis glances my way. Her steady presence at my side is a comfort. When she brought me to Olympus, she and I formed a friendship that has spanned centuries now. I am her right hand, and she is my protector.

"And what research would you need?" Athena states slowly, losing her patience with me. Several sets of male eyes fall on me as their curiosity spikes.

"I have found something within the text that talks of a possible new star formation, one we haven't named yet."

Athena nods at that, and the men go back to barely tolerating me, which I prefer.

"A new star?" She nestles further back into her chair, mildly interested in my discovery.

"Yes," I say excitedly. "If I'm correct, in two months, our world will rotate just so, so that I am able to confirm for sure. I would like the ability to do the calculations to determine if I am correct. This would take me away from my normal duties, but I assure you, I could perform both tasks. The current scrolls talk of the possibility, but there isn't proof. I would like to—"

"Where would you need to conduct your research?" Athena interrupts.

This is the tricky part of my plan, and I glance at Artemis, whose face is unreadable. I need to convince the goddess to allow me to leave and convince Artemis once I announce where I'm wanting to go. While I'm not a prisoner of any kind here in Athena's home, I am somewhat of a prized guest. My position as curator of the new Library of Alexandria keeps me employed and out of the way of the gods. Athena's palace is protected, one of the few places on Olympus gods have to be invited to enter. Many others have no such rule.

I am free to roam here, my position respected, as my duties as curator are many. Losing that time to research for something that may turn out to be nothing could set Olympus back in the progress it has made—advancements I, and the twelve other scribes, have helped to bring about. Progress I am proud of, that make the empire of Olympus technologically advanced in comparison to the human realm.

"I would need somewhere high. Somewhere above the clouds, where I could get a clearer view of the sky to conduct the research and gather accurate calculations."

The Tellus Province, the one ruled by Athena and Ares, is in the plains region of Olympus. The empire is split into four provinces, with a fifth, the Golden Estate, surrounding Zeus as its own entity altogether.

"I would like to go to the Cosmis Province." My voice cracks as I dart yet another look to Artemis. "I need a high place with a clear view of the night sky."

"Apollo's province?" Artemis scowls. Her large diaphanous wings—shimmering silver in the sunlight that streams in through stained-glass windows—flap irritatedly several times, and her red hair flames. I haven't told her where I'd like to conduct my research, and she isn't all too pleased.

"And yours, if I recall," Athena says dismissively.

My protector stares at me, and I do my best not to shrink. I knew convincing her wouldn't be easy.

"Yes, but I do not trust Apollo to conduct himself appropriately. She is my right hand, Athena. I wouldn't allow one of my nymphs in his palace unprotected, but Hypatia . . ." Artemis huffs. While she may love her twin, Apollo has a reputation. One that isn't just hearsay and gossip. And one Artemis actively does her best to keep the women of her court far removed from.

Athena shakes her head. "Of course not, I don't trust any man, god or human. However, we are coming upon the summer solstice celebration. Since scribes are barred from participation, Hypatia would have several months to conduct research without getting behind on her duties here. If she wishes to conduct research, now would be a good time."

Artemis scowls. "I do not allow her to leave."

Flicking my gaze between them, I worry my proposal may die on the floor if I can't convince the goddess I am not in any danger.

"I believe Apollo isn't in residence," a deeper voice chimes in. All three of us look in unison as Ambassador Elatus stands. Ambassadors belong to the old gods instead of beholding to certain provinces, like council members. Ambassador Elatus is the ambassador for Poseidon. "From what I understand, the young god is off with Dionysus, half in the barrel I assume, and defiling whoever is near." He sneers at me.

Elatus is vile and the few run-ins I've had with him left me feeling uneasy. He is always quick to remind me of my lower status and my insignificance on Olympus.

"The scribe would be unbothered, as long as she knew her place." He barked the last of that sentence at me. Artemis curls her fingers into a fist, and I can only imagine what she's thinking. Athena doesn't seem bothered by the rude insinuation or insulting manner of my position. She nods.

"If Hypatia needs a high place, with a clear view of the night sky, the Cosmis Province is where she needs to go. Apollo's palace is the second highest point in our realm." Her eyes dart in my direction. "She can conduct her research in the Hyperion mountains, and you can send along a warrior from my court to watch over her if you are worried, Artemis. Will that be amenable?" She glances at me, lowering her chin. I swallow and nod reluctantly.

"I will make the necessary arrangements with his council," is all Athena says.

Artemis frowns. She can fight Athena on the matter, but I did such a thorough job convincing her I need to research my findings, that she wants me to succeed. It was hard enough getting a meeting with Athena to discuss my thesis. My friend nods, the matter settled. Athena gives a dismissive wave of her hand, and we rise. I salute and fall in step behind Artemis, intent on the door. I barely make it to the hallway before she lets her displeasure be known.

"You never mentioned Apollonion when we discussed this!" she hisses, turning the corner, heading for an alcove so we can speak properly. In all these centuries, I haven't thought of Artemis entirely without reason. My opinion is swiftly changing.

"I knew you would react this way, Artemis," I say innocently. "I need somewhere high with a clear view of the western sky."

"But at Apollo's home? Hypatia! And during the solstice."

"He isn't there, and I'll have a guard. His palace is the second highest point, and if I'm right, I'll add a new discovery to the library."

"Apollo isn't known for decorum."

Nervously, I twist my fingers into my palm. Artemis glances down and lifts an eyebrow, before covering my hand with her own and sighing. I am winning.

"This is what I wanted. A place to do my research without interruption. I'll be fine, Artemis."

She makes a noise in the back of her throat and gives in. The goddess doesn't like those under her protection around any men, but Apollo is different. And she and I both know why. He is someone that I can't trust myself around.

"His archives are better and more intact than most other gods. It's rumored he has all of the recordings of the Oracle. He also doesn't employ a scribe, so the information held in the archives would be all new discoveries," Artemis says, giving in to the idea of my spending any time in Apollo's court. "He's a jackass to be sure, but he is the god of the Oracle of Delphi. And that is something you've been missing from the library."

The prospect of discovering new information for the library is thrilling and one I hadn't thought of. I could conduct my research at night and spend my days lost in a sea of discoveries we could use in the future. And with him gone, avoiding one of the most flirtatious gods in the empire would be easy.

I have only met Apollo once, briefly, when he came to a summons from Artemis. But once was enough to leave an impression. He isn't just beautiful; Apollo rivals Adonis, and in my opinion, outshines him. He is everything lyrists sing of. His golden hair, his command of a room, and his impressive white wings are all reasons women fall at his feet. But those weren't what I noticed. It was the way his smile was slightly off-center when he was being smug that burned in my memory. The way his nimble fingers plucked the strings of the lyre, making it sing in a way I'd never heard. The way he teased Artemis until her annoyance turned to laughter at his playfulness. He occupied my thoughts for much longer than anyone knew.

He sat one table over that fateful night and still, I felt as though I sat too close to the sun. I tried to concentrate, but I found myself stealing glances all evening. Being in his palace for weeks on end with him in residence could be detrimental if I allowed myself to get caught up in his charm.

It is better he is gone, and I can stay hidden among the stacks of scrolls and dusty books, so my silly heart stays firmly intact. A god like Apollo wouldn't just burn me. He'd consume all of me until there was nothing left but him.

I am glad he is away, or I might just indulge my curiosity and discover what it must feel like to be plucked like the strings of the lyre.

Chapter 2
The Scribe

With each province preparing for the solstice festival, followed by the games, I am left with little time for me to truly wrap my head around coming to the palace. I continually assured Artemis of my decision, and we learned his right hand, a prince from Amyklai, was in charge while the god was away

In the last few centuries, I've seen very little of the empire I call home. When travel to other provinces or even to the Golden Estate comes up, I routinely decline. I mostly know the land geographically and am content to continue to stay in the Tellus Province. Most of the gods can travel from one end of the empire to the other with only a thought. Some open portals to move about. All other beings on Olympus use the impressive, interconnected bullet trains that snake through the realm.

But Artemis, not wanting to rush, chose a slower form of travel: a large swan provided by her twin's court. I lovingly name my flying steed Orion. While the saddle isn't uncomfortable, keeping my balance atop a bird has its challenges. I have never ridden an animal, fowl or otherwise, so being astride for the first time in the air is an experience.

Artemis, on the other hand, took to the air alongside me. Her silvery wings, shimmering against the sun, move in time. The land spreads out below me, changing from grass and patchwork farms to lush forests, then rolling hills, and finally mountains. A network of life that exists far beyond the walls of my home.

Apollo's palace sits tucked into the side of a mountain range, golden in every sense of the word. White marble, impossibly round columns trimmed in gold, and enormous halls are all bathed in a golden light that emanates from everywhere. Going from Athena's home, which is a richly decorated citadel, to the opulence of this palace is as if I entered an entirely new realm. I settle into my temporary home rather quickly.

From my chamber balcony, I can see far into the Hyperion mountains, a range so sharp in its incline, that parts of the village surrounding the palace are built directly into the rock—a marvel of ingenuity I hope to explore.

The gardens surrounding the home are plenty, and each more beautiful than the last. Tonight, I chose this particular spot for its abundance of shrubbery and lack of tree cover to obscure my view while I begin my calculations. Around me bloom yellow flowers of various kinds. My favorites, though, stand merrily at my feet. Happy yellow daisies wave in the light breeze as I set up my telescope. I glance into the scope and take in a breath, feeling as though I am breathing night air for the first time.

Crisp and clean, it stings in my lungs at this altitude.

Dusk claims the atmosphere in colors of purples, pinks, and glorious oranges that I have never seen before. A true display symbolizing Apollo giving way to Artemis dances across the sky before me as I peer into the scope and select my heavenly body. If I am correct, it will be a few weeks more before I can finally see the star. Since the telescope I brought from Athena's palace only has so much magnification, I have to wait until the rotation of our world is just so. But as it is, I enjoy the anticipation.

I have almost gotten the instrument into position when I let my girlhood wonder take over and stop to pluck a daisy from its place at my feet.

"Our gardener has done a tireless job of keeping fields of daisies in bloom, and here you are, standing among them, plucking one from the ground."

Freezing, the aforementioned flower still in my hand, I turn to see the biggest man I have ever seen standing just inside the hedge that encircles this part of the garden. He strides the short distance between us and takes the flower, tucking it behind his ear.

"Good thing I don't care a wit about the thoughts of the gardener."

I stare up into the slowly fading day at the giant before me. Handsome like most Olympians, his shoulders seem to stretch for yards on either side. His chest, thick and round, blocks my view of his full face. His arms are bulky, placed on each side like muscled ropes. His jaw looks chiseled from marble, strong and defined, covered in a thin layer of beard. He is tawny, with dark hair and dark eyes.

I am tall for a human, but he is taller, towering over me as warriors tend to do. He donned a modification of the warrior garb worn by most of the men in my life. Leather skirting encircles his hips, greaves on his shins, sandals on his feet, and leather cuffs cover both forearms. But the chest in front of me is covered with a golden breastplate. It fits him perfectly and the hammered design is expertly crafted. The bulk of the center of the breastplate holds a half-sun with a crescent moon intertwined and an arrow shooting through both celestial bodies. Apollo's symbol is evident, the half-sun with the arrow, but the moon is Artemis. Only one rank would be allowed to wear the symbol for both who rule this province. Someone who isn't an Athenian warrior at all.

"Your Royal Highness." I bow my head low, twisting my fingers into my hand. He acknowledges my reverence with a half-tilt of his head.

"I haven't been bowed to in several centuries," he says, his deep voice rumbling from his chest. "At least not in this public of a venue."

"I apologize, Your Highness. I assumed this part of the garden wasn't occupied by anyone." I eye him as he reaches out and touches my telescope, biting my tongue to keep myself from saying something out of turn. He peers through the scope and then the eyepiece, adjusting the focus and tilting the instrument.

"Stop that," I snap before I can stop myself. "I had that adjusted just right, and you'll ruin the angle."

"What are you looking at so early in the evening?" he mumbles with one eye closed as he continues to turn the knobs and move the instrument. I swat at his hands and am met with a half-chuckle. "Reactive little thing, aren't you?"

"First of all," I huff, using my shoulder to push him away from the telescope, "I am not little. I am a grown woman, not a child that needs your condescension."

"And second of all?" he says a bit too close to my ear.

"Second of all," I say into the eyepiece as I squint with one eye closed, looking for just the right place in the space above to begin my discovery, "I had this adjusted to where I wanted, and now you've gone and manhandled my instrument." I adjust the knob under the star finder, opening the mirror wider. I turn to scold him, but he hasn't moved away to a proper distance. His face is mere inches from my own. I narrow my glare on him to accentuate my displeasure at his actions. He's staring at me with hard, dark brown eyes that have specks of bright blue in the corners. His gaze searches my face, tracing my features before he stands to his full height and frowns.

"You're the scribe sent by Athena." He looks up into the heavens, and I can't help but follow his eyes. Scratching his beard, the sound of the stiff hairs punctuates the softening world around us.

"Yes," I say to stars that are now starting to peak out in the gathering night sky.

"I don't believe your calculations will be accurate, then."

"Pardon?"

He crosses his arms over his wide chest, still looking up. "If you use that simple of an instrument, your calculations won't be as accurate. You need something larger that can magnify, see further, I assume."

"I'll have you know I'm capable of calculating just fine using this telescope. I have an astrolabe to judge the distance and a chart to ensure I am in the correct position of the night sky. Athena has enchanted the lenses, allowing a magnification far surpassing its original capabilities. And furthermore, my calculations are almost always correct."

"Almost?" He lifts an eyebrow, and one of his eyes sizes me up.

"One must allow for human error, of course. But I assure you, I am most capable."

He plucks the flower from his ear and examines it. Thick fingers come towards me, and I jerk my head out of his way. He grunts, catching my chin with one hand, refusing me an escape, and brushes my wild hair back with the other. A calloused finger traces a line behind my ear as he tucks loose ends that have escaped my tight braid, leaving behind the daisy. It sends an odd tingle through me. He releases my chin, and my skin burns where his fingers gripped.

"I never said you weren't capable, just that there was a better way." He puts his hands behind his back. "Apollo has an observatory."

I can't help the gasp that escapes, and he seems pleased with himself at his surprise. My face lights up at the thought of using a telescope that powerful for my research.

"Why don't I show it to you, and you can see if it's to your liking? No one but myself or Apollo uses the facility, so you would have access to it whenever you need."

I frown. In Athena's court, to gain access to certain areas, she has stipulations. Rules. Stepping out of line means certain death.

"Do you not want access to the observatory? You could continue to use your telescope, I just assumed someone of your stature would want a better instrument."

"My stature?"

He shrugs. "Your station, then."

"And what is my station, Your Royal Highness?"

His eyes twinkle. "Curator of the library and scribe of Athena's court, of course," he says, almost bored.

"And what do you want in return?"

The prince smiles wide and gives his head a shake. "You're bold to think I would want something of you, little scribe."

I grit my teeth at the unwelcome nickname. "In my experience, those in positions of power rarely give without consequence to the receiver."

A frown turns his full lips down. "In mine as well." He eyes me. "I may not know how Athena's court works, but here, I have the authority to give you access to a powerful telescope that would aid in your research. The entire reason you're here. That is all. No quid pro quo."

"All right," I say cautiously. "I would like very much to use your observatory, Your Royal Highness."

Something passes over his face, a shadow, for a fleeting moment before it's gone. "The name's Cinthus, or Cin, if you may."

"Thank you, Prince Cin," I say with a bow of my head. His finger finds my chin again, lifting until my eyes meet his.

"No prince, just Cin. I haven't been a dutiful prince in a very long time."

Chapter 3
The God

My mind is elsewhere and my ability to pretend to listen is waning. I returned empty-handed yet again from my latest quest. Many in the court grumbled about my absence, calling me irresponsible and arrogant. Maybe so, but I am a god undeterred. I have been on a singular mission for the last few centuries and am once again without answers.

Council members have droned on for hours now. There is a new Epsilon warrior assigned to our province. I have yet to meet him, but the council seems to be very passionate about it. Whatever happened to the last one, I care even less about than this meeting. Athena and her righteous temper usually abolish one every hundred years or so. Another would come along, be in her good graces, and then piss her off, and the cycle continues. As long as she keeps to her province, she can continue treating her elite warriors any way she wants. I stifle a yawn behind my hand.

The doors at the end of the room open, and in he marches. Tall, broad-shouldered, narrow at the hip. Gods he is beautiful.

Beautiful and mine.

He wears a shorter chiton, showing off those muscled legs I so enjoy wrapped around me. A tooled leather strap encircles his waist and hanging from that is his sheathed sword. The one I gave him as a present years ago. His dark hair looked particularly ravishing earlier this morning, bent over, sucking my soul out of my cock. But that beard of his has gotten long in my absence. We will need to rectify that today. I make a mental note to tell one of my stewards.

"Your Majesty," I call, a little more enthusiastically than I mean to. Council members who once cocked a brow look on in uninterested boredom. Prince Cinthus has been my right hand for centuries and my bed partner for almost as long. He stops a respectful distance away, crosses his arm over his chest, fist to his heart, and bows—a salute worthy of my standing. But it is the soft curl of one side of those full lips that has me smiling in return. In public, we are the epitome of decorum and rank. I, the god of light, the son of Leto and Zeus, responsible for this province. And he, the prince, stolen because of his beauty, my adviser on all matters. But behind closed doors, we both know who is in charge.

"My God," he says in an even tone.

"Gentlemen, are we about done here? I believe my adviser and I have much to discuss since my return."

Tucking several scrolls into a leather carrier, the council members begrudgingly pack up and file out of my private chamber. I prefer to conduct my business here, away from the prying eyes and ears of the myriad of warriors and guards that call my palace home. I nod to one such guard who stands at the entrance waiting for his dismissal. Long ago, when my palace was new, I employed several white-winged guards. Donning them in Roman Centurion armor instead of Greek gave me an odd thrill; the fact it pissed off Ares was a bonus. Over the eons, I have collected as many white-winged, blond-haired Athenian warriors as I can employ and keep them well-outfitted in Roman garb. This simple act has effectively kept Ares from my doorstep.

Asshole.

Cin crosses the room, intent on the dais my throne sits upon. Pushing up from the marble table, white, like everything in my home, I ascend the risers.

"Bored, My God?" he says, taking his position, and opening the small desk—one that seems to shrink as soon as he sits down—and takes out parchment, quill poised in his thick hand. Most times, Cin transcribes my thoughts from the various meetings and councils I attend, but as the afternoon wore on, I listened less and less, until their voices became murmurs in the background. I shrug and flop onto the throne.

"I have been in my fair share of monotonous meetings but am at a loss as to the importance of keeping me so long from my activities."

"Activities?" He cocks an eyebrow, and I playfully roll my eyes.

"While *that* would be a respite from the last few hours"—my response is met with a deep chuckle—"I more meant joining the warriors outside. A friendly discus competition or a foot race, perhaps. Practice before the games."

Cin places the quill in its holder. "Or you could introduce yourself to the scribe Athena has sent to conduct research."

I scowl, fiddling with the end of the white cape affixed to my shoulder. "Another stuffy, pompous scholar who cares only about his work? I think I'd rather call the council back and start the meeting over."

"I believe *she* would be rather insulted you called her a man."

That catches my attention. "A woman?"

Cin nods, sitting back in the desk chair, pleased with himself. "I was just as surprised as you."

"I had no idea Athena employed a human woman as a scribe. She hardly accepts their input on anything, let alone elevates them to such a position."

"I met her last night, in the hedged garden. She's not what one would expect. I believe she is the right hand of your sister, My God."

I sit up. Years ago, Artemis saved a human woman from a certain gruesome death. Few interact with her and even fewer have seen her. I have, once, only once. And that was enough to send me to the far corners of the empire looking for her. I tamp down my eagerness. If Cin is right, the woman I have been searching for has landed on my doorstep in an odd twist of the fates. He told me centuries ago to call off the search after Artemis chased me from her palace for the fourth time, but I couldn't.

"I thought her a myth. One in the same vein as a unicorn or a phoenix."

"She is very real. Although she isn't keen on anyone touching her instruments."

My eyebrows shoot up my forehead at his insinuation. Cin snorts.

"Not in that way, Apollo. The woman has several instruments she is using to conduct her research. I told her she may have free rein of the observatory in the evenings if she wished."

"A scribe." I'm in awe. So that's where Artemis hid her. In the only place I wasn't allowed to go: Athena's. *Clever bitch.*

"Not just a scribe." Cin interrupts my musings. "She is also the curator of the Library of Alexandria. I believe you may recognize her."

"I believe I may," I say to the otherwise empty room.

Half an hour later, I find myself in the archives. I used to employ a scribe, as many of the gods do. He did fine, meticulous work and was an asset, especially when it came to transcribing the ramblings of the Oracle of Delphi. But as it goes, he was out on the training field one afternoon and met the wrong end of a sword. An accident, to be sure. Immortal humans aren't as immortal as one would believe. They can be killed, harmed, maimed, and many other afflictions the gods don't worry over. Ever since, the massive rooms have sat empty of an occupant.

As I make my way down the corridor, light pours into the hallway. Golden streams wave in the darkness as dust dances among the beams. I had to see for myself if the woman from that fateful night is indeed under my roof and if she is as beautiful as I remember. Trying to cross the threshold, I'm stopped by one of Athena's warriors, but noticing who I am, he steps aside.

Well played, Artemis. Sending a guard to protect your precious commodity.

The racks of scrolls, both used and unused, reach towards the ceiling. A rustling comes from behind one such rack, and I head towards the sound. Glimpsing a light-colored chiton, cream, with a bright blue himation slung across, I round the edge of the rack and admire a rather perfect, albeit smaller than I like, ass. She is leaning over one of the large tables in the middle of the miles of shelving. Mumbles come from her general direction, and I lean against a rack to admire her for a moment.

She is tall enough that even bent over the wooden table, she isn't on tiptoes. Her hair is neatly pulled back in a familiar style with two ivory combs on either side. She straightens quickly and, with a quill in her left hand, begins drawing something in the air. The feather flits across the transparent page and she makes an odd little squeal before she bends again. One foot tucks behind the other, and unashamedly, I allow my eyes to travel the rather nice silhouette she's making against the late afternoon sun. Again, she pops up to write in the air and again folds herself over the large wooden table. A table, I notice, that is long enough to hold her should she lie atop it. That thought sets my feet in motion. She's popped up again and as I gather closer, she is muttering a series of numbers quietly to herself.

"When I was told the palace had a scribe, I assumed a man," I say, a cheeky smile tugging on the corners of my mouth.

She sighs loudly. "Yes, a man," she says with her back to me. "It's always a man. I wonder why so many of you are impressed when a woman can read"

My head tilts. "Read, yes. But not many can calculate in midair."

Another loud sigh. "I'm sure it's rather interesting. But I have to do half my calculations in the air because I require more scrolls. Whoever used this blasted archive last, left it in such a disarray that they should be flogged for their inattention to detail."

"Is that the fate all should meet if they fail to be as meticulous as you?"

"Maybe flogged is harsh, but at the very least catalog the information so that others may benefit."

"So, you believe the former scribe of this archive a dimwit? One that should have been punished?" I tease and pray Cin's right. That this enchanting, quick-witted creature is her.

"I didn't say—"

"You most certainly did. Or rather, that is what I heard."

"Excuse me, but just who do you think you are?"

She stops miming mathematics, and I can tell just by the straightening of her shoulders, she is about to turn and give me a tongue-lashing. And for some reason, that thrills me. I don't have to wait long. She whips around and glares at me.

"I believe most would address me as My God, but you may call me Apollo."

Recognition blooms in those wide eyes of hers, and she reactively bows. This causes that nice ass of hers to bump into the table and the pot of ink tips from its precarious perch, spilling onto several scrolls.

"Oh!" she exclaims, turning around as she hears the pot hit. "Oh, no!"

Her shawl is off in a flash, and she uses it to mop up the mess. Trying to right the pot blackens her fingers and ink soaks into the lovely blue color of the himation, ruining it. Splotches of black now coat her fingers, palms, and wrists, and she curses as she moves the parchment.

"My God!" she salutes, one hand coming to her heart. Unfortunately, that hand is hopelessly stained black. The reverence to my station leaves a handprint at her heart that is half on her skin and half on the chiton tied across her chest and pinned at one shoulder. The offending hand then travels to her hip, where it rests, leaving another print in its wake.

She twists her lips. "I wasn't expecting you, My God. I was told you weren't in residence."

"I'm just as surprised to find you are a woman as you are to find me in my home." The prince was right, crafty bastard. He knew exactly what he was doing mentioning her. I have frequently talked of her, devising plan after plan. And now, here she stands, under my roof, and even more beautiful than I remembered. I briefly wonder if she remembers that night as vividly as I do. Scratching my chin, I prop my hip against the wood, intent on teasing her.

"I see. Is that why you've come? I am said to be gone, so Athena thinks this is as good a time as any to send a scribe into my home. I should hold a meeting and try you for trespassing."

Her brows jog up her forehead. "I assure you, My God. I had permission," she sputters.

As I step closer, she shrinks back, and for some reason, the act tugs at something in me. I had planned on keeping up the ruse, but she looks so much like a hare snared in a trap that the joke loses all steam.

"I have papers. I have the appropriate paperwork from both Athena and Artemis, My God. If you'll allow me to return to the chamber I am using, I can fetch them and bring them back. I am here for research. Research only. It's just your home is the second highest spot, and Athena agreed it better I have an adequate vantage point. And—and His Royal Highness was allowing me the use of the observatory. I have only used it for a better view. I promise, My God, I am not here to cause trouble."

She's speaking so fast I barely have any time to interject and come clean. Retreating, she backs towards the door, ready to run should I press the matter. The guard from the corner, seeing the ruckus and sudden outburst, marches forward to protect his charge.

"Guard," I shout a little too loud, "stay."

The poor woman squeals in fright and scampers to run, but she misjudges the distance and collides with a large rack when she turns. The sickening thud cuts into the room and scrolls rain down atop her. Her arms flail as her sandals slide. I'm to her in a breath, catching her before she hits the ground. Fear in her eyes, she claws at me like a wildcat.

"Madam," I say right before her fist finds my cheek and makes contact. The punch explodes under my eye, and I cry out in shock. "Ow! Fuck!"

She fists my chiton as I tighten my grip.

"Hold still, woman," I hiss. "I was only joking."

Cradled in my arms, her breathing stalls.

"Joking?" she croaks.

I nod. "Yes. Joking."

"About the Apollo part or the trespassing without papers part?"

She tilts her head, and her neatly arranged hair brushes my forearm. It sends an odd little tingle firing up my arm. My hands tremble, actually tremble, holding her, knowing she is very real and not some figment of my imagination I conjured up and have been chasing for centuries. Loosening my grip, I'm secretly delighted she stays pressed in place. Her eyes search mine face for any indication that I might not be telling the truth. And for those few seconds, I lose myself in deep gray eyes—the color of a steel blade. I don't know I move until I feel her soft skin under my palm.

"You'll have a bruise." My voice comes out lower than I intend, raspy. My thumb strokes her cheek of its own volition, and for a few fleeting seconds, she allows it, sinking into me as if this is where she belongs. Where I want her to belong.

"It'll heal, My God," she says quietly. It takes more willpower than I thought I possessed to not react to the sound of my title from those pretty lips. "Hypatia."

"Pardon?"

"Hypatia. My name is Hypatia. You called me madam, but my—my name is Hypatia." Her long, graceful fingers skim along the fabric covering my chest, and I have the sudden desire to feel those fingers against my skin.

"Welcome to Apollonion, Hypatia," I reply absentmindedly, still lost in those wide gray eyes that are set a bit too far apart.

She pushes off, and the spell she has me under is broken. She crosses the room so fast that I have to remind myself I had her in my arms. That I hadn't hallucinated on moly root.

"I am here to conduct research, My God."

"Research?" I'm trying to act casual, but I feel like I'm gasping for air. The only thing I can focus on is the feel of her fingers through the linen a moment ago. And how those oh-so-intelligent eyes saw into my soul. I held her for seconds, mere seconds, but I'm sent reeling as she moves around the room.

She rescues the unusable parchment from the ink-soaked wood. Angrily, she pushes the ruined himation aside.

"Damnit." And another slap rings out. This time, it's her hand over her mouth. "I apologize," she says, her words muffled behind her hand.

"For cursing? Or for punching me?"

This is met with a groan, and it makes me smile. She's an odd woman, this scribe. Intelligent, clearly, but the mix of softness and brilliance leaves me feeling drunk in her presence.

"Both."

"I accept your apologies, Hypatia."

The way her name feels on my tongue is an omen of sorts. I returned home to dry myself out. To stop the search and actually do my duties as they are assigned, something Cin is constantly telling me I shirk. But this woman. This charming woman. How am I to go about my normal day knowing she is within the walls of my home? She will be quite the distraction.

Chapter 4
The Scribe

The palace is alive with excited energy. Apollo's staff has been decorating almost since I got here for the summer solstice celebration. I've been trying to keep hidden, but the hallway outside the archives rings with feminine voices. I have approximately three seconds before they burst in here and seize me. A glance at the ever-present guard for help tells me I am on my own. He yawns and adjusts his armor when they descend upon me. The nymphs, merry and giggling, burst into the archives with a flutter of female comradery that floats to the ceiling. These women attend to the needs of the palace. The nymphs are like ladies in waiting, if Apollo a wife. They and the Sisters of the Eternal, a sorority of women born from the muses but protected by the god, are the only women amongst a sea of warriors. Nymphs are in every palace of the gods, besides Ares, as he prefers the company of his men. In Athena's home, they are seen as a nuisance, silly and forgettable. Here, the god has elevated them to a position of respect. They are free to move about the palace and its grounds unfettered. Free to find unsuspecting scholars and attach themselves to her as if she required rescue.

I did. From them.

"Hypatia!" one squeals as she enters. Her pink-and-red chiton is beautifully made, coming to her ankles and fastened to her shoulders with pins. "Are you ready?"

The gaggle of women that follow have me smiling despite myself. Dramatically, I roll my eyes to the high ceilings.

"Must I? I would much rather toil here in the archives, away from such activities as the festival."

Another in a blue himation waves her delicate hand at me, pointing her index finger. "None of that talk. You are coming with us to the opening ceremony if we have to drag you out," she scolds playfully.

I've only been in the palace a short time, but these women found and adopted me, and no amount of protesting deters them. I tried many. All failed. I am part of their company whether I want to be or not.

Spending my life as I do, I rarely make female friends, and I have never been included outside of prayer in the temple in Alexandria. Well, not counting Artemis. So, when these ladies found their way into the archives one afternoon and forced me to accompany them to the training fields to watch the warriors, I didn't put up much of a fight. I secretly adore them and their loud antics. It is a glimpse at another life I could have lived had my father allowed me to choose differently. Looping a hand through my arm, one in purple tugs me towards the door.

"Come along, Hypatia. We need to ready ourselves for the lighting of the fires."

Helplessly, I'm pulled along like a raft carried out to sea with the current. If I try to resist, I'll be scolded; best to comply. Truth be told, it has been ages since I celebrated summer solstice, and I am keen to be part of the festivities.

Hours later, dressed in a borrowed peplos and himation, my sides hurt from laughing, my cheeks are sore from smiling. These nymphs take having fun seriously, and I can't remember the last time I let myself have this type of fun. The women find another group and all dance wildly around a blazing fire, feet and arms flailing about. Reasonable as I am, I stand back and watch, drinking wine, and talking among the other sideline spectators. As the night wears on, the amount of wine these delicate wisps consume is impressive.

"They are quite the sight." His timbre sounds like a beckoning to my ears. Closing my eyes, I allow myself to indulge for a moment. Carefully, I disguise my enjoyment with a sip of wine. His Royal Highness eyes me.

"How many have you had, little scribe?"

"Enough to know I need to switch to water." I wink. "Not enough to make impaired decisions." A giggle bubbles up at my wittiness, and the prince frowns.

"I see."

"You're so serious, Your Highness," I tease and pout my bottom lip. Perhaps I've had more wine than I realize. His dark eyes watch me, and I get the distinct impression he doesn't approve. One of the nymphs squeals as her dancing has her coming close to the fire. One of the other women pulls her back.

"See, Your Royal Highness, the nymphs know how to have fun. Maybe you should join them. Take lessons."

He snorts in derision. "Should I?"

I sloppily nod, and he fights a smile. For some reason, I want to make him smile. I want to see those full lips curve because of something I said.

"Why aren't you dancing, little scribe?"

I slam one fist on my hip dramatically. "Hypatia. I'm not little, I'll have you know."

He nods, unaffected by my outburst, and scratches his cheek. "Whatever you wish, little scribe."

Shrugging, I set my wine goblet down at the base of a marble statue. My gaze travels up the stone legs to the gloriously naked male form gleaming in the firelight. The sculpture is bent, mid-spin, a discus gripped in the marble hand. I find myself staring at the carved lines of the statuette's forearm, veins chiseled, muscles beautifully designed.

"Like what you see?"

I blink as though the statue asked the question, only to remind myself it was His Highness. "Pardon?" I say, giving my head a shake.

He inclines his head to the sculpture. "It's an incredible likeness, do you not agree?"

It is then I notice the face of the figure and all but gasp as my eyes travel down.

The sculpture is the prince.

The prince throwing a discus.

The naked prince throwing a discus.

I avert my eyes quickly and blush.

"I hadn't noticed," I say, clearing my throat. A smile teases across his scruff-covered cheeks.

"Don't be embarrassed, Hypatia. Apollo only employs sculptors that carve the nude form."

"I'm not embarrassed," I say indignantly. "I was admiring the crafts-manship."

He hums a noise, and a smile finally appears. He's beautiful when he smiles.

"I see. And what part of the craftsmanship do you find most fascinat-ing?" His dark eyes twinkle the same they had in the field upon that first meeting.

"Your"—I glance back at the naked figure—"arms."

"My arms?"

"Mmm. The way the artist chiseled the stone along your forearms, the grip your fingers have on the discus, it is beautifully done." My words come out soft for some reason, and I touch the figure, trailing my fingers along a formidable marble arm. "It exudes strength and poise and . . . something."

When I tear away from the powerful beauty before me, I notice the prince. His expression is hooded, cast in shadows from the fires. His lips part and his chest heaves, and I wonder if he will scold me for being so bold to tell him what I truly thought. The wine is making my head fuzzy, and I'm having a hard time keeping all my thoughts in my head. His throat bobs.

"Fancy a walk"—his husky words ripple across my skin—"Hypatia?"

I can only follow, the air between us changing, sparking to life as if embers from the surrounding fires have caught us aflame.

We walk along the gathering of warriors jumping the flames, proving their manhood for all. Several feet away, a smaller group of women are giggling, intently watching the warriors. The prince walks with one hand gripping his sword, the other tucks a thumb into his leather breastplate. A formal stance on such an informal night. We come across a buffet table, several yards long, laden with food, and I pick up a skewer of chicken. Pulling the meat off in chunks, I plop one in my mouth. I grab another dram of wine, and His Royal Highness intercepts it, setting it back down.

"Water," he commands, lifting a goblet for me to take.

"Am I to do everything you say?" I huff. Teasingly, I bow my head and rising, lift the goblet at him. "Command me then, Your Highness."

His sharp intake of breath is my only answer. His hand juts out, grabbing my chin between his forefinger and thumb, effectively halting our walk. When our eyes meet, heat flashes in his, and he leans forward just enough.

"While you are under this palace roof, you're under my care." His eyes flick lower, and tingles run across my lips. I wet them, curious if the feeling is related to the wine or the hungry stare His Highness holds me in. "And I take great pleasure in taking care of you."

Letting go, he continues his walk, and I, dumbfounded, continue along beside as if his look didn't send my pulse racing. I stumble over an imaginary root, and his large hand takes hold of my bicep. It's soft and sure, and he pulls me to him, steadying me.

"Careful."

I'm so close I can smell whatever scent he's wearing. It's an intoxicating mixture of clean and spice. Without thinking, I lean in, wanting to bury my nose in his skin and drink him in.

"Hypatia," Cinthus chokes out as my fingers curl around the leather at his neck, pulling him down.

"You smell like . . . something familiar."

He stiffens, and I can't help but notice his thumb sliding ever so slightly against my arm.

"Laurel soap." He clears his throat. "I washed with laurel soap this evening. Perhaps it's time to get you to your chambers."

The moon catches my attention, and I turn my face up. "But the moon hasn't crested yet," I whine, and he smiles again. This time, I smile back, and my silly heart flutters. "I'll miss the dance with the clay phalli. I was so looking forward to it."

This time my pout is genuine, and he chuckles. "As disappointing as that is, the men will continue to drink, and you, little scribe, don't need to be privy to that spectacle. You're a guest after all."

"Will you not join them? I hear they dance naked and howl at the moon." My eyebrows wiggle, and he shakes his head.

"Hardly. How much wine did you have?"

Closing one eye, I try to remember. We had a glass as we got dressed, another upon entering the field. I lost track after the dancing began. "Two. No, three. I think. Three."

"So, four?" he arches a finely shaped brow. His features are pretty, too pretty for me to concentrate on anything but his face. My hand reaches forward and strokes his bearded chin by its own power, and a sigh escapes me. His eyes close at my touch and when they open, the look is pained. "Maybe five."

"I'm allowed an indulgence one time a year, I believe. I'm not reckless. Do you not drink, Your Royal Highness? I would think as big as you are, you could drink more than the average warrior and still remain upright."

His hand slips around my waist. It is possible he's trying to steady my stumbling feet, but I take advantage of his nearness and sniff him once more.

"I only drink at the evening meal. And only one glass. I know far too well what happens when drink impairs judgment. I'd rather have my faculties about me in the company of warriors." He eyes me one last time, leading me to my chambers and away from the growing crowd. I allow him, for as much as I enjoy an evening of unfettered enjoyment, I am not one to indulge often. Following along the hedges, I turn towards shouts coming from a pyre. Apollo and several men are stripped down, trying to jump the flames that lick at their wings as they leap. He follows my gaze. Studying his profile in the flickering firelight, I notice his features soften as he stares after the god.

"You truly love him." His head comes round to face me. "I can tell."

He smiles again and my heart flutters. Again. "Can you?"

"Yes. By the way you look at him."

He arches an amused brow. "And how do I look at him?"

"As the moon looks at the sun. As if you were in darkness, and he is your light. His brilliance reflects in your eyes." I lean forward a tad too far, almost off balance. "Such beautiful eyes."

The prince clears his throat and continues on our walk. "Come along." It's a rough command. I crash along the dewy grass beside him.

"You should join once you leave me safely in my chambers. Be naked as they are. And that way, I can watch."

He shoots me an odd look; one I can't place. "Watch?"

Looking up, I grin. "I can see everything from my balcony."

"Ahh, so you're secretly a voyeur, are you?"

"If it's you or Apollo in nothing but your finest skin, I think I shall become one." My hand slaps over my mouth with a pop as I realize the thought I had was now running free in the night air.

Cinthus laughs. "To your chambers, little scribe, before you say something you might regret."

Chapter 5

The Scribe

After recovering from the solstice festival and my subsequent headache, I spend more time with my newfound friends. Although I need to work, the company of the nymphs is too enticing.

That and the two men who occupy my thoughts more and more. One afternoon, my friends and I wander onto the training field, intent on watching the warriors. It is fast becoming a pastime I didn't know I'd enjoy. Warriors from all over the Cosmis Province have been coming for the last few weeks in preparation for the Olympic Games. In Athena's court, these games are the height of competition, and many warriors train specifically for them. In Apollo's palace, it seems more of a time for boasting and puffing of chests. The growing swarms of men spend more time preening and badmouthing each other. It is refreshing. It feels more like a display of skill and friendship, than a pitting of company against company.

As I hide from the heat under a shade tree, the prince strides over from a wrestling match. His long, muscled legs move with grace and precision as he makes his way to me.

"I've been instructed to ask if you would like to judge the discus throwing competition tomorrow."

I hear his words, but my focus is taken up by his bare chest. His dark, rugged physique glistening from exertion, is slick with a thin layer of sweat. I watch a bead roll over his defined chest, sliding through the dark hair that peppers his pectorals. A leather-clad forearm waves at me, breaking my concentration.

"Hypatia, did you hear me?"

"Hear you?" I repeat.

His Royal Highness tilts his head and gives me a knowing look. Then, taking a cloth from his belt, he wipes the sweat from his chest.

"Yes," he says absentmindedly as he wipes a broad shoulder. My eyes drink in every movement. "I asked if you would like to judge tomorrow's discus competition." His hand stalls at his abdomen, and I snap my eyes up to meet his. His smile sends butterflies loose in my belly.

I clear my throat. "Of course, if I can."

One fine, dark eyebrow arches. "If you can?"

"My research."

"Of course." He nods, looping the cloth once again at his side. "Although, if you'd like, you could stall your research for a day. We need someone with a mind for numbers to help with calculations. It would be perfect for someone with your intellect."

"If I am needed, Your Highness, then I shall do my level best to come."

A flash of something crosses his face. "Oh, little scribe, I fully expect you to come."

Watching him walk away leaves me fanning myself as I'm sure the temperature has soared in the span of our conversation.

And that is how I find myself in the judge's box, sandwiched between a nymph and a councilman, furiously scribbling notes onto papyrus. While I agreed to judge one competition, I have been sitting in the stand for hours, judging event after event. So, when Apollo flops into his raised seat and motions for me, I welcome the reprieve.

"Enjoying the games, Hypatia?" he says with a sigh, drinking from a golden chalice.

"Immensely." That isn't a lie. Athena has official hellanodikai, or judges, and only those participating in the games can spectate. Since women aren't allowed to participate in the games, I have never been privy to the festivities. But as I am learning, things at Apollonion are done with fewer restrictions and more fanfare. He points his chin at the men lining up for the discus throw. I watch for several moments as their arms glide through the air, swinging a rhythm so as to make the most of the throw.

"Cinthus hasn't lost a competition in several years," he says and offers me a chalice. Bowing my head, I take it and gulp, grateful for the cool water.

"Are you trying to sway my vote, My God?" I say and quickly, my eyes meet his. I didn't mean for that to come out. I forgot my place for a moment, and I worry he will see it as a disrespect. Instead, he frowns playfully.

"If it involves Cinthus winning, and I not having to listen to him whine about the loss for the next year, I would." He winks. "But something tells me you are too upstanding to take my bribe. So, I'll have to allow the call to be made by the judges and suffer the bemoaning should he lose."

I laugh. My delight glides through the wave of male voices.

"Come, Hypatia, as my guest, I ask you to move next to me so that I might sway your calculations."

I gasp in fake shock. "Absolutely not, My God. I'm insulted you would think so little of my character." I sit in the empty seat next to him with a hard thump and tap my fingers along the wooden table. "Now, how much to call the prince the winner? I accept gold, crowns, and candied fruit as payment."

A boisterous laugh tumbles out of the god. "Quite the negotiator, aren't we? I'll need to remember that."

I nod and turn my attention to the first contestant. Each man takes their position, twirling in a dance only their feet know. Competitor after competitor, each doing his level best to send their iron pieces flying and into the sand. When Cin steps up, I straighten myself in my seat. He approaches the throwing circle with a swagger to his step, leather skirting sways with his movements, grazing his toned thighs. His honed, athletic body moves in a ballet of precision as he twists, his arms in a perfect arc, his muscles contract with fine movements. When he lets go, the bronze discus flies straight and true. It glimmers in the sun, catching the light as it sails towards the target, landing with a thud in the sand.

My attention is captivated, not wanting to miss a second of the brawny prince and his preferred event. Each step, each grunt, keep me enraptured at the perfect display of athletic masculinity. I hardly breathe through each try, hardly blink for fear I'll miss something. When the third discus hits the sand, the cheers from the crowd spring me into action. Quickly, I try to scribble something down.

"He's beautiful, isn't he?" Apollo asks. I jump, my quill skipping along the page. Letting out a shaky breath, I gather my wits. I shouldn't be caught staring at the prince in the god's presence. He belongs to him, and while Apollo may seem boyish and charming, his temper is infamous, and I refuse to be on the receiving end. I turn to the other judges, conversing with them and tallying length. Three men come out winners and will advance to the next round. One warrior, one captain, and His Highness. Looking to the stands, the prince nods in Apollo's direction, and I watch as they share silent words with subtle facial movements.

Catching him staring at me, there's a wistfulness to his expression. "He's in his element like this."

I glance at the competitors readying themselves for the next round and the sun god breathes softly as a memory shades his sun-kissed face.

"I first saw Prince Cinthus in a discus competition many years ago. He was so magnificent; power, precision, athleticism. I couldn't take my eyes off him. I was completely captivated. I wanted him for my own, wasn't going to leave without him, and so I stole the prince. I have loved him ever since."

Nodding, I sip my water and try to avoid staring at the claimed lover of the god of light. These two share something so special and rare on Olympus that my silly daydreams of the way Prince Cin gripped my chin or the way his fingers felt brushing hair behind my ear are a fleeting fancy. Cin belongs to Apollo, and I belong in the archives. He watches me, and I try to busy myself scoring the contestants.

"Do you not agree?"

Clearing my throat, I watch His Highness take the circle. "He is a very beautiful man, My God."

My heart is pounding out of control, and I wonder if I've been in the heat too long.

"The way you are staring—"

I whip my head to look at him.

"I know that stare well." He grins wickedly. "Admire him, sweet Hypatia. You aren't the only one." He casually flicks his finger at the crowd and that's when I notice that His Royal Highness doesn't just have my attention, but most of the spectators as well.

"I apologize, My God." I bow my head, trying to return to some semblance of decorum, but Apollo shrugs.

"I see no reason for apologies. I'm admiring His Highness myself." He bites his lip at me, winking. "But I'll get to admire him more fully later and up close."

My cheeks heat, and I take a sip of water to the sound of the god's chuckles.

We watch as Cinthus twirls twice more, his discus sailing through the air. After all, three have finished the round, there seems to be a tie, and the contestants could go on for a third. Tallying up the numbers, I hand the sheets to the official judge who reads them and claims Prince Cinthus the winner.

His Royal Highness lets out a roar and runs full speed at the raised stand where his lover sits. In one leap, he scales the wooden sides. Reaching for each other, the two embrace, Apollo kissing both golden-brown cheeks. The prince jumps down, running off to celebrate.

"Congratulations, My God. Now you won't have to hear moaning all night long." We both whip around to stare at each other as my mind catches up to what just flew out of my mouth. "BE-moaning, My God. Bemoaning. From the prince. About losing." I turn to face the crowd and the next contestants as the god roars with laughter.

The afternoon wears on and by early evening, I'm hot and tired and ready to be back in my archives. Apollo and I have exchanged quips most of the afternoon, and I can't think of a time I have enjoyed myself more. When he turns those cloud-colored eyes on me with that hint of mischief, my heart flutters wildly against my ribs. I've watched as council members and warriors alike approach him with an ease of familiarity. They respect his position, but he is truly liked by the men in his home. During one event, he excuses himself to address several priestesses of Delphi who had made their way to the games. The way he cares for his people reminds me of Artemis and her care of the nymphs.

We've been waiting for the last event, a foot race, to begin calling participants.

"The foot race is my favorite event," he says, catching my attention. The fading sun leaves streaks of burning oranges and reds blazing across the sky. His beautiful white wings are lit from behind by the bursting of color. He might be the most beautiful man I have ever seen. Sitting this close, I feel like I did the first time I saw him: tongue-tied and awestruck.

"Do you enjoy participating in group activities, Hypatia?" Bringing a golden chalice to his lips, I notice a coyness tugging at one corner.

My brows furrow at the odd question. "I am usually in the archives, My God."

He shrugs, rustling the white cape. "I assume you come out of the archives from time to time. What is it you do for fun?"

"I enjoy looking at the stars, and I've been known to tinker."

"What do you do for exercise?"

I shrug and rearrange the papyrus in front of me. "I like to walk, My God."

He turns and there are crinkles in the corners of his eyes. "In the gardens?"

"Yes. And along the palace walls. But I'd really like . . ." I stop myself before I can say it. I've never expressed this particular wish to anyone, and I certainly am not about to start with Apollo. He is only being nice because I'm a guest and his sister's right hand.

He waves a hand. "Go on."

Turning, I face the gathering crowd.

"Hypatia, look at me." His command sends an odd shiver through me. "Tell me, what would you really like?"

He isn't going to let it go, so with a sigh, I give in. "I've never been this far outside Athena's palace. I'd like to explore the mountains, walk the village surrounding the palace, see the agora."

Lines form along his forehead. "Is that all?"

"Yes."

"That can be arranged, you only need to ask."

Turning towards the crowd, he yells something at one of the contestants who begins taunting the god. Apollo stands with a jolt, waving his arms and shouting. His cape and breastplate are off in moments. Next, come

40

the greaves and leather armbands. I gasp as he loosens the belted pteruges around his waist.

"My God! What do you think you're doing?"

"I've been challenged." He grins as the leather skirting drops to the wooden stand with a thud. "I never back down from a challenge."

Grabbing the lip of the stand, he swings his legs out and over, dropping to the dusty arena below. I squeal and rush to the side.

"Where are you going?" I call to the god below. The god who has clearly lost hold of his senses.

"It's called participation, Hypatia. You should try it sometime."

"Women aren't allowed to participate in the games, My God." I scoff. He leaps into the air, his wings stir up dust from the arena, and suddenly he's eye level.

"Women may not, but you, sweet Hypatia, are allowed to participate in any *activity* you choose." Reaching out, he taps my nose, and my cheeks heat. "In fact, I insist that you do."

The way he says the word *activity* sends a host of butterflies loose in my belly. I stumble over words as his wings push currents of air that dance around us.

"Participate? With—with all those warriors?" Looking around him with worry, I pray he doesn't force me to race. He shakes his head; grabbing the wooden ledge, he leans closer.

"Warriors, no. I'll not have you participate in activities with them." His face is dangerously close to mine. My eyes wander down to his lips for a split second, linger there, wondering what they would feel like against mine. I flick them back up. "The prince may join us if you wish, but never would I allow a warrior."

Then he drops out of sight.

Again, I peer over the side of the stand. The only thing left on his body is a chiton and sandals. Unlacing the straps at his back, he whips off the chiton, and I cover my mouth. Before the crowd of warriors and Olympians alike stands a naked Apollo.

A gloriously naked Apollo.

The sight of his posterior, tan and looking as though it is dusted with gold, does something to my insides. My fingernails bite into the wood and sound escapes my lips. I bite my bottom lip to keep any more embarrassing noises properly in their place. I have seen plenty of naked men in my day. Even now, as runners line up at the starting line, many of the men are naked. We are Olympians, being naked is normal.

But the god of light naked. I don't want to admit how many times I have fantasized about what he would look like, his perfectly toned body on display for my hungry gaze. Heat spreads through me at a frightening speed. He turns, and I let out another low sound.

"Hypatia!"

I can't answer. My tongue is too busy wetting my lips.

"Cheer for me. I need your screams as motivation."

He flashes the cheekiest smile I have ever seen and runs to the start. His Royal Highness greets him with shoving and good-natured ribbing. Meanwhile, I am speechless, captivated by the god who has occupied my thoughts.

I don't know who won the race. I was too busy watching a prince and a god run.

Chapter 6

The Prince

She is rustling around behind me, and the sound is comforting. A light scent wafts on the breeze. It is lemony and soft, sort of like her. Her slender hand touches my shoulder.

"It's beautiful," Hypatia marvels, her hand staying in place, tenderly.

Weeks have passed since the solstice festival, and she and I have fallen into a comforting routine. My evenings are spent in the observatory with her as company. They're some of the most delightfully filled evenings I have spent in a long time. While I enjoy the god, time with him differs from time with her. Apollo enjoys chess and card games, watching me paint. I enjoy making him submit to me as I fuck the god of light into oblivion. But, this woman, she brings out a side of me I haven't allowed to surface in some time.

"Is that the lower gardens?"

I nod. "Mmm."

"You're so talented, Your Royal Highness. Your brush creates a masterpiece."

I find myself preening under her genuine praise.

"I'm so impressed."

Her lips find my cheek, and I can't help but lean in. She straightens, her eyes wide in surprise and an odd little squeak comes from somewhere behind her hand.

43

"Your Highness," she mumbles between her fingers, "I'm so sorry. I never meant—I didn't mean—we aren't that familiar . . ."

"It's quite all right, little scribe." I capture the fingers of her opposite hand and kiss them reassuringly. "You may kiss me anytime you please."

To that, she blushes, and I turn to my art to examine the monstrosity I'm working on. I stare ahead with blurred vision, the feeling of her soft lips against my rough cheek sends shock waves through me. I want her to kiss me again. I want all her damn kisses.

"I'm still not happy with it," I say, pointing with a brush handle at the painting I should burn, trying my best at casual conversation, "but I suppose it will do for the night. Shall I walk you back?"

"Is Apollo still sending you to be my nightly companion?" Her cheeks pink prettily when she realizes the double entendre. The embarrassment is endearing.

"I meant merely the man who sees me nightly. Nightly in the observatory. Not my chambers." She's all red now, and the color crawls down to her slender neck. "Because I'm here for research. For the star."

I can't help but laugh and it fills the room, bouncing around us. It's deep and clear and feels good. Freeing. It's odd to laugh with someone who has only been here for such a short time, but she is fast becoming a fixture in my daily routine, chipping away at my stoic nature one smile at a time.

Hypatia shakes her head. "I'll be quiet now."

"By all means, little scribe, continue talking. I quite enjoy the verbal hole you're digging." I clean my brushes as I tease, setting them to dry on the table I had brought in. She is rolling scrolls and laughing at herself. It's dainty and feminine, and I want to make her laugh more often.

"I still detest the nickname you insist on calling me." She changes the subject.

"I know," I confess.

"I would much rather you use my name or at the very least my title of right hand."

"So, little scribe, you'd rather I invoke the titles you insist on subjecting me to?" I playfully bite back. No matter how many times I've corrected her, she continues to call me Prince or Your Royal Highness. Centuries of distancing myself from everyone but Apollo has made me a master at being seen and yet unseen at court. I am merely his right hand or the prince, never Cinthus. I want to hear her say my name, say it with familiarity, as if I'm as important to her as she is becoming to me. Instead, she uses my title as a barrier I can't vault over.

We are standing on the top step of the observatory, side by side, looking out into the dark. Apollo had this built for his own amusement. White marble that matches the rest of the palace lie end to end across the floor. The outside is a soft pink and orange, the colors of sunrise. Inside, the walls are adorned with frescoes. Depictions of the god of light run in a circle around the room. Some of war. Some conquests. Some myths.

All naked.

Every last one.

She looks up into the sky and squints as if she's trying to catch a last glimpse of the object of her obsession. Saying nothing, we both descend the steps and make our way through the gardens. I know the path well by now. A turn around the flower garden, past the hedges, rounding the oversized fountain of a naked muse, and up three marble steps to her wing of the palace. My chambers are further away, but I insist on accompanying her to the corridor. Hers are the first set of doors.

A palace is not a safe place for a woman, and I refuse to allow her to travel the relatively short distance alone. She protested at first but gave in after the third night. Our routine is comforting, and I now must end the evening walking Hypatia to her rooms. Truth is, I refuse to give any of these assholes that live with us an opportunity. Hypatia has been splitting her time between us: me in the evenings and Apollo in the mornings. By now, the warriors and guards have seen that she is favored amongst us. That is enough to put her either within the protection of the warriors or invoke their jealousy.

Dead is the man who lays a hand on her.

As we round the hedges, a loud breaking clap interrupts our quiet walk. Light streaks across the sky. Both of us freeze in place.

"Is that thunder?" she asks, and before the words leave her lips, rain is pelting down on us. Freezing, driving water soaks our clothes in seconds as ice stings our faces. Her hand is in mine as we run. Shivering against the freezing rain, I hear her shouting something, but thunder drowns out her words. We take the stairs, careful not to slip, and are under the protection of the palace once again. Hypatia is shaking, her breathing coming out in puffs of smoke as she brushes wet hair from her forehead.

"Rain?" Her teeth chatter as she speaks. "It doesn't rain on Olympus."

Lightning makes a liar of her statements, followed by thunder. The grounds are soaking up the rain as a layer of ice forms along the marble steps.

"Must be one pissed-off gaiamancer," I state, looking to the freezing water pelting the stairs. Grabbing her hand once again, I tug her towards her chambers. "Come along, little scribe, let's get you warm."

"A gaiamancer? A warrior that can control the elements?"

I nod.

"I've never known any that control this element." Picking up a cluster of frozen rain drops she examines it. "Ice in summer." Shrugging a shoulder, she lets it fall to the marble. "Just in case, I better remember to drink my tea."

Pausing, I give her a quizzical look. "Tea?"

She's nodding but her cheeks round as she smiles. "Could be a warrior, could be Zeus. Either way, I'd rather not end up pregnant."

The laughter that bursts forth rings through the corridor. I have to brace myself against the wall. Warriors, myself, hell even Apollo make jokes at The King's expense, but never once have I heard a woman. She looks like the cat who caught the canary. That little smirk is doing things to me.

In her chambers, I ring the bell for the maids to light her fire and instruct them to draw her a hot bath. Looking around, I see her room is neat and yet messy. As all the chambers have, there is an oversized bed, chairs, and a dressing table, but she has added a large wooden table. Scrolls are piled on one side, rolled and tied, while the other end holds piled parchment not yet rolled into scrolls. The astrolabe lies in the middle, along with a quill and inkpot. It is all situated nearest the open balcony, easiest access to the heavens, should she need it.

"I-I'm sor-rry for th-the mess."

Hypatia stands in the middle of the room shivering. As if she can't figure out what to do next. I march past her.

"Little scribe, for the gods' sake."

I rip the blanket off her bed. As I throw it over her, I regard the soaked linen peplos clinging to her skin. She moves grasping the blanket edge and two pert nipples poke out from behind the cloth. I pretend I haven't noticed and wrap her up, pulling her to me. Rubbing her arms vigorously, she rests her head against my chest, the top coming to my sternum. Selfishly, I breathe her in. Her whole body shakes, and I do my best to warm her as we wait for the bath to be drawn.

Along with furnishings, every chamber has a modern bath. Heated water from a spring comes from the ceiling and fills a large rectangular pool. It could easily fit three adults and is used primarily for private bathing.

Cleansing and ritualistic bathing are done in one of two bathhouses on either side of the palace.

"Hypatia," she insists as her teeth rattle hard enough to make mine shake.

"Stubborn woman," I softly scold.

"I'm a grown w-w-woman, Cinthus."

I pull her closer for no other reason than this is the first time I have heard my name on her lips. I desperately want to hear it again. That thought gives me pause as my hands rhythmically rub up and down her arms. I haven't wanted a woman in centuries. Apollo and I have an understanding. We are both free to see whomever we like. Men, women, wings, horns, tails, it matters not. Frequently, he'll add someone to our bed, but it never lasts long. In a matter of weeks, we are back to just the two of us, as it has been since the god stole me from my family and brought me here. Happily stole, I might add. But she is different.

One of the maids inclines her head at me, indicating the bath is filled.

"Come, get warm."

"I'm fine," she insists.

"Your shivering is rattling my teeth, little scribe. Either go willingly, or I'll toss you in."

She mumbles into the blanket and begrudgingly unwraps herself. Her peplos sticks everywhere, outlining her lithe body, obscured by linen. It's beautiful, and I can't help but stare. As I follow her into the bathing room, I am hard. Like a damn rock.

She turns to see I have followed and asks, "What are you doing?"

My gaze immediately goes to her breasts: small, round, and suddenly mouthwatering. Glancing down, she makes a sound in protest and covers them with crossed arms, but it's no use. I now know the outline of them, and I can't for the life of me focus on anything else.

"I need you to leave, Your Royal Highness."

"We're back to Your Royal Highness, are we?" I say smugly, crossing to sit on one of the benches. Both sandals come off, and I rise to unlash the belting around my waist. It plops to the floor. There is no denying how I'm responding to her now. She blinks when she catches sight of my erection, hard and upright under the chiton. The wet linen is sticking to me, and I can't hide anything, nor do I want to. Her chin rises to the ceiling.

"What do think you're doing?"

"Bathing," I say as I whip off the soaked chiton. "If you recall we were both caught in that storm."

"You think I'll let you bathe with me?" She turns her back and that round ass is playing peek-a-boo with the cloth, and I have the sudden urge to know what it feels like to smack it, to see it pink. I lower myself into the pool, letting out a groan as I sink.

"Come, little scribe—"

"Hypatia."

I can tell that correction is said between clenched teeth, and I enjoy the insistence on her name. Images are now dancing across my mind, ones I've kept at bay. She will be so lovely when I have her under my direction. I want to make her bloom and see her take what I give. Watch her respond to Apollo. Under my hands, she will become what she is meant to be. She will be exquisite for both of us.

"Hypatia." I lower my voice, giving her a one-word command. "Come."

She turns her head to look at me, and I wait. I want to see if she'll accept the terms. I know she'll submit, but a part of me loves the challenge she's currently giving. Several seconds tick by before she growls. It's fucking adorable.

"Fine." She looks at me again. "Don't look."

"I make no such promise, little scribe. Now. Come."

Again she growls, but she slowly unfastens the pins at the shoulders of the chiton. It falls heavy to the floor. Those long, lean legs, that ass, the curve of her back, all on display for my hungry gaze.

Fuck.

"Leaving would be the gentlemanly thing to do."

I shake my head. "I never professed to be a gentleman. I'll go, Hypatia, if that's what you truly want. But you need to tell me."

She grumbles, and I think for a moment she will order me out, but she reaches up and pulls two combs from her hair. It falls below her shoulders in a cascading river of silky chestnut. My fist clenches, wanting to grasp a handful and watch as she gasps from both pain and pleasure. Instead of turning to face me, she steps back, then again.

"What the hell are you doing?"

"If you won't grant me the privacy to bathe on my own, then I shall enter the pool where my most private areas aren't on display."

"Oh! For fucking Zeus' sake, Hypatia. Get in the damn water. You will catch pneumonia taking this long."

She straightens her back and continues her backward path. *Stubborn as a damn centaur.* Once she's in, she sinks to the step and relaxes against the side, her back still to me.

"Is this how all our baths shall be?" I tease, and she glares at me over her shoulder.

"There will be no other baths, Your Royal Highness. I am adamantly against this one."

"Is it me you truly detest or the being naked with me?"

Sighing, she relaxes further into the side of the pool.

"I do not detest you, Your Highness. I'm annoyed with you."

Her honesty makes me smile, and I watch her lean her head back, letting the water ease the muscles along her back.

"You'll not come closer so we may talk about your day? I would love to hear about your walk with Apollo this morning."

I'm having more fun than should be allowed but the woman keeps her back to me. Several moments tick by, and I watch her curiously.

"My day was fine. Apollo was the perfect gentleman. Maybe I shall ask him to instruct you. You seem to need lessons." She glances over her shoulder, but her earlier irritation is replaced with a playful glint in her eyes. Gods, this woman is making me want things.

"Are you getting warm, little scribe?"

"I'm warm enough," she states. While her teeth have stopped their chattering, she is still shivering even in the heat of the water. "If you'll excuse me." She moves to stand.

I've reached my limit of her obstinance and scoot close enough to grab her by the hips, pulling her down. She lets out a squeak of surprise and then bats at my hands, but it's too late. The water sloshes over the sides and runs onto the tiled floor.

"Let me go, you brute!" she protests, but I refuse. "Prince Cinthus, if you please."

"It pleases me very much, Hypatia. Now, you'll stay here with me until I'm satisfied you won't die in your sleep."

"You can't die from being cold."

Twisting my head so I can meet her eye, I give her a look. "Ever heard of hypothermia?"

A disgruntled puff of air is my answer. "Yes, but I would be under the covers and warm if I were asleep. I meant I can't die from being wet."

"Oh, on the contrary, being wet can lead to death. I believe I heard a French warrior once refer to it as *la petite mort*."

She gasps and turns to face me, her side profile on display. I want to nip at that jaw of hers. Her glare softens by degrees as the gray in her eyes glint.

"You are a brute." Her tone scolds, but the hint of a smile gives her away. She doesn't shy away, instead, she rests against my chest, and I can't help but enjoy the feel of her curves. I don't know what I've done to earn her trust, but I'm determined to keep it.

"I suppose. I'll not take a chance of you dying, little scribe. Best to stay here."

Reaching up, I massage her shoulders as she further sinks into me. A soft sound urges me on, and I move her wet hair aside to dig my fingers into the muscles of her neck.

"Do you like this, Hypatia?"

She nods. "That feels nice, Cin."

Her murmurs of appreciation along with my name are sending lightning straight to my cock. She tilts her head the opposite way so that I may loosen muscles there. My hands move down her shoulders, to her back, then lower, under the water. Leaning back, I cradle her as I find her hips.

"You are very tense for someone who looks at stars," I say low in her ear.

"Hmm, maybe it's because I have to deal with a certain pompous royal."

Her wit is intoxicating, and without thought of the consequences, I kiss behind her ear. The little gasp will be the end of me. That pink tongue of hers flicks out from between parted lips, and I want so badly to know what she kisses like.

"Cin."

It's a raspy whisper and one that fills my head with visions of her rasping my name.

"May I?" I have to ask. I can't have her giving me complete control without a bond of trust forged beforehand.

"May you what?"

I rub my nose along her temple. "May I kiss you?"

She swallows, and I'm reveling in how her breathing is coming out in little pants. I skim my hand across her belly under the water, and I have to remind myself to control my eagerness.

"I shouldn't," she says low.

She's responding to me with the tiniest of arches in her back, causing her ass to find my rather eager cock. It wouldn't take much. A word, a look, and I could have her straddling me, begging for release.

"May I?" She nods, and I demand again, grasping her chin in between my wet fingers. "Say the words. A nod isn't sufficient. I need to hear you say you want me to kiss you."

I ache to kiss her, to tangle my tongue with hers, taste her. Her eyes have fluttered closed, and my mouth finds her ear. A nip on the edge has her gasping.

Gods the things I want to do to her.

"And then what?"

"Whatever you'd like."

I give her time to catch her breath and think. I want her willing and enthusiastic. Twisting around, her pretty mouth finds my jaw, then my neck, and I lose myself to the feel of her lips against my skin.

"More kisses?"

"Yes."

Her lips tease a line to my jaw.

"A little death?"

Fucking Zeus! "Yes."

"Apollo will mind, I fear."

"Apollo won't, I assure you." Her eyes catch mine, and she bites her bottom lip sending pulsing desire coursing through me.

"You're his, Cin."

"I can be yours." I say, barely touching her lips with mine. "Let a man who knows what he's doing worship this beautiful body of yours. I can have you shaking under me, calling to Zeus."

Her breath stalls and something crosses her delicate feature. Her eyes pop open. "You can't make those types of promises. I can make myself call out to Zeus without a man in sight."

Sitting forward, she slips from my grasp and is out of the pool. I clutch at air and water droplets.

"I don't want a *little* death, Your Royal Highness," she spits at me as my mind tries to comprehend how she is out of my arms and wrapped in a toweling cloth so fast. "I want to be dragged to the Underworld to dine with Hades. Unless you can promise that I'll stick to what has served me well in the past."

She is in the doorway before I can even rise from my spot in the pool. Turning, she gives me one last annoyed look.

"See yourself out."

Chapter 7

The Scribe

I've read this sentence three times. Earlier, I found a scroll from the Oracle, my first in the endless stack. I was eager when I saw it, but my mind refuses to focus. It's been days since the prince climbed into my bathing pool. His command has been echoing in my mind like a siren song beckoning me closer.

Come.

. The deepness of his timbre is like an aphrodisiac, and I want to hear him say it again. My fingers find my clavicle as I recall him behind me, his thighs on either side of my hips, holding me in place. His fingers found every sore muscle I had from all the hours bent over a table or hunched looking through instruments. I wanted to give in that night. I wanted him to kiss me, touch me, to make good on his promise. But I stopped myself.

Prince Cin belongs to Apollo, and as I have learned, the gods do not take kindly to others playing with their toys.

The last few nights I've been restless. Memories of His Majesty's hands, his breath, his words have bored themselves into my mind. I'm trying to ignore the way he makes me feel. How they both make me feel. Between Cin's words in the bath and Apollo's perfect naked body at the games, I'm losing the battle. Dreams of the two of them in my bed haunt me. Dreams I have no business having.

I have avoided them trying to gain a semblance of control. To stop wondering what their lips taste like. Cutting myself off is what I need to do until I can trust myself. But if my midnight desires are any indication, I'm losing a grip on that control.

It isn't just those moments of meeting their penetrative stares or catching them looking at me with expressions I can't read. It's the genuine interest in me that has endeared them and made my time here more pleasurable. Apollo began seeking me out after the games. Each morning, he walks with me around the gardens, listening to me carry on about findings. Each evening, the prince meets me in the observatory, and we share quiet moments in comfortable company. They ask about my home. About my human life. I am not just a scribe, I'm myself. I make jokes, laugh too loud, and am relaxed around them. As if I fit. As if I belong. I enjoy their company, but it comes with a cost; the cost of secretly wanting both.

And I know I can't have them both.

This only ends one or two ways. With my heart in tatters or Artemis finding out and trying to kill both. Either way, I lose.

Clearing my head of my previous thought, I begin reading once more. A drawing of a naked warrior in battle has me back in the pool in my mind. All of his beautiful body, honed to perfection by war and drills, flashes before me every time I close my eyes. I might have told him not to look, but I made no such promise.

The memory of the prince's teeth nipping my ear invades, sending my reasoning flying. His hands were large and surprisingly soft on my shoulders. I let my hand follow there next, retracing his path.

Hypatia.

I want him to call my name. To know what it sounds like from his lips as he explores me. I enjoyed the sensation of his beard as I kissed his neck and jaw. Rough. Masculine. Erotic. Closing my eyes, I give over to my fantasy. My fingers skim the tops of my breasts. Without any thought to my constant guard, I pinch one pert nipple through the fabric of the chiton and bite back a moan.

"You've been avoiding me."

My lungs freeze, and my eyes fly open at the familiar masculine voice. Apollo is leaning against a rack, staring, his brow furrowed. I will myself to act natural. And, if I'm honest, scold myself for allowing my imagination to lead in such a public place. He gives no indication he saw what I was doing, and I play along.

Coming closer, he strokes my cheek with a finger; it causes me to shudder.

"You're flushed. It's quite warm in here. Perhaps your guard can open the shutters." He snaps his fingers, and the warrior moves.

Concern builds a wall of lines across his forehead, and I remind myself that Cin is his and not mine. That Apollo is a god, and gods don't choose women like me. That my fantasies are not my reality. That wanting either is wanting heartache.

Clearing my throat, I move. "I'm fine, My God. Is there something I can help you with?"

He's staring, and I realize where his gaze has landed. My chiton this morning is thin, keeping me cool in this heat. It's only one layer, which means my hard nipples are puckering under the fabric for the god of light to admire.

"My God?" I repeat, hoping my casualness forces him to look at me. But the longer he stares, the darker his eyes become. When those eyes snap to mine, I forget any logic I previously had.

"You've been avoiding me," he repeats. I shake my head and his tilts, giving me a knowing look. I hate that he can read me so well after such a short time. I wonder briefly if he can read my thoughts because the way he's looking at me makes me think he can see deep into my most private fantasies, ones where it's Cin and Apollo and me. Like one I had last night that had me crying out so loud I was sure the entire wing heard me.

"I—I haven't," I sputter, flustered and hot, and desperately wanting to retire to my chambers to take care of a sudden ache between my legs.

"Three mornings. I haven't seen you for three mornings." His thumb skims my hand, and I'm instantly on fire. "Are you so busy here that you can't spend time with your host?"

"Is there something you need, My God? Something I can help you with?" I desperately try to change the subject. Trying to get him out of the archives before I do something impulsive.

"I wanted my companion this morning."

"I apologize. I had found some of the Oracle's prophecies and decided to transcribe them instead." Skirting around him to the next table has me secretly wanting him to touch me. He doesn't. Gaining my composure, I busy myself by making a show of moving scrolls around. My mind is blank as his stare prickles across my skin. He needs to leave.

"Have I done something to offend you?"

I blink, quickly raising my head. Apollo looks genuinely concerned, and I deflate. I've dreamed of this man for centuries, and my damn private dreams may ruin our delicate friendship. I'm embarrassed he almost caught me doing something rather indelicate.

"Of course not, My God."

He raises both eyebrows, and I have the overwhelming urge to ruffle his hair. I am supposed to be keeping my distance, but I've missed our early morning talks. The way the sun catches his wings, illuminating the white to a celestial brilliance. Those golden curls, tossed about on the wind, shining under the rising dawn. Three days of avoidance and I'm back to replaying stolen moments as I have for centuries.

"I assure you."

He shrugs and leans against the table. "What is it you've found that has kept you hidden away for days?"

"Oh, that! I have found a few things that bridge some gaps in the knowledge I've obtained for the library." I launch into an excited retelling as Apollo looks on. He nods. He hums. But most importantly, he listens. I roll out a scroll and show him where I found one instance of the Oracle's prophetic word coming true in later accounts. Another scroll shows a grouping of constellations. Excitedly, I wave my hands and unroll several more scrolls, but he isn't looking at the parchment. His large hand dances across the wood and settles close to mine.

"You are incredibly intelligent, have I told you that?"

I'm taken aback by the odd compliment. "I'm aware I'm intelligent, My God."

"That isn't what I said." His fingers skim over my ear as he tucks hairs behind it, and then they travel the line of my jaw, lifting my chin so I am forced to look up. Tiny electric shocks buzz against my skin. "I asked if I had *told you* how incredibly intelligent you are."

I swallow, my heart pounding against my ribs. "You just did."

He smiles and it is like the brilliance of the sun. I want to soak up its radiance. I want all his smiles.

"What's next?"

My gaze shifts to his lips, and I wonder how soft they'd feel. "Next?"

"What have you to do next? This morning?"

His thumb finds my lower lip and methodically begins tracing it. Those cloud-blue eyes are dark, lidded, and unashamed of whatever thoughts he's entertaining. I know because I'm having them as well. I'm a woman obsessed with the way he is looking at me. I jerk my chin and release myself from his hand.

"I have some calculations I need to do from the measurements I took, but I was going to do them after midday meal." The words tumble out between clearing my throat.

"Humm. So, you have time then, to spend with me."

I can only nod.

"There are many things we could do to pass the time. Have any thoughts, scribe?"

I tilt my head up and scowl. "My name is Hypatia, My God. Scribe is what I am."

"Intoxicating is what you are." He comes closer so that we are a breath away. "Alluring and intoxicating."

Again, he smiles, and my heart flips in my chest. Or stops beating altogether, I'm not quite sure. Instead of backing away, I slide closer. If he notices, he says nothing. Leaning forward, he's intent on my mouth.

I snap my head back, and everything in me screams in protest.

"What—what are you doing?"

He breathes a laugh, and it slips over my lips as if he's kissed me. His eyes dart lower and back up.

"I assumed the intent was clear." He hasn't moved. His mouth is tantalizingly close.

"Are you going to kiss me?"

"Would you like a kiss? May I kiss you? Is that the game you play, little scribe?"

I ignore the drumming of my pulse in my ears. "I don't play games, My God. And my name is Hypatia. Seems to me, one should address the one they intend to kiss by their name."

He blinks. But my mind has fixated on his words. The nickname. *Prince Cin's nickname.* He's using His Highness' infuriating nickname. After weeks of daily walks, not once has he called me that. That can only mean one thing.

They are toying with me.

Suddenly everything is screamingly clear. They are discussing me in private. I must be the latest object of their attention, not an equal like I was beginning to think I was. They must be mocking me and my silly belief that I am important to them. Getting involved with the gods, any god, only leads to heartbreak at best and death at worst. But dreaming of a god and his partner, wanting them both? I must have lost hold of my senses. I had fancied the idea of them. Of me. Of us.

I fooled myself for a moment, but logic is screaming to the surface. Apollo claimed a lover in Prince Cinthus. He would never claim one in me. I would only be burned by him and eventually tossed aside, thrown over for the next obsession.

"May I kiss you, Hypatia?"

The sound of my name thrills me, and I want so desperately to believe this is real. I lean forward.

"No," I hear myself say as my intellect wins this round over my idiot heart. Apollo pulls back, creating a chasm of space between us.

"No?"

"No, My God," I say, but my feet betray me. They step forward, wanting to bridge the gap. "No, you may not kiss me."

His hand darts out, grabbing hold of my chin and tipping it up so I'm forced, once again, to look him in the eyes. I want him to kiss me anyway. I want him to prove that I have only jumped to conclusions.

"Humm. I'll respect your refusal for now, but I believe soon you will ask me, no beg me to kiss you." His gaze roams lower, and I can feel heat moving south as if his mouth is on me. His hand skims my side, coming to rest on my hip. "Beg me to touch you." His hand slides to my thigh, slipping the fabric of my dress between his fingers. The throbbing between my legs resumes with vigor, and I forget to breathe, forcing myself to continue holding his gaze. "Beg me to taste your skin."

"I doubt that, My God," I challenge with a well-timed sniff. "I've never needed anything from an Olympian bad enough to beg. Besides"—I move closer, enough that if I wanted, I could press my body to his. And I want to. Fiercely. My mind may have put the pieces together, but my body craves him. This doesn't go unnoticed, and his beautiful mouth twists into a knowing smile. Unable to stop myself, I let my words land—"I am the right hand of Artemis. I hear she can be quite the tyrant when one of the women under her care is defiled."

Testing his resolve, I rise on my tiptoes and lean even closer so that our mouths are almost touching.

"The answer is no," I whisper, lowering down and stepping back.

Apollo sways forward, chasing me before he steadies himself. He smirks, and I have the sinking suspicion I am about to eat my words.

"Very well. I suppose I'm now forced to tell you the other reason I came, although my loneliness these past few mornings was part of it." He jerks his chin at me. "I am calling you to my chambers. I have been told about an incident with Prince Cinthus a few nights ago. I need to hear your side of things."

My eyes widen, and I swallow. Panic sets in. Jealousy is one emotion gods are skilled at, and if Apollo is calling me for a meeting, he knows about Cin and me. My heart hammers against my chest now for an entirely different reason.

"I'll see you this evening."

His feathers rustle as he leaves, his footsteps heavy on the marble.

Chapter 8

The Scribe

My fingers twist into the opposite hand. Two guards come to retrieve me. Sandwiched between them, it feels more like a death march than a simple summons. I don't know how the god of light will react. Worry mars lines across my face as I walk.

Instead of entering the main throne room, we turn just before an enormous archway decorated with Apollo's symbol of a half-sun with an arrow through the middle. The guards open tall double doors to a set of private chambers. We stop near a large, white, round marble table with chairs ringing it. To one side is a floor-to-ceiling wall with an open hinged door, displaying weaponry of all kinds. All in gold. Before us, atop a small platform sits a large, simple, white marble throne. Apollo is seated, beside him at a desk is the prince.

The sun god is dressed formally this evening, and that worries me. When we meet in the mornings, he wears a chiton or tunic, armor, and sandals. Tonight, he has added a white cape, affixed to one shoulder and flowing to the ground. His demeaner is guarded, and I can't read his face. I have secretly prided myself on being able to decipher his moods but now, seriousness cracks the veneer of friendliness, and for the first time since coming here, I'm afraid. If the god thinks I am trying to somehow take his partner, he could do anything to me, and no one would blink. I try to calm my erratic heartbeat, but it isn't any use. By the time he flicks his fingers, dismissing the guards, I'm trembling.

His Royal Highness locks eyes with me and frowns. He moves to stand beside his god, his hand on the back of the throne. It doesn't matter that Cin got in the pool first. Or that I stopped myself and walked out. No explanation will matter to him if he's made his mind up that he's been slighted.

I'm alone with no one to speak for me.

"It has been brought to my attention, that you had quite the evening with my prince."

I look at said prince whose face is unreadable and hold my breath. I don't trust my voice.

"He tells me it was an interesting encounter."

My mouth is dry.

"Why did you leave?"

I blink, my mind deciphering what he asked. "Ex-excuse me?"

"Why did you leave?" He touches the prince's arm and levels his chin at me. "I find His Highness to be a rare specimen. If I had him naked and wet in my bathing pool, I wouldn't leave. Do you not find him as attractive as I do?"

I don't know how to answer. Looking between them, I open my mouth to say something, anything, but only garbled noises escape. Nothing in the way of actual words.

"Is he not the one you want?"

I'm frozen to the ground by the absurdity of his questioning.

"Would you prefer a god, perhaps?"

"My God?" My voice sounds from somewhere else as if it's thrown from my throat. "I am unsure what you mean." I finally respond, shaking my head. Apollo stands and descends the steps to stand before me.

"I'm curious, how you came to resist Prince Cinthus. I've never been able to. If he nor I are to your liking, maybe it is that you prefer women to men."

I am so stunned I shake my head at his inference. "I prefer men."

Why I answer is beyond me. This isn't how I expected this evening to go. I expected him to rail and accuse me of stealing his lover. I expected the god to throw me out. Or kill me. But asking why I left a naked prince in my bathing pool was not something I had prepared myself for.

"Good," he says, pleased for some reason. "So, my question remains, why did you leave?"

Taking a deep breath calms me some. "Because, My God, I respect his position."

"His position?" He turns slightly to look over his shoulder at the prince, who shrugs. "And what position is that?"

"Yours, My God."

"How do you mean?"

I frown. Why isn't he angry? Why does he seem pleased, somehow? I can't tell where he's leading me, and it makes me leery of his intentions. If I had stayed, I would have given in. I would have let Cin do any number of wicked things to me, consequences be damned. And I would have enjoyed every second.

"His Royal Highness is yours. Your lover. And he is off limits, to me." My voice trails off at the end as I lower my eyes. "I was afraid of your jealousy."

The truth, as inconvenient as it is, comes out. I didn't leave because I didn't want Cin. I left because I feared what would happen if I gave in. Raising my chin, I look at him. At least, if he threw a tantrum, I'd know I didn't cower.

He moves closer, and I resist the urge to step back. Inside, a spark of irritation grows. I can't shake the feeling that they are playing a game, and I do not know the rules. That infuriates me. His finger traces my jaw and something low sparks to life.

"I am jealous, *little scribe.*"

"Stop calling me that," I grit out. "I am not a girl. I am not little. I'm a woman with a name."

"Oh, I'm well aware of the woman you are. And that is why I'm jealous." Several fingers stroke down my neck, and my body betrays me. Closing my eyes, I lean my head back just enough.

His mouth grazes my ear, and I take in a sharp breath. "The prince has been insufferable. He has refused to tell me any delicious details besides the fact he likes the feel of your lips on his neck. I had hoped I'd be the first one you showed affection to. I'm jealous I haven't shared a bath with you yet. I'm jealous he got to hold you. Touch you. Kiss you. So yes, I am jealous, but not of you. Of him, Hypatia."

My eyes fly open at my name. Why it thrills me each time they use it when I insist is beyond me. Cinthus is watching me intently, and I can't help but notice how he's also watching Apollo. Darkness shades his face, and I wonder who he's mad at.

Me for leaving that night.

Or the god for his little display currently.

The god is standing so close, the air between us grows thin. His mere presence is choking my ability to breathe, until I forget altogether how my lungs work the second his lips touch my neck. He lays one slow, steady kiss on my pulsing artery before he raises his mouth just enough that his breath tickles my ear. I shiver.

"I have had dreams about you," he confesses. "Wonderfully vivid dreams of you and I and Cin."

I gasp and my eyes dart from him to His Highness and back. A god wouldn't confess such a notion, would they? He watches me, and his expression changes slightly as he gives a tiny nod as if he's reading my thoughts.

"Does that surprise you? That I've been thinking of you? You are a treasure, Hypatia. A gift sent by the fates. One I've been waiting on for quite a while. A mere mortal man would claim he could make a woman like you call out to the gods." He *tsks* and lets his hand wander down. At his touch, my head slowly falls back, betraying me. My nerve endings come alive, and I can feel him everywhere. It's as if he's stripped me bare, exposing my secret desires. My body hums to life. Cinthus tilts his head around the god's looming frame, and I see the fire blazing in his eyes as he watches Apollo with me.

"But the gods of Olympus do not exist here, Hypatia, only me. I'm not one to share what I claim as mine, and I plan to make you mine in every way. I long to hear my name called from those pretty lips of yours."

Stopping his assault, he leans back and and removes his roving hands. I glare into his darkening expression, like storm clouds rolling in. His lips curl as they hover over mine. He's pleased with himself for playing with me like a cat with a mouse. I desperately want to tip forward and kiss his lips, show him that I've been thinking of him too. But I know he will never claim a lowly scribe for anything so daring as a lover. Let alone share her, as he's alluded to, with the prince he finds himself infatuated with. I am a distraction for them both. Something to occupy their time between the festivities. Someone they laugh at behind closed doors. As much as I dream of the two of them, having them would be a mistake. One I can't afford to make. As my tongue darts out to run across my lips, he watches, and his stare grows hungry.

Two can play this game.

"Mmm," I purr as if he does not affect me. "Make sure you do, My God. I'd hate to call the wrong name by mistake."

His expression jumps from surprise to something else in moments. A flame lights behind those eyes piercing my very soul. I hold my ground.

Arrogant god.

"I am not a thing to be possessed. I am just a pawn to you"—I look at His Majesty—"both. You see me as the next conquest, not anything of importance."

He snaps to an upright position as if I've struck him. It gives me the courage to continue.

"I refuse to be some sort of prize you claim at the end of this game you two are playing. I am here with a singular mission in mind that does not involve either of you. For the rest of my time here, I request to be left alone to do my research in peace." The words fly out of my mouth before I have time to think about them. I might have entered this room in fear, but I'm leaving pissed. Calling me by the same infuriating name, discussing me as if I am in their bed already. I'm angered I fell into their trap.

"Hypatia." Apollo says my name in a pained tone but His Royal Highness interrupts.

"Concede, Apollo. I believe she has won this round," he says quietly, but the deep timbre bursts into the room. It's as if I've been struck by lightning. I'm paralyzed and burning, a shocking jolt of electricity shooting down my spine. I wait until the tingling subsides before I move.

"Your Highness," I snap in the prince's direction, turning abruptly, and heading towards the door.

"I haven't dismissed you," Apollo demands.

I stop my escape and refuse to turn around. "Then force me to stay," I say, my back straight. When no one responds, I look over my shoulder at the pair. "I thought as much."

Leaving a god's presence without permission is a blatant disrespect, but I was done being respectful to either of them. I was not the timid woman they chose to see.

I marched from the room without a backward glance.

Chapter 9

The God

A god can do many things, but my least favorite is hearing those who call my name shouting inside my head. I have learned to block it out, all gods have to, or we'll go mad. Except, I can't with her. I heard her thoughts in the archives this afternoon. I heard them last night as Cin fucked me. They are quickly unraveling any rational thought I have.

Sighing, I let her leave in a huff. A guard comes in quickly, and I instruct him to follow. I wanted her to say outright that she felt something as I did. I should just let her go, but I can't. She's in my blood, curling through my veins like too much wine.

"Was that necessary?" Cin scolds in that way he does. Taking a seat on my throne, he leans forward, his forearms on those thick thighs of his.

"Which part, bringing her here under guard, or trying to force her to voice her thoughts aloud?"

"You're being an ass, Apollo." When I turn, he is looking at me pointedly.

"I'm tired of waiting for her to make a move. Damn it! I have never had to work this hard to get a woman's attention."

He wrinkles his nose and sniffs. "Now that she's here, do you want her, or are you, as she said, toying with her?"

"And if I was?"

He's serious as he sits up and crosses an ankle over his knee. "I would command you to stop."

"You? Command me?"

Cin's chin lifts slightly, and his fingers flex, pulling at the muscles in his forearm. I know he is aching to put me in my place. He could have me on my knees if he wanted. On my knees, submitting to a punishment I'm sure I deserve. Heat races through me at his stare.

"Are you toying with her?"

Rapidly, I shake my head. Sinking into the marble, Cin looks like a king holding court, and I'm beginning to feel more like the court jester. I know I'm being irrational. I know I've got to give her time but dammit, I've spent centuries looking for her. I don't want time. I want her.

"Because I won't stand for it, Apollo. If you plan on continuing to confuse her, I order you to leave her alone completely. She is too important. She isn't a prize to me."

He's studying his fingernails, but I know what that means. He's pissed, and he's doing his best to hide it. One shake of my head, and he relaxes back into the throne.

"It's her."

Something flickers in his eyes, and I wonder if this is madness. If wanting her, searching for her has left me teetering past obsession and into mania.

"That night, in Artemis' court. I thought her another of my sister's nymphs, but she's the woman, the one I tried to find. The one who's occupied my thoughts. It was her, Cin, all this time. And now she's here. I can't let her get away again. And I'm—it's her, Cin."

He scratches his chin. "I'm aware, Apollo. I knew it that first night in the gardens. But I'll ask you again: Is she important to you or is she a conquest?"

"No." I soften. "She's so much more."

"Good, because she isn't to me either." We stare at each other for several long seconds before he continues. "She is important to me, as well. So important, I was going to request she join us."

Sputtering on air, I cough at his admission.

"*You* want to add someone to our arrangement?"

A jerk of his head is my only answer. I knew he had formed an attachment to my Hypatia, but I assumed it a friendship. Cin never asks to include someone else. He doesn't mind when I do, in fact, I think he enjoys dominating me in the presence of others. But to request means the other night was more than just him playing along. He feels something for Hypatia, just as I do. The prince is discerning. When he falls, he falls hard and remains loyal. The fact he wants her too is telling.

"I am not looking for a quick fuck. I enjoy her company outside of anything I might want, and I have many thoughts on what I want." I snort a laugh at myself. "She is effervescent, a breath of fresh air. So clever. Gentle. Kind."

"Intelligent and funny," he chimes in. "But I refuse to be a party to someone you will tire of in a week. I'm not in this for a fling."

"Neither am I."

"We need to cherish her."

"Those are your terms?"

He nods. "Those are my terms. And if you agree, I take the lead. I can't have you ruining this with your eagerness. We need to take this one step at a time."

"I accept. We both are interested in our alluring house guest."

"More than interested," he says, scratching his chin. "Infatuated is more like."

I move to leave the room to find her now that I know he wants her too, but Cin barks at me. "No." I turn to face him; my lips twist in displeasure.

"Give her time to breathe. She will no doubt retreat into the archives to mull over your little stunt this afternoon."

He's right, of course, but I selfishly don't want to wait. My lips tingle from kissing her neck. I want more of her. I want her like I wanted Cin all those years ago. It's a burning ache, consuming my thoughts. I want her in our bed, in our lives, and not just for the fleeting time she has been here. Hypatia has haunted my thoughts for centuries, and I need to know if she feels the same.

"I take the lead, it's what you agreed to."

"And the first step?"

He relaxes further into the marble. "Asking her what she wants."

Nodding, I ascend the stairs, and Cin makes room on the arm of my throne, beckoning me to sit. My hand entangles in his hair as his eyes close, a low hum of approval coming from his lips. This man has been my obsession for centuries and tonight he confessed to wanting someone else as much as I do. I bend to kiss him, wanting his lips, his hands on me. His beard scratches my chin as his tongue tangles with mine. He's grasping my head, holding me in place. I will give him anything he wants as long as he keeps kissing me like that.

The Prince

Fucking Zeus! Apollo is such an ass. Good thing I like taming that ass of his. He had been allowed to revert to his old ways, the ways he was before he let me in his bed. He needed to be reminded who held his reins. His admission this evening has given me pause. He has frequently talked of the woman who held his attention during that dinner so long ago, but when she showed up here, I knew we needed to tread carefully. He isn't thinking of the consequences. He's only thinking of his desires. Artemis will be furious if she finds out. Moreover, he can come on strong, reacting to his desires the way a god would, not the way a human would and that could send her running. We have to tread carefully here. It's why I need to lead. Hypatia, *our Hypatia*, is a rare woman.

Our bold Hypatia.

She didn't fold under his touch like so many have when he turns on his charms. She didn't just resist, she called his bluff and pushed back, forcing him to let her win. She has held steadfast for weeks, driving the god out of his mind, and truth be told, driving me out of mine. I thought her timid when we first met, but I know better now. It was a marvel watching them interact. Exhilarating. She has no idea the power she wields over us. Hypatia slid under my skin that first night. I fully admit that I crave her, want her in ways I haven't felt in years. But Apollo. Her thwarting his advances so expertly held me captivated. Nymphs, sirens, hell even me on occasion, bent to the god of the sun's flirtation. But not Hypatia.

She has bite.

Bite I am eager to tame. I want to see what she can take, push her past her limits, and set her free.

Claiming her will be a challenge, and I fucking love a challenge.

Chapter 10

The God

I groan with his repeated thrusts. Pulling against the ties that bind my hands above my head has me arching my back and taking him deeper.

"Fuck, Cin." I moan, breathless, as he keeps me on the edge. He isn't talking; isn't dominating the way he usually does, and I take this opportunity to try to flip. "You like me at your mercy?"

His dark eyes flash as they open, and he growls in response. His thick fingers come around my throat, putting pressure on the sides, letting me know he's in charge of everything, even the very air I breathe.

"I am using you, you arrogant ass. This is for my pleasure, not yours. Don't you dare come until I say, Apollo. You'll take this cock of mine as hard as I need."

His fingers tighten, and I can't help the delight that tugs at the corners of my mouth. I enjoy all sides of my prince, but this side I know only comes when he feels out of control. And I have an inkling why. He slams into me, and I teeter on insanity. Focusing on the shape of his mouth, his fingers around my throat, I'm not prepared when her thoughts invade my mind. It's an image of my prince in her bathing chamber. Then his face close in proximity to hers. When the image dances through, I let out a desperate whine. Being fucked by Cin while I can hear and see my sweet Hypatia's thoughts sends me over the edge. Her moans get closer together, and suddenly, she climaxes.

"Fuck. Gods," I yell from deep within my chest. "Fuck."

Cinthus would normally enjoy this sight of me losing all control, but he begins shaking and falls with me into the fucking abyss. I wonder for just a half second if our alluring house guest has somehow invaded both are minds, but I know that isn't possible. We both come back to Olympus together, his head on my shoulder, panting into my skin. Flopping over, Cin lies still for several minutes, and I revel in the sounds of our mutual exertion. Several minutes more and I'm untied, cleaned up, and my prince lies beside me, staring up at the ceiling.

"Twice," I say to the room.

"What's twice?"

"You." I roll to my side. "As if my mouth wasn't enough, you needed to fuck me as well." Placing a hand on his chest, I trace a carved pectoral, chiseled to perfection by centuries of exercise. You are wound tighter than usual, Cinthus."

His eyes roll in my general direction, but a grunt is my only answer. I sniff and notice something dancing on the soft breeze. Leaning closer, I breathe him in.

"What is that scent?"

This question causes him to roll over on his side. "Laurel soap."

I wait impatiently for further explanation, but he offers none, so I push. "Are we out of soap in the palace? I wasn't aware you preferred the soap sold in the agora."

Cin sniffs, then sighs. "Hypatia."

Raising up on my elbow, I look over at him and wait again. Normally, my prince is full of answers and truths, but tonight he has been in that head of his, and I know why. That woman is turning us into desperate, needy men.

"You know I rarely care about such things. The other evening, I spent too long in the training fields and bathed in my chambers instead of the bathhouse. I didn't notice which soap I used, but she did. She commented more than once on the scent, and I—"

"I see," I say with a lift of one shoulder. "So, it's for her."

He nodded. "I can't get her out of my head, Apollo. I find myself gravitating towards her throughout the day and then reminding myself we are to give her space. I'm trying to be patient, but I'm beginning to think you were right, we should have went after her when she marched out of the throne room."

I flop back onto my back, placing a hand under my head. "I'm following your lead, and you're starting to crack."

He chuckles and tucks a pillow under his head, shifts a blanket around his waist, kicks it off, pulls it back on, and then finally turns to his back. I turn back to my side.

"Come here, you—what did you say she calls you?"

"Brute." He wiggles closer.

"Come here, you brute." We both laugh, and I wrap my arms around him, holding his head to my chest and running my hands through his hair. I know this is what he needs. As much as my prince likes to make me submit, he enjoys snuggling more. I feel his body grow heavy, and he sinks into mine, relaxing into me as we both succumb to sleep.

The pounding of footfalls jolts me awake. Looking beside me, she lays fast asleep, her red hair spilling out from under the covers. The pounding gets closer, and I quickly rise to my feet, bow in hand. My arms are thin and scrawny, shaking as I move to the end of the makeshift palette we've made on the cavern floor. Everything in me is freezing, even my blood, as we can't make a fire, lest Hera find us.

"Apollo." Her tiny voice has me looking over my shoulder.

"Shhh, Arte, get back into the cave."

The sound of an army gets closer, it rattles around us and stirs my mother.

"Apollo?"

"Get back, it's Hera. She's found us."

The women scurry further into the cold, wet cavern, and I stand ready, the bow I can barely pull back gripped in my icy fingers. I had forgone the furs so that I may always be ready to defend my mother and sister. My teeth rattle as I shiver in the dark. Light bursts into the cave, and Hera stands at the entrance, an army of warriors behind her.

"Kill them," she growls between gritted teeth. "Kill them all."

"NO!"

"Shhh, Apollo."

Hands grab me, pulling me somewhere, and I fight against them. Raining blows down upon my captor, I can feel the crunch of bone under knuckles.

"Fuck!"

"LET THEM GO!" I scream as the man reaches around my waist, pulling me away from my mother and sister. I'm wild now, clawing and scratching, doing anything to get away, to protect the most important people to me.

"Don't touch her!" I shout, and it echoes off the rocky walls. I'm so small, they can pick me up, landing me on my side. I try to fight but they wrap their arms around me. I can't defend. I can't fight back. I can't move.

"Apollo! Apollo!"

Cin's voice calls to me in the cave, and I wonder why he is part of the army.

"Apollo. I have you. You're safe."

Shaking, tears fall as I try to fight my way out of the man's grip.

"Open your eyes. You're safe."

When I open my eyes, I'm in my chambers, shaking, tears spilling like golden raindrops onto the floor.

"Artemis." The sob tears from my throat.

"She's alive. Shhh. Artemis is alive. She's alive, and so are you, and so is Leto. You're on Apollonion. You're home. I have you."

Cinthus strokes my sweaty brow and comforts me, rocking my torso back-and-forth.

I'm home. I'm home. They're safe.

I repeat this over and over, reassuring myself that my family is indeed alive and safe.

"It was just a nightmare. I have you, Apollo."

He kisses my hair and continues rocking, keeping me locked in his arms and grounded to this realm. He shifts into old, ancient Mycenaean as he rocks and I let the familiar language sooth my racing pulse.

"You aren't alone anymore, my love. I'm here. I'm right here.

Chapter 11

The Scribe

Days have passed and still no sign of either of them. Neither His Majesty nor the god of light have darkened the threshold of the archives. I have spent my mornings alone and my evenings observing the heavenly bodies above me. I have stayed the course, keeping my mind occupied with facts and figures, not mouths and hands.

And I miss them.

I don't like the idea of being their newest conquest, but I also don't like the endless days that stretch out before me. I had the ridiculous notion last night to march into the dining hall and demand they speak with me. But halfway down my corridor, I lost my nerve. I commanded them to leave me alone, but I never expected them to listen.

This evening, I've decided to forgo dinner and take an extra-long-time bathing during the evening meal. The women's bathhouse is tiled in blue tesserae, creating a soothing pattern along the walls. The pool is in the center, surrounded by marble and bronze loungers. I bypass the hot room knowing the women would be filing through the cooling room and into the palace.

I wanted the pool to myself.

Throwing off my robe, I sink into the heated, mineralized water and sigh as the warmth seeps deep into my muscles. It calms my mind, and I cup water over my shoulders. I haven't dared to let myself think about

Apollo or Cin. They proved that I was nothing to them, just as I suspected. The quietness of the bathhouse rings in my ears, and I try to focus on anything other than the loneliness I feel. No one tells you when a goddess saves you and makes you immortal, that living amongst the Olympians, while beautiful and thrilling, is heartbreakingly lonely. I have only Artemis as a confidant when I'm in Athena's court. Being here has shown me friendships are possible. With the nymphs and warriors, I have found companionship. My most treasured company is theirs; it is a balm to my soul and what I imagine being courted feels like. I never had the privilege in the human realm, too wrapped up in my students and my work. Athena doesn't allow scribes to fraternize, and so I stayed amongst the scrolls. I learned to accept my position, but being here for the last month has shown me how I yearn for companionship.

My wet hand cups water and pours it absentmindedly over my shoulder. Apollo's lascivious flirtations come beckoning to my mind. His lips on my skin is a memory I should erase. I imagine his lips lower. I want to run my hands through his hair, smell his gold-dusted skin, skim my hands along his chest. A familiar throbbing between my legs begins again.

My hand finds my breast, and I pinch, playing with one nipple, then the other. I imagine Apollo's mouth on them, his touch.

As my fingers walk lower, it's Cin's mouth I fantasize next. Easily, they find my clitoris. I'm aching and, even underwater, I'm aroused by these thoughts. I begin a highly effective technique, perfected after years of wanting release and no man I want to have coitus with. I ache to replace my fingers with theirs. My actions get tighter, my hips rolling in time. My imagination conjures up their eyes, their mouths, their touch, and heat courses through my veins as I continue to pleasure myself. I pinch and roll the nub between my fingers, and my head rolls back. *So close.* Speeding towards an orgasm I've been avoiding for days, I buck at a rather rough pinch. My ass slips on the marble step, and I plunge into the water. Sputtering as I surface, reaching for the edge.

"Fuck!"

I don't curse. My father frowned on it, but it seemed the appropriate word for getting oneself to the brink only to be accidentally waterboarded.

"Such language, little scribe."

My teeth clamp down on my tongue to keep another curse at bay. They stand at the edge of the pool looking at me as though I am a meal.

"What do you two want?" I snap as wet hair gets angrily wiped from my face. My annoyance at their walking in on me is palpable. Glaring at their smug faces, I turn my back. "This is the women's bathhouse, or can neither of you read?"

"This is the men's pool."

I whip my head around. "Men's pool?"

They both nod, and I growl in frustration. *Of course it is.* This side of the palace has smaller pools and the men's and women's pools stand close together.

Zeus on the throne!

"You're awfully angry, little scribe," His Royal Highness teases.

My teeth gnash together. "Hypatia," I grit out over my shoulder. "My name is Hypatia."

They come to the edge and begin removing robes.

"Am I to bathe with both of you now?"

"You may leave if you wish, but we need to bathe before the evening meal, same as you," the prince chaffs.

"Are you averse to bathing with us? Or is Prince Cinthus the only one you allow?" Apollo questions as he splashes behind me.

"I'm not allowing this." I keep up my annoyance, but something in the air around me changes, coming to life. "I know from previous experience that simply asking you to leave is foolish." I shoot that comment at the prince. It doesn't have as much bite as I want.

Cin is before me, beautiful, naked, and staring with an expression I can't read.

"Would you like us to leave? Say the word and we will."

I shouldn't let them stay, but curiosity is a powerful motivator. I opt for nothing, lest I betray myself and ask them to stay.

"We've come to ask you something."

"I believe the proper way to ask a house guest something is fully clothed, in front of others." I cross my arms over my chest.

"I prefer this way," Apollo says, and I shoot him a look.

"I'm sure you do. What is it you want? I have strict, ritualized bathing to attend to. One that doesn't include men."

The god of light lets a roguish smile lift one side of his lips. "You."

"Me?"

"Yes, you." The prince's deep voice sends shock waves through me. It's different, more commanding, more sultry.

"You both have made it abundantly clear that I am just a conquest. I'm only a game to you. I thought I made myself clear, I want no part of whatever this is. I fooled myself into believing"—I pause, meeting their inquisitive gaze—"that doesn't matter. The point is this isn't what I thought it was."

Water settles as they watch me. Something has changed in their demeanors. Neither man is teasing, both wear an expression of seriousness.

"We aren't playing games," the god says to the settling water.

"You are. I'm of no importance to either of you."

With the prince before me, blocking the step to get out, and Apollo at my back, my pulse thumps in my veins.

Cinthus brushes wet hair from my cheek. "Oh, sweet Hypatia, I fear you are of great importance to both of us."

"We have thought of little else but you," Apollo says softly. "From the sounds you were making, I hope it was one of us, or both, you were thinking of."

I blush clear to my toes. I can't possibly tell them. I can't admit that it's Cin's arms I long to feel around me. That my neck burns as if Apollo's lips have branded me. How, even though it's wrong, I want them both.

"I don't know what you mean, My God."

The fight is gone the second I'm touched. Apollo traces my spine with his fingertips. Heat blooms low in my belly. Shifting my weight underwater, I can't deny how my body responds to having them near. I should push them away, but I can't.

"I'm sure you do."

"I have a confession; would you like to hear it?" Cin draws my attention away from the god's rhythmic stroking. Licking my lips, my gaze meets the prince's hungry one.

"I have thought of little else but you since that night in the garden. Every evening in the observatory is delightful torture. Having you respond to my touch days ago, has left me a man dying of my own need. It's you I need, Hypatia."

I can't breathe. The air in the hot bath is suddenly suffocating. Cin's confession dances on the tendrils of steam like tiny pixies of lust, compelling me to hope.

"This is improper," I say to the steam.

"I revel in impropriety," he says with a little grin. "I have a proposition for you, little scribe." He's staring at me so intensely, I believe I may melt here in the pool. Despite the warm water, I shiver. "One that mutually benefits all of us."

I don't know why I ask the question. Curiosity? Possibly. Lust? Probably. "And that is?"

"First, tell me what you were thinking just now." Cin moves closer, and my heart thunders in my ears. "My mouth?"

"Or mine?" Apollo pipes up.

"Or my touch?" Cin traces my neck, and I sigh.

I can't take it anymore, so I blurt out. "Kissing you."

"Kissing?" Heat blooms in Cin's eyes. "Would you like to kiss one of us?"

I don't know why I nod. I don't know why I haven't kicked them out and yelled to make them leave. The god of light is so close that I can feel the heat coming off him. He strokes his fingertips along my skin, while the prince slides nearer.

"What's the proposition?" My throat runs dry with them so close. I shouldn't want them as badly as I do. I should leave the bathhouse. There are several paths I should choose but all deny what I want most. One night. Give us one night to explore, to taste, to indulge, and then, by morning, you can decide if you want more." Cin brushes my cheek with wet knuckles as he softly mumbles to himself. "I fear one night will not be enough, little scribe."

"If I do, decide I mean, then I insist you use my name. If you want me as you say, I demand my name." I raise my chin and Cin reaches out, tracing my jaw with one finger.

The smirk that dances across Cin's lips is wicked. "Hypatia."

His deep voice rolls through me like a wave, and I shudder. Apollo lays a kiss on my shoulder, sending goosebumps across my skin.

"We need to ask her. Ask if she wants to be kissed," Apollo whispers, tenderly moving my hair, exposing my neck.

Zeus on a throne, the things these two do to me should be studied. I'm an intelligent woman but they reduce me to my primal desires, make me dare to want the forbidden. Liquid fire is coursing through my veins as Cin's eyes penetrate mine.

"One night?" I wet my lips and lock my eyes with his. I'll not back down. I'll surrender for the evening, give in to what I desperately want, and by morning go back to the way things were.

"One night," Apollo says, flicking his gaze between the prince and me.

"Only one evening then."

Something shifts between them, an understanding unspoken. If one wicked smile was enough to leave me panting, two had me reaching for the tiled edge of the pool to ground myself to this realm.

"Which of us would you like to kiss first?" The prince runs his thumb over my bottom lip and the words fail on my tongue. My eyes shift from the god to the prince and the decision feels impossible. I want them both, I want both their lips at once. My hunger for them roars, and I whimper in response.

"Cinthus or me?" The god is running his fingers over my shoulders.

Everything in me screams to choose Apollo first. To let the sun god burn me, but I choose His Highness. He seems safer than the man who has occupied my thoughts.

"Cin?" My voice sounds timid as I ask instead of demand. My head is swimming.

"Then come here. You'll need to kiss me; I'll not make the first move."

I move close and pull him down to me. My mouth finds his, and I can't help the explosion that follows. I meant for it to be a peck, a point proven so they will leave, but instead, I devour him. Like a thirsty woman in the desert, I drown in the oasis he brings. His lips slant across mine, soft and inviting, moving as one. Exploring, tasting, feeling. When his lips part, his tongue strokes mine, and I fist his hair, clinging to him. A deep moan rumbles from somewhere, and he releases me. I want him again.

"Would you like Apollo next?"

Cin is living up to his nickname as I stand in consecrated water and commit these acts. I lick the taste of him off my lips and turn to meet the object of my frustration and desire.

My mouth meets the god's, and my right hand grabs his curls. He backs me into the wall, his body pressing to mine. His erection is thick and warm pressed against my belly and for some reason, I move against it. He groans into my mouth, and it is the most heavenly sound. Stars burst behind my eyes, and I can't catch my breath. I have wanted him for so long, and the feel of these soft lips has reduced me to nothing but base desires. My other hand hasn't left His Majesty's hair as my fingers weave themselves further. I'm holding both men and wondering why I hadn't kissed them sooner. When Apollo's tongue meets mine, he lets loose a sound so primitive it causes my skin to prickle.

"Fuck," he exclaims, releasing me. His lips trace my jaw, and I mewl at the contact. My eyes lock with Cin's, and he lowers himself down to kiss me again. It's needy, taking, and ends way too quickly. The prince's devilish grin has me rolling my hips under the water.

"Gods, Hypatia," Apollo mumbles as his tongue traces down my neck. I can't help but notice how the god of light is trembling under my touch. The water level comes to under my breasts, and he wastes no time taking advantage. One hand cups one side as his tongue finds my nipple. I am nothing but whimpers and moans. Cin's nose brushes my cheek.

"Would you enjoy the sight of a god between your thighs, Hypatia?"

Fuck all the gods.

"Yes," I manage to say.

"Do you want both of us?"

I whine.

"We have rules. And before we begin, we need to know yours."

"Rules?"

He leaves kisses down my neck as he speaks, his beard scratching. "Rules. Boundaries. Things we can't abide. We all have them, what are yours? What don't you want?"

I know the answer as soon as it's asked. "I don't want coitus. Not yet."

Cinthus pulls back, his dark brown eyes gleaming. "No penetration?"

"No."

"Of any kind or only our cocks?"

I'm taken aback by the boldness of the question. A shyness creeps over me, and I suddenly feel the need to dip below the water level, hiding myself from them. His Highness notices my sudden apprehension and gently grabs my chin, forcing me to look at him.

"There is no wrong answer."

"Of"—my voice cracks—"your members."

He shakes his head as he fights a smile, and Apollo softly chuckles beside me. "Say cocks. No need for pleasantries now."

"Your cocks, Your Royal Highness." My cheeks flame. "I haven't prepared the pennyroyal tea, and I would prefer to avoid pregnancy."

It's a simple request, and one I'm not afraid to make. Living among the land of immortals beings means I don't have to worry about colds or flus, infection or disease, but pregnancy is not something I am ready for. I might have fantasies about them, but if I want this, them, fully, I have to protect myself.

Cin frowns but it is soon taken over by a crooked smile. His thumb rubs my swollen lip. "I have been hard for days thinking of these lips wrapped around my *member*. But that's for later," he teases. "Call me Cin. The time for Your Royal Highness is over. I want you saying our names, calling them out as you come, do you understand?"

"Yes."

"Yes, what?' He's stern and his voice sends butterflies loose low in my belly.

"Yes, Cin."

"That's our girl."

He grabs me and lifts. Water runs in torrents down my body as he climbs out of the pool and sets me down on one of the marble loungers.

"What if someone comes in?" I say, looking past the men to the open doorway.

Apollo kisses my skin. "Anyone who dares interrupt will feel my wrath." Heat bounces in his eyes, and I know he means every word.

"Focus on me, Hypatia, and allow us to show our devotion."

Cin makes good on his promise. His thick fingers dance along my hips, brushing low, and I lift my hips wanting contact.

"Ask me to touch you." His highness breathes into my cheek and I feel as though I'm drunk.

"Touch me, Cin."

We are both panting, breaths mixing as his fingers find my center and slip between my most intimate part. When he finds my clitoris, I arch.

"Such a needy thing for you, Cin." Apollo smiles against my stomach as he nips.

His Highness nods, his mouth finding my neck. "And so wet already. Taste."

He brings his fingers, coated with my arousal, to Apollo's lips. I watch them disappear into the god's mouth. He moans, relishing the taste. Those same fingers get sucked into the prince's mouth, keeping his dark eyes locked with mine.

"Apollo," he says, his eyes still on me, "You want to feast on our girl, don't you?"

I'm burning under his intensity. I want to grab his head and shove him between my legs. I fear if I'm not allowed a release soon, I'll spontaneously combust. Gathering both my hands above my head, Cin holds me to the marble, and I strain against him. Teeth catch my shoulder, a warning not to resist.

Apollo looks up at me from between my legs and smirks. "Beg me."

"No." It's a breathless statement.

"Beg. I want to hear our needy girl beg her god to taste her."

"I told you, I won't beg for what I need." I lift my hips in protest of his torturous tongue gliding down my thigh.

"Beg me, Hypatia," he says again as he trails kisses along the inside of the other thigh.

"Fucking taste me, you arrogant god. Now!"

Both men laugh darkly. The vibrations move through me, tearing at my dignity until all I want is them. Apollo licks, teasing, before he does exactly what the prince commanded. He feasts.

I'm so lost in the sensation of his mouth, his tongue, his hands gripping my thighs that I forget the prince is in the room until he touches my body. He holds my hips to the marble, restricting my movements as Apollo continues his pace.

"I'm enjoying the sight of our god between your legs."

I hiss at his words. His mouth claims mine as his hands roam up to cup my breasts. At this moment, I am their plaything. I buck as I get closer to my orgasm. Cinthus' lips are slowly making their way down my neck.

"Gods!" I cry out when his warm mouth closes around the hardened peak on my breast. The sensations of teeth and tongue leave me teetering on the brink.

He stops, his perfect bow mouth curls upwards, and he scolds me with a shake of his head. "Your release is ours to control. You'll only say my name. Or Apollo. Call out to the gods again, and I'll make certain our god keeps you on edge until you break."

I nod. I can't form words as the god slows his assault to an irritating pace. His tongue lazily circles my clit, and I wiggle closer to where I want him. Desperate need claws through me, and I realize I will let them both do whatever they want. I am at their mercy. And Cinthus knows it. He flicks my nipple with his fingernail and the sensation brings me closer to the edge. Lowering his head, he keeps eye contact. When his mouth hovers above my breast, I arch my back aching to be released from their torture. Apollo stops altogether, and I feel as though I am fracturing into pieces. My toes curl into his plumage as he readjusts me higher on his shoulders.

"Cin," he coos, and he reaches a wet hand out to caress the prince's cheek. "Is she deserving of release this evening?" Apollo's gaze finds mine, and I realize he's making me pay for not begging. Fear sparks down my spine. They could leave, both of them. They could leave me here on the side of the bath, hungry and aching and driven half-mad with lust.

Damn them both.

"Please, please, My God." I hate the sound of my timid plea, but he sparks alive. His grip on my thighs tightens.

"You're so pretty when you beg for us." The prince's face is inches from mine. He lays a soft kiss behind my ear. I'm reduced to whimpers, rolling my hips. "Use your words, Hypatia."

"Please." My voice is raspy from desire flooding me. "Please."

"Please what?" Cinthus asks, his kisses trailing lower. Apollo chuckles as I writhe against him. His fingers have found my sensitive clit while his glorious mouth antagonizes me.

"Please, command him to let me release."

"Mmm." His Majesty's mouth is on me, vibrating against my skin. "Say come."

I bite my bottom lip. "Come."

"So compliant. Begging her men for a taste of their depravity."

He threads his hand through the god's golden curls, a look of wickedness passes between them, and I hold my breath in anticipation. His hand joins the god's at the apex of my sex. They both bring me to the edge again, only to stall, refusing to allow me to fall from the precipice I now teeter on.

I hear myself growl in protest.

He hooks his finger under Apollo's chin, pulling him up for a kiss. For several seconds I watch them, enamored by their passion and feeling every bit like a voyeur. Releasing the sun god, he turns to me, crawling up my body, ready to devour.

"You taste like ours," he says, positioning himself above me, holding me to the marble. I'm completely at their mercy, unable to move without permission. Unable to orgasm without their say. A sacrifice on the altar of their choosing.

And it thrills me.

"Our god's tongue will make you see the Elysian Fields." He leans in, his breath hot against my mouth. "While your prince will drag you to Tartarus, keeping you as my obsession."

I whimper when Apollo returns to his task, and it isn't long before I'm writhing against him. A tightness pulls at my core, and I spring loose, crying out as I shatter into pieces. My hips grind against his mouth, and a second one builds on the heels of the first. Cin's hot breath finds my ear.

"That's right. Fuck his tongue. Ride his face as you scream my name."

I'm so close again so quickly that I can only do as he says.

"Cin!" One syllable rings out against the stone walls of the bathhouse. A cry from the very depths of my soul.

"There, that's right." He's stroking my hair as my legs clamp around Apollo's ears. "Such a good girl for us."

The euphoric high feels like a blanket of clouds as I float back to this realm, but my captors aren't done. His Highness roughly rolls me to my side as the god moves, changing positions. I'm too limp to protest.

"You are so lovely like this, rewarded for being so good. But earlier you were disrespectful to our god. Leaving his throne room without permission." He *tsks*. "Are you accepting of your punishment before more pleasure, Hypatia?"

Uncertain of what he means and still recovering from what they just did to my body, I answer in the affirmative.

"Two spanks, do you agree?"

"Yes." I nod.

A loud slap to my ass fractures my consciousness, and I squeak in shock. It doesn't hurt, not in the way one would think. It's almost as if it releases something in me. His hand raises again and connects once more, and I emit a low moan; a sound I didn't know I was capable of. It isn't pain that I feel but something freeing.

"One is for leaving the throne room without being dismissed," Cin growls as he moves down my body. "The other is to see if you enjoy it. Do you?"

I open my eyes and rise on my elbows as he positions himself between my legs. Apollo is next to me, his hand stroking his cock at the sight before him.

"Yes," I respond emphatically. "Yes, Cin."

His smile at my approval has my hips rolling, wanting contact. Immediately his mouth is on me, and I'm racing towards another orgasm. He doesn't play, doesn't keep me on edge, and when I buck, he tightens his grip on my hips, restricting me from anything but the feel of him. I grab his hair, doing exactly what he commanded me to do with Apollo. I fuck Cin's face until my cries ring out again. Apollo beside me is stroking his cock with such vigor that when he orgasms, his head throws back. His lower, deeper moan, mixes with mine until the crescendo is deafening. My entire body is shaking, and I am unable to do anything to control it. I vibrate for several minutes, lost in the sensation.

Both men are surrounding me, cooing platitudes and stroking my hair, arms, and hips. They sound far away as I stay in this state.

Once I am done shaking, a drying towel wraps around me, and I am once again scooped up against His Majesty, being carried to gods know where. I don't care. I can hardly protest, my limbs limp, my body in a state I've never known. Then I'm in a bed, soft cushions are under me, warm blankets around me, and my body gives over to exhaustion.

Chapter 12

The Scribe

Low, deep voices are around me, dancing on the air in mumbled syllables that I can't make out. Someone brushes my hair away from my face.

"Did we wake you?"

Opening my eyes, I catch the soft blue of his as he passes something over me.

"My God?"

"Mmm."

Sitting upright, I tug the blankets up to my chest, realizing as I move that I'm naked, unwrapped from the towel from earlier. "Where am I?"

"My chambers," His Majesty answers as he brings me a golden chalice. "Drink. You need to replenish after what we just did."

I roll my neck and take the offered glass, sipping water and watching him prepare a tray. I use the opportunity to look around his room. The furniture is similar to mine, but his has paintings hung around. Drawings in charcoal and ink sit stacked on one side. Another side sports a plain stretched canvas on an easel, while beside it sit canvases five or so deep. A wooden unit has been custom-built for him. Brushes of all sizes are grouped in clay pots. Color palettes line up neatly. It is the chamber of a talented artist, his softer side on display in private.

He positions the tray next to me. Apollo is lounging on the other side. He has tied a chiton to his waist and left his golden chest bare. He looks relaxed and at ease in this room, and I realize, as if for the first time, that these two must spend time in each other's chambers. They aren't just lovers who meet secretly under the shroud of darkness and hushed whispers. They are open, loving, and intertwined in each other's lives to the point that they are almost one and the same.

And it suddenly feels like I'm intruding.

"May I have a robe?" Apollo gives me an odd look but retrieves one from the end of the expansive bed. I shrug into it, the silk caressing my skin as it slips over my shoulders. It's too large, made for the men, but I'll need it if I'm to walk the halls. My garment is abandoned on the floor of the bathhouse. Tying it, I remove the covers and begin to slip from the bed. These two need to eat their dinner, and I need to return to my chambers. Moonlight floods the open balcony, letting me know I'll be going hungry tonight as the evening meal is over.

"Where are you going?" His Highness asks as I try to maneuver around the tray, careful not to topple it.

"My chambers," I state. "It is late, and you have cared for me long enough."

"Sit." He uses that tone of voice he used in my private bathing pool. The commanding one. "You'll not leave."

I turn to give him a look. "Am I not allowed to?"

"No."

"No?"

"No. Not until you have been fed and rested." He's standing before me, blocking my escape from the bed. "Your body experienced a lot, and from what I suspect, for the first time. You need cared for. Get back in your spot and let me do just that."

"Better to listen, Hypatia," Apollo says. "Cin has a way of getting what he wants, and he isn't above putting you between us, bodily."

I glance over my shoulder at Apollo who winks and then up at the prince. He isn't budging. He's a wall of solid muscle and determination. I huff. I have no fight in me after the intensity of the bathhouse. Crawling back into my place between them, the prince seems satisfied and returns to fussing with the tray. I prop up pillows and wait.

The food smells delicious. It is a simple dinner and one that makes me miss my human life. Fasolada, salted fish, and crusty eliopsomo—a bread made with olives that happened to be my favorite.

"It looks wonderful, Your Highness."

He lets a smile crack his seriousness for a moment. He serves Apollo his bowl first, acknowledging his position. Then he dips the ladle in the pot, comes up with beans and carrots, and empties the contents into a waiting bowl. The aroma makes my stomach growl. My mother made this particular soup most of my life. When she died, I continued. It is a tether to my old life and memories I've held onto for centuries. He sits beside me, scoops and then offers me his spoon. I pull back on instinct.

"I am perfectly capable of feeding myself," I say, looking up, but he shakes his head. His broad chest is on display, around his hips he has tied a cloth. He crosses his ankles determined to wait me out. I give up easily as the soup looks more inviting than protesting my ability to take care of myself. Opening my mouth like a hungry bird, I resist the urge to tweet. As he pulls the spoon out, I mumble my satisfaction.

We stay like this for a while, none of us talking, just peaceful enjoyment of each other's company. For every spoonful I get, Cin gets three, and I quickly realize the man is a bottomless pit. We share one bowl and several of the fish. As I tear a hunk of bread off to pop in my mouth, he and Apollo eat two more bowls of soup, more fish, and two loaves of bread. I'm astonished by their appetite.

"You two are like ravenous wolves," I joke, munching on my piece.

"Only for you." Apollo leaves a sloppy kiss on my cheek on his way to more fish. I laugh and wipe my cheek.

"Men need food and sex. We are quite simple creatures." He looks up at Cin who nods. I break into giggles at the two of them. They playfully fight over the last fish which erupts into a semi-wrestling match with forks, and I worry they'll upset the entire tray. They laugh, deciding to split the fish, and then spend several minutes arguing over who got the bigger half. It is a side of the gods rarely seen. So used to Athena and her role as a leader, I forget they can be silly behind closed doors. At least Artemis is with me. She and I have laughed until we cried, and as I watch the men, I'm reminded how much alike Apollo and Artemis are when they don't have to be the roles they play in the pantheon. Cin, ever the prince, has hidden much of his true self behind his confidence. But here he can relax, and the way he teases Apollo endears him to me.

"Have you had enough?" Cinthus asks.

I arch a brow at the ransacked tray. "If I hadn't, I have now."

"I can call to the kitchens if you'd like." He is truly in the role of care-taker, and it is odd to be in the position to be taken care of.

Is this how he is after they are together?

Shaking my head, I finish my piece of bread. "No, I'm quite full."

With a quick jerk of his head, he removes the tray. I excuse myself to ready for bed in my chambers and when I return, the prince grabs me and turns me around, lifting the oversized robe.

"Do you mind, Your Highness?" I pretend to be annoyed, crossing my arms.

"Not at all, little scribe."

I emit a low growl and both of them laugh at me. Cin's hand caresses the side of my rear end he spanked. I twist to see.

"It's not as red," I say and shrug.

His frown deepens. "Does it hurt? It wasn't my intention to leave marks. My excitement got the better of me."

Placing my hand inside the perfect pink outline of his, I shrug again. "It doesn't hurt in the slightest."

I smile reassuringly, and he touches my cheek, satisfied with that answer. Apollo comes round to inspect the prince's handiwork as oil is rubbed along the mark.

"His hand is so big," I say absentmindedly.

Apollo snickers. "Other parts of him are big as well."

I laugh. "You're impossible."

Cin agrees as the god lifts the other side of the robe, exposing my full ass to the moon, and gives the other cheek a light smack

"Insolent woman."

"Your insolent woman," I say before I can think better of it. My cheeks pink at my presumption but they both agree. I am their woman.

"To bed?" the prince asks with a lazy yawn he makes no attempt at hiding.

"Yes. And thank you for the meal." I make my way towards the door when I'm stopped once again by a wall of prince.

"*Our* bed." He points behind me. Apollo has joined his ranks, his arms crossed.

"To bed, Hypatia. *With* us."

"You said one night, that was the deal. We had one encounter."

"Four," His Royal Highness says with a smug rise of his chin. "I believe it was four orgasms in that one encounter."

A blush warms my cheeks and runs its way down my chest.

"Cin's right, four."

"The amount of . . . release . . . was never part of our deal, gentleman," I say diplomatically, swallowing loudly, and clasping my hands. If they can speak plainly then so can I. "Our arrangement was one night, and—"

"The sun hasn't risen, Hypatia. Bed. With us." It was Apollo's turn to point. "I'm not above throwing you over my shoulder."

Confused, I stare at their formidable frames blocking my path, then back to the bed. I assumed they would ask me to leave once the event of the night was over. That the expectation was the experience and not the aftermath. I never expected one night meant the whole night. "But our arrangement."

"Our arrangement was for one night. We get you for a whole night not just a few hours of pleasure." Apollo stepped forward, touching my cheek. "Although, I fear I'll want more than that."

I can't help but lean into his warm palm as his thumb caresses my cheek, my heart fluttering against my ribs. And so, I do the only thing I can. I obey.

Returning to bed, Apollo crawls over me, and his wings brush my forehead, sliding over my legs. Cin flops down beside me, and the mattress sags with his weight. Apollo is settled on my other side, stroking my arm as he watches the fire. Cool night air dances in from the open balcony, smelling of citrus and dew. It is comforting and relaxing, and I feel as though I belong.

"Are you comfortable?" The prince's question is filled with tender concern.

"Yes, almost too relaxed." Stretching like a cat, my belly full, my men beside me, I could sleep here all night. "I'll need to go in a few moments. I can't be caught here in the morning," I say, stifling a yawn.

The prince grazes his fingers over my exposed thigh rhythmically, relaxing me further. My robe must have come open, and I no longer care at the moment as exhaustion settles into my bones.

"I care not of the opinions of others, little scribe. In the morning, I'll have the pennyroyal tea sent with the morning meal if you wish."

I nod sleepily.

"Ours for the entirety of the night." Apollo pulls me into him, my nose touching his. I giggle as he wiggles closer. "You're ours. Can't you see how we need you? We are helpless to your charms, my dear Hypatia. Let us worship you."

He playfully smothers my cheeks with kisses, and I give in.

"Fine, fine. But if one of you snore . . ." I look accusingly over at the prince, who has wrapped his large frame around me from behind. I am sandwiched between them.

"I do not snore," he protests into my hair.

"Liar," Apollo says, and he threads his fingers with Cin's over my hip, caging me in. I couldn't get free if I wanted to, as both men are entirely entangled around me. His Highness pulls Apollo's wing over all of us, encasing us in down and arms and legs.

As the men settle and ease into sleep, I stay awake, listening to their breaths even out, feeling their limbs grow heavy.

Any fear I had has dissipated, and I allow myself to finally admit, this is what I wanted all along.

I am theirs.

They are mine.

And the truth is, I'll never be satisfied with just one night.

Chapter 13

The Scribe

Well before first light, I untangle myself from a heavily sleeping prince, who did, in fact, snore.

"Good morning."

Apollo greets me outside my chambers, and we make our way to the gardens. He wears more formal attire this morning, his white cape affixed to one shoulder, his sword at his hip. His day is filled with council members and godly duties, and he needs to dress the part, or so he says with a wink. We walk along the hedges of yellow roses, talking of what the day will bring, side by side but not touching. His hands remain clasped behind his back, and I wonder what he would do should I reach over and thread mine through his arm. The waking of the palace is beginning and warriors shuffle along the path to the dining hall, their weapons clanging as they go.

"You need to begin your day, My God, and I need my morning meal," I say, watching warriors pass us on the gravel walkway. We are almost back to where we started.

I clasp my hands together, keeping them to myself. After what transpired between us last night, one would think I would feel comfortable, but the truth is, I feel more uneasy. I don't know what they expect of me or us. Was last night really a one-time thing, or will I be spending every night with them? Do I want that?

I turn over questions while Apollo looks up into the bright morning sky and then down at me.

"I remember you, you know."

My brows furrow as he meets my look with a sheepish one of his own.

"I had come to Artemis' palace once, centuries ago, for what I can't recall now. But she held a small formal meal after, and you were there. I remember your intelligent eyes from across the room. You watched the lyrist play his ballads with such intensity." He touched my cheek. "You entranced me. You watched him, but I watched you."

He reaches for me, and I step into his arms before I can contemplate his confession. That was the first and only time I had seen Apollo, and I chastised myself most of that evening for wanting to drink him in. To take in those broad shoulders, those high cheekbones that made silly women like me weak in the knees. He was a beacon, calling me from across the room. One I had to ignore for the sake of our positions. He has lived in my fantasies ever since, a whisper of a man I am not allowed to have.

And all the while, he had been thinking of me.

His lips touch mine, and the world around us stops. He kisses me like I am the air his lungs need.

I sink, grasping his armor as if it would save me from falling from the precipice I've climbed upon. One where, if I jump, I might crash into a sea of heartache below. His hand finds its way into my hair, holding me in place as he deepens our kiss. My hands run up his chest and neck, coming to cup his face, his mouth moving against mine. When he releases me, my head is fuzzy, my breath comes in pants.

"I have wanted to do that for weeks," he whispers against my swollen lips.

"You wanted to kiss me?"

"Mmm."

"You did more than that not but a few hours ago."

His chest rumbles with a low half-chuckle. "I haven't forgotten. But now I can kiss you anytime I want."

He rests his forehead against mine as I desperately try to control my rapid breathing. After last night, the act of a simple kiss is oddly more intimate than cunnilingus.

"Do you have any idea what you do to me? You have intrigued me for far longer than you know. Centuries. Having you here . . . you're a distraction, Hypatia." His fingers dig into my hair, and I let loose a soft moan. "A beautiful distraction."

I let him massage my scalp, let his lips lazily wander where they will. I let him tell me without words that I am more to him than I thought. That I am not someone bending his charms. But this might be real.

"You aren't a plaything."

I open my eyes to find him looking at me with such a tender expression that my heart squeezes. "What?"

"You accused me of toying with you. That you weren't important to me, but that isn't the case." He brushes hair from my temple and rubs his nose against mine. "I admit Cin and I are over-eager, but it isn't because we think of you as a conquest. You are so much more than that to both of us. I'm not playing games, Hypatia. I want you. In my bed. In my palace. In my life."

"You need to go," I mumble as more warrior's footsteps crunch along the path. He lays gentle kisses along my cheeks, nuzzling down my neck.

"I don't want to," he says into my temple as he places gentle kisses there as well. "I have half a mind to carry you back to my chambers."

The determined glitter in his eyes tells me he is seconds away from just that. I wouldn't protest if he did. He kisses me, soft and slow, and I melt under the rising sun.

"The warriors will see," I mutter against his lips.

"Let them. I don't care." His head rests against mine once more, and he breathes in the dewy, sweet air. "Let one of them say something. It will be his last word."

I giggle at the absurdity, but the look on his face tells me he means it. His arms tighten, and he reluctantly lets me go.

"Will I see you this afternoon?"

"If you wish it, My God."

"Apollo." He wiggles my chin in a soft reprimand. "I know what your thighs feel like against my ears, what you sound like as you climax. I think we can use first names."

I blush a deep red. "Apollo," I say quietly to his armor.

The sun sinks low in the late afternoon sky when I finally emerge from the archives. In between transcribing Oracle accounts and having a breakthrough in the mathematics of the nearest star cluster, I thought about them.

Cin. The way his dark hair looked in the low firelight. A frown on his lips, his large hand curled under his scruffy chin. Sometime in the night, he had shifted positions, pulling me with him. His body a protective shield to the night that crept in through the open balcony.

Apollo. He was light emanating from everywhere. His golden curls caught the early morning sun, shining in hues of yellows. The way his blue eyes had looked into mine, affectionately, as though I were something precious. His kiss, his admission this morning played in my head most of the day.

They were the sun and moon of my world. My sun and moon. Heavenly bodies pulling me into their orbit.

Eager to see them both, I gather two scrolls, intent on showing them what I'd found. As I walk the halls to the god's private rooms, a soft smile tugs at my lips. I plan to ask them to dine together for the evening meal. It is bold of me, as Apollo frequently takes his meals in the large dining halls. But I selfishly want more time with them alone. Entering the smaller throne room, I find it empty. For a moment, I wonder if he's decided to go down to the hall early, and I can't hide the disappointment gathering across my face. Studying the room for a moment more, I turn to leave when I hear a male voice just beyond the door on the opposite side of the room. I'm to it in a few steps. Another male voice, hushed and low, comes from the other side.

Athena's palace has places I'm not allowed. Behind doors sit important council members or warriors discussing the state of the empire. If Apollo held similar rules and was in a private meeting, I would be interrupting. And while he said he didn't care what the warriors thought, he may if I disrespect his court.

In the end, I decide to take him at his word, hoping my interruption isn't met with his wrath, and open the door.

And freeze in place.

Apollo is seated, Cin kneeling before him, his head slowly bobbing.

My mouth falls open. My body is stuck in suspended animation, one hand holding the door open, the other holding scrolls. Apollo had his head tipped back when I opened the door. Tipping it forward, he catches my stare. An unholy smirk crosses those beautiful sun-kissed lips.

"Enjoying the sight?"

"Oh! Oh! My—fuck Helios," I blurt out, whipping around and bumping into an enormous statue of the naked god. His marble endowment is inches from my face, while the low moans of the flesh and blood god come from behind me.

"Come to admire or join?" His words are strained, and a satisfied groan follows.

I blush from head to toe. "My God. Your Highness. I can come back. You're obviously . . . occupied." I tear my eyes from the marble phallus to the door. It closed when I turned, and the room suddenly feels too small.

"Did you curse Helios?" It's Cin's voice.

Nodding, my cheeks and neck are burning. I need to leave. They certainly don't need me at the moment, and I can't add voyeur to the list of sins committed under this roof. Apollo laughs. It's loud and boisterous and fills the room.

"I'd say I agree, but Helios is so damn temperamental, he'd be in my chambers raging and ruining my pleasant afternoon," the god teases.

"What is it you've brought, Hypatia?" Cin asks.

My breath stalls in my chest. My name on his lips when I know the state they are currently in sends heat coursing through me.

"Scrolls," I say to the marble. "Scrolls I can leave for you . . . um . . . for later."

I look around for a desk or shelf to lay them on. Hastily, I set them on the nearest flat surface. I'm too preoccupied with leaving the two of them to their *pleasant afternoon*, that when Apollo speaks, I jump.

"Stay. If you'd like."

Stay!? I can't stay. And do what? Watch? They obviously need to be alone to finish what they started. They don't need me. The image of the prince before Apollo replays, unwelcome, in my mind, and I shift my weight.

"We'd like it if you stay." Cin's words are just that. Sinful.

I war with myself until I give in and turn to face them. That same unholy smirk has fixed itself to the god's mouth. His Royal Highness is watching me with hooded eyes. His expression dark, hungry.

"Come here, Hypatia," the prince says in that commanding tone of his. Helplessly, I step forward, something is pulling me, a line to the two of them. Cin moves, exposing a naked god to my gaze. The chair he sits in is tall, accommodating his wings. He seems content to be at the prince's mercy. His wrists are tied to the arms with strips of silk. The prince is half-dressed as he rises to stand.

"He is quite beautiful, is he not?" Cin asks darkly, and my mouth goes dry.

"Do you enjoy the sight of our god before you?" he says in my ear.

My body flushes, heat running through me, straight to my core. I can't think of anything intelligible to say. Wetting my lips, I try not to focus on the seated and bound god. He's even more beautiful up close. Thick fingers brush my hair to the side, and I take in a sharp breath.

"You can touch him if you'd like," he whispers, softly kissing my shoulder, his beard tickling the exposed skin. "Explore him. Taste him. Would you like that?"

I shift my weight, my head spinning from the images the prince has conjured with his words. While I have seen plenty of males in various states of dress, I have rarely touched them. My experience, limited as it was, never lent itself to anything like this.

Until now.

"You may leave." Cin gently kisses behind my ear, and I gasp. "We want you to stay, but you are welcome to go. Leave or go. Your choice."

My fingers burn to touch him. Run them over his muscled torso, chiseled to perfection by years of training. Skim them down those thighs that had entangled themselves with mine last night. My mouth waters at the sight of him, and I can't deny how much I want to stay as I grow flushed with each ticking second I stare.

"Don't be shy, sweet Hypatia. Make our god submit to you. He is at your mercy."

I am drawn to him by forces unseen. Apollo whimpers when my mouth meets his. My hands explore of their own accord, tracing his chest, moving over every ridge and valley of his stomach. He's panting, whimpering when my lips find his jaw, his neck, following the trail my fingertips have left. He looks as though he is in agony, and I stall.

"Do you want her to touch you, Apollo? Taste you?"

He nods and my fingers curl against his muscled torso as my gaze meets his. He is barely breathing, staring at me as if he's afraid to blink. For a god who usually has something to say on every matter, finding him speechless is exhilarating.

"Have you ever wrapped those lips around a cock?"

Something low clenches in my belly, and I bit my lip. Cin is leading us with his questions. Apollo's breath hitches and a sudden jolt of power runs through me.

"Would you like that?" I whisper.

The god moans. "Yes," he breathes, emboldening me.

I let my gaze wander over him, caressing him with my eyes before my hands, taking in his size, his body. A slow smile spreads across my face at the thought of making him submit as Cin called it. And I want to. I want to be in control of him.

When I touch him, his cock jerks and a low groan comes from somewhere. I sink to my knees and Apollo looks as though he'll come apart. He shudders. His wings open quickly to their full expanse before folding neatly behind.

I palm him; he's warm and thick in my hand. Every movement is slow, every touch a caress. I map the god's body with my fingers, fully aware of how they both are watching me with heady eyes and parted lips. Apollo's head lays back against the chair when I add pressure to my ministrations. Wood creaks as his hips buck when I wrap my hand around, sliding down to the base. I explore him this way for several breathless minutes, marveling at how he grows harder with each slow stroke.

"Hypatia." His voice is gravelly as I slide my hand back up, a bead of cum gathers at the tip. "You're killing me."

He hisses, and I stop, letting go. I didn't realize I'd hurt him.

"For fuck's sake, don't stop." His half-laugh is breathy.

Cin stares down and points his chin, encouraging my continuation of the slow torture of the god of light. "Taste him," he orders, the edge of his mouth curling in a smile. I willingly obey.

One lick sends Apollo's hips thrusting out of the chair. Another runs down his shaft slowly, feeling every pulse of his racing heart under my tongue. My mouth surrounds him, and I'm lost to the sensation of it all. Unsure of what would feel good, I try to mimic what I've seen. While I may have never performed fellatio, it doesn't mean I'm ignorant of it. My head bobs slowly, as I use my tongue to slide around the sides. Sliding back up, I release him. My eyes lock with his and Apollo moans so deep and low it vibrates through his body.

"Stay still," I command out of nowhere. Both sets of eyes widen. "Don't move. I like the way you taste."

I'm met with only moans and curses as each man loses his mind at my words. This empowers me, and my head spins as I continue. I've become drunk on the power they give me.

My pace quickens.

"Don't stop." His low whisper does something to me, and I adjust my hips in response.

Cin's fingers have twisted in my hair, encouraging my actions with a slight tug. My hips roll, desperate to release the throbbing ache that is building. I've never felt my heartbeat pulsing that low before.

"You look so lovely with our god's cock in your mouth," Cin coos, dragging his fingers across my scalp. The gentle sensation causes me to moan, and Apollo cusses. "That's right. Take as much as you can."

My tightly held decorum snaps. I slide down the length of the god's cock as he arches his back, driving more of him in my mouth and down my throat. It is more than I can manage, and when the tip hits the back of my throat, I gag.

"You're doing so well," Cin soothes.

My cheeks hollow on the pull back up, and Apollo gasps, his knuckles white as he grips the arms. I slide down, and this go, I try to take him further. The sound he makes is beastly, somewhere between a howl and a growl as he thrusts his hips. My eyes water when he hits the back of my throat again, but I'm determined to keep at it. My tongue circles around, and he is nothing but moans.

"Not yet," Cin says before he reaches for me. I am pulled off the god, and he comes between us, his hand fisting the god's thick cock as he roughly strokes him. Confused, I try to return to my task but he growls.

"No, he'll not come in your mouth. He doesn't deserve that yet."

He's tugging hard and fast. Apollo cries out as cum flows over the prince's fist, shimmering in the low light. Cinthus continues to stroke the god of light until every last drop is spilled.

"Look at the mess you made of our god. You should be proud."

He licks his fist clean, and I'm mesmerized by the glistening release. I didn't know ichor ran in more than their veins.

I have no time to ask questions as Apollo is let loose, and he grabs me, pulling me in for a kiss that steals my breath. I kiss back with a fever I didn't know I possessed.

"You are magnificent," Apollo praises and his lips smash into mine once more. "This mouth. Fuck."

Suddenly, Cin grabs me, hoisting me to my feet, picking me up so that my legs wrap around his waist. My butt hits a table and his mouth is everywhere. My neck, my cheeks, my cloth-covered breasts.

"No fucking, right, Hypatia?" he growls in my ear.

Chapter 14

The Prince

I lost control. This afternoon started out as a stress relief for both of us, a way to cull our mutual desire for her. We agreed that we rushed things the night before.

I rushed things.

I was gaining my composure edging Apollo like I was, and then she entered the room. Now all I want is her. She's in my blood, racing through my veins at break-neck speed.

Watching her suck Apollo's cock in that tender way she did everything, had lust clawing at me from the inside. I thought she would need more instruction, virgins generally do, but she surprised me. She wasn't intimidated by the god's larger-than-normal dick. Nor did she shy away. She would have sucked him dry had I let her.

But now she's under me, writhing and melting at my touch and all I want is to bury myself in her. I'm starving for her, desperate, and now that I've had a taste, I don't want to stop. Breathing her in, I calm myself enough to remember her limits.

"Gods, Hypatia," I groan into her hair, as I slide her chiton up, exposing those soft thighs to my grip. Yanking her closer, the only thing between us is the thin layer of linen still around my waist. "No cocks. Is it still no penetration with cocks?"

She whimpers and rocks her hips against me.

"I want to fuck you. I need to fuck you. Hard. Now. Answer me," I snap, my resolve crumbling to nothing the longer she stays silent.

"Yes," she whispers.

"Yes, what?" My teeth nip her neck, as my fingers work free the top of the chiton. It falls, exposing one breast, and I waste no time claiming it. Hypatia's eyes roll back, and she moans loudly. We are both reduced to panting breaths and hurried kisses. Her fingers find themselves tangled in my hair holding me in place as I suck her nipple.

"Cin."

It's a breathless whine that sets me on fire.

"Is coitus still your boundary? I'm losing control, and you aren't ready for that," I warn her. She hooks her ankles around my back, grinding against me, and I fist the end of her chiton, ready to rip it off.

"Yes," she whispers again. "Yes, it's my boundary."

It takes power I didn't know I possessed to slowly let go. I can't cross it. I can't force her. That isn't how I conduct myself. I might dominate, enjoy controlling those in my bed, and even edge them close, but I never cross their lines. Red-hot need courses through me causing my hands to shake. They skim her legs as I remove myself from between them. I'm so damn hard I'm in pain. I need release. I didn't get any last night, and I fear I may be driven mad if I can't get any now.

"Cin," she whines as I step back from the edge. My name is music when she says it, a symphony when she screams it.

I need her to scream it.

"Cin."

I will abide by her limits. I will respect her boundaries and pull myself back from the brink, but as I've told her before, I'm no gentleman.

"I want to watch."

It isn't a command or a question. It's a statement of fact. If I can't bury myself in her just yet, I need something else to satisfy this monster begging to be free. My hand tugs at my hard-as-fucking-steal-cock, pumping while she contemplates my words.

"Watch?"

She's looking at me with dark, heavy-lidded eyes.

"You told me you didn't need a man to make your legs shake." I can't help the dance of sin that moves across my face as I watch her pupils swallow that pretty steel color. "Prove it. Show me. Let me watch. Touch yourself for me. I want to watch you come."

She closes her eyes, choosing whether she'll comply. When they open, they are the color of stone.

"Please," I whisper. Apollo touches my cheek, his hand replacing mine. His tongue is in my mouth, stoking the lust that is now a raging fire. He lays kisses on my neck, my chest as I study her.

I am never the one who begs. I make others beg, that is my specialty, but for her, I will. I will do anything she asks. She has all the power and right now, she's bringing me to my knees. I'm ready to pray to this goddess laid out before me on a wooden altar.

Her hand slides from her knee to her thigh as she opens to me. My cock is in Apollo's mouth when her fingertips reach her clit. I watch every tease, every circle, every movement, committing to memory exactly how she likes it.

Apollo slides his tongue around me, and I harden further filling his greedy mouth.

"Deeper," I command him and grip his head, pushing myself further down his throat. His groan reverberates, and I grab his hair in desperation.

Hypatia's light, feminine sounds mixing with our deeper ones is a heady combination. She's stroking her pussy with fury, watching us, and I can no longer be a voyeur.

"May I touch you?" My voice doesn't sound like my own, it's coarser and strained. She bites her bottom lip keeping her moans at bay.

"Yes."

Reaching for her, I drag a finger along her slit. Her hips tilt as I tease her wet pussy. Slipping inside her is euphoric. With each stroke, she loses herself more. Apollo is working my cock as I work her, and the parallels leave my head spinning.

"Take all of me, you cock whore of a god," I grit out. He palms my balls on the next stroke, and I am gone. I'm a drowning man in a sea of desire these two create.

"More," she begs, and I'm helpless to comply.

I add a second finger, and Hypatia's hips jerk off the table. I want to come with her, feel our mutual orgasms slamming into us. She's gripping my fingers as I pump in and out, and I don't know how much longer I can hold out.

Apollo does that thing with his tongue that he knows drives me insane, and I teeter on the edge of madness.

"Fuck! I love that pretty mouth around my big cock." I grunt, thrusting hard into the mouth I love. "You take me so well. Take my cock down your throat like the greedy fucking god you are."

Hypatia is shaking, and I explode right before she does. Apollo swallows deep, taking every last drop I give as I watch our girl fall apart in front of me.

Several minutes pass and the only sound is panting from all three of us. Apollo wipes his mouth daintily, kissing my inner thighs as we both come down off the high. Hypatia is the first to move and grabs my face with both hands. Her mouth slams onto mine leaving me breathless, wanting her all over again.

"I want more, Cin." Her husky whisper breaks the silence. "I want more from both of you."

"More?"

She looks down at the god of light seated at my feet and runs her fingers through his hair. He smiles up at her and takes her hand, kissing the palm.

"I want you. Both."

"You have us both. We are entirely at your mercy." I kiss her, a reassurance that neither of us wants anything that doesn't include her. But she's shaking her head.

"I want intercourse, Cin. I want your cock in me. I want both of you."

Chapter 15

The Scribe

Several days have passed since the study. I try my best to keep my mind occupied, but it keeps returning to them. To that room. To mouths and hands, kisses and groans. To the feeling of completion, and the admission that I was ready for more. But more hasn't come.

While our meetings haven't decreased; in fact, the god and the prince seek me out frequently, I am confused as to why they both pulled back from anything improper. As Apollo put it, they know what I sound like when I climax, so why I'm not a fixture in their bed is a mystery to me. But I do enjoy our simple interactions just as much.

Getting up early doesn't bother me if it means I can walk the gardens with Apollo. He is an expert at stealing kisses, and I enjoy them being stolen immensely. His playfulness has my silly heart thumping erratically whenever he's near. His Highness, however, is different. He sits and watches me work in the observatory in the evening as if my very existence enamors him. His kisses are thoughtful. To my disappointment, he only walks me to my chambers, never passing the threshold.

Our interactions are the best part of my day. This afternoon, the prince wandered into the archives with a bouquet of daisies in a pot. He placed them on my workstation before he swept me up in those massive arms of his and kissed me until I was breathless. My silly heart will never recover if they keep up this attention. Tonight, I have been asked to dine with both and so, I find myself quickly rejecting any of the clothing I brought with me. Since I brought only sturdy, simple dresses, I asked a nymph if I could borrow a dress. Somehow, this leads to several of them in my room, styling my hair and dressing me, as if I am important. The peplos they choose is beautiful. Detailed jeweled embroidery edges the softest linens I have ever worn. The light purple color makes my skin look rosy under the soft candlelight. Two pins are affixed to my shoulders, both adorned with the symbol of the Cosmis Province, a sun and moon. They drape a darker purple himation over one shoulder, tucking it into a gold-embossed belt. Simple jewelry, a cuff on my upper arm Artemis gave to me as a present, and bangles on my wrists are my only adornment. Instead of winding my hair back as severely as I normally do, they pin plaits back with two combs, leaving the rest of it flowing below my shoulders. Their brushes bring out a sheen to the chestnut, that in a certain light, looks as though I have auburn highlights.

"Are you sure Apollo will approve?" one asks as she brushes, tossing her chin at the other.

"Is there something wrong with this? Is it not formal enough?" My hand skims the embroidered trim on the himation.

"It's quite lovely, and the color brings out your eyes," the second nymph answers. "It's just, Apollo enjoys his women dressed in something more . . . sheer."

"And less of it," the first interjects.

I finger the trim between my index and thumb and wonder if they are right. *Should I wear something more revealing to our dinner?* I assumed, given the station of both men, formal attire was required, but possibly I had misjudged.

"Don't worry, you look lovely, dear. A word of advice. Apollo can be enthusiastic, and he has a voracious appetite, particularly for virgins."

I whip around to face them. "Virgins?'

"Yes of course. Don't be alarmed, he knows his way around a female body. Allow him to guide you, let him set the pace. Lay back and let him do the work. You are in for a treat as he's especially nimble." She winks, and I grind my teeth. "Watch out for his prince, though. He'll have you agreeing to things you have never imagined. His tastes are darker, and your gentle person can't take what he gives."

"I always refuse his company. The way he looks at a person." The first shivers. "I'm convinced the man made a deal with Thanatos."

The women finish, chattering on, telling me all about intercourse as though I am ignorant of it. When the door shuts, I have no time to think about what they meant. I have never once felt uneasy in the prince's presence, quite the opposite. Grabbing a piece of parchment, I scribble down my thoughts. The guards will be here to collect me soon. The prince mentioned boundaries in the bathhouse, and at the time, I had only one. But with days of nothing but kisses that left me wanting and nights where only I could satisfy my lust, I have thought of what those might be. I need to discuss this with them before their lips touch mine and I forget why I need anything called boundaries, to begin with.

Half an hour later, I am escorted into a small chamber off the main dining hall. It's quiet here, having just passed the ruckus of all the warriors gathered together. My escorts part, and His Royal Highness sees me first. The smile that lights his deep brown eyes has flutterings bursting in my belly.

"Beautiful," he breathes. No nickname he insists on. Just one word that had me blushing from the intense pronunciation.

"Enchanting, more like," Apollo agrees, turning beside him. Both men had been addressing council members when I came into view. They stare at me as if I am an apparition and any moment they might blink, and I'll disappear.

"Evening." I incline my head, noticing that several council members have joined them in gawking. I twist my fingers into my hand, uncomfortable at being the center of attention.

Apollo reaches me first, taking my hand in his, he leans down and kisses my cheek in greeting. His Royal Highness is next, placing a kiss of greeting on the opposite cheek.

"You may go in." He motions to the council members who have begun to shuffle their feet. No doubt anxious at being held up from their evening meal. "We'll join the processional shortly."

"Join the processional?" I look around the god's wings at the members making their way to their designated tables.

"Never mind now." He guides me to the table in the middle of the room. "I thought we'd have a drink in here before the meal."

Flashes of what happened the last time I was in a room with a wooden table and both men dance through my mind, sending excitement racing down my spine.

Cin and Apollo grab a goblet, but I leave mine sitting on the golden tray. Pulling the parchment from my pocket, I swallow and unfold the paper.

"What have you there?" His Royal Highness asks, and I glance up at him before taking in a breath.

"The first time we were"—my eyes shift to Apollo who looks rather amused—"um, together, you asked about boundaries."

Cin sets his goblet on the table with a clunk. "I did."

"I have thought of some," I say to the paper, embarrassed now, for some reason.

A frown and then an odd crooked half-smile cross his face before Cin nods twice. "Okay, let's hear your boundaries."

Both men take their seats, leaving me the only option of the seat between them, or cross to the opposite side. I had hoped I might be able to look at both men, as I feel it would be more diplomatic, but I choose the seat between them.

I clear my throat. "I would like permission—"

"There is no need to ask for permission," Cin interrupts. "What you want or don't want isn't up for debate. You may always change your mind, of course, even during sex if you feel uncomfortable, but Hypatia, what you say no to, we respect."

I frown; I didn't expect that. He makes a motion, and I continue. "I would like—I mean, my first boundary is I require a robe that fits."

They share a look around me.

"I left my clothing in the bathhouse, and the next morning, I had to go to my room in a robe that was too big. I wouldn't want to accidentally show myself to some unsuspecting warrior."

Cin sits back in his chair and looks shocked at first before he chuckles. "You are aware boundaries mean things you are unwilling to do in bed, Hypatia."

"Or the study," Apollo chimes in. I catch his eye as he wiggles his eyebrows at me.

"I'm aware. I just want it to be known that I require a robe."

"Consider it done, little scribe." Cin winks.

"While I did enjoy the spanking"—I gulp, powering through to my next point—"I don't believe I would like it every time, or with objects like belts."

Cin nods.

"I don't believe I could . . . fit both of you at once—"

Apollo gasps, choking on his wine. Droplets sputter to the wood as he coughs, pounding his chest.

"Fucking Zeus, Hypatia," he croaks as Cin regards me with wide eyes. My head swivels, studying them, as they both seem very taken aback by my request.

"I only meant—"

Prince Cin holds up a hand. "That never crossed our minds."

"But there are two of you?" I insist.

"And there are ways to enjoy each other without that," His Highness says patiently.

I frown and look at the paper. I may have overanalyzed what might take place between us. Shrugging, I continue. "I would, however, like to explore things. I have very little scope as it is, but this arrangement is very different than my first. My partner was painful, and I'd rather go slower—"

"Painful?"

"How do you mean?"

They both interrupt at once, and I swing my head from the prince to Apollo and back.

"How do you mean?" Cin repeats.

"I would think you, of all people, wouldn't need it spelled out for you, Your Royal Highness. I've had coitus, I don't prefer it. Every time was painful and uncomfortable."

"It might hurt at first, but it shouldn't be painful every time," Cin replies, his handsome features darkening as he shares a look with Apollo. They exchange words with just a flick of an eye, each knowing what the other is thinking.

Apollo scrunches his face, twisting his lips as he does, his expression hard and unyielding. "So, you're not a virgin? Was it consensual?"

"Excuse me?" I shove my chair back from the table. At the scrape of the wood, both men leap to their feet. "Is the only way I might have a sexual encounter through force? I couldn't possibly want it?"

Apollo opens his mouth but slams it shut. They share a second look, and I gnash my teeth, frustrated at their intimacy. The words of the nymphs float in my mind. Up until now, I could have sworn neither cared whether I am a virgin or not, but their reactions show a different side.

"Is it so shocking I wouldn't be untouched? Or am I only valuable to you if I am a virgin; is that it?" I glare at them, determined to defend what little dignity I have left. If this was their plan all along, to want me simply because they view me as innocent, I will march back to my room. I am not about to enter into some arrangement with men who value my hymen more than my mind.

"Your virginity or lack thereof isn't in question, Hypatia." His Royal Highness' deadly tone sends a shiver down my spine, but the way he touches my hand has me softening by degrees. "We don't care who you choose to share your body with, as long as it was a choice. We ask because if it was by force—"

"He'd be dead," Apollo finishes.

I fold my arms, cutting my eyes to His Highness. I don't want, nor need defending, and their instantaneous anger seems misplaced.

"It was centuries ago," I challenge.

"Hours or a thousand years, the time matters not." He flicks his chin at me. "The man would die, simple as that. Anyone who dares lay a hand on you in harm will pay a heavy price."

"Without question or remorse," Apollo says, reaching for me. His rough hands slide to either side of my face, tilting it up so I can see him. There is pain in his eyes, as if the possibility of my body being defiled hurts him deeply. "We defend what's ours, sweet Hypatia, and you are ours. I have burned cities to the ground for far less. Hear me, you are my priority. You are the one I will always protect." Whatever bluster I mustered vanishes like smoke. "I ask you again, were you raped?"

"No." My voice shakes as I speak. "No. It was consensual but not pleasant."

"How so?" the prince asks.

Apollo tucks me into his side, folding an arm and a wing around and resting his chin atop my head. Relief washes over him, and I feel it hit me in waves. His Highness retakes my hand as if he needs my reassurance more than I need comfort.

"Do you really want details, Cinthus?"

"I guess I don't, but I'm curious. If it was consensual, and you found the sex unpleasant, why change your mind now? I'm delighted"—his wry smile and wiggling of those dark eyebrows causes me to roll my eyes playfully—"but I'm wondering what it was. Our technique? Or simple curiosity?"

I snort, pulling away from Apollo, who keeps a hand on my hip. "You're a brute, Cinthus."

His smile widens. "So I've been told."

"The first time, I approached it scientifically. While I might have been employed by a virgin goddess, warriors are certainly not. I had accidentally caught enough in the act to wonder about it myself. So, I asked a warrior I had become friendly with to assist."

"Assist. And?" Apollo's voice strains. His lips disappear into his mouth, and his eyes dance merrily. Hiding his amusement, he clears his throat.

"I performed the act three times to get a control base, but it was, as I said, unpleasant."

Cin coughs. "Right."

"And bumpy."

"Bumpy?" Apollo squeaks out.

"Yes," I say, making a sharp back-and-forth motion with my pelvis, demonstrating the undesirable technique. "Bumpy."

They break. Laughter fills the small room as both men's tightly held amusement snaps. I cross my arms and huff. I don't see what is so funny about my less-than-stellar experience. Cin kisses my forehead as he laughs.

"Dear Hypatia. Only you would look at sex as an experiment to perform." His nose brushes mine, and I give in, softening by degrees. "I vow to make this next experience quite less *bumpy*."

"An experiment, really, Hypatia," the god of light scolds. "Wait, is that what we are?" Feigning insult, Apollo gasps. "Are we your latest experiment?"

The prince laughs harder and mockingly throws his hand to his chest. "Madam, I beg you, say it isn't so."

Rolling my eyes, I growl. "Continue to mock me, and I shall quantify your performances."

This causes Apollo to sober quickly. "How so? With rulers?"

"Or orgasms?" the prince quickly adds.

"Technique?" Apollo continues.

"Is it out of ten?" Cin asks.

"I'm certain I could beat the prince," Apollo says confidently.

Throwing both hands in the air, I forfeit any idea of making my men pay for their transgressions.

"You both are impossible," I whine.

They are still teasing when the door opposite the table opens, and a servant scuttles in, nodding at Apollo. I look around us, expecting others to enter and bring in our dinner. Several seconds tick by as the men straighten their formal garb, and Cin slips a crown onto his head. They are acting as though we are entering the hall, and I shuffle my gaze from one to the other. We are to eat in his private dining room, that's why Apollo received me here. He won't want to parade me into the hall, have warriors and Olympians alike see me with him. Or Cin. I was a temporary indulgent, not a permanent relationship. Another servant enters, and Apollo wings an elbow at me. Stunned, I stare at the offered elbow.

"Will you accompany me, sweet Hypatia?"

I blink.

"Oh, I almost forgot. One can't sit at the high table without proper adornments. You need something more formal."

I touch the bangles. They are pretty but old and surely nothing in the way of what formal guests wear in the presence of the one who rules this court and his prince. Twisting my fingers into my hand, I step back.

"I apologize, My God." Another step back, away from the open doors and the sounds of music and deep male voices rushing into the room like a river of comradery. "I assumed we were dining together. My mistake. I'll return to the archives and wait for you to call for me when you're finished with your meal."

I retreat further and bump into a solid wall of leather-covered muscle. His Royal Highness grunts.

"Hypatia, we are dining together," Apollo says, pointing with his index finger at the table on a dais at the end of a long marble runner, "in the hall. I know you prefer the archives, but it is time I show you off. Make these assholes jealous I have the most beautiful woman in the room."

The thundering of my heart drowns out the roar of the hall. Scribes aren't allowed in great rooms. We aren't warriors or anything of such stature. No magic, no powers, no abilities of any kind. We simply exist because some Olympian wished us to. To have a scribe in such a position is scandalous. The palace may not care who Apollo and Cin share their beds with, but they most certainly care who sits beside them.

"Hypatia?" He touches my arm, and I realize I'm holding my breath. I gasp as if it's the first time I've ever breathed.

"I dine in the archives."

Tilting his head, he studies me. "Yes, but I'm asking you to join me in the hall."

"No." I shake my head. "I dine in the archives."

Sharing a look with the prince over my head, Apollo turns my head, forcing me to look at his for the second time. "Meaning?"

"Scribes eat in the archives. We aren't to mix with those of more importance in the great hall."

His crystalline blue eyes search mine. "You are important to me, Hypatia. You sit at the high table and anyone who so much as flinches will taste my blade." He smiles before waving his hand. "Now, as I was saying, you can't sit at the high table without a special adornment. Will this do?"

Wiggling his fingers, a delicate crown appears between his palms. A golden sun with glittering rays and a diamond crescent moon sits in the center, surrounded by stars of various sizes made out of gemstones. Pearls line the sides as laurel leaves twist around the pearls. It is dainty and delicate and expertly crafted. It's a crown fit for a goddess or a princess, not someone like me.

"My God," I whisper, "it's beautiful, but I can't wear it."

"Of course you can. You need a formal crown, and I have another for every day."

I'm shaking my head, but he ignores me and places the crown of jewels.

"My God," I insist, but he bends down and kisses me, leaving me breathless.

"Exactly as I imagined." Leaning in close, he whispers, "I've fantasized about you in this. Only in my fantasies, you are naked wearing only this crown." He places my hand on top of his.

I stumble, and he smirks, knowing exactly what he's doing to me. My eyes slide to the prince, and by his look, he is thinking the same thing. Cinthus flanks me, taking my other hand and placing it on his. He nods at the servant, and they propel me forward, down the runner, and into the great hall.

The crowded hall comes to a low murmur as we walk in, announced by the palace caller. The murmur grows when warriors and Olympians realize I'm the one between their god and prince. By the time we reach the dais, I'm shaking. They split, leaving me clinging to Apollo to round the table. Chairs are pulled out as we come to our spots. Apollo in the center, me on his right, and Cinthus next to me. I want to run. I want the room to stop staring at me. My chest tightens and all I hear is screaming in my ears as the room gets darker.

"Breathe," Apollo leans over and whispers as I somehow find the chair and sit. "Breathe." He rubs my hand under the table and His Highness touches my shoulder.

"Focus on my voice," he says as he arranges the goblets and plates that magically appear before each of us.

I do and pray I don't pass out.

Chapter 16

The God

I am enchanted by Hypatia of Alexandria. Enchanted and wondering if she'll ever be as at ease with me as she is with the prince. He leans over once again, and she rolls her eyes at whatever he says. When we first entered the hall, I thought she'd run from the high table. Her trembling squeezed my heart, and I wondered if I was once again too hasty. Cinthus says I'm guilty of plunging headlong into whatever I want. And I want her. I have tried to be more human in my attention, softer, gentler. To her, I want to be more than a god of the pantheon. I want her to see the man behind the god.

As the evening meal wanes, she relaxes more and more. I like her this way; her hearty laughter flits around me on wings of mirth. She is light and carefree, and I catch glimpses of who she is when she lets her walls down—when she lets us in. Once the music begins, His Highness asks her to dance, and my lovely Hypatia takes the floor with my equally lovely prince.

As they are preoccupied, I take this moment to judge the crowd. Cinthus had mentioned that some may question my choice to bring her into the hall. He warned it may raise the eyebrows of a few Olympians, as scribes are notoriously low in social standing in the palaces of the gods. Warriors might grumble between themselves, but none would challenge me. The councilmen, however, will have something to say, I'm sure. Ask me how many fucks I give for other's opinions. They can advise me all they want, but in the end, I'll choose her. Just as I chose the prince.

The music changes from an easy gathering melody meant to entice people to the floor, to a rousing one. Holding hands, Hypatia and His Highness join the others. Warriors, nymphs, fauns, and other creatures form a line, hands on shoulders, ready to spend the remainder of the evening in dance. Hypatia and Cin are in the middle of the line, surrounded by those in the palace. The brightness in her cheeks gives way to her excitement, and I find myself smiling along with her. Until the music begins.

I wince as my beauty steps on the poor prince's feet. She trips herself as the line of dancers bends and sways. Pulling herself upright, she's out of step quickly and rapidly disjoining the dancers around her. I've never seen anything like it. She is a brilliant mind with intelligent eyes and a mouth that makes me want to fall on my knees and worship her, all wrapped up with the graceful ability of a minotaur on roller skates. Her arms are back atop a warrior on one side and Cin on the other; the line of dancers wraps inward, and Hypatia steps on the warrior's toes. He yelps. Cinthus pulls her aside, leaving the fray, to keep her from injuring anyone else, I imagine.

I'm enthralled by the worst dancing I've ever seen, refusing to tear my eyes away, and I try to decide if it's lack of rhythm that made her first attempt at sex so *bumpy*. I was inclined to blame her unfortunate experience on the eagerness and inexperience of the warrior she chose, but by the way she moves on the floor, her terrible first experience may not solely rest on the man's shoulders. This tidbit I'm saving for later when we can have a private lesson. I am so captivated by the two that I don't notice the councilman until he thumps the table.

"My God." He inclines his head, and I resist the urge to roll my eyes. "I'm glad we have a moment," he says, rubbing his nose. The motion reminds me of a rat.

"Are you? Perhaps I'm occupied, councilman."

His thick hands rest on the table. "I would like to discuss the maiden you have brought here—"

"There is no discussion." I wave my hand dismissively and plop a grape in my mouth. "Hypatia eats with Prince Cinthus and me from now on."

His thick fingers again tap the wood. "She is a scribe, My God. While the council normally looks the other way when you indulge in your different tastes, exulting her to a higher position without notice to the council—"

"I wasn't aware the council was to be informed each time I engage with someone," I snap.

Hypatia is far more to me than a fleeting fancy and having her reduced to her position is pissing me off. I am proud to enter the grand hall with the spitfire who deflected my advances by telling me she may call out the wrong name. The woman that turned my prince's head. Instead, the council only sees her as a problem, someone who might try to advance within my court, and who needs to be reminded of her position. The woman almost fainted not an hour ago from the attention in the room. She cares little for social climbing, only for her stars and planets and mathematic equations that leave my head spinning.

It makes me want to wring the bastard's neck.

Her position is beside me.

Or under me.

But not hidden away again.

"The advisement of the council—"

"The advisement of the council can fuck themselves." The words punctuate the music as a warning. Glaring, I wait until he breaks eye contact. I'll not be told what I can and cannot do in my court when it comes to who I share my bed with. "It is my advisement that you scurry back to your seat, councilman, before I show you the wrath the gods are famous for."

He bows, hand coming across his heart in a salute, rushing back to his seat on fat, little rat feet. Rolling my head against my neck, I take a swig of wine and sit back, my mood sour. Again, I watch the dancers, hoping Hypatia has improved in the last few minutes, but she's busy at a set of tables. Several warriors are gathering around, handing her parchment. One is rushing back from somewhere with a model of the solar system. Another waves his hand and her astrolabe appears. Whatever is taking place, I enjoy watching her commence teaching amongst the free-flowing wine and rousing dance. Cinthus is beside her as she talks, taking the planets of the model and manipulating them. Every so often she glances at him and the way her face lights when she smiles sends shockwaves to my heart. Shockwaves and pings of jealousy.

I don't know how long I watch her, long enough for the music to fade to the background, and the hall to begin to clear. A bump to my chair breaks me out of my trance, and His Highness gives me a look as he sips from a chalice.

"Out with it."

Hypatia is now bent over, scribbling something on parchment with about five warriors enthralled beside her.

I shrug. "Out with what?" I can't take my eyes off her.

"You have been brooding all evening."

Sighing, I push back into my chair. Lying would be futile; Cinthus would see right through it. "I have been intently watching, Your Royal Highness. I'd hardly call that brooding."

"By this time in the evening, you're either halfway to intoxicated or engaged in the night's music. Yet, here you sit, wine glass from dinner in hand, half full, and staring at our exceptionally lovely house guest. So, I say again, out with it."

"It's nothing, Cin," I lie.

He points the rim of the glass at our mutual obsession. "I'll concede if you ask me to."

I jerk my head around and gape. "Concede?"

"A jealous god is a dangerous god, Apollo. As much as I want her, I want you more. I'll not let her come between us. For this to work, we all have to agree. I love you, you pompous ass, but if our choosing her makes you jealous, then I will walk away."

"I'm not jealous," I say, and even I don't believe it. "Fine, I'm a little jealous, but not enough to force you to step back." The back of my head hits the tall chair with a soft bump. "I have never had to work this hard to gain a woman's attention. Just when I think she's giving in, she retreats. I see the way she looks at you, and I can't help but wish she'd do the same for me."

"You're impatient, My God." He eyes her and takes a last swig of the water I know is in the glass. His strict rules around alcohol haven't wavered in centuries. "Perhaps you need to romance her a little. Woo her. You can be quite charming when you want to be. She needs to see another side of you. Not the naked side."

Snorting, I take a gulp of wine.

"You've wanted her for so long that you are freezing at the threshold. Woo her. You can do this, My God."

I shrug again, staring at the object of my obsession. Pushing back, I stride over, a plan forming with each step. *Romance her.* That should be easy, I can do that. When my shadow falls over her model, Hypatia greets me with the softest of smiles, and I suddenly feel tongue-tied.

She's finishing her point, and I silently panic. I'm a damn god. I can do this. I'm going to sweep my sweet Hypatia off her feet. Until she turns those gray eyes my way.

Shit. I have no fucking clue how to be romantic.

"My God." She inclines her head, and the warriors in her company all salute in unison. "Is there something you need?"

My hand finds my curls and, for the first time in my life, I'm speechless. Resting my hand on the back of my neck, I stumble over my damn words.

"Are you—teaching?" The warriors stare, and I cough. "Men. Warriors. I mean, are you teaching the warrior men . . . planets?"

Her brief nod is both delighted and confused at my odd question. Unfazed, she picks up the model and turns one of the planets, rotating it around the sun.

"I was showing the men how I came to my conclusion that there is indeed a new star." She sets the model down and meets my gaze. A flicker of heat leaps in her eyes. "But I can be finished, if you'd like my attention."

She isn't challenging me this time, isn't running. She's standing before me, offering a reason to break up this impromptu educational lesson. Telling me she's ready for the rest of the evening, the evening I promised when we entered the hall. An evening I have wanted since I first saw her. And now, the idea of taking her back to my chambers seems absurd and crude. I suddenly have only one thing in mind, and it has nothing to do with the promised crown and nakedness. Now, all I want is for her to smile up at me as if she sees me. I meant what I said, I don't want a quick fuck. I want her. All of her. I want her heart.

"You're dismissed, men," I say, coming near. Noticing the drawings she made on the parchment, I pick it up and study it, giving my hands something to do besides jam behind my back.

"That's nothing, My God." She waves a hand as she straightens the table.

A drawing of a cone ending in a point is surrounded by several equations on all sides. I turn my head, trying to make sense of what I'm looking at.

"It looks like something familiar," I say to the paper, turning the drawing back around.

"A lens."

We look at each other for a minute; a wordless conversation falls heavy between us.

"For what?" I say, like a damn idiot.

Clearing her papers into a pile, she sets the model on top of the stack, the astrolabe next to it. I motion for a steward to take the things away, instructing him to return them to her room. She softly breathes and comes to stand beside me. The lemony scent of her perfume wafts through the air, driving me crazy. I return my attention to the paper in hand as she points.

"For the telescope. The one in the observatory. I can only get so much magnification and need something stronger. I'll give the calculations to Athena to have her make one for the one in her palace. That way, I can finish up with my report when I return after the closing ceremonies."

The closing ceremonies.

She says it so casually, and I have the sudden urge to command her to stay. She has to stay.

I want her to stay.

"Come with me." It's the only thing I can think of as I wing an elbow in her direction. We pass the prince, who is still sitting where I left him.

"Is His Highness not coming as well?" she asks with a tilt of her head.

"Not for what I have in mind," I say as we walk through open doors leading to the gardens. She frowns as we pass under the archways and out into the warm summer night. When we pass a hedge of yellow roses, she stops and turns to me.

"This isn't the way to your chambers."

"How do you know where my chambers are, sweet Hypatia?" I try to be coy, to return to the ease I had around her not hours before, but something between us has changed. Electricity hums just under the surface and I wonder once again if this is madness.

"I thought we were going to your chambers." She steps back. "Our agreement, my boundaries." She looks down at the tender blades of grass. "I assumed, that meant—have I displeased you, My God?"

When she says it that way, it sounds as if she's a concubine, as if I want her only for sex and damn the rest. Is this what she thinks of me?

"No"—I shake my head as I take her hand—"I thought you would like to show me the observatory."

"But you built it, My God. I hardly think you need me to show you your own building." Her thin eyebrows pinch together. "My God?"

She's staring up at me and I can't resist any longer. Sliding my palms on either side of her cheeks, her eyes close at the contact, and I gently pull her near. My mouth brushes hers, and I hear that hitch in her breath.

"Call me Apollo," I rasp and watch her pink tongue dart out, tasting my words. "I need my name uttered by your lips, sweet Hypatia." My forehead finds hers, and I close my eyes, breathing her in. "I may have built it, but I've never seen it through your eyes. Please, show me the thing that sets your heart on fire. Your obsession."

I can no longer tell if I'm talking about a building or something else. I kiss the bridge of her nose, her eyelids, her cheeks. A soft hum floats on the cool breeze. Her teeth graze her bottom lip, and I keep myself from nipping that very lip. When she looks up, her eyes are the color of stone, dark and heavy-lidded.

Somehow, we make it to the observatory, and I watch in awe as she flits around the room, showing me everything the large scope can do. Her skin flushes with excitement when she adjusts some knobs and lenses and identifies an object far above us. Her hands move with precision as she tells me about her research. I can do nothing but soak up every smile, every glance, every thrilling sentence that starts and ends with words I'm unfamiliar with. I am drawn into her world, and she makes sure I understand everything. She teaches and I listen, and I am enamored by her beauty and her brains. With bits and bobs, rocks and chalk found around the room, she makes a model of a star grouping. She has come alive letting me have a glimpse into her world, and I feel as though I am the luckiest man on Olympus.

"So, if you're right, it should be right between that asteroid belt?" I mumble my question as I close one eye, squinting at the planet that remains within the lens' view.

"Yes, and no."

"And the lens you drew up, you'd need that to get a clearer picture?"

"I think so," she says from behind me. I straighten and turn to face her. Her crown glints in the low light, and I can't help the damn butterflies that fly loose in my stomach at her in my crown.

"So, why would you give Athena your sketch?" This I'm curious about. She could ask me. I would pull down the entire cosmos if she asked.

She brushes past, and I gently touch her arm. She lets me linger, and it sends tingles racing through my fingertips. When she looks at me, I can't help but notice the slight changes in her demeanor. She isn't nervous and isn't looking for a place to retreat. I hope this means she feels comfortable enough to allow me in. I think she's going to respond, but I catch a glint in her eye, quickly passing across her iris. Before I know what's happening, her fingers are in my curls, running her trimmed nails over my scalp. They slide through my hair and behind my ear, tracing my jaw. I can barely breathe. I stand so still, I'm certain I rival every statue in the gardens. Jolts of desire run the length of my spine. Again, she reaches for me, but this time, she buries both hands into my hair, and I am a man undone. Tugging as she follows my scalp to the back of my head, her fingers rest at the nape of my neck.

"So soft," she breathes, pulling me down toward her. When she smiles, I'm blinded by the radiance. "Apollo." She sighs.

Her lips find mine and what starts as gentle, questioning pressure erupts into need. Feverish need. One of us moans as both our mouths open, tongues twisting, tangling themselves together. I don't know how, but her back has met something hard and sturdy, a wall somewhere in the room. She arches into me, and I run my hands into her hair, pulling the strands and keeping her close. My lips find her neck, her jaw, her ears; anywhere I can kiss her, I do. She's tugging at my shoulders, grabbing a fistful of the cape draped across me and keeping me pressed against her. Reaching down, I gather fabric until her thighs are in my grasp. I hoist her up, keeping her positioned against the wall, and her legs close around my hips. The observatory hears every low groan, every moan, every sound we make as I grow more desperate with each passing second. Then she stops.

"Take me to your chambers, My God."

She says it so low, in such a husky whisper that I shiver. Our lips find each other again, rough and wild. Her hips flex against me and it drags a moan deep from my ribs. Her fingers are in my hair, her thighs clamped around me, and that delectable mouth kisses places I never knew were sensitive. My breath is coming shorter, my heart thumping against my chest.

"Please," she whines, teeth scraping my neck.

And I explode. One minute, my hands are full of her delicious thighs, the next, I'm thrusting against her, spilling cum and shaking, groaning in her ear like a beast. Like this is my first encounter. *Damnit.* My hard breaths ruffle fine hairs along her neck, and she moves her head to look at me.

"I wasn't aware men could finish without touch." Her lips lazily skim mine. A cheeky smile tugs at the corners as her feet hit the floor.

"I could finish from just one look from you, sweet Hypatia." I nuzzle her neck, raking my teeth across the top of her shoulder. "I have been walking the edge all evening."

"I didn't know I had that kind of power over such a fierce god." She isn't coy when she says it, states it like a fact. It's endearing and sweet. I want to ruin her. Ruin her for any future man. Wreck her as she is doing to me.

"You have more power than you know. I'm under your control. Command me, and I'll fall to my knees in worship."

When she moves, I brush against her core, harden again, ready for more.

"What separates gods and men, is men need to recover after coming. Gods have no such restriction." I kiss a line to her mouth. "I want you in my bed. Let me take you back to my chambers so I can properly fuck you."

So much for romance.

Chapter 17

The Scribe

The moon is a crescent sliver that gives very little light. Several torches are lit around the balcony so Cin and I might work. Hours ago, pressed against the wall of the observatory, I thought for sure Apollo would take me there, claim me as I've been aching for him to do. He'd all but flown back to his chambers, towing me in an eager attempt to finish what we started. Well, finish again. For him.

When we burst into Apollo's chambers, Cin looked just as surprised as the god to see us. From what I gathered from their discussion—something I half-listened to as I walked the perimeter of the room, learning all the stories his chambers told about the god who occupied it—Cin fully expected us to end up in my chambers. He had come to find a set of paints he needed and was returning to his room when we appeared.

I have little understanding of how this works. How being one part of a third looked in terms of nights and beds and sharing, but what I realized was time alone with each other was expected. Something I hadn't thought of. I'd just assumed it'd be the three of us always, in whatever endeavors we pursued. I suggested and Apollo insisted Cinthus stay and that was how we ended up on the balcony surrounded by torches in the thinnest of moonlight.

"Is drawing something you've always pursued, or had you learned it here?" I stand beside His Highness, watching him work. The more time

I spend with the prince, the softer he becomes. The rigid, harder persona that he wears around the palace is a barrier he puts up. I want to reach across it. Reach across and drag him to the bed.

"I've always been interested. I had an interest long before I came to Olympus, but here I have more time to pursue the medium and master it," the prince says as his thick fingers delicately hold charcoal. I clench low, remembering those fingers filling me but not enough.

My eyes meet Apollo's from across the room. I haven't cooled as I thought I would, as the night wore on. The longer I remain in the chamber, dressed and not under one or both, the deeper the ache. I am trying my best to pretend I don't want what he's promised—a proper fucking.

I am failing.

This is torture.

A flush creeps across my skin, and I scold myself, trying to concentrate. Looking up at his handsome profile, I long to run my fingers through his hair, tug his face down to mine, kiss that mouth that's speaking words I'm unable to hear as the pounding of my heart becomes a thunder of want. Once more, I glance at the god of light who is wearing a knowing smirk as if he can read my thoughts. On instinct, I bite down on my bottom lip, and he slowly nods. He's stretched out on an oversized chaise lounge, made exclusively for the god's tall frame and massive wings. Taking fruit from a nearby golden bowl, he pops a grape into his mouth, and his look turns heated. Flutterings deep and low in my belly cause my thighs to rub. The slight rise of one of Apollo's light-colored eyebrows tells me he knows exactly what he's doing.

"Did you hear me?"

Jerking my head, I stare into deep brown eyes that momentarily block my view of the flirtatious god.

"What?"

The prince's eyes crinkle at the corners as he shoots a quick look at Apollo who winks. I don't know which is more agonizing: pretending I don't want to reach over and entangle my tongue with the prince's or enduring every seductive look the god of light sends my way. Apollo eats another grape. I watch, entranced, as his full lips close over the fruit and he chews slowly. His throat bobs when he swallows, and my heart flutters against my rib cage. Heat prickles along my collarbone when he grabs another.

"Are you listening Hypatia, or are you busy eye-fucking Apollo?" His Highness says with a smirk, and I blink in response. Unable to think of anything coherent, I open my mouth several times but close it and look sheepish. Cin grips my chin between those fingers I was admiring and lifts my head.

"Is there something you want to say, little scribe?"

I'm frozen in his hand, there's nothing I want to say. Words have no place here. The scent of his soap is on a breeze that ruffles his dark hair.

Laurel soap.

It's mixed with something, a spice I can't place. Stepping closer forces me to arch into him and Cin's pupils expand. His breath is mixing with mine, and I want him closer. I want him to lean down and kiss me. I want to bury my nose in his skin and taste him as my tongue runs down his neck. I want to be bold. To kiss him first. To take control. To lead. His lips part and those two, soft, pillowy lips entice me from inches away.

"Fuck it," I mutter before I grab his face and pull him to me, kissing that mouth. It isn't the kiss of a woman who is timid and unsure. This is the kiss of a woman who knows, infallibly, what she wants. And she wants a prince and a god.

Here.

Now.

Tonight.

I don't stop when he comes up for air, gasping and slamming his mouth back on mine. Instead, I tug at the leather breastplate trying my best to free the latches at his shoulders. They come loose despite my stumbling fingers, and I pull the armor off. Smoothing my hands along the linen chiton, my next foe is the leather skirting. His nimble fingers beat me, and the skirting hits the floor. Cinthus spins me around to face Apollo who is stalking toward us. My hair is pulled to one shoulder, and kisses are laid along my exposed neck. Reaching back, I thread my hand through the prince's hair. Someone moans, soft and light. Possibly me. The two of us ignite, no longer willing to wait. I want this. I've been dreaming of this.

My himation is pulled over my head, as Cin kisses my neck and works the pins free of the dress. The crown that has been on my head all evening feels too heavy suddenly; I reach up to take it off before it winds up tossed to the floor.

"Don't you dare," Apollo growls. "I meant what I said, I want to fuck you with my crown from my court atop your head." His mouth claims mine, and his tongue pushes past my lips. I groan, yanking him closer.

"Boundaries," Cinthus says into my neck, and I whimper from the vibrations. "Our boundaries."

"I want you both, Cin," I explain, punctuating my point with sloppy kisses to Apollo's jaw. "Now. Sex. Penetration. Cocks. I've been drinking my tea. I'm ready."

"Yes," he breathes, and Apollo traces my hardened nipple poking through the fabric. "But ours." He spins me again to face him. We are both panting, both seconds away from combustion. Swallowing I nod.

"What are yours, Cinthus?"

At the whisper of his name, he whines, low and soft, as if it were both a beautiful sound and the sweetest torment. My hands find his cheeks, and he kisses my palm.

"No domination. No spanking by anyone. No blindfolds. No restraints," he says, and a shiver runs the length of my spine. He doesn't say it as a command but as a request. It's a quiet, telling moment that squeezes at my heart. His mouth finds mine. I lean in, wanting to reassure the prince that I have no intention of breaking any of his boundaries. His fingers go back to work freeing me of my clothing.

When he releases me, the peplos falls to the floor, and I am naked before them. Apollo turns me slowly, drinking me in from head to toe. He's barely breathing again, and I wonder if I'm enough for him.

"You're more than enough," he says, and I jerk my head. "So much more than enough."

"But I—"

He softly kisses my shoulder. "Gods can read minds, sweet Hypatia. And reading yours has been delicious torture. Every fantasy you've had, I'm willing to indulge every single one if you'll let me."

"I didn't know."

"Mmm," he hums against my skin, his hands caressing my sides. "In the archives. In your chambers." He nuzzles my neck, burning me with kisses. "The bathhouse was particularly bawdy."

Heat flushes across my skin, and I fear my entire body is blushing. Apollo stops his sweet torture and gazes down at me.

"My thoughts have been the same." Stooping down, he hoists me up, and again, my legs encircle his waist.

"I have only one boundary, sweet Hypatia," the god says as he strides to somewhere in the room. "You. My boundary will always be you, and I dare anyone to cross it. "

I feel the mattress under me, sagging under both our weights as Apollo moves us to the center. He's gone for a second, and his bare skin brushes mine when he returns. It's electric, sending jolts of white-hot need straight to my aching center. Arching, I glide my hands over the gold-dusted beauty that is the god of light, and he settles between my thighs. His hips rest on mine, and I wrap my legs around him, securing him to me in case he decides to flee.

His mouth is everywhere his hands are not, and I'm nothing but whispers and whines. When that mouth clasps onto my nipple it wrestles a strangled gasp from me. He's plucking me like strings, playing my body with the same impressive expertise he plays the lyre. Calloused fingertips turn velvet as they glide harmoniously toward my core. His fingers find my clit, and Apollo moans in my ear.

"So damn wet." Laying kisses on my collarbone, he moves down my body. "I have smelled your desire for hours, an intoxicating aphrodisiac. But had I known you were this ready, this needy, I would have taken you the moment we entered my chambers."

Gasping as his teeth rake over a nipple, I rasp. "You—you can tell?"

He nods, slipping a finger into me. "Gods come with many attributes." He stops his assault for a moment and meets my lidded gaze. "You are beautiful." A kiss between my breasts. "Intelligent." Another pressed into my belly. "Enchanting."

He works me slowly, lazily, as though he cares not of the torture I'm under at the languished pace. Inserting a second finger, I lift my hips, taking him to the knuckle. He curls them, massaging a certain spot. I rock against his hand and the delicious ache it builds deep within. He does it again, over and over, curling his fingers until I am half out of my mind, bringing me quickly to the edge. It's fast and hard, and I come with a scream, my body going taut before exploding. Arousal coats his finger and when he brings them to his mouth, he groans.

"Fuck."

Spreading my thighs wider, his cock is next to rub against me, and I become slick just from the tip of him.

"You're sure?" He's paused above me, ready to do just what he said he would. What I want. I nod.

"No. Words." His hand finds my cheek. "I need words."

"Yes."

Slowly he slides in, and I tense. Every muscle contracts, and my breath catches. The fear of pain rushes in over my want of him. "Look at me. Look at me, Hypatia." Stroking my cheek, he waits until my eyes open.

"I'm sorry. I'll try to be better." I grip his biceps, and Apollo shakes his head.

"Not like this. You have nothing to apologize for. I'll wait until you relax; until you trust me." He's panting, his face lined with intensity, but he retreats giving me time to catch my breath.

"I want this, Apollo. I want you. I'm saying yes. I'm just scared it will hurt." I confess, and he brushes hair off my forehead.

"Then we'll go slow." He places the tip back at my entrance, and I tense again. "Breathe. We can stop at any time," he says, pushing in. I stretch around him and wait for the inevitable discomfort, but I'm so slick with arousal, that he glides. "Look at me," he commands in a husky whisper, and I look up into eyes the color of an early morning sky. "Move with me. Let us do this together." His touch is gentle, soft, reverent as though he's afraid this isn't real. "Are you in pain?"

Shaking my head, I touch his face, but Cin's voice comes from somewhere beside me. I had forgotten momentarily he was in the room.

"He needs words. *We* need words." His large hand finds mine, and I look over at a concerned prince's narrowed expression.

"I'm fine." To accent my point, I lift my hips, angling us and causing him to hiss. He buries more of himself while my body adjusts to his size. There isn't pain, just fullness. Glorious fullness. "It feels good."

The words leave my mouth before I have time to think of something better, more articulate to say. Sexier. Both men groan at my admission. Apollo slides further in, and I can't help the eager noises I make. He's moving slowly, driving me out of my mind. I want more. I clutch at him, but that only encourages him to slow down. "Do you want me to stop?"

"No." To make my point, I nip his shoulder. "Please," I beg. I'm desperate. I grab at his ass and try to force him to understand.

"Slow. I want to make sure there isn't pain."

I shake my head. "There isn't. Please."

My begging is met with a deep chuckle.

"My Asteria is a needy one, desperate for me." I look at him in confusion, but his face is tender and sweet, in awe of me. He's calling me by an old god's name. "You are her, sweet Hypatia. Goddess of the falling stars. My Asteria. My falling star. My heart. Mine."

"Yes." A soft smile crosses my lips at the honor he's given me. "Yes. I am yours."

Gods do not bestow their title on anyone. To be a god is to be born into privilege and royalty, it cannot be spoken with words, it is a birthright. But here, now, I am worshipped by the god of light and called one of his own He kisses me and thrusts deeper. Pulling out, his hands find my thighs and lift.

"Any pain, Asteria?"

"No." I tremble as he thrusts, pleasure building.

When I whimper, he kisses me. "You are magnificent like this. I have wanted you for so long. Craved you. Gods, you're made for me. Made to be fucked by a god."

His lascivious words leave me breathless as his motions pull me further along.

"Look down, sweet Hypatia. Look at where we're joined. See how well you take your god."

I do as instructed and watch his cock disappear inside me. A primal feral sound rips from my chest.

"Faster." I can only whisper. I don't realize the word is spoken until Apollo growls in my ear, and his tempo becomes punishing. He's pinned me to the mattress, stretching my body along his, my hands gathered in one of his above my head. I'm at his mercy, and I am finally where I want to be. Each thrust brings me closer; each moan is like a melody only our bodies know. I am his.

His falling star.

"Fuck yes." His hiss brings me back to the room. "I'm never letting you go."

We both tumble head over wing off the clif. Falling together as my body clenches around his. Our cries mix as well as our orgasm, and I shake as it rocks through me. We float back to Olympus together.

The back of his head is damp as I thread my fingers through his curls. He rests on top of me for a few moments, allowing me time to catch my breath. Then I'm on my side and Cin's face is in view. He kisses me, pulling me to him.

"Do you want more, little scribe?" His dark eyes are sinful, and I know if I nod, he'll make me answer.

"Show me."

149

Lifting my leg, his head is between my thighs before I can protest. His tongue, mouth, fingers, are all poised to fling me back off into the abyss. His groan vibrates through me, rippling up my body like a wave. Two of his fingers slide inside, and my hips flex as he moves in and out. Stopping, he slips both fingers out.

"Taste both of your releases. Your cum is sweeter than ambrosia," he commands.

I take the offering and suck them into my mouth. Our combined release makes for a heady combination. My head is swimming as the prince goes back to lapping up every last drop. His tongue works my clit until I swear I see stars burst overhead.

I explode again, clawing at him, keeping him in place. When the shaking subsides, my limbs are heavy. These two will be the death of me if I'm not careful. I will truly die a *little death*. This thought causes me to giggle, and Apollo nuzzles my ear.

"Care to share what is so funny?" He playfully nips my earlobe.

"Between you two, I'm being dragged to the Underworld and dining with Hades," I answer to a confused Apollo. Cinthus grins so wide, so brilliantly, that I think his smile may outshine the god's.

"In that case," Apollo teases, lifting my leg and thrusting into the hilt. I arch. No pain. Any apprehension is gone. I am in their hands to do with what they may, completely trusting. "You can take me again, can't you, sweet Hypatia? One more. I need to give you one more."

My head swims, and I make a barely audible noise.

"Tell me you're okay. Tell me to keep going." He rotates his hips as he asks.

I raise my head just enough to look Apollo in the eyes. "Fuck me properly, just as you promised."

He's moving as I whimper, lying on my side. Cinthus kisses my breasts. When he takes a nipple into his mouth, I shudder. I want to explore him; I want him to lose control as Apollo is doing. My hand finds his cock, and I swear he stops breathing. Long, slow strokes begin and Cinthus tosses his head back.

"Make him come," Apollo says as he slows, the sight of us exciting him.

The prince is big. Bigger than the god currently filling me, and I wonder how he will fit. I'm pumping him faster and faster, matching the tempo the god has set. I'm crazed, erratic, as my fist slides up and down.

"Let me taste you."

Cin's eyes fly open, and he regards me as if he hadn't heard what I said. In case he didn't, I repeat myself. "Let me taste you."

At first, he shakes his head, but in a momentary burst of coyness, I grab his chin.

"Use your words, Your Highness. I can't give you what you want unless you tell me."

I'm not sure who cursed first, Apollo or the prince. Emboldened, I grab for the cock I want in my mouth. Cin wastes no time climbing to position and as soon my lips flower around the tip, his tight controls snaps. "Suck my cock, greedy little scribe," he says behind clenched teeth. "Take me while our god fucks you. That's a good fucking girl."

I don't think, I just react. I wanted both and tonight I'm determined to have what I want. Cin's hips piston down as my tongue circles his shaft. Apollo increases to a feverous tempo. I hold at the edge, not wanting to fly into the unknown without my men. I swallow deeper and gag when his cock touches the back of my throat. Cin coos approval at me. Using my tongue, I slide it up the shaft, and he loses himself.

"Fuck. Yes. Fuck." He fists my hair and his cum is flooding my mouth, down my throat. I can barely swallow fast enough. Apollo and I fall together into a euphoric heaven. Their moans send me off the cliff once more before I even landed from the last. I want them to moan again, all night, both, together. For several long minutes, neither of us move. The only sounds are our raspy breathing and soft crackles from the fire in the fireplace. Cinthus breaks the silence.

"Holy fuck!" He flops onto his back, and I wiggle to him, wanting to be closer. Wanting to reassure myself that this isn't another of my fantasies. Resting for a minute more, both men set to work cleaning us up and fitting me in bed between them.

Because it's where I belong.

With them. Always.

They are mine, and I'm never letting them go.

Chapter 18

The Prince

I awake sometime before dawn and untangle myself from my partners. Brushing hair from Hypatia's cheek, I kiss it. She mewls something in her sleep, smiling sweetly. Apollo awoke when I did, but he remains wrapped around our girl, tenderly keeping her warm under his wing.

The gray morning's misty fingers stroke the edge of the balcony, gently calling to me. Hypatia had fallen asleep almost instantly once I got her settled, leaving time for us to talk about what this meant. His jealousy last night had been a wake-up call. He had feelings for her, same as I, but the difference between us is I love him more than my feelings for her. I will do anything for him, even walk away from Hypatia to keep our relationship intact. Apollo reassured me that his jealousy was short-lived. That he'd still choose me. That his love was not fickle when it came to us.

If he decided I was competition, I could lose both of the people important to me. The people I loved. It was a risk I wasn't willing to take. Placing both hands on the cool stone, I look out into the mountain range surrounding the palace. My heart beat wildly in my chest at the realization.

I love them.

Hypatia of Alexandria and Apollo the god of light.

I fell in love with her the moment she pushed me out of the way of the telescope in the field of daisies. Hypatia isn't just someone I want in my bed; I want her in my life. *Our life.* I have never wanted another person until her. I didn't know my heart was capable of expanding the way it has in the short time she's been here. But even so, I'd give her up to keep him.

With thoughts tumbling around in my mind, I lose myself to my art. Across the canvas, I use paints to express my uncertainty. The rosy glow of the first beams of sunlight falls across the balcony as I paint into the canvas what I feel.

"Morning," she says, keeping her voice low. Our eyes meet and she smiles, and my heart squeezes as if in a vise. She's snuggled into a thin blanket she's stolen from the bed, one bare shoulder peeking out. Beautiful gray eyes match the last of the mist that is quickly fading in the sunlight. Her hair is mussed, her cheeks bright. She is glowing this morning.

God's she is beautiful.

Please be mine too.

"Mind if I peek?" She points at the canvas with her chin, and I move aside. Her interest in artistry is something that I find endearing. One of her dainty hands finds my chest, and her palm warms the skin it touches.

"Oh, Cinthus!" she breathes, excited. "It's beautiful. You're such a master at oils." Her eyes catch mine, and I melt under her genuine praise. "Is it the agora in town outside the palace?"

I nod, speechless as she moves and wraps her arm around me, placing her cheek on my bare chest. I tuck her in tight, wanting her near. We stay like this for a few minutes, admiring the painting and silently telling secrets to each other's hearts. I kiss the top of her head as I move to put the brush down.

"I think I need a new subject." Replacing the half-finished painting with a sketching pad, I touch her nose. "Perhaps it's time I drew you?"

She wrinkles that pert nose and shakes her head. "I'm not a subject for such a fine artist. You should draw one of the nymphs."

"Hypatia"—my tone causes her to look up at me, and I fall all over again—"I don't want any of the nymphs. I want you."

She blinks. "But I'm a scribe."

As if her position within the hierarchy of the Olympians means anything to me. Does she truly believe that her entire existence is defined by the duty she holds?

"Do you think that matters?" She doesn't respond. "I want you. Just you. The woman before me is bold and brilliant. I don't care about your position; I care about you. Scribe is what you do, not who you are."

Something in her eyes flickers. She is hearing my words for what they are, truth. Whoever has drilled into her that her value is only as high as her position is an asshole. I want to erase that idea and replace it with what Apollo and I have been trying to tell her. That she is far more important to both of us. And that, if she'll let me, I'll happily spend my eternal life next to her loving the same man.

"Let me draw your beauty."

Twisting her lips, she thinks for several long seconds, longer than I would like. But a coy smile curves her lips, and she closes one eye, squinting.

"This is all a ploy to see me naked, isn't it?"

"It's a bonus, I'll admit."

Her giggle sets my heart alight. Taking a deep breath, she looks around the room.

"Fine, Prince Cinthus, where shall you have me?"

I can't help the smirk that crosses my face as the thought of bending her over any number of surfaces plays across my mind. Ultimately, I decide on the settee and point to it.

"There, little scribe."

She moves and turns to face me. "And in what position?" The look on her face tells me she knows exactly the question she's asked.

"Now, now, this is strictly professional. None of that behavior." I bring the stand and sketching papers closer, dragging a table over to lay charcoals and pencils on.

"Lie there, on your back," I instruct. "Now, one hand over your head, that's right. Let the blanket go, down to your hips. Take your other and under your chin. Yes. That's my girl."

I'm all business as she does as she's told. Fitting the thin fabric around her waist, she places her arm above, and I forget what I'm supposed to be doing.

"My breasts are quite lovely, are they not, Your Royal Highness?"

"Shhh, subjects aren't supposed to talk," I playfully scold and she giggles again. It is mellifluous and tinkles in the room like crystal. Scrunching my nose, I pause, hovering above the paper, charcoal in hand. The only subjects I can focus on are two perfectly round breasts that I'd rather be holding. I do my best to pretend I'm not thinking of them.

"No giggling. Hold still."

I take my time, first sketching her likeness and then moving on to the medium. Apollo has been awake this whole time, watching us.

He leaves the bed with a pout. "It's too early to be awake."

"Says the god of light," Hypatia teases over her shoulder. He sits next to her and softly swats her ass.

"Insolent woman," he reprimands as he bends over and blows air into her neck. She squeals, kicking her feet and swatting at him. The blanket ends up in a heap on the floor.

"You two have no sanctity for the greatness before you. Quit! Let the artist work."

"He's sure in a foul mood," Apollo says, wiggling his eyebrows at Hypatia who suppresses a laugh.

She shoots me a coquettish look, and I resist the urge to abandon the whole idea for more enjoyable endeavors. "Shhh the artist is working."

"Do either of you mind?" I say with a humph.

With that, Apollo peppers her shoulder with kisses before he gets up and rings the bell for the kitchens. It's almost an hour before trays are brought up and placed in their rightful spots. Apollo leaves to bathe and dress, leaving me and the gloriously naked Hypatia to our task. When the servants come in, I assumed she will scramble to cover herself, but there is a boldness about her this morning. She stays just as she is, lounging while they set to their task, never taking her eyes off me.

My charcoal sketches the line of her torso, the graceful slope of her hip, her thigh, her calf. All places I have yet to explore. The way she's staring has my breath sticking in my ribs. Each time our eyes meet over the top of the stand, hers darken further. I am supposed to be the one in control, but she is shredding that control one glance at a time.

"You're so serious, Cinthus."

Every time she says my name, I want to capture the sound and bottle it. It does something to me that no other word could. She moves her hand and traces the edge of her jaw, slipping down her neck to her collarbone.

"Have you drawn here?"

My mouth is dry. How can this woman have me tied in knots on the inside? I watch her index finger trace lower, down the center, stopping between her breasts. She follows the rounded edge of one, coming along the full bottom.

"Or here?"

I've stopped drawing, entranced, fully under her spell. I belong to her, every move a torment until she allows me to touch her. Truly a goddess among women. Her finger slowly climbs the small mound of her breast and encircles her areola.

"Or here?"

It's a husky whisper that has my cock standing at attention. I'm out of my element. Last night, I came so damn fast with just her mouth. But it was her command to use my words that had made me almost lose control without her touching me. And now this.

"You keep saying I have to ask for what I want." She crooks her finger at me. "You. I want you, Cin."

My mind races with all the reasons I shouldn't move. They come tumbling out uncharacteristically. "Not—not yet. You'll be sore. I'm larger than Apollo. It might be painful. I don't wish to cause you pain, Hypatia."

Why I'm trying to talk her out of the one thing I've wanted since she got here is beyond me. Her taking the lead is spinning my head round. She has reduced me to a fumbling lad in four words. *I want you, Cin.*

"Please."

Fucking Zeus! I'm a man undone. I'm to her in two strides, my mouth colliding with hers as I hungrily devour the noises she makes. She kisses me back with a need that teeters on insanity. Her hands are on me, pulling at the cloth around my waist. Her nails leave marks along my biceps. Pulling her in my arms, I flip her on top, and her hips hit mine when she bounces.

"You want me? I'm yours." Rising, I capture her mouth. Her tongue pushes past my lips, tangling with mine. She is writhing on top, desperate for friction against her clit I know is swollen. I seal my mouth over one of her nipples and she arches her back, moaning and bucking against me.

"Take me like this, Hypatia. Use me." My hands grip her hips, and she rocks, slipping over the tip of my cock. She's soaked, and I want nothing more than to bury myself in her. Grasping me, she settles back and rubs the tip along her slit, teasing.

"This, your arousal it's all because of me. I enjoyed watching you with our god, but never doubt who holds your reins. Now, you're going to do as I say and ride this cock. Fuck me and come when I command it." She has me at her entrance and then sinks slowly. Inch by fucking inch. Her face contorts, and I grab her chin.

"Is it too much?"

She shakes her head, and I tighten my grip. "Words," I remind her.

"No, Cin."

"Good girl."

She's about halfway and slowly taking more. I watch as I fill her, her breathing rapid. Tilting her hips, she drags back up, and we both moan.

"Yes. Fuck me."

She feels so good wrapped around me. So fucking good, I almost come here, halfway in. On her next stroke, she does what she's told, taking me to the hilt, and my hips push up.

"Fuck."

She is riding so slow, each stroke agony and pleasure. I need to wait for her to get used to me before I encourage her to increase her movements. I'm trying, but as her ass meets my hips, I lift mine, driving myself into her. Her head throws back, her hands on my chest. The tempo increases gradually until she is at a speed that has her thighs shaking.

"That's my girl, taking my big cock like you are." I grip her hips as she pumps up and down. Her moans turn to whimpers, and her inner walls clamp around me. "Keep going. You're going to come like this, on top of me, aren't you?" She nods. Her breath is coming in short pants, her lips parted as she gets herself to the orgasm we both want.

"Use your words, Hypatia. I'll ask again, you're going to come for me like this, aren't you? Make a mess all over me."

A high-pitched groan is my answer. I thrust my hips up, driving into her. Then I slow her down until her body is shaking keeping her on edge.

"Words. I'll keep you here, your release just out of reach. Is that what you want? You want me to tease you?"

Her fingernails leave half-moons in my skin. "No. No. I want to release."

"Come," I demand. "Say come."

"I want to come." Her voice is raspy. "Yes, I'll come for you, Cin."

Thrusting up hard, I twist us until she's under me. I keep pumping, wrapping her legs around me. It takes her seconds before she explodes. What she doesn't know is I have no intention of coming with her. I'm back in control, back in myself. I give her a moment to recover before I move. Rocking, I pull her legs up, and drive into that pussy that is made to take me.

"Pain?" I rasp in her ear.

"No." She looks at me, touching my face before she leans up and kisses me. "More."

All the fucking gods. This woman is my equal.

That control I prided myself on not seconds ago shatters into a thousand pieces. I forget about wanting to hold back, forget about distancing myself so I can last longer. I'm erratic and wild and barreling towards an orgasm like no other. Punctuating each thrust with the only words that matter.

"You. Are. My. Undoing."

We both career off the sharp cliff that sends us into the beyond. Her scream echoes in the room, bouncing off the walls. Her pussy convulses in waves, pumping every last drop of cum out of me. Collapsing on top of her, my arms are no longer able to hold my weight. And she does the most shocking thing of all.

She holds me. She holds me and whispers in my ear.

"You're mine as well."

Chapter 19

The Scribe

Mid-morning sun filters through the slats of the large wooden shutters, which keeps the brightness at bay but does little to reduce the heat. Taking a wet cloth from a porcelain bowl, I run it over my brow and behind my head, cooling where I can. I found a treasure trove of information in a stack of scrolls earlier and am happily copying the words onto scrolls I plan to take with me back to the library once I leave Apollonion.

I pause, mid-step at that thought. I've gotten the very thing I wanted, needed even. I have both my men. And in a few short weeks, Artemis will send a message saying she was ready to collect me. A deep ache forms just behind my heart at leaving here. Leaving them. Shaking my head, I scold myself into being practical. I knew this was temporary, that coming here always had an end to it. I just never expected to find a part of myself that I didn't know was missing. I allowed Athena to hide me, seeking comfort in the shadows, but Apollonion brought me into the sunlight. Into the sun and into a world I want to keep.

The last few nights I've done very little in the way of research. I've spent my evenings at the high table and my nights being worshipped by my men. The nymphs were right, Apollo is very nimble. His eagerness to ensure I have "one more" orgasm, coupled with his boyish charm touches tender places in my heart, making it bloom. But Cinthus. What that man can do with words and fortitude should be scientifically studied.

Lost in a wave of wistful dreaming, I don't hear them enter.

"Oh!" I exclaim when they both appear from behind a tall shelf. The smile that rounds my cheeks is instant at the very sight of them.

"Gentleman." I try to play off my excitement as coyness, but it fails miserably when I lift my lips to kiss Apollo and then Cin in greeting. I just saw them not hours before. Had engaged in rather enjoyable intercourse with both. And yet, I missed them until they came into view. They are dressed formally, and both make my heart skip a beat. Cin is dashing, dressed in the golden breastplate, leather armor, greaves on his shins, sandals, and a deep blue cape, fastened to one shoulder, slings across his chest and flows down the other side. His beard is tidied, his hair styled, accenting the rugged planes of his handsome face. Apollo, however, looks every bit the regal god he is. Golden armor, greaves, sandals, anywhere there could be gold, there was. His white cape flows off one shoulder, pinned with his insignia. His formal attire is quickly becoming my favorite of the styles he wears, but it is playful mischief that lights his eyes and has me melting in the warming day.

My men.

Equal parts beautiful and masculine. A silly woman such as myself could easily fall for their charms if she isn't careful. A silly woman such as myself is already doing just that.

"What are you two about?" I begin rolling a scroll. "You seem to be up to no good."

Apollo chuckles. "We came to rescue you from a day of toiling away in the archives."

Grabbing another, I roll it as well. "I enjoy the archives; I don't need rescuing."

"Then maybe we are here to steal you," Cin offers.

I feign a sigh of disappointment. "If you must steal me away, what have you in mind?"

"An activity for all of us to engage in." Cinthus grabs a scroll and begins rolling it.

"I believe all of us have already engaged in an activity, rather vigorously if I recall."

The smug look they both shoot me is priceless.

"Although, now I have data to compare and contrast. I'm certain I can quantify a sure winner," I say to the scroll in my hand. "If you'd like, I can get the—"

"You insolent little daemon of a woman!" Apollo exclaims, picking me up and setting me down atop the table. I try to wiggle free, but he tickles my sides, and I am lost to giggles. "Continue to threaten pitting one against the other, and I shall be forced to outperform His Highness."

Cinthus scoffs, undeterred. "We know who would come out the winner, My God. I happen to be the one with the bigger endowment."

"Asshole." Apollo playfully shoves him.

"Where am I to be stolen?" I laugh and hop back down with the god's help. Placing my hands on my hips, I turn to look at the mess I've created. I need to straighten before they take me and keep me occupied for hours.

"You said you wanted to see the village and agora."

I whip around to a grinning Apollo who seems overly pleased with himself.

"The market?"

They nod. Cin leans against the wooden table.

"With me?"

They nod again.

"But gods don't go outside palace walls."

Apollo tilts his head and scowls. "Gods don't what?"

"You don't go outside the walls. You don't mix with the commoners and immortal humans and creatures. You are revered. You're holy. You stay inside the walls where it is safe."

Cinthus is shaking his head, while Apollo frowns.

"You and your rules, Hypatia," the god says. "Such arbitrary nonsense. Athena's palace sounds as if it's a land of no spontaneity, no comradery." He touches my shoulder. "Take a chance. Be bold."

Moments later I'm in my chambers and there is a rather robust debate about whether to leave my hair in the twisted bun at my nape or have it down. I ultimately win, when I refuse to entertain any thought of wearing my hair down in this heat. They both insist I wear the crown Apollo crafted for me. That battle I lose. I pick out my nicest dress made of soft, lightweight linen. I fasten the shoulders with pins the god gave me and drape the fabric so it will flow and not touch my skin. I decide against any shawl or secondary fabric for keeping cool, that is until we are heading down the steps of a side entrance and the sun peaks out around the stone walls. The linen of the peplos is so thin, that the silhouette of my body is highlighted by the rays. Both men stop in their tracks, eyes wide, pupils swallowing up deep brown and bright blue respectively.

I toss my head and give them a sly grin. "The agora, remember."

Apollo slides his hand along my waist. "By way of my chambers?"

"By way of the palace entrance, My God." I slip from his grasp and grab the prince's elbow. "Now, if my escorts are done gawking—"

"Never." Cin's deep timbre tickles my ear.

"Escort me to the marketplace."

The agora is teaming with life. Colorful banners wave half-heartedly in the soft wind that does nothing to cool the temperature. A mélange of canopies and fabrics crisscross overhead as peddlers and craftsmen sell their wares below. Stones pave a walkway through the village, as centaurs, pegasi, and humans atop various carts and wagons rule the streets. As we walk, humans and creatures, warriors, and councilmen, all greet Apollo and Cinthus and in turn, me. Many come out of their shops just to shake the god's hand. Apollo doesn't mind the attention but keeps his hand on my lower back guiding me as we wade through the crowd. Cinthus introduces me to several craftsmen and one in particular who designs all the stands and holders for his brushes. They all are delighted to show the prince any new pieces they made, and Cin buys several.

Walking with the god, I feel light and happy as the sun beats down on us.

"Has it met your expectations, sweet Hypatia?" he asks, his hands behind his back.

"It's just as I envisioned it to be."

Several children—two humans, one minotaur, and one faun—run around us shouting and kicking a ball between them. Apollo stops and guards one child, allowing the small faun to kick the ball. The child's smile warms my heart, and I slip my hand into his as we continue our walk.

Resting my head against his bicep, I ask him the burning question I've been dying to ask. "So, my thoughts?" I glance up quickly. "Can all gods read minds?"

Apollo slips his hand around my waist. "Yes. But Hypatia, please know, while we have the ability, it is considered uncouth to read the minds of those on Olympus."

"But you read mine."

He sighs and stops, turning so we are face-to-face. "Not at first. I can hear anytime someone calls my name. I ignore it mostly; it's a skill of the gods to block out the invading thoughts of others." His handsome face leans close. "Yours were hard to ignore. Particularly when you screamed it."

I flush despite the heat. Knowing he could hear my lascivious thoughts should embarrass me, but for some reason, it excites me. Before I can fully enjoy the moment, seriousness crosses Apollo's handsome features.

"Go ahead, sweet Hypatia, let your thoughts be as wild as you like. Be warned, I will do whatever occupies those thoughts, and I'll not control myself as I have so far." His heated gaze travels slowly down my body, and I wet my lips. "I look forward to the next time you're alone."

He rubs his nose along my temple, and I hold myself back from pulling him into an alleyway. I'm a respectable woman, I can't let a god take me against a stone wall, at least not in the middle of the day.

We return to walking, and I do my best to think about anything other than him.

After several hours, I find refuge under the shade of one of the canopies and wait for Apollo to finish speaking with a man who has an issue that needs the god's attention. As he speaks, women of the village come up and touch the god. Rubbing his wings, his arms, his chest. They touch him with boldness but instead of rebuffing their advances, Apollo preens. He smiles, flirts back, even teases. I, the sensible woman that I am, want to remain aloof of the whole thing. He is a beautiful god, one many admire, men and women. Being jealous of a god for acting like a god is ridiculous.

Very ridiculous. As ridiculous as my sudden need to march over there and scratch out the eyes of anyone who so much as breathes in his direction.

But I am sensible, of course.

I focus on sipping cool lemon water given to me by the shopkeeper when Cin appears at my side.

"Are you enjoying yourself, little scribe?" His gaze follows mine to the god and the pretty daughter of the man he is speaking to. He looks down at me with one lifted eyebrow, and I fake a grin. I am hot and sticky with sweat, and the heat is doing nothing for my mood. But my heart is elated. Seeing this side of them, as the men they are not the titles they hold, I want to hold this day close for fear it will shatter.

"Yes." I sigh and take a sip.

"He loves you, never worry about that."

I turn my head up and catch His Highness looking at me.

"What did you say?"

"Apollo loves you, Hypatia. He loves you the best he can being what he is. He doesn't love like humans do. When he falls, it is all-encompassing and overwhelming, all or nothing. He is reckless and selfish. He loves like a god, with his whole heart, never cautious, never questioning. But to love him back, means you have to love all of him."

I stare after the god that has lived in the secret parts of my mind for centuries. The one I had tried to forget.

"This . . . us . . . isn't something temporary for him. Or me."

I look back up into Cin's deep brown eyes and notice, for the first time, a flicker behind the usually stoic prince. A softness tugs at the corners of his eyes, and a shy smile creeps across his face.

"Cinthus." It's a word with so much meaning, that it can only be breathed.

"I bought something for you."

My tongue seems stuck to the roof of my mouth. "You did," I rasp, taking a large gulp of the lemon water.

"I didn't know whether you would appreciate such a small token, and seeing as you wear minimal jewelry, I wasn't sure you would like it. But I want you to have it all the same." He is talking fast, one hand on his sword, the other clutching a small object in his palm. When he opens his hand, he smiles, and I catch a glimpse of him as a boy. Ruffled dark hair, rounded cheeks, sheepish grin. I want to wrap my arms around him and reassure him that I will cherish whatever it is. That this isn't temporary for me either. That whatever this is we are doing, whatever these feelings, I feel them too. I can't help the little gasp that comes when he shows me what he bought.

"It's beautiful, Cinthus," I say in awe, picking up the delicate golden chain. On the end is a beautiful pendant, an arrow pointing down through a half-sun, with sapphires placed just so.

"It's the stones of Delphi," he says as I examined the setting. "The sun is for Apollo, the arrow, for me, for my kingdom. It's the symbol of my homeland. I wanted you to have something that will remind you of us."

I run my fingers over the ornate design. "You had this made?" I ask.

He nods once. "Shortly after the summer solstice celebration." He smiles again, his bearded cheeks rounding. "Do you like it?"

"Very much." I touch the intricately made arrow. "So very much. Will you put it on me?"

Turning, he clasps the necklace, his fingers lingering on my neck. Leaning down, he kisses my shoulder and wraps two strong arms around my waist. My mind catches up with what he said. He had this made after the solstice celebration. Before e slipped into my bath, before

"I love it, Cin." I choke out, not wanting to spill the tears that rim my eyes at his thoughtfulness. A shadow falls across us.

"I see you finally gave it to her," Apollo says, clapping Cin on the shoulder.

"You knew?"

He leans down and kisses my forehead. "Of course. I was the one who thought of the sapphires. They'll protect you, Hypatia, when we can't."

I clasp the pedant, running it through the chain. "You enchanted them?"

Apollo nods and looks at His Highness with a satisfied grin. "Mmm. I protect what's mine, Hypatia, and if that means using magic, then so be it. As long as you wear it, I can always be summoned. Home? Shall we?"

I kiss him and turn in Cin's arm, pulling him down for a kiss of his own. We walk back to the palace, me between the men who have equal parts of my heart. That evening, we take our meal in Cin's chambers. He paints and Apollo teaches me to play the lyre. To which Cin complains that it sounds like I am torturing a small animal. We laugh and eat and love. And when Cinthus takes me, I keep my eyes on him, telling him without words, that I, too, love them.

Chapter 20

The Prince

I wipe the sweat running down my face. The sun is already blazing, and it is barely two hours since the morning meal. Sheathing my sword, I clasp the wrist of the warrior I'd been sparring with. I hadn't been out on the field in days, preferring to spend my mornings lazily in bed with her and him. Last night, Hypatia chose to return to her chambers alone, wanting time to do calculations for preparations for the next few nights. It felt odd to be abed without her, the missing piece I didn't know was missing until she filled it. I make plans to visit her in the archives later this morning, maybe bring her the afternoon meal, and have her tell me in great detail all about her calculations. Nodding greetings to several warriors, I tidy my armor and begin my way back to the palace. The training fields are busy, the clanging of swords and armor, the grunts of men in action. I always find it soothing to be amongst the men, preferring to sleep in the warrior barracks versus my bed in the place of my birth—something my asshole of a father hated and reprimanded me for. A prince was a commodity to him, not a son.

I gain the rise of a small hill, upon which, the warriors set up rows of targets. Some are for the archers, some for spears, all hay-filled and badly dressed forms made to resemble opponents. Having come to the crest, I notice one archer at the end has a small gathering of women surrounding him. A smug knowing smile makes its way across my lips at the man who could capture the attention of the nymphs this early in the morning. Their feminine voices carry further than the deeper timbre of the men around them. I am ready to turn when one such laugh catches my attention, stopping me in my tracks.

My Hypatia.

She stands next to the warrior, holding a bow as he demonstrates a stance, miming his own weapon at the distant target. Her laugh floats over the others as he makes some remark and moves so she may take the spot. Raising the bow, she adjusts her body, twisting one way and then another, and shoots the arrow. It sails precisely two feet in front of her and weakly slides into the grass. She laughs again at her terrible aim, the nymphs joining for a round of teasing. Seeing her interacting with others gives me a little thrill. There is an ease at which she enjoys those around her, a softness. Aiming once more, the warrior comes along behind her, placing his hands on her hips. Touching her, twisting her, then he steps closer than he needs, his arms encircling her as he grips the bow with her. His face is beside hers. Way too fucking close.

Asshole!

Some of these men have been warriors for far too long; they've forgotten their manners. I know what they are capable of. I've seen far too much in my life, the cruelty of men who take without permission. His hands roam all over her body, the body that belongs to Apollo and me. I march over, not out of jealousy; no, I'm not jealous. Hypatia is free to learn any weapon she wants. No, that warrior is too handsy with my little scribe. She can learn the bow with my help, not some young warrior who only sees her as a means to an end. It is my duty to protect her.

"You know, these would go further if they were made of composite metal versus wood," I hear her say as I approach. "I could get you some prototypes if you'd like."

The warrior thinks for a second. "Is that something you would use for only weapons? I have a warrior that needs—"

"Remove your hands from my scribe!" I bark, my glare reserved for the warrior who grasped either side of her waist. "Or I'll do it for you."

My hand is at my sword as I come close, and the warrior has the good sense to back up three steps. Slowly she turns, and her expression could have cut me in two. I didn't know she could make those gray eyes flame. If she wasn't human, I am certain I would have been blasted with a magic of the umbramortis variety—deadly magic that would kill me on the spot. I don't understand why she is angry; she deserves respect.

"Come, Hypatia, you are needed inside," I order. Not a single nymph or man moves as she stares me down.

"I assure you," she says coldly, "I am not needed anywhere, Your Royal Highness."

The way she addresses my title has me wondering briefly if she isn't magical. I have never heard it said as a curse.

"Little scribe," I warn.

"I have a name, and you shall address me by it, Your Highness," she snaps.

The battle lines are clearly drawn, by her mostly. She is mine to protect, and I'll be damned if I'll let a warrior manhandle her.

"Hypatia," I try again, but she marches forward bow in hand, and points the end at me, looking deadly, "I said come."

"I am not your possession, Cinthus," she hisses. "Either talk to me in a civilized manner or return to your god."

The hillside grows so still that not even the wind dares to blow. All eyes are upon us when she thumps the edge of the bow against my armor. For the whole of my life, men have done as I said. Even here, on Olympus, being Apollo's right hand and lover, has awarded me respect worthy of my title.

While there might be grumblings, none outright ignore a command if I give it.

Hypatia, however . . .

"You are causing a scene, little scribe," I say behind clenched teeth, warning her of her unfavorable behavior. Instead of surrendering to my warning, she steps closer.

"What is it you want exactly, Your Highness? Seems I recall you had duties needing your attention this morning. I was not one of the duties."

Seconds tick by as we stare at each other, neither bending.

She swings back around and marches to her previous spot, raising the bow, and pursing her lips together. "Now, Captain Lucci, show me again how to manipulate this weapon. I understand the physics in theory, but the application is my downfall."

The warrior in question stands at attention, no doubt wanting to avoid getting in the crosshairs of the battle of wits before him.

"Capitan Lucci," she calls.

He stares at me, unsure. Swallowing, he takes a step.

"Don't," I growl. Hypatia turns around again. "You are coming with me, Hypatia."

"If you want me, Your Highness, you'll have to remove me bodily."

"If you wish."

"Am I not allowed to learn a new skill?" She raises a perfectly shaped eyebrow.

I cross my arms, eyeing the good captain. "Of course. Without another man's hands on you."

"To learn the weapon well, Captain Lucci needs to manipulate my body so that I may shoot correctly. If you find my behavior so grossly inappropriate, you may have a seat in the grass over there"—she flicks her chin to a spot yards away—"and observe. Unless you are willing the fling me over your shoulder, and carry me to the palace, I'll continue my lesson, if you please, sir."

"It isn't your behavior I object to," I say, continuing to glare at the captain.

She lets out the longest, most exasperated sigh I have ever heard. "Observe then, Your Highness."

I have never been spoken to in that matter. Had she been Apollo, I would have him in his chambers bent over something, accepting whatever punishment I thought he deserved. But Hypatia? I knew she would be a challenge to tame, but I never expected that under that soft demeanor, she is a fireball. A woman who can stand on her own. Fierce and foreboding. Pride strikes through me at her resistance to obey, even though it pisses me off. I like a challenge, and she is giving me one hell of one at the moment. I don't know how to make her submit without looking like a complete barbarian in front of Apollo's men. The idea of throwing her over my shoulder has promise, but her defiance has an interesting effect. It sends blood coursing through my veins, straight to my dick, now rock solid. If I get my hands on her now, I'll fuck her so hard she'll come in seconds, and she certainly isn't deserving of that after this outburst. Reluctantly, I decide what is best is to let her think she's won. I'll make her pay this evening. I make my way to the spot she pointed at and flop into the grass.

Raising the bow, Hypatia lifts her chin as well, smugly. "Now, Captain, teach me."

Captain Lucci returns to his task, saddling up next to her. I watch, shredding blades of grass in my fisted hands, as she looks me squarely in the eyes, and raises her elbow, forcing the captain to touch her. His hands are everywhere, hips, shoulders, waist, elbows, fingers. With each tiny adjustment, we lock stares. She makes sure I witness every single one.

Chapter 21

The Scribe

As I walk the corridor between meeting chambers on the west side of the palace, the sun stretches its long golden fingers along the marble floor. I've always liked this time of day—the golden hour—when the sinking sun sends the world into a fantasy land. Taking a breath of whatever magic is being created by the late afternoon radiance, I slow my steps. Apollo won't be out of his meeting for another hour or so, and Cinthus hasn't come to visit all day. After this morning, I should continue on my way, cut through the lemon gardens, and back to my chambers. I had never seen him possessive before outside of the bedroom. His behavior confuses me. Does he assume my lesson would make me want to learn weaponry? Or does he suddenly not trust me? It isn't as if he and I are monogamous, certainly, but does being involved with them mean I am to keep my distance from any man? If that is so, when I return to Artemis, I will chalk this summer up as a fleeting occurrence and move on.

I had only asked the good captain because the nymphs struck up the conversation first. I hadn't sought him out. If that is how Cin acts now that we are, whatever this is, I want no part in it. I am not about to be ordered back to the palace as if I am a concubine. My feet stall on the white marble.

Is that what he sees in me?

Shaking my head, I dismiss that thought rather quickly. The prince gave me a necklace—had it specially made. He is constantly showing me with action how much he cares about me. I am not just a fuck to him.

This isn't temporary.

Cinthus' words from the marketplace come back to mind. I'm not temporary to either of my men. So why the hell did he act like a possessive jackass?

I do feel a little guilty making him watch my impromptu lesson with Captain Maximus Lucci. Forcing him to sit as I deliberately moved my body so that the captain had to correct me. I shouldn't have enjoyed his increasing annoyance as much as I did. My eyes locked on his like magnets, making sure he caught every bit of my defiance. When I left the hill, my body tingled from the intensity of his gaze.

Heavy footsteps pound against the smooth floor. I know those footsteps well. His Royal Highness is coming towards me with two council members, no doubt from a meeting. He slows the moment he sees me and a flash of sheepish boyish charm crosses his face. His handsome face. The face that is frequently between my legs as of late. *Zeus on the throne*, so help me, I flush at the sight of him.

Damn the man.

"Hypatia," he says in greeting. Softly. Gruffly.

"Your Highness. Gentlemen." I incline my head, and the councilmen eye me as they pass, leaving us alone in the hallway.

He places his hands behind his back and tosses his chin. "Care for a walk?"

"I suppose." If he is willing to make peace about this morning, then so am I. We trail slowly along the path I just traversed, silent, both waiting for the other to cross the narrow divide.

"I've thought about this morning." He cuts through the silence with a gentle tone. "I understand you may not know how things are done. For that, I'm willing to forgive—"

"Excuse me?" I pull up short. "You believe I'm in the wrong?"

His eyebrows crease as he studies me. "Yes. When I give a command, I expect—"

"Oh! Do you?" I throw my hands in the air and march back down the corridor, away from the arrogant damn prince. *Commands? I refused to be commanded.*

"Hypatia," he calls, but I continue. "Hypatia."

Stopping suddenly, I whip around, and he almost crashes into me. "I am not some servant you can order around, Your Highness."

"Of course you aren't, but—"

"You stormed up the side of that hill as if you were storming the citadel at Troy, Cinthus. Shouting at me. Ordering me inside as if I was beneath you. I was taking a lesson in something I know nothing about. It was harmless."

"Yes, but his hands—"

"For the last damn time, I needed correcting to be able to shoot an arrow. I was learning to use a weapon."

"Hypatia, I—"

"And furthermore—"

"Would you let a man finish a damn sentence!" He pulls a hand down his face and scowls. "He had his hands on you, Hypatia."

"Correcting me," I say slowly, enunciating each syllable.

Cin turns away, marching to one side of the corridor and back. His hands flex into fists and relax.

"Fine. Correcting you. But you—you made me sit there and watch. Watch as some fucking *captain* manhandled you. Your hips. Your shoulders. Fuck, he gave instructions in your ear. His damn mouth was so damn—and what's worse, you enjoyed it. You enjoyed forcing me to witness that little display. You made sure your eyes were on me, not the target, Hypatia. Made sure I caught everything." His nostrils flare and his eyes blaze.

It suddenly dawns on me what he is trying to say. The man was jealous. Jealous. Of *me*. Not angry because I was learning a skill. Not annoyed because I had a warrior teach me. None of what I initially thought. He was jealous someone else could take an interest in me, and it would turn my head. As if anyone else could ever make me feel as I do when I'm with him. With Apollo. With them. It should have fueled my anger, I should be enraged, but I'm not.

I enjoyed making him watch. Making him sit idly by as I teased him with a warrior I cared little for. A better woman would feel guilty, she would apologize, but I am not a better woman. I had made a man like Cinthus—handsome in ways that are otherworldly, intelligent, stoic—jealous. The idea invigorates me and for reasons I don't fully understand, makes me want to do it again. To bring him to heel. To make him desperate for me. To tame me as he had Apollo.

"What are you smirking at?" he snaps, stepping closer.

"Nothing," I say, trying to hide my elation at discovering my newfound power. Stepping closer, I look up through my lashes, trying to seduce him.

Creases deepen along his forehead. "What are you doing?"

I fail.

Sighing deeply, I purse my lips and cross my arms. "I'm going back to my chambers. Apollo isn't finished and *that* is who I came looking for. Not you." I add the last part to wound him.

"Is that so?"

"Yes!"

I try to slip past, but I fail at that too. He grabs my arm, refusing my escape. He runs a hand through his dark hair and lets out a long sigh then pulls me into his arms. My hair ruffles as he buries his nose at my crown. His big arms squeeze, and I melt. I want to tease him further, but I can't, lost in the feel of him around me.

"So, you didn't like my lesson?" I say into his chest, resting my cheek against the armor. I look up, but his trimmed chin blocks most of my view of that lovely face. "You're a brute."

"So I'm told. I didn't like someone else's hands on you. You're mine, little scribe."

I breathe him in; the scent of his soap fills my nostrils along with that spice I never can put my finger on, lingering in the background. Lifting on my tiptoes, I nuzzle my nose into his neck.

"I love the way you smell," I confess to his skin. My lips find their target, and I leave tiny little appreciations of his bathing practices against his wonderfully sensitive neck. A noise, softer than a growl but more robust than a groan, rumbles through the prince's chest, rattling me in the process.

"Little scribe, I'm warning you. If you want to continue, we should find somewhere a little more secluded than the hall."

"Continue what, Prince Cinthus?" I tease, raking my teeth across his jaw. My back finds the wall, and he cages me in, lowering himself several inches so we are at eye level.

"You know damn well what."

A half-giggle bubbles up, and he lifts both eyebrows in response. I shrug innocently. "I was just smelling your soap."

The sexy grin that slides across his lips tells me he isn't buying my claim. I peck a kiss on his lips.

"You're going to be the death of me, aren't you? I'll let you get away with murder as long as you continue kissing me."

"Then find me a sword, Your Highness. I feel quite bloodthirsty."

I'm not sure who kisses first, but the wall behind me became a rather annoying hindrance as I grab the prince and pull him closer.

The Prince

She had me so distracted that most of the afternoon I spent tense and on edge. I snapped at anyone unlucky enough to come within any distance of me. Not that I was normally welcoming, but Hypatia was messing with my head. But now the damn woman is kissing me, and all I can think about is her misty eyes, pinning me to the ground, proud that she had the upper hand. My lips trace the line of her neck, and she whimpers, pulling me closer. I push against the wall, all my strength goes into not taking her in my arms, not giving her what she wants.

"Cin." Her breath feathers against my lips. When her lust-filled gaze meets mine, her eyebrows meet, questioning. "Take me to your chambers."

"You think you can just kiss me and that makes up for your behavior this morning? You kept moving on purpose, little scribe."

Those gray eyes widen as she makes the connection. I knew exactly the game she was trying to play, and she's in over her head. Grabbing her hand, I tug her back down the corridor.

"Where are we going?"

Gone is her earlier aplomb. My plan to make her submit this evening is quickly shredding in favor of now. Opening a door, I usher her inside. Her wide eyes take in the room and come round to meet mine. It's sparse, as this room is mainly used for overflow. One long table sits in the middle. A row of stained-glass windows, depicting the cycle of the sun from dawn to dusk, filters light in rainbows. She's chewing on that bottom lip, and I spark alive. But she doesn't retreat, instead she straightens her spine, squaring off with me.

Fuck all the gods, this woman is my weakness.

"You kept your eyes on me, Hypatia. Each little adjustment, you defiantly moved so the captain would have to touch you again, manipulate you. You knew what you were doing." I *tsk*. "And you thought I wouldn't figure it out?"

"You are jealous, Cin," she accuses.

Nodding, I pull her by the belt she wears that cinches the billowy fabric of her dress. It's off in two flicks of my wrist. She doesn't flinch.

Good.

"I am jealous. I'm jealous of the man who came before me. I'm jealous of Apollo when he's inside you. I'm jealous of anyone who touches you. Looks at you. Yes, I'm jealous. Because you're mine."

Lifting her chin so our eyes meet, she purrs, "Did you not enjoy being made to watch? I rather thought you did, what with the intensity of your stare."

"Fucking temptress."

I can't help the growl that breaks free when my lips meet hers. It isn't the gentle, leading kisses of before. I possess her mouth, claiming it, reminding her who she belongs to. She kisses me back with just as much need and intensity. I back her up, and her ass hits the table with a bump. She catches my lower lip between her teeth and bites down, her need turning animalistic, hungry. Tearing my mouth away, I leave her panting.

"You make me so fucking crazy, Hypatia. I want to punish you for forcing me watch your little stunt on the hillside." Grabbing my chin, my untamed scribe has the audacity to smirk.

"Prove it."

Need screams through my veins, tearing at my control that is seconds from snapping. My next words come out dark and low.

"Turn around," I command. "Hands on the table."

Uncertainty flickers, but then it's gone. She turns, hands in front. I place mine at her shoulders, gently pushing until she's bent before me, hands outstretched. I slide one hand into her hair, tugging as I run the other over that fine ass. Flexing her hips, she tries to rub against me.

"None of that," I say, regaining my control. "You haven't earned any rewards yet. Here's what's going to happen. You're going to take whatever I deem appropriate. You're going to do as I say. You're going to use your words, and you're going to tell me if it's too much. Do you understand?"

She nods, and I smack that ass of hers. A low moan, the same one from the bathhouse, rolls out of her. I lean down, my body covering hers; her breaths come in slow, steady puffs.

"Words."

"I understand."

"That's my girl."

Raising my hand, I smack again and a guttural moan from her sends electricity straight to my cock.

"This is what you needed all along, isn't it? You want me possessive and jealous."

"Yes, Cin."

"Fuck! Of course it was. Gods, you've had me in a cock hold since this morning." Bending down, my mouth brushes her ear. "Do you see that door?"

She looks up. "Yes."

Fuck. Answering might be the sexiest fucking thing I make her do. "Right behind it is the meeting Apollo is in. The room is filled with men from all over the palace trying to pay attention. We both know how loud you can get. If you moan, if you cry out, they'll hear you. Keep quiet little scribe, or the entirety of that room will know how you enjoy my company."

"Brute." She tries to whisper but it comes out breathless, and it takes every ounce of control not to lift the hem and fuck her now.

"I suggest you keep your pretty mouth closed." I release her hair and drag both hands down her body. Skimming her hips, I fist handfuls of fabric, until she is exposed to my gaze. She flexes her hips again, wiggling, rubbing her thighs together. My palm meets her flesh, and her skin warms. I watch her fingers claw the wood, but she doesn't make a sound save the sharp intake of breath. Sliding over her rounded ass cheek, now pink, I admire my handywork. No marks like last time, just coloring. Perfect. I trail a path up the back of her thigh, and she parts her legs ever so slightly, wanting me.

"You think that's all you'll get, Hypatia? That's the only punishment you deserve?" My words are gravelly, and I'm dangerously close to losing control. "You had me so distracted. I had to fist my cock several times to keep myself from seeking you out. All I could think about was this." I smack her again on the other cheek. This time, she moans but it's short-lived as she tries her best to remain quiet. "I wanted to fuck you on that damn field for making me watch. Hell, I wanted to fuck you in that damn hallway, the second I saw you. I've thought of little else."

My fingers brush along the outside of her hip, her thigh, then back up, skimming close to her core.

"Cin," she whines, and it's like music to my ears.

"Yes, little scribe," I tease. Once more, I caress her skin, coming close to where she wants me. She is begging for anything I can give, anything to ease the ache I've created. I dip a finger along her opening and find her slick and oh so ready.

Of course, my girl would enjoy this.

Her head comes off the table as I slowly fuck her with a finger. Adding the second has her spreading her legs, making room for me.

"Gods, you're soaked. Do you feel that, how swollen, how needy I've made you? You want me to fuck you, ease that ache."

"Yes"—she nods—"I want you, Cin."

"Not yet."

I tease, making the rhythm uneven until I begin to pump slow and steady, keeping her on the edge of the knife, not allowing her to fall. She's writhing, trying to get friction where she needs it, release of my torture, but I deny her. When I stop, she lets out a low whimper.

"Please, Cin," she begs, but I ignore it. Kicking her legs open wider, I squat down and run my nose over her thighs breathing in her scent like a damn fiend. She shifts back, and I can see how aroused she is, practically dripping.

"You want my mouth on you, don't you little scribe? You need my tongue to make you come. Tell me."

"Yes." It's barely a word.

"Tip your hips for me, I want to see your pretty pussy." Her obedience elicits a primal growl deep in my chest. "Such a fucking good girl."

I devour her like this—from behind, ass in the air. She is my obsession, my undoing, my everything. The sounds she makes start soft but grow louder the closer I bring her to orgasm. Abruptly stopping, I rise, and she growls in frustration.

"You taste divine, Hypatia, wild and unencumbered. Keep quiet or they'll hear my needy girl." Grabbing her, I force her to stand, then spin so she's facing me. Her fingers clutch my armor, steadying herself.

"Take me back to your chambers, Cinthus. Please."

Brushing a few strands of wild hair from her temple, I deny her request. "No, my beautiful Hypatia. We're going to stay right here, and you're going to learn the consequences of teasing me." I flick my chin to the table. "Get on the table, I'm not done."

"No." She lifts her head defiantly, and it's my turn to moan. "I demand to go back to your chambers, Cin."

"I demand you get on that table," I order, but she shakes her head.

"I'll not let them hear me."

I smile. "Oh, little scribe, they already know. You forget, Athenian warriors are made with abilities. They can smell your arousal, hear your hushed moans. A chamber full of warriors all acutely aware of how desperate you are for me." I run my nose down hers, and she licks her lips. "Why do you think I picked this room? I want them to know who you belong to, so next time they'll think twice about touching what is mine. Now, get on the table and open your legs for me."

The look on her face goes from panic to irritation to a spark of something else, something akin to revenge. Excitement pulses through me at that. I hope she tries.

Lifting her chin, she unfastens the pins at her shoulders, and those eyes, now the color of steel, meet mine. "You win, Cin. It seems to me this dress is cumbersome to navigate. Better to be bare, if I'm to be made a meal."

Fuck every single god in this fucking realm. My knees buckle at that statement, and I catch myself on the edge of the table.

The dress pools at her feet and she hops onto the table. Rising on her elbows, making eye contact with me, she slowly opens her legs, showing everything she has to give.

She's beautiful laid before me, mine for the taking.

Yanking her calves, I lift her legs over my shoulders and bury my face between those luscious thighs. At first, her cries are muffled behind a hand, as she desperately tries to keep quiet. Chuckling between laps, I delight in her desperate attempts to hide what I'm doing to her. Her hips move, and I realize if she keeps going, she'll fuck my mouth and come before I want her to. Placing my hand on her lower belly, I pause her movements.

"Be still, little scribe. I'm in charge of your release."

Opening her legs wider, I bring down a palm on her inner thigh, turning her flesh pink, before I kiss the hurt away. She lifts her hips, seeking release that I know isn't coming anytime soon. After several minutes of driving her to madness, Hypatia goes quiet.

She's giving her body over to me, trusting me to find her path to orgasm. I've seen Apollo do this during intense sessions, but it was years before he could get there. My girl, however, calms her breathing and surrenders easily. Truly a born submissive. She bucks against my mouth, and claws the table when my fingers enter her, but otherwise, no sound. It's remarkable. Freeing. I set to work again, this time, intent on allowing her to orgasm when the door bursts open and slams against the wall. It flings shut just as hard, rattling the room.

Looking over the rise at the junction of her hips, I find a pissed-off god glaring at the two of us. He's glowing a golden hue, filling the room with his radiance, something he does when he has been pushed past his limits with no reprieve. Reaching out, he grabs Hypatia's hands and tugs her taut between us.

"You," he snaps at her. "All that moaning and calling my name in your fucking head . . . I fucking came in that damn meeting in front of my court." He flicks his gaze to me. "What the hell, Cin!"

She raises her head and looks me square in the eye.

"You told me to be quiet, did you not, Your Royal Highness?"

A smug grin crosses Hypatia's face, and I realize too late that the revenge she invoked involved driving Apollo out of his damn mind while I drove her out of hers. The glowing god glances between the two of us, pride written across his features.

"It seems our girl has learned a new trick," he says before kissing her.

Chapter 22

The God

I've never really cared for the moon. The old gods placed the stars in the sky long before my existence, and I paid them little attention until Hypatia taught me to love the moon's luminescence with its silvery glow—to marvel at creation far above our heads. Her obsession became mine, which was why I am heading to her room.

The prince has been occupied for days, preparing his painting for the annual Solstice Court Feast. Hypatia has also been busy, creating something she called, "a tinkering I was intrigued by"—whatever that means. We have been going on as a threesome, tied together by invisible strings, for the last few weeks. After my Asteria's brilliant stunt in the overflow room that brought me to orgasm in front of my men, and Cin admiring the shit out of her cunningness, we have become inseparable.

Inseparable. Until we separate.

Artemis will soon call for her; time is running short. Once she finds out how important Hypatia has become to me, I hope she sees reason. Part of me is nervous Artemis will become furious and refuse to allow me to plead my case. Or worse, take Hypatia and hide her from me once again. As much as I love my sister, starting a relationship with her right hand does ensure I bring down her wrath. She isn't one for allowing the defiling of her nymphs to go unpunished, and Hypatia is far more important than one of her nymphs.

Wrath or not, Hypatia is mine. My Asteria. My goddess reincarnate. She has become everything to me, just as important as the prince, just as needed. Which is why I am seeking her out while Cinthus works. Coming to her door, I pause, breathing in the soft scent of lemons that seems to follow her everywhere she goes. I hesitate at her threshold, studying her door for several breaths. Opening it, I find her room dark.

Her fire is glowing, but the only light comes from the open balcony. The moon in its brilliance is putting on a display, and her curtains are tied back to allow as much of the show as possible. Instruments are scattered about: a telescope angled just so, her astrolabe, metal construction of the universe, and all its planets. Upon a wooden table lies a large object covered by muslin cloth, hidden from view. I shift my gaze from one side of the dark room to the other, trying to find my astronomer. When I see her, it brings a soft smile to my face.

Peeling back covers, I sink into her bed wanting to be next to her. She startles awake and for a brief second, fear lights in her eyes.

"Shh, it's me. Apollo."

Her hand rests on her chest. "My God! What are you doing here?"

Gathering her to me, I roll her onto her back, settling myself along her body, my head on her stomach, my chest resting between her thighs. I flap my wings as I settle, and she huffs until the plumage calms along with me.

"Go back to sleep," I whisper into the thin garment she's chosen for bed. I prefer what she's worn most nights in my chambers—nothing.

"What are you doing here?" she repeats. "I thought you were with His Royal Highness this evening."

Yawning, she makes no move to stifle it and instead, runs her delicate fingers through my hair, twisting the curls methodically. I snuggle in closer, melting. She is softness and curves whereas Cinthus is hardness and muscle. And both are my obsessions. My two sides. My comfort and my peace.

I take a deep breath, letting it out slowly, ruffling the fabric of her night dress.

"Where is Cinthus?" she whispers to the night.

"He's busy painting his masterpiece for Solstice Feast. He is all a tizzy, worried it isn't his best. The man is crazed. Everything he paints is his best work."

"Mmm," she says dreamily, and I nestle my head into her midsection, enjoying the massage of her fingers against my scalp. Lifting my head, I tip my chin at the muslin-covered object on the table.

"Is that your contribution?"

"Yes." She opens one eye and glares at me. "And if you lift the cover to peek, I'll have you flogged."

A deep chuckle rumbles out and over the thin gown. "Flogged. Such a serious punishment."

"It's a serious offense, My God." Closing her eye, she smirks in the dark and wiggles down so she can reach my back. Her fingers work over my shoulders, reaching between my shoulder blades where my wings attach. I arch into her and groan. I didn't know I enjoyed being touched there until her. She has taken to lazily drawing geometric shapes on our muscled backs after sex. It is soothing in a way I hadn't expected, tattooing us with her knowledge.

I reposition myself so she doesn't have to reach down so far. Tonight, the shapes intersect. The last several nights, I'd become good at guessing, but now I am stumped.

"Why aren't you waiting for Cin to come to bed?" she asks as her fingers climb my spine, dancing between my feathered appendages.

"When he gets like this, he will stay awake for days sometimes. In those instances, I seek solace from someone in the palace." I kiss between her breasts, and she sighs. "But now, I only need you, Asteria. I need your comfort wrapped around me like a woven blanket."

She smiles with her eyes closed. "You could sleep alone, My God."

"I don't sleep alone."

This causes her to giggle. "Why not? I enjoy it from time to time. I get this whole big bed to myself. Until some god comes round and interrupts my sleep." Her eyes open, catching mine, and I watch as she lazily grins, then shuts them again. Every time she smiles, I see stars as if they burst overhead.

"Firstly, these beds are made for multiple people. Its massive size holds both of us and if we were lucky, Cin as well. Secondly, I have never slept alone."

She opens her eyes again, and this time, she shifts to look at me. "Not one night?"

Shaking my head, I watch her. "No. Never. I wasn't alone in the womb. And when Hera chased our mother to the island, we hid in a cave. I slept with her and Artemis to ensure our safety. My mother protected us from the queen's fury, but with no fires to keep us warm, the only memory I have is cold. Hera was on a mission to kill us both before we had matured, and my mother refused to let that happen. Zeus refused to protect us, allowed his wife to chase my mother from one end of the earth to the other." I shuddered against the memories flooding in. Of being cold. Of icy hands and threadbare garments wrapped around us in that dank cave. Of the darkness. I hate the dark. Hated night, until her.

"Once we were mature, Artemis and I lived together for a short time, sleeping in the same room. I protected her from Olympians sent to violate her as punishment for our mother falling in love with The King. I was barely matured, barely able to pull the bow back, but I stayed awake many nights waiting to kill any man who tried."

Hypatia frowns sadly and brushes the hair from my forehead. Her quiet breaths bring me back from the fear that lies just beyond the dark edge of every shadow. And I fall, wanting her to be my landing place.

"Nightmares plagued me for centuries after, but I found if I had someone to share the dark, my nightmares were less frequent. I found company easily once I settled here in the Hyperion mountains. My bed was never without someone to fill it. Sometimes, several someones." I wiggle my eyebrows at her, and she twists her lips. "But then I fell in love with the prince, and he has been my bed partner for longer than I remember." I'm serious now, making my point by meeting her gaze. "I no longer want just anyone in my bed. You have captured more than my attention, sweet Hypatia. It is you, you and Cin. You're all I need."

"Me?"

"Yes, you," I say to her stomach, inching up her gown. I want her skin next to mine.

"What are you doing?" She looks down awkwardly, catching me with a handful of fabric.

"I want nothing between us, now get this garment out of my way." I hike up a portion of the gown over a hip and she lifts her ass while chiding me.

"I was perfectly happy in my sleeping gown, My God." Her voice is flat as she purses her lips in a scold. "Some of us prefer to sleep in gowns, not walk the halls in the nude."

"I don't know if you're aware, Asteria, but I'm quite handsome. Some would say a rather fine specimen. Nude is best for hall walking late of an evening."

She shoots me a look before playfully rolling her eyes as I laugh. "You are a ridiculous god."

Her gown is free, and I unceremoniously toss it. It floats silently to the marble and lands in a heap somewhere off the side of the bed. "I'm your ridiculous god, Asteria. I'm whatever you need me to be, so long as I can feel you beside me."

I settle back in my position, her warm skin next to mine, as it should be. She wraps her legs around me, her heels at my back. She hugs tight, like a python wrapping itself around its prey. I would gladly let her devour me if it would keep her here. I stroke the outside of one thigh, before hitching it up, so I can lay a gentle kiss to the inside of her knee. "I don't want to sleep without you, Hypatia. I don't want to be without you at all. Ever. I need you."

"My God," she whispers. "Artemis . . ."

"Is coming, I know. I plan to petition for you to stay. You can finish transferring the scrolls in the archives for the library. I'll convince Artemis. You have to stay here, Asteria. Stay with me. With Cin. We need you more than she does."

"Artemis will be coming, and Athena will call me back; we can't stop it. I need to return to the library, to my duties, to my life in Athena's court."

I kiss under her breast, trailing my hands along her sides, breathing in her sweetness. "I'm going to find a way to keep you."

Moving up her body, I kiss a trail to her mouth, before I claim her once again as mine. She breaks my kiss, holding my cheeks in her hands.

"If I stay, I have one request for you, My God." The seriousness in her voice gives me pause. "While I'm here, it's just you, me, and Cin. No others."

I lay a peck on her cheek. "In this bed? Done."

Shaking her head, she gives me a look. "No. I mean here in the palace. While I'm here it's just us. Cinthus said to love you is to love all of you, but I'll not share you with another woman. I might be inclined to claw at her eyes if any so much as looks in your direction."

I blink. *Did the woman I have been infatuated with for centuries—who I now have in my bed—just confess to loving me?* Rising, I look at her. Her serious expression squeezes my heart.

"Of course," I agree cautiously. "While you're in the palace, it'll be just you, me, and Cin. Just us. Always."

Her smile is achingly sweet, and my heart nearly stops. I didn't know it was possible for a god to be this dumbfounded, this *human*. While I have never said it aloud, I have loved Hypatia since I laid eyes on her. I'm desperate for her to feel the same, to love me back, to stay. I meant it, I am never letting her go—not willingly anyhow. I will fight Artemis if it comes down to it. Fight Athena. Hell, I'll fight fucking Zeus himself if he tries to make me give her up. I fought for the prince; I'll fight for my scribe.

Her fingers find my back once more and the drawing continues.

"Are you writing me a letter?" I tease, huskily.

She breathes slowly. "No. An impossible shape."

"You and shapes," I say, grazing my thumb over her nipple. Her breath hitches, and I delight in the sound. Her next words are strained as I lightly run my hands over one breast and then the other.

"In Euclidean geometry"—her breathy explanation is music to my ears. I nip at the underside of her breast, kissing her nipple—"there is a pyramid that should work in three-dimensional space, but it will only ever be a concept. One draws it using three different shapes. The center of each needs to be just so, intersect in the right manner, the right slope to form a pyramid." She arches her back; I take advantage and move her leg, trailing my fingers lower.

"My God." It's a needy plead.

"Continue, Asteria. Teach me about shapes." Skimming my fingers over her creamy inner thigh, I take my time teasing her.

"The only way to mathematically make it work is if the heart of the circle is tilted, then all three centers can align." She shifts her hips, wanting me to touch her. My fingers brush back up in an agonizing pattern. Swallowing a whimper, she continues. "When I taught this, I would often say the masculine heart of one shape had to rise to meet the feminine heart of another to achieve the height of the great pyramid. All three shapes work perfectly in tandem to create the impossible."

I stop my torture when she gently touches my chin.

"We are the impossible. An improbable equation that shouldn't work, shouldn't fit, but we do. All three of us fit." Her eyes glitter in the moon-light. "We fit as if we were made for one another—crafted by the old gods."

Leaning down, her lips find my forehead, my cheeks, and when they find my mouth, they sear right through me. Burning me to my core.

"Make love to me. Cherish me while I'm here."

And I do. Flipping over, I have her take me like this, put her in control. I watch in awe as she rises, gliding up and down my cock like the goddess she is.

The goddess that's mine.

Chapter 23

The God

The palace is decorated in full regalia. Banners of gold hang in straight lines from the ceiling, running the length of the white marble runner that leads to the dais. The throne room has been a hive of activity, with villagers lining up to offer gifts for the Solstice Feast, and warriors and palace guests alike gathering to celebrate. Hypatia stood beside me most of the day taking gifts offered generously and meeting villagers. That first night at the high table, I thought for sure she would faint, but over the last few weeks, her confidence has grown. Confidence in herself and her position here in my home, beside me, as she should be.

Her gentle presence is calming on a day that isn't all that enjoyable for me. While I don't shy away from a party, Solstice Feast isn't about me; it is for those outside the palace walls. One day a year, they come into my home and are fed, celebrated, dance, and enjoy their god. I don't mind shaking hands, meeting my people, or even any of the festivities, but it is exhausting. In the past, I have leaned heavily on Cinthus to help in the numerous tasks. Hypatia offered to greet the guests when Cin remarked that warriors from the mountains were coming, and he was needed out in the fields. But if I am honest with myself, having her participate as an extension of my crown feels like a puzzle piece fitting into place. As if she was always meant to.

Nodding at a man who brought vegetables for the palace to use, I happen to glance at Hypatia, who is accepting a large jar of honey. She compliments the woman who hands it to her and then kneels to a small girl with dark hair who hides behind her mother. Straightening, she catches my attention and smiles, and my damn heart does that thing where it feels as though it is in a vice. *Butterflies.* Fucking butterflies in my stomach as her eyes lock onto mine. Just as it was that night.

Other women would have worn their finest dresses and jewels for a day such as this, but Hypatia chose a simple, yet elegant, chiton that goes to her ankles. She wrapped a shawl around her torso and pulled it over the back of her neat bun, covering part of her chestnut hair. Even though Cin and I insisted, she refused to wear the crown I made her. Instead, she has a gold cuff on her upper arm and the necklace Cinthus gave her.

And she is a damn vision. A goddess divine wrapped in blue linen. My goddess. My Asteria.

Something between us has changed as of late, and I feel her pulling away. As much as I want to keep her with me, there is a gnawing fear that settled in the back of my throat, telling me she is saying goodbye. I can't lose her, not when I've only just found her, but if her words the other night are any indication, I am going to do just that. I don't know how to make her see she is important to me too. That I care about her, love her just as much as Cin. I've never had to try to capture attention, but she's different and I'm failing. I don't know how to woo her and because of that, I might lose the only other person who holds a piece of my heart.

Cherish me while I'm here.

One of the guards moves to stop the flow of villagers and give me some reprieve. Acknowledging the break with a sharp nod, I shake my shoulders, ruffling my wings.

"I've never seen anything like this," she says in awe to the crowd. Her gray eyes are alive and dancing as she looks at me.

Butterflies. The woman sets loose thousands with just words.

197

"Does Athena not participate in the Solstice Feast?"

"Oh, she does"—she stretches her arms above her head and rolls her neck—"but the villagers come to a courtyard and are given items to take with them. Ambassadors or Councilmen are there, but rarely Athena herself."

"So, she feasts with the warriors?" I stretch my wings to their full extension, covering most of the dais in a shadow of feathers. They lie back in a comfortable position, and I ready for the next round.

Hypatia half shrugs. "No, not really. She eats with her Epsilon warriors and a few council members, some honored humans, but she keeps those feasts private. The large one is held in the grand hall."

"And you?"

I know the answer before she says it.

"I stay with the scribes. Sometimes I eat with them, but mostly, I eat alone in the library or archives. It's quiet in there and I enjoy my own company. There is a beautiful clay jar salvaged by one of the warriors, and I take my meals where I can admire it."

She says these things with such certainty as if her lonely existence in Athena's court is normal. Again, I feel the tug, the one that makes me want to take a holiday away from palaces and courts and show her the Olympus I know. The one with mountains and streams, oceans, and forests. I want to view the world through her eyes. I want to wring Athena's neck for hiding away this precious jewel in the name of status. My heart breaks thinking of my Hypatia, bold and alluring, with her intelligent eyes and stubborn pride, being forced to spend an eternity in such isolation. And, not for the first time, I wonder if I could bring a portion of the library here, so she may work, and I won't have to be without her.

Movement at the end of the room catches my attention and before I can respond, he's flying towards me with a giant smile plastered across his youthful face.

"Hermes!" I meet him at the bottom of the stairs leading to my throne and clutch his wrist in greeting. "I didn't think you were coming this year."

He's a happy surprise, one I didn't know I needed until I saw him. He tosses his light brown hair and lands on the marble, his sandals fluttering at his feet.

"I got held up but I'm here now. I wouldn't miss your feast, brother." His dark eyes climb the three steps to the dais where Hypatia stands with her hands clasped in front. They snap to mine and back to her, glinting in the afternoon sun that streams through the windows. "Hypatia of Alexandria."

She inclines her head, fist to her heart in salute as she bows, and I follow him.

"Hermes. I didn't know you were attending tonight's feast." Smiling, she greets him as he gains the last step.

"You two are acquainted?"

"Very much so. Hermes helps me give messages to the warriors from Athena."

"Ahh, yes, but I have been known to deliver secret messages as well." He winks and Hypatia blushes.

"Those weren't secret."

"They weren't from Athena," Hermes teases.

They both laugh, and I suddenly feel like a third wheel. He greets her warmly with a kiss on her cheek, and I grit my teeth. Of course, they would know each other, that makes sense. Hypatia works for the library, and she would need to deliver messages to warriors on behalf of Athena. Sure. Perfect logical sense.

Why the fuck is he standing so damn close?

"I'm so happy to see you, Hermes," she says warmly, and it needles me. She still calls me by my formal address, even in private, but she says his name? How long had he known her before she dropped the formality? I wonder if I will ever have the closeness she seems to have easily with others. I'm desperate for her to see me for who I am. Not the god. The man. I might have her in my bed, but she still puts up walls, and I'm locked out pressing my hand against the stone, begging to be let in.

I move to stand next to her and slide my hand to the small of her back.

"I'm delighted you'll be staying; I've missed our conversations." She glances at me through her eyelashes and steps closer. I have to will my hand to stay where it is and not pull her against me. Hermes responds, but the only thing I can focus on is her nearness, the faint smell of lemons, and the way the fabric of her dress feels against my palm. This is utter madness, I'm sure of it.

A lull in their conversation allows me to cut in.

"It's getting late in the day, sweet Hypatia. Do you need to get ready for this evening?"

Her eyes light with excitement. "Yes! And may I have two warriors to bring my gift to the hall?"

"Of course, anything you want, you only need to ask." I tap her nose, and Hermes gives me a sideways glance.

"You eat in the hall?" He frowns for a second. "I don't believe I've ever seen you in a dining hall."

She turns and looks up at me, her cheeks glowing softly with a rosy hue. "I do here."

Bowing her head, she excuses herself, and Athena's warrior and my guard follow her out. Hermes takes a nanosecond before he turns to face me fully, with raised eyebrows and a smug look.

"Four hundred and eighty-three."

"Excuse me?"

"Four hundred and eighty-three," he says slowly, shaking his head. "Four hundred and eighty-three and only one of those inquiries went to Athena."

I open my mouth several times, but I only have an unintelligible groan as an answer. "It wasn't that many."

"It was exactly that many. I had to deliver every single one." His tone turns mocking. "Oh, where is the woman with the dark hair? Artemis won't tell me. Here, Hermes, I have another stack of messages begging for information. I can't send them by raven feather because that would be too damn easy. Fly over the entire empire and ask around for a girl I saw once at an evening meal. I'm obsessed."

"Piss off."

"Two centuries and four hundred and eighty—"

"Fine. Yes. It's her. Happy?" Sighing, I look to the side door she disappeared into, already missing her. Her company is a lot more enjoyable than Hermes is at the moment.

"Ares threw a damn spear at me, Apollo. Eros threatened to join the hunt if I didn't stop flitting around trying to find this damn woman. The gods were more than annoyed at my inquires. And she was under Athena's roof the whole time. Fucking Artemis, of course she was there."

"Artemis refused to tell me. What was I to do?"

He crosses his arms and the wings on his shoes flutter. "How is she here?"

Taking a deep breath, I make a face before I answer. "Athena sent her. She's here for research."

"Research?" He eyes me. "For the library, I presume? And you've clearly fu—"

"Yes."

"And Artemis?"

"Doesn't know."

Shaking his head, Hermes turns to the line of villagers as I point my chin at one of the guards to continue the processional.

"You are fucked, brother."

"I know."

"Artemis may not be able to kill you, but she will damn sure try."

"I know that too."

"Royally fucked."

I turn and accept a beautiful tapestry from a woman.

"I know," I say out the side of my mouth.

"Hypatia of fucking Alexandria. Royally fucked."

Chapter 24

The Scribe

The dancers spin in tight circles in the middle of the ballroom. Apollo opened a second and third room in the dining hall to accommodate everyone. Villagers, warriors, place guards, nymphs, all mingling. Two ensembles are placed in two of the rooms, giving dancers and the uncoordinated music for their evening. I am staunchly in the latter and have given up on dancing after several mishaps with Cinthus. A prick in my chest comes at the thought of never having danced with Apollo while I am here. The last few days, he has been distant. One night, he hadn't come to bed until well after Cin and me. I reached for him; he pulled me close for a moment and then turned away. I am beginning to think I did something to upset him, but our morning walks remain the same. Delightful, sweet. His kisses are still passionate, but we haven't been together intimately since he slept with me in my chambers. I catch him looking at me with longing as if he is trying to relay some message telepathically.

I've never wished to be magical more than now so I can read his thoughts.

Even during this morning's activities, he was more stoic, more reserved. The Solstice Feast is the last ceremony before the closing ceremonies. After that, Artemis will come, and I will leave my men. Apollo keeps telling me he is going to keep me, but I don't see how that is possible. His current behavior leaves me utterly confused. I want a future with them, but does he want the same thing? Is his affection waning like the late summer sun?

Grabbing wine from a table, I twirl the goblet. The crowd in the hall gives me some anonymity, and with Apollo and Cinthus busy with their duties, I have time to myself to think. Hermes catches my eye, and I lift my glass to him. He responds with his own lifted glass and goes back to his conversation.

Do I want to stay? In the last few weeks, I haven't done as much research as I would have liked, trading stars in the sky for the ones that burst behind my eyes when pleasure overtakes me. But so close to the end, I need to return to the task.

Stay or go?

My heavy heart won't let me think of much else. My work with the library is important, respected. I have a life in Athena's court. I have a job. Rebuilding the Library of Alexandria is my project, one I am solely responsible for. I can't be here and keep the library running at the same time. Can I give up my passion for these two men? If I do stay, what will my life look like? A few years of transcribing the Oracle's writings and then what? A fixture in the god's bed until he gets bored with me.

Is that what is happening now?

I gulp wine at that last thought. What if his distance means he is ready for me to leave? That all this talk of keeping me is just a god being a god. Plying me with sweet words because soon I will be nothing to him. I worry I may never recover if he decides I am a fleeting fancy. Do I want to stay with Cinthus if Apollo will soon find another? I want us, the three of us. Only. Always. My idiot heart has jumped off a cliff, clutching these two as it plummets to the earth. Cinthus loves me. He hasn't said it, but he shows me over and over, but Apollo . . .

Did I want this without him?

Thoughts swirl in my head as I run my necklace through the chain. I need both of them. I am happy with both. I want the security and comfort of Cinthus and the light and flirtatiousness of Apollo. I want the painter and the musician. The prince and the god. I need to belong to them. I want Apollo to make a gesture, some sort of sign, to reassure me. I don't want to give up Cinthus, but I won't stay if I have to watch Apollo with someone else.

It is the three of us or nothing.

A horn sounds, and the room grows quiet. I search for the men who occupy my troubled mind and find them close to the high table. Threading through the crowd, I make my way to them. I catch both scanning the room and a small smile curls the corner of my lips when our eyes lock and their faces soften. Once I am to them, Cin gains a small platform. Behind him sits three easels with a cloth draped over them. He is in his formal attire, a blue cape swinging over his shoulder. He addresses the crowd, loud and clear, his baritone punctuating the quieting room.

"In the past, I have presented one painting, but tonight, I'll be presenting three." That smirk of his crosses quickly before he continues. "I was inspired, as of late, and felt three a better offering for My God than one."

Moving to the first painting, he grasps the cloth. "I wanted to showcase Apollo in his best light."

"If it's naked like last year, I'm crying foul!" Hermes yells from behind us.

Cinthus chuckles, as does the crowd.

"He isn't naked, no. But I hope it's an honorable depiction." He removes the cloth, and the revealed portrait causes the entire room to collectively gasp. The portrait shows Apollo with outstretched wings. He is backlit in a golden paint that glimmers in the overhead light. He rises off the ground, bow in hand, battle armor on, helmet in place. Golden.

White cape. White wings. The picture of destruction with rays of sunlight streaming from his fingertips. It is a beautiful painting of Apollon: Apollo's war persona. Exquisitely terrifying; a side of him I've heard about but never seen.

I have burned cities to the ground for far less. His words from our first dinner come to the forefront of my mind.

Cin stands unsure for several long seconds, his hand gripping his sword, before Apollo begins clapping. The crowd erupts, and I watch the god of light gain the platform to kiss his only love.

Only love.

That thought leaves an ache deep down.

"You are masterful," he says, kissing him again. Those rugged, bearded cheeks turn ruddy at the praise the god showers on him.

"Go on!" Apollo shouts over the crowd. "I'd love to see your next piece, Your Highness."

Full of confidence now, Cinthus tugs the cover off the second, and I stand in awe of the lemon orchards. Long, sweeping rows of trees filled to the brim with lemons. The painting is so vivid that I can almost smell the tang of the fruit. This earns him a second round of applause. Before he tears the cloth off the third, his dark brown eyes find mine and hold me captive. The corners crinkle, and my heart flutters against my chest.

How can I leave him?

"This last is what I find most beautiful."

The cloth lands on the platform in a heap and my jaw falls.

Before the crowd, sketched in charcoal and lined in drawing pencil, is me. Naked me. On the chaise lounge in the god's chambers. Both hands tossed above my head, the necklace settled against my sternum, just above my bare breasts. Above that sketch is another of my face soft and relaxed, lost deep in thought. To the side is another sketch my back bare, my hair mussed from the nights activities, a blanket from Apollo's bed around my hips.

Both men look at me with wide, endearing eyes for several moments as I struggle to catch my breath. The room has lost oxygen, I am sure of it.

Me.

Not a beautiful nymph or a god or even a warrior mid-battle.

Me.

I touch my lips and tears prick behind my eyes. I fight to keep them contained. Cin's face falls, and he pales at my reaction.

"Do not agree, Hypatia?"

Every villager, warrior, councilman, and Olympian disappears and for those moments, it is just me and my men. Trembling, my feet move before I command them to, and I am before Cin. He takes my hand and holds my gaze, waiting for an answer.

"Thank you, Cin," I whisper. The crowd must have cheered, I'm not sure. The blood in my ears pumps louder than their clapping.

"She's stunning, Cinthus." Apollo agrees, sliding his hand around my waist as Cin showers me with a smile that turns my world on its axis.

Several minutes later, collecting myself from the stunning display of my portrait before a crowd, one I should be embarrassed about if I were any other woman. But I'm not any woman. I'm the woman Prince Cinthus sees as beautiful.

A small gathering of village children is seated before my gift. Two warriors carry it to the table while I arrange the last few things needed for my presentation. I was excited to show it, hoping the god of light would enjoy the theatrics, but as the seconds tick down, I begin to get nervous he will see it as silly and frivolous. I'm not his love, only his lover. I don't know if he'll react like he did to Cin. A sharpness pings my heart at the idea of his indifference, or worse, flat-out rejection. I twist my fingers into my hand, keeping my feet firmly planted instead of running as my heart speeds up.

Our eyes meet as I grasp the edge of the cloth, and I hold onto his gaze like a lifeline. With a flick of my wrist, the cover flutters off, waving slightly before landing on the ground. Apollo's eyes light from within, blazing, locked on mine with admiration. Small gasps came from around me and the children began chattering all at once.

"It's Apollonion." I walk around the large, metal mountain rising from the table. Built into the metal is a massive glowing, golden palace, every turret and column, every balcony intricately designed. Small scale warriors cover one hill, fruit orchards cover another. I crafted the upper and lower gardens out of the same composite metal. On one side is the observatory, the other the stables. The mountain is set against a backdrop of half-night and half-day. The sun's rays slice into the sky, turning clouds orange and pink, and the moon's silver glow lights the night, giving way to glittering stars. Carved into the mountain is the village and below that, the Hills of Hyperion, with tiny homes and villages dancing along painted hills. A herd of pegasi graze on one far below the palace. Turning to my helper, I take a small packet and empty it into one side, then round the piece and empty the other. I glance at both men. The look of adoration written across their faces is all I need to complete my presentation.

"It is magnificent, Hypatia," His Highness says.

Apollo steps forward but I stop him with a hand.

"Long ago," I begin, glancing at the children who settle themselves for a story. "Long before the old gods had burned out like stars in the sky, there was a set of twins."

Apollo's expression when I look up is one of utter astonishment. I never leave those wide, sky-blue eyes as I speak, telling the story to the inspiration.

"Their mother was a beloved goddess, and she gave the twins dominion over the sky. The princess would raise the moon every evening and the prince would raise the sun every morning. One day, the siblings wanted to race their chariots to see who could raise their celestial bodies the best, and they asked their mother to be the judge." I click a knob, and two doors open on either side of the piece. "The prince of the sun came flying out on his side, his chariot, pulled by four strong swans, moved so fast it looked as if it were on fire. The swans flapped their wings in great strokes, cutting the night from the dawn and leaving pink and purple colors in the sky." As I speak, the first chariot of Apollo and his swans streak across the makeshift sky. Behind the chariot blaze red and gold dust, which turns pink and purple as it settles. The children gasp and giggle, clapping their little hands. Apollo's smile is like a beacon, calling me to him.

"Not to be outdone, the princess of the moon took her chariot pulled by four strong bucks and began to raise the moon. The strength of her animals caused the moon to shine, full and silver in the sky, leaving silver stardust in its wake. The pounding of their hooves pierced holes in the fabric of the night so that stars may shine." The chariot representing Artemis bursts out of its spot, silver dust trailing behind metal bucks. The two move to the center where they stop, dumping the last of the dust on the palace. "When the prince and princess reached the center of the sky, their mother declared both winners, for she didn't want to choose between her children she loved so much. She told the prince he may raise the sun every morning and the princess may raise the moon every night. And this is how it has been from that day to this."

The children clap and chatter at the end of my story, excited little faces looking up at my crafted masterpiece. Apollo's eyes glitter like the first signs of stars in the dusk fallen sky, his smile hauntingly sweet. He makes his way to me.

"Do you find this gift acceptable, My God?"

He stops in his tracks at my address, and a piercing pang hammers in my chest at the expression that crosses his handsome face. I feel it then, the pulling of his affection, like a snap to the fragile line we have woven between us. As if I have somehow hurt him. Confused, I twist my fingers and wait for a split second before he speaks in wonderment.

"It is more than acceptable, sweet Hypatia. This is exquisite in every sense of the word, and I am honored to be the recipient of such a gift."

The crowd cheers and begins to swarm my creation, asking a multitude of questions. Apollo reaches me before the prince. He slides his hands on either side of my face, tilting my chin up.

"Apollo," he says softly. "I ache for the day you only call me Apollo." He slides his hands along my waist and kisses my forehead, turning so Cin can come to congratulate me on my work. My heart thumps in my ears, drowning out the room. He kisses my forehead again.

"My heart is full this evening. My two favorite artists need a celebratory drink, I believe." He eyes Cin, who nods.

"You never cease to amaze me." I blush under his praise. "That mind of yours is wonderfully inventive."

"Thank you, My God," I say quietly, embarrassed by his words. He kisses my cheek and preens when several villagers came up to coo over my contribution. Turning, he leaves to go gather drinks, leaving Cin and I to deal with the villagers.

I settle into a conversation with one, all about how I designed the small chemical reaction when a familiar gruff voice causes me to turn.

"Quite impressive, Hypatia. Then, you were always quite impressive, weren't you? Although I doubt when Athena assigned you, she meant for your talents to be used in the manner they currently are."

Stiffening, I look at the voice. Cin turns as well; he ticks a sharp look in my direction, his hand instantly on his sword.

"Ambassador Elatus," His Highness says coolly. "I didn't know we were to be graced with your presence this evening."

The ambassador salutes, hand to his heart, giving Cin respect for his position, but his beady eyes never leave mine.

"I thought it time I made the rounds in the Celestial Legion on behalf of Poseidon. He sends so few of us, that the task is ever taxing." He flicks those dark, judgmental eyes to me as he speaks, letting them roam my body. I shiver.

"And you are acquainted with our house guest?" Cin steps to the side, just out in front, placing me behind. I want to reach forward and pull him back to me, back to protect me from whatever the ambassador is about to say. Of all the ones I have met, Ambassador Elatus is by far the nastiest. He is a deadly combination of haughty and direct, always putting those he deems beneath him in their place. I was a frequent recipient, in Athena's court, of his opinion, being the only female scribe in a revered position.

"Very much so, though I have to say, she knows her proper place in Athena's court."

He addresses me with a jerk of his chin. "I wonder what Artemis would say if she saw what her right hand had become. A scribe belongs in the archives, not here in a great hall and certainly not at a high table, dining with gods and princes." He shuffles forward, his robe of dark blue covers the white chiton all ambassadors wear. He has a navy-blue sash slashed across his shoulder, held on by a pin bearing the emblem of Poseidon. "But it is clear from the portrait exactly how you acquired that position." He scowls. "Just like a damn woman, opening her legs wide enough to let two men in just to move beyond her station."

I hear the sickening crack before I know the prince moved. Cinthus growls, shaking his fist, his sword drawn. The ambassador flies back a foot after the blow, grabbing his face and snarling. In a breath, the world spins, a flurry of movements and shouts. Golden light, rays so thick they blind, shoot through the air on white wings. Warriors rush to their feet. The deafening sound of hundreds of weapons being drawn at once makes the hairs on my arms stand on end. Nymphs and village women shout, scuttling children out of the way.

Before me in golden armor, helmet on, golden bow in hand stands the live embodiment of the painting I viewed just moments earlier. Apollon raises his bow, glaring at the ambassador.

"Need I remind you, Ambassador, in whose court you stand," he says, his voice lethal. I had feared Apollo the god. I feared his wrath all those weeks ago when I bathed with Cinthus. But seeing the terrifying creature before me, I stand in awe, not fear. He is glorious—golden light and fierce protector.

Elatus lifts his jaw with a sneer. "And you forget who I answer to, young god. I am not intimidated by the likes of you. Defending a ruined scribe as if she were anything important. Your duties seem to be between her legs, instead of on tasks important to the crown."

Apollon lowers his weapon and chuckles. *Chuckles*. Eerily. Stony. "I'd advise you to watch your fucking tongue ambassador, or I shall separate it from your mouth." Raising the bow, he aims a golden arrow at the man. "I may be a young god, but my aim never misses. You have a choice. Bow before her, honor her position in my court. Or run."

"Excuse me?" he scoffs.

"Bow or run."

The ambassador looks as though he doesn't believe the war god and for a split moment, I think he might retaliate with even more spews of nastiness.

"Bow or run." He straightens his stance.

"This is an insult!" the man rails, fear bursting in his eyes.

"Run or—" He pulls the string taught to his chin.

The ambassador takes off toward the doors, the crowd parting down the center of the dining hall as he runs. Heavy, thudding feet against the marble is the only sound against the backdrop of his heavy breathing.

"Die."

The golden arrow flies, gold dust streaking off the end looking as though it is aflame. When it hits, he is steps from the open door leading to the corridor. He is thrown forward with the force, his head jerking back as his body crashes to the ground with a deafening thud. The hall is deadly quiet, an entire room witnessing their god eliminate an ambassador in front of his court. Cinthus has his sword raised, ready to lead men into battle. Turning, I catch warrior after warrior, weapons raised, ready to defend their god. Ready to defend *me*. All because their god sees me as important. As more than just a scribe. As his.

"If anyone else has objections with whom I share my heart, I give you the same choice. Bow or run." He steps in a circle and one by one, all in the hall fall to one knee, leaving Cinthus and I standing. An entire crowd bowing before the loves of Apollo.

Apollon slowly turns to face me, returning to the god I know in the blink of an eye. Back to the god I am falling in love with despite my best efforts. His eyes are dark, determined, unapologetic. When he reaches for me, *Zeus help me*, I should shrink back. I should be furious or embarrassed or rail against him—*my Apollo*—for such a display of pure unyielding wrath. But I don't. I step into his arms. I step into his damn arms and breathe him in.

"Cinthus," he says over the top of my head, "send a raven feather to Poseidon along with a note. It seems he will need another ambassador."

Chapter 25

The Prince

T he late afternoon sun beats down on this part of the orchards, ripening the fruit in the trees. He is up ahead a few yards, pacing under the shade of two and muttering to himself. A councilman stopped me in the corridor concerned because Apollo has missed several meetings this morning. In the last few months, he has been the god I always knew he was, believed him to be. Caring, attentive, present. I know why.

Hypatia.

She has both of us wanting to be better men, wanting to prove we are worthy of her. He hides the change from her, from everyone, but I see it; the positive change she has made. In such a short time, she has made all the difference in both our lives. Our days are filled with her laughter and her stories. Her observations, her math. Our nights, with her between us, softly cradled in our arms, fragile and delicate because any moment we know the bubble we are in will burst. She completes the two of us in ways I never imagined. Ways I never wanted. I was content to live my life secure in the fact I was the lover of Apollo. She makes me hope for more. I now want a future with her and me alongside Apollo, the three of us, loved beyond measure. I hadn't gone looking for a second partner, but I found my equal in her.

"I thought I'd find you here." I snap a twig off a low-hanging branch, and he jerks his head up.

EM MEYERS

"Cin." Twirling a leaf by the stem, he flings it to the ground. "So, they sent you to find me."

"You missed meetings. You haven't missed one in months. The council was concerned you may have reverted back to—"

His wings snap open, a sign of his frustration. They beat several times, causing the air around us to move in swirling currents before they return to their position.

"You've been agitated as of late. Are you contemplating a return to Dionysus?" I ask the question knowing full well what the answer is and why the god of light is acting this way. After his display during the feast and the subsequent killing of the ambassador for being a right dickhead, Hypatia retreated. Her initial reaction that evening had me thinking they would both open up, but the last few nights, she has refused to come to either of our chambers, stating she needed to focus on her research. The god, in turn, had become increasingly temperamental. He has been short with me and anyone stupid enough to get in his way the longer she stays away. And so, the two people I love most in the world are silently retreating into themselves. Protecting themselves from hurt by avoiding the inevitable.

He twists his lips and snorts. "No. I have no intention of returning. Is that why you've come? Afraid I'll leave you too?"

When he becomes like this, the only thing to do is to let him work it out in his own time. Taking a deep breath, I cross my arms.

"You're not going anywhere, and neither am I, but you know that."

"She's leaving, Cin." he blurts out, snatching a lemon off a branch. "I know I shouldn't have, but dammit, at the feast, I read her thoughts and she . . . she's leaving."

"You know this for sure?" I try to calm the beating of my heart against those words. I didn't expect that. Hypatia's confusion, yes, but to return

216

to Athena's when she could have so much more with us. I don't want her to go.

"No, but she's contemplating it. She has a life there, Cin. A life that doesn't include either of us. She has respect and a position. What can we offer her here?" He tosses the lemon to the ground. "She is the curator of the library and Artemis' right hand. Here, she is a fixture in my bed."

"She said that?"

He points to his temple with a gruff, "Thoughts."

I nod, it's the only expression I can think of that doesn't involve running back to the palace and making Hypatia see she is so much more than a bedmate. Begging her to stay. Shaking her by the shoulders until she listens to me when I tell her she isn't temporary. That we need her, both of us in equal measure.

"It's because of me." He ruffles his hair and paces. "I'm fucking this up, Cinthus. If she goes, it'll be because of me."

Apollo is the god others adore, the beautiful one. Charming. Outgoing. Charismatic. But he isn't like that with me. He rarely lets others in. Sex is an action, a thing he does and is excellent at. Feelings aren't something he allows, choosing to leave the other person before he is left. Being hunted by Hera left a lasting impression, one he deals with by pretending sex is meaningless.

With her, it hasn't been meaningless. Not once. It is why I insisted on taking the lead, because I know him. I knew he would burn as bright as the sun and then retreat like a dramatic ass.

With me, he had been attentive from the start, but true feelings hadn't developed until he brought me here. He didn't want to admit I was his weakness. Gods couldn't have weaknesses. Not when other gods and Olympians were spiteful and destructive and had been known to plot to destroy. We spent too much time in those early years frustrated and lonely, until we both admitted that this wasn't just sex for us, that we were the best versions of ourselves when we were together. That we were in love. Perfect, all-consuming, accepting of the other person, flaws in all—love. He may have other partners, but he never feels the same way about them. Never lets them into his heart, into his soul.

But now.

Hypatia managed to crawl under his skin and open him up, leaving him bleeding ichor in her wake. He is terrified of her. She is ruining him, and he needs ruining.

"I'm going to lose her. I'm going to drive her away because I don't know how to be like you. And I've tried, Cin. Fucking hell, I've tried."

"You can't make Hypatia stay by imitating me."

He holds out his hands. "I don't know what to do. Just the idea of her leaving and my chest grows tight. I've given her a crown. I've given her a position, a place beside me, honor, and she is slipping through my fingers because I don't know how to make her see me." He thumps his chest. "Me. Not Apollo. Me! Fucking Zeus, she still calls me My God."

He turns away, his wings glowing white in the hot sun.

"Help me, Cinthus." He speaks the words to the soft breeze that carries the scent of lemons, her scent, with it. "I can't have searched all these years and finally have her, only to lose her. I can't bear living here without her, knowing who she is. Knowing the color of her eyes matches the mist coming off the mountains in the morning. Knowing the sound of her laugh when you say something particularly bawdy. The quill she likes to use. I feel as though a part of me has finally fallen into place. I want her to look at me like she looks at you. How can she have such a connection with you and keep me at arm's length?"

Time for the truth. "Because you keep her at arm's length."

He whips around and marches to me, emotions clouding his blazing eyes. "I do not. I pursued her. I sought her out, gave her things, had my entire court bow before her. I claimed her first."

"And you fuck her, not love her. Sex and making love are two very different things, and Hypatia is smart enough to know the difference."

He steps back as if I struck him, narrowing his glare, but he doesn't argue. The truth hurts but it needs to be said. Apollo has continued to be a persona with her and not a person.

"You dominate her, and I'm the one who fucks her?"

If I wasn't used to his venom in these moments, I would be insulted.

"Simple. She trusts me. She doesn't trust you."

Rays of light radiate from his skin, his wings rip open, and he hisses. "Lies."

"I'm not, and you know it." I won't back down, haven't uncrossed my arms. I am ready for this conversation, ready to pull his head out of his ass. "Why do you think you enjoy me making you come to heel?"

My response is a quiet glare that borders on deadly. I have to tread lightly here, or I could provoke him too far and have to deal with Apollon making an appearance.

"You are a god, every day, all day. You can't take a break. You can't show weakness. You can't back down. Your family is deadly and ruthless and will hunt and kill the ones you favor just for spite. So, you are selfish and demanding and, left unchecked, an infuriating ass. Despite all that, I love you, fiercely. You enjoy me dominating you because it takes the pressure off you having to be anything but mine. Mine to control. Mine to command. Mine to punish. Mine to soothe." Picking a lemon off a tree, I examine the textured skin, the bright yellow color, before I continue. "Hypatia is different. She is curious, intelligent and so fucking stubborn it's intoxicating. She enjoys it because she knows she can test me, push me, make her own rules, and turn this entire thing on its head. And she does. Frequently. "

His glare softens.

"She knows that because she trusts me. She knows I care for her. Fucking Zeus, I'm in love with that damn woman, I fully admit it. But she doesn't trust you yet. She wants to. I see it in the way she looks at you. She is in love with you, desperately, but she doesn't trust you. She won't give over fully until she does." Throwing the fruit into the air, I catch it in my palm with a smack. "She'll leave because she believes you are still playing games with her, and she won't be a prize. She said it in your throne room that first time, challenging you and your arrogance."

He deflates as I lay out exactly why the woman we both need protects her heart from him. Closing his eyes, it takes him a few steps before his head hits my chest. His arms find their way around to my back, holding me. And he breaks in the only way he will allow himself. Privately. With me.

"Do you wonder why you haven't had a single nightmare since she started sharing our bed?" A slight shake of his head tells me my words are sinking in. "She soothes a part of you just as she soothes parts of me. I told you before, let her see you, not naked you. Let her inside your heart, Apollo. She isn't putting up walls, you are. You always have." My arms encircle him, gripping him, needing him near. "It's time your walls fall."

Chapter 26

The God

"You wanted to see me, My God?"

Her delicate voice echoes in the empty room, along with my thoughts. It has been days since the feast, and she continues to avoid me using research as an excuse. I went to the archives earlier to ask her to meet me in the observatory, and the nervous way she rustled scrolls reminded me of the first time I saw her in that room: ink splashed across the wood, her dress, and her skin, when she punched me.

Call me Apollo.

Cinthus was right, taking me to task in the way he always did. I am the one who built walls, and they need to come down. The bringing down of said walls, however, is unnerving. Trusting Hypatia means knowing she will leave. Leave with pieces of my soul in her possession. I ruffle my hair unsure what to do with my hands suddenly.

"Did you have a celebration in mind?" She eyes the setup I presented. I had a table brought in: wine, candles, and fruit. I wanted to show I was serious, that I was exactly what she needed, but looking at the spread now, I feel ridiculous. What the hell was I thinking?

"No." My voice breaks, and I clear my throat. "I wanted to—I'm not sure." Picking up a glass, I raise the decanter. "Wine?"

Hypatia's lips twist. "No, thank you. I think I prefer Cin's adherence to a glass with the evening meal and one after."

"I see."

We fall into an awkward silence, and I resist kicking myself for this idea.

"Is there a reason you wanted to meet in the observatory?" She cocks her head.

"You."

"Me?"

I set the wine glass down and round the table, deciding to lay it all at her feet. "I missed you." Admitting the truth is a good place to start. I have missed her in more ways than I can count. "You've been preoccupied with your research, so I thought I'd keep you company while you gaze at the stars. I didn't know how long it might take, so I had food brought in. I admit now this all seems a bit silly. If you wanted to be alone—"

A sad smile tugs at her mouth. "No. No, it's very thoughtful. If you want to, you should stay. I'd enjoy the company."

Raising my eyes to the enormous telescope, I clasp my hands behind my back. "Tell me, what is it you are admiring tonight?"

Her face glows as if from within and those damn butterflies set loose inside me once again. Gods she is beautiful when she's enthralled in her obsession. I could listen to her rattling off numbers and constellations until the stars themselves burn out.

"Oh, well, that. I figured our world is at the right angle to finally see what I think I see. If I'm correct, the star should be visible tonight."

"That's exciting."

She nods enthusiastically and clutches her hands together. "It is. I may be wrong; I haven't been able to finagle the magnification—"

"That." I walk back to the table and grab a tin box. "I think you might find the contents useful."

I present it to her, and tentatively she takes the box. Her brows come together, pinching creases into the soft skin of her forehead. "My God?"

"Open it," I say, ignoring her address.

Tugging on the golden ribbon, her fingers tremble as she lets it fall to the polished floor. Lifting the lid, she peers inside, and up at me, then back. "It's glass?"

"Lenses." Reaching in, I lift one out and hold it up to the candlelight that softly illuminates the observatory. "That first night in the dining hall, you drew lenses—"

"You understood my calculations?" Her wide eyes glow with intrigue.

"Admittedly, no, but a god needs not understand to create."

A soft gasp steals her breath, and she gently takes the lens from me. "You created these?"

"You said you would have to wait until you returned to Athena, and I"—looking up at the telescope once more, I shrug—"you shouldn't have to wait. I can provide whatever you need, sweet Hypatia."

"Lenses for which . . ."

I incline my head to the instrument that takes up most of the room. Looking over, she looks back at me, and then back to the telescope once more.

"I did my best, but if all else fails, they are enchanted. It isn't cheating if they're magical, right?"

"Apollo," she breathes as though in prayer, and I can't help my eyes from closing at the sound of my name. Placing the lens back in the box, she sets it on the table and turns, her features shifting between awe and appreciation. Her arms slide around me, her lips finding my cheek before I can react.

"Thank you." A murmur of adoration said into the leather of my breast-plate as she squeezes my midsection. Wrapping her in my arms, I kiss the crown of her head, wanting to soak this moment into my bones. She looks up at me, and I melt.

"Do you know how to change the lens? I don't know that I have ever looked through the instrument until you came, so I shall be useless in that department."

Giggles are her response, and it's melodious. "I'll have them changed in minutes, My God."

The address pricks my heart, and I remind myself that she called me by my name, and it will have to sustain me for now.

A few minutes later, tools set aside, and lenses in place, I'm standing beside her as she's adjusting the multitude of knobs, squinting as she adjusts one of the plates underneath. I marvel at her excitement. Beauty and brains, and I get the privilege of loving her.

"Can you see it?" I'm impatient to see if I created something useful. All this time and she's only asked for small favors. I wonder if she knows that I would rearrange the cosmos for her. I would do anything she asked.

"I'm not sure." Raising her head, she looks up into the ceiling-covered heavens, then back into the telescope.

"I hope I created them correctly. I'm not sure what you had on the page was math, but I tried all the same."

"They are correct, My God, but I'm not seeing what I think I should be." She straightens, and her finger taps her lips. "It's possible I'm in the wrong place in space." Brushing past me, she rustles scrolls left on a table nearby, pulling one out and laying it atop the others.

She mumbles to herself in numbers too complicated for me to understand, and I can't help but appreciate her grace. Grace like the calm in the middle of a hurricane. One that has torn through Cin and I, upsetting our lives and throwing us both off kilter. The quill in her grasp looks more dangerous than blades as she scratches out her calculations. She is power and beauty, intelligence and wiles. A contradiction who cares for the protection and the preservation of knowledge and history all while hating acknowledgments and accolades of her accomplishments in front of courts. She is a woman who could birth a coming storm that would likely destroy us all if she willed it, and I would bow at her feet because she smiled. The wrinkle of her pert little nose and the squinting of one eye against the endless array of equations running through her mind give way to her softness. Hypatia is a force to be reckoned with. A force that is eroding my heart and making me a man worthy of her.

Determined with whatever she's figured out, she marches back to the massive instrument and huffs. Adjusting the mirrors and angling the lenses, she is back to mumbling. If she can find the star using what I've made, I'm fairly certain I can win her over. And if she does, she can write Artemis and—I stop dead in my tracks, my heart pounding in my ears—go home.

Oh, fuck! Oh, *fuck!* I created the very lenses that would allow her to make her findings and send her back to Athena's court sooner. If she finds the star, she can leave before the closing ceremony. Artemis will come and once she sees how Cin and I look at her right hand, will surely try her best to kill me for fucking Hypatia. And falling for her. And wanting to keep her here. And refusing to be sorry for any of it.

Zeus should have thrown me off Olympus for being a right dumbass.

Holding my breath, I pray I screwed up my gift so badly that right now, the only thing she can see is the tops of trees beyond the building. If I wasn't such a fucking idiot, I would have inverted the calculations and maybe she'd be staring into the Underworld instead of into the cosmos.

"I'm wrong."

I barely hear her words through my panic. "What?"

"I'm. Wrong." Suprise coats her words, and she stares past me in disbelief. "I'm wrong. I'm wrong. My calculations, my research is . . . wrong."

Her gaze meets mine finally and neither of us know what to say.

"How do you mean, you're wrong? Surely if you look . . ."

But she shakes her head. "No. I mean I found something, a series of stars in a constellation, but with the new lenses and the magnification, I can see exactly where I thought. But what I thought was wrong."

"Hypatia?"

She trembles, her gray eyes turning red at the rims. "All this time, I—I thought it was . . . but it never was . . . I'm wrong."

I reach for her, wanting to comfort, wanting to hold her and tell her this isn't a setback. That science is discovery instead of absolutes. But she rushes past, heading for the door.

"Hypatia," I call, turning quickly.

"I—I want to be alone, please." Her voice is thick with emotion, and I can see her wiping her face as she speedily walks away. "Please, Apollo."

The last thing she says before her voice cracks and a strangled sob reverberates off the stone walls. An echo of her heartbreak as she leaves me. I wanted her to say my name, I never meant for it to be attached to disappointment.

Chapter 27

The God

The evening wind that blows my hair is crisp tonight. The solstice ceremonies will be over soon, and the summer will fade into autumn, and then the mountain will once again be covered in snow.

And she'll be in Athena's court.

My hands rest on the stone balcony, and I breathe in the evening. I am royally fucked, just as Hermes said. When I returned from the observatory, I demanded Cinthus leave me to my thoughts, but I knew in a few hours he'd return. He always returns. He was giving me space to turn over my epic failure of winning Hypatia over. Her muffled sob as she left the observatory ripped at my heart. I didn't know how to help her, or what to do when research and experiments didn't go as planned. I had gone to her chambers in hopes she'd let me comfort her, but her room was empty. So here I stand, looking out over the mountain range I called home, at the village that surrounded the walls of my palace, unable to ease her disappointment. Unable to ease the sickening truth that lodged itself deep in my gut.

Hypatia wouldn't stay.

In mere days, it'd be Cin and I again. Each wounded, with a hole in our hearts.

Three soft hollow sounds rupture the silence of my chambers. Turning, I pinch my brows together, confused as to what that could be. Again, the noise rattles softly from inside. Marching into the room to investigate, I hear her, not aloud, in my mind.

If he isn't in his chambers, I'll go to Cin's. Answer the damn door.

Relief I didn't know I'd feel washes over me knowing she sought me out. Although, the knocking on my door is an odd custom. My chambers are private and those allowed in can open the door and enter. Her repetitive knocking is so fucking cute. Yanking the metal handle, I catch Hypatia mid-knock for the third time, her fist raised, and her shocked expression is slightly comical.

"My God!" She blinks and I resist the urge to pull her in my arms. I've never been so happy to see anyone at my door this late. For several seconds, we stare at each other before I move aside, and she enters. She glides to the center of my room, her fingers twisting in her palms in an action I now know well.

"I'm sorry about my . . ."

"I was wondering if you . . ."

We speak at the same time, and both trail off together.

"Do you truly believe your research isn't salvageable?"

She sighs and nods twice. "Yes. I've gone over my calculations, and charts and"—her hands flop to her side as she shrugs—"I'm simply wrong. There isn't a new star, just a cluster of existing ones."

We fall into silence again. I want to say something clever or witty, but the unsureness starches my usual charm.

Fuck this! I am to her in three strides and wrap her in my arms, where she belongs. For a moment she stiffens, but it is short-lived, and she sags against me, sliding her hands around my waist and burying her little nose in the crook of my neck.

My damn heart feels as though it could burst.

"I'm so sorry. I know you're disappointed," I say into her hair, wanting her closer. The moonlight is our only companion as I rock her back-and-forth, letting myself get lost in the feel of her.

"I came to tell you that I have sent notice to Artemis of my failure—" she mumbles into the linen of my chiton.

I freeze and instinctively tighten my grip on her waist. "What?"

"I told Artemis of my findings. Or rather, none. When the closing ceremonies come, she'll be back and—"

Pushing her away, I march to the fireplace across the room, clasping my hands in front to keep from reaching out and clutching at her like a man out of his mind. She has made her choice. She is going to leave. Leave Cin and I and return to what she knew before as if nothing between us had happened. I pace back and then away again. I want to rail, I want to yell, anything to get her to see reason. To choose us.

"Why?" I finally say.

Creases form along her forehead. "Why what?"

"Why—why would you cut me like this," I blurt out.

"I'm not."

"Are you trying to hurt me, Hypatia?"

She steps back and I can't help the fear and desperation mixing in my veins. I am finally ready to let her in. I have been trying to make her see me, but she is going to leave no matter what I do.

"I'm not trying to do anything, My God."

"Apollo!" I shout. "I'm Apollo. Just Apollo to you, forever, always. Your Apollo."

"I don't understand."

I grunt. "You don't understand. Of course you don't. I gave you honor, a position, crowns, your place beside me. I made lenses, and you'll still leave. It's because he loves you, and I fuck you, is that it?"

229

Oh, good. Insult her and yell at her. That will make her stay, asshole.

She opens her mouth to say something but snaps it closed, her eyes flashing in the low light. "I didn't realize your kind gestures came with a contingency that I stay. Were they bribes then, so you could continue, as you say, fucking me?"

Utter, undeniable shock slams into me like a gut punch. It steals my breath.

"I think I'll leave."

Nodding, I snort derisively. "Yes. Leave. Leave us both."

Her arms cross. and I swear, if I didn't know she was human, I would have thought she'd hit me with magic, enough to knock me on my ass. I deserve it. I'm being fucking unreasonable.

"This was always temporary, *Apollo*." She spits my name at me and glares.

"Not for me. Not for Cin."

"And when you find another woman or man or dryad? What then? I stay here, warming your bed, until you tire of me and kick me out."

It's my turn to cross my arms, which I did. Then uncrossed them. Then threw them in the air for good measure. "Gods, is that what you think? That I'll replace you so easily?"

"You said yourself your bed is never cold."

She threw my confession back in my face. I stutter in response. It is true, I've never slept alone, but it isn't because I am some out-of-control, horny ass god who needs his cock rode. I have fears. Fucked up fears and having a body near—any body—is better than waking up alone during a nightmare and not knowing what is real and what is in my mind. But now? I no longer desire anyone outside of the three of us.

Tell her.

"I told you. I want us. Only us." Her voice drops into sadness. "I don't think you are made to commit to that type of request."

"I don't want anyone else, Hypatia. Not since the night you sat three feet from me and the candlelight made your cheeks glow."

She narrows her eyes and tilts her head. All the bluster puffs out in one sigh as I realize she doesn't know what I mean. She doesn't know the truth.

"I didn't give you gifts and place you beside me expecting sex as payment. Or because I was lonely. Or waiting for someone better to come along. I did it because I'm in love with you. I have been for centuries. I don't just remember you from that dinner." Grabbing her by her upper arms, I lower my head, so we are eye to eye. I want her to hear every word I say. "I was enchanted by every move you made. I couldn't take my eyes off you. I can't tell you what my sister said or what the musician played, but I can tell you I memorized the sound of your laugh. That you were wearing two ivory combs like what you're wearing in your hair now. That your chiton was blue like the night sky and made you look regal, like a goddess. That your eyes shone like stars as you watched the musician play. I have committed to memory every second of that evening. "

Those eyes widen, and I lay everything at her feet.

"After that night, I searched for you, Hypatia. Four hundred and eighty-three. That's the number of inquiries Hermes delivered asking who you were. I traveled to courts all over the empire looking for you. I begged Artemis to tell me. I had to find you, had to know you."

I grip her waist in my empty hands as the weight of my confession has untethered me from reality. She has been a singular thought in my mind, and I have never spoken it aloud to her.

"Please, Hypatia, see me. Not the god, the man. I'm desperate for you to see me, and I am fucking this up. Don't you understand? That night, you took root in my heart, and ever since, it has felt as if a piece of me is missing.

Your name is written across my skin, tattooed in stardust for centuries. You are etched into my bones. I can't bear to lose you again. To know you, love you, and not be with you is a fatal blow. Please. Stay."

"Artemis will come—I have to return."

"It's because of who I am, isn't it? Because of my being a god. You don't trust me. I can be gentler. I can be anything you need, let me prove it. Let me be whatever it is you want."

Her eyes crinkle at the corners. "I have thought of you too. Dreamed of you. I've memorized every moment of that night and replayed it in my mind. You are my most treasured memory." A low, guttural noise claws its way out of her throat. "I don't want you to be any different. You think I only see playfulness, your charisma; they are masks you hide behind." She palms my cheeks, and the pain in my chest grows, like a hot knife slicing open my heart. "I don't want those parts of you. I want the chaos inside you—the sides of yourself you conceal from others. I want both Apollo and Apollon, the god and the warrior. I want the man you stash away deep inside because he is vulnerable." I have ceased breathing as those gentle gray eyes search mine, finding truths I've hidden. "I want to know your secrets and share your pain. I want to be your comfort—someone you trust. Give me the battered pieces of your soul and let me keep them safe. "

"Hypatia." I breathe her name into the space between us. "I want—" I sigh, my fingers tearing through my hair. "Never mind what I want. What do you want?"

"You. All of you." Her mouth is so tantalizing close that I don't know whose breath belongs to whom.

"You have me. You've always had me."

"Ask me to stay, Apollo."

I crush my mouth to hers. She's kissing me back with intensity and hunger and need. I can only think second to second as her hands slide to the back of my neck to entangle themselves in my curls.

Lifting her, I stride to my bed. I don't want sex, I want love. I want a connection. When I lower her to the mattress, she rises to her knees and grips my shoulders. Her lips are on mine, and the moan that snakes its way around us tethers us together, stitching her heart to mine. She presses kisses into my cheek, my jaw, my neck, walking her way to my earlobe, where she tugs it with her teeth. Her fingers are nimble as they work my chiton open.

"Hypatia," I whisper to the woman who is untying my resolve string by string.

"Hmm."

"Stay."

If I were a different god, I would never allow a human to see my weakness. As her gaze turns watery and glimmers in the moonlight, I need her to know that she is one of my weaknesses. Her palms burn my shoulders through the fabric, turning me to ashes. Leaning forward, her teeth nip the underside of my jaw.

"What are you doing?" It's a low, gravelly whisper that I can't control. Gods, I want her. I'm addicted to her, like moly mixing with the ichor in my blood and spinning my head.

The sexiest of smirks sides across her lips, and I'm undone. If she asks me to fuck her, I'll be unable to say no.

"You confessed to admiring me for centuries." She fists the edge of the chiton, tugging it off. "To searching for me. To loving me." The fabric pools onto the polished floor. My breath is hitched, sticking to my ribs. "I want you bare: your heart, your soul, your skin. Bare, next to mine."

My trembling hands rest on her hips, and I let her explore as I haven't allowed her before. Her hands brush my shoulders, and I flinch. They build bridges between the gap of my soul and hers. Her piercing eyes meet mine, and I can't help but crumble. I've not been touched with such gentleness, such tenderness, from any woman. The pads of her fingers skim across my chest in such slow, graceful movements that it's hard to breathe, like ice in my lungs. I'm not a stranger to the touch of women or men; I don't care where their hands roam. My body is a thing to use and discard with others. Not with my Asteria.

With each delicate pirouette of her fingers against my skin, I become more unraveled, more tortured, more freed. She is cutting me open with her tenderness and leaving me bleeding in her compassionate arms. Her touch makes me feel alive as if I have a home in her. As if I could rest my trust in her delicate palms and know she will give me refuge.

She moves to untie her garment, and I gently stop her hands.

"I want you in my bed, next to me, but I'm not looking for sex at the moment. I only want to hold you."

I'm a damn fool because the disappointment that crawls across her face has me rethinking my stance. I'm trying to show her I can be serious, but as her chiton slides down over the rise of both breasts, I start to forget why I don't already have her on her back, full of my cock. The garment falls to the mattress and her luscious, naked body makes my mouth water.

"Are you very sure?"

Fuck all the gods, including me. This woman is mine.

I lift her by her thighs, and her legs wrap around, hooking at her heel, and we move to the middle of the bed. I can feel her center hot against my lower abdomen. Our mutual desire would ignite the room if I let it. Her tongue slips across my neck, and I have to remind myself I am doing the noble thing. That I am proving to Hypatia how committed I am to her. When we settle into bed, her leg flings over my hips, right over the erection that is betraying all the good intentions I have. She flexes her hips and places kisses on my shoulder, clavicle, chest. My arm curls around her back and swats playfully at her ass.

"Sleep, Hypatia."

"I know one way to get me to sleep that has proven very effective in the past."

Her sly smirk is akin to a fox in the hen house.

"I'm sure, but tonight, I want to hold you."

"You could hold me after." She wiggles her eyebrows, and I realize she's picked up tricks from me. It makes me love her all the more.

"Enough, impertinent woman. I'm trying to show you the man I am. The better me, not the naked me." She whines and rains kisses down on my cheeks. Laughing, I swat her ass again.

"I enjoy the naked you."

"Where was this Hypatia moments ago when you were ready to cut me in two with a look."

"You were being an ass, Apollo. I was reacting accordingly."

Sighing, I pull her closer. "Apollo. I have waited so long for you to say my name."

Done teasing, she sweeps one finger side to side methodically, her head on my chest. "Cherish me while I'm here, Apollo."

And I do. I hold her until she settles, and her limbs grow heavy. Until the moon crests and begins its descent. Late in the evening, Cin climbs in next to us. I haven't allowed myself to sleep, fearing I'd wake up to an empty bed and empty arms. He catches my eye over the top of her head and the relief that fills every line on his handsome face tells me everything I need to know.

You've told her, I see. He says in his mind, so as not to wake our mutual love. I nod and kiss the crown of her head. Hypatia mumbles something that sounds like numbers before a sharp intake of breath has her opening her eyes for a second.

"Cin."

Dreamily she murmurs, rolling over and snuggling into his wide chest. He looks at me, holding my stare.

She's staying then?

"If I can help it," I mouth.

Good.

I want to say something in the way of thanks for helping me remove my head from my ass, but it seems small in comparison.

"I love you," I whisper as I wiggle closer, letting a wing cover us. Cinthus half-smiles and touches my face.

I'm aware.

Chapter 28

The Scribe

The dawn has come too early, and I want to throw a wing back over my head. Coming awake, but refusing to open my eyes, I hear soft snoring rumbling next to me. It's familiar and comforting, and I roll on my side nearer the noise and the man who claims he doesn't snore. As I roll, the light blinds me behind my eyelids, and I smack a hand over my face. Mumbling surrounds me, filling in the gaps between each wave of noisy breath.

Opening them, I find His Highness lying on his back. One muscled arm is slung over his head, the other is somewhere on the other side of that barreled chest of his. His full lips are parted, dark eyelashes rest atop bronzed skin. He snorts on the intake of breath and licks his lips, returning to his snoring seconds later. His normal stern expression is softened in his sleep, and I resist the urge to play with his hair. Reaching forward, I choose to stroke his arm, which usually gets him to roll and the snoring to stop. Pulling me into his embrace is a delightful reaction to turning over. A shout next to me catches my attention. I shift to look, and a foot juts out from nowhere, kicking me hard enough to bruise my thigh.

Yelping, I sit up just as Apollo screams. His arms flail as he fights whatever has invaded his dreams. He's breathing hard, his fists meeting monsters midair, and his gold-dusted skin is slick with sweat.

"No! No! Stay away from her!" he yells, and I realize it isn't the sun, but the god of light glowing that woke me. I don't know how long the three of us have been asleep—I barely remember Cinthus coming to bed—but my eyes dart to the open balcony and the sinking moon. It's still night, not morning as I thought. Apollo shouts again.

"Shhh," I soothe, trying my best at comfort. Rubbing my hand over his chest, I have just enough time to feel his thundering heart under my fingertips before I go flying across the room and land somewhere close to the wall on the far side with a crack. I don't have time to react or even get my bearings before he's on me. Apollo's face is mere inches from mine. His cloud-like eyes are wild and unfocused as if he is looking right through me and into the depths of the beast he's fighting. Suddenly it's hard to breathe. His strong fingers curl on either side of my throat cutting off my air.

"Get away. Get away from her!" he growls low, tightening his grip. Stars burst behind my eyes as I try to say something, anything but the only sound is an odd gasp. My heart beats in my ears, and I claw at the vice grip around my delicate throat.

"It's Hypatia!" I hear my name two heartbeats before the god is pulled backward and slammed into the marble floor by a wall of solid muscle. "Hypatia!"

I sputter, gasping air into my lungs and drooling as I cough. The air stings my throat, and my eyes water as I rise on all fours, struggling between breathing and coughing. The marble is cool under my hands, hard, un-yielding, like his fingers. It grounds me, bringing me back to the chambers. Cin yells something to a wild Apollo who is shouting and growling like a wounded animal. I hear the smack of flesh hitting bone, and he yells again. The god of light fights against His Highness' hold before he yields. A howling cry comes from beside me, and I finally gasp enough air into my lungs to force my mind to work. Looking around, Cinthus is on the floor, Apollo clutched in his grasp. I don't remember hearing furniture topple, but a chair is flung across the room while a table and its contents lay upset on the floor. They sit atop the blue carpet that makes up a sitting area nearest the fireplace. Cinthus watches me with a distressed expression whispering something to the god as I stumble to my feet, clutching the wall for support lest I faint.

"Hypatia?" the god of light breathes before he bursts into a heart-wrenching sob and crumples in Cin's arms. I can only watch as one of my men comforts the other who falls apart. Sunlight drips onto the floor in golden splashes. Light emanates from every pore of his skin radiating a golden hue into the dark corners of the room. The scene before slashes at my heart.

"He didn't know it was you, Hypatia," Cin says, half-apology, half-shock as he rocks the god, whispering. "He didn't know it was you."

Parts of my soul break at the sight of my god and my prince. Even though I am not fully recovered, my feet move of their own accord, and I kneel next to them. Placing my hands on either side of his damp cheeks, I let golden tears wash over my knuckles as he sobs.

"You're safe," I croak out. "You're safe, my darling Apollo. Safe. We have you. Cin and I have you."

An hour later, wrapped in my silk robe and sitting on the settee, Cin is inspecting my neck and bruises thoroughly and frowning.

"I'm fine, really," I rasp, my voice having not recovered as quickly as I had. He runs his hand softly over my neck, and then exposes my shoulder. Letting out a deep breath, he rubs the purple-and-blue bruise. Grabbing his hand, I kiss his fingers reassuringly. Dark brown eyes search mine for signs that I'm not as okay as I keep insisting. He's trying his best not to fall apart, but I can tell he's just as rattled as the god.

"Did I leave a mark on her, Cinthus?" Apollo's worried question pricks my chest. He hasn't come near me since he awoke to see the carnage his nightmare left. I know guilt has taken root. I look around Cin's large frame and try to smile.

"No marks. I'm okay, gentleman."

A sigh of relief comes from deep in his ribs and he sags against the stone archway leading to the balcony.

"He didn't know it was you, little scribe," Cin repeats for the hundredth time. I'm unsure if he is trying to reassure himself or me. I pat his bare chest and walk over to the god, whose expression has become increasingly troubled.

Shaking his head, he hugs his well-toned arms around himself. "Perhaps you should go back to your chambers, Hypatia. I don't know what caused it tonight, I have been without one for months." He glances at Cin and continues, "It would kill me if I hurt you again." He refuses to look at me, but I'm not going to let him retreat. I wanted all of him and this is part of him. I softly take his chin and force his eyes to meet mine.

"I'm not going anywhere, Apollo." Stubbornly I refuse to loosen my grip, and his blue eyes look as though they may water. "What was the nightmare about? Let me comfort you."

We stare for a few breaths before I force him to comply in another way. I open his arms, and he reluctantly allows me to fold them around my back before he tightens them. He grunts as I squeeze, lowers his head, and sinks into my embrace. I knew this would work; holding me is his comfort. I want to cry at that realization, but I keep quiet.

"Hera. Always Hera," he says into the crook of my neck. His breath is warm and steady, and I can feel him gain strength just having me near. "This time she had Artemis, and I couldn't protect her. I was too scrawny, too young. She was trying to kill her, and I couldn't stop it."

He speaks to the chamber over my shoulder and the only thing I can do is press myself tighter to him and close any gap between us. I let my soul speak to his, reassuring it again that it is safe.

"He used to have them frequently," Cin offers from behind. "Several times a month. It would take me hours to get him settled. But you . . ." He trails off, and I lean back to look at Apollo's worn face. Smoothing the frown lines that have formed along his brow, I pull him down, kissing his forehead.

"But me what?" I say over my shoulder.

"You make all the difference, little scribe. For both of us."

Nodding at that, I slip my hand into Apollo's and then Cin's, tugging my two oversized boats back to our bed, to the safe harbor we have built. Apollo stalls just at the edge.

"If I have another—"

"Then I shall comfort you again. And again. And again." Letting go of his hand, I kiss his lips, and then lightly push his shoulder. "Now, get in that bed. You've denied my earlier advances, and my subsequent release, and then woke me up in a rather unsettling way. You may not know it, My God, but I need beauty sleep, and you are keeping me from it."

Cin snorts a soft laugh beside me, and I smile up at him. I refuse to allow either to feel guilty for tonight. I refuse to allow Apollo to set up the walls he had in the beginning. Now that they are down, now that he is finally letting me in, I will stubbornly stay inside.

"You are a demanding little thing, aren't you," His Highness jokes as he crawls into his spot. I crawl over him, wedging myself between my men. Turning, I peck kisses on Cin's lips, and he mumbles something. I look up and it hits me then that the prince and I are the same. We are both in love with the god of light, we are his weakness and his strength. His constant and his comfort. We are his. But we are also separate. We are ours too. That Cin is my equal, my partner, and I am his. I didn't know one could care for two hearts the same, but I do. And I never want it to change.

Pulling a wing over us, and arms and legs around us, I make sure they have thoroughly twisted themselves with me at the center before I answer.

"Yes, I am. Now I demand we sleep." Apollo rests his head near my shoulder, and Cin fully encases me in his body. "Remind me, gentlemen, to take up boxing in the morning."

Slamming my eyes shut, I fight a grin that threatens to erupt.

Chapter 29

The God

"You're a brute, Cinthus!" she playfully scolds, laughing as my prince scowls in her direction. They are focused on their tasks this evening, tossing quips between them. The palace has been preparing for the closing ceremonies, which means I have been inundated with meetings. Many of the warrior companies want to meet with the council to discuss everything from grievances to allowances. Cinthus had rescued me from one such meeting that would have taken us to the evening meal claiming he needed my assistance. We took up sanctuary in the private library off my chambers, partly because the lighting was better for Cin's painting and partly to hide from those at court. Hypatia happily came along, as whatever she was tinkering with in the archives could wait until morning.

The late afternoon sun washes one of the balconies in light, bringing out the gold veins in the marble and making it shimmer. And so, I lounge here, watching my loves as they do what they do best.

Be brilliant.

Cin is working on a portrait of the three of us. He has painted many such portraits over the years. Looking around the room, it tells the story of the two of us—oil painted depictions in various states of dress and actions, along with stills, gardens, and anything else he fancied. Two such paintings hang on a far wall he had presented last year: One of me naked out in the lemon orchard, and the other of him in the nude in the bathhouse. Eyeing the wall, I cut into their playful banter.

"Your Royal Highness, might you do a portrait of Hypatia? Maybe one similar to your paintings from last year." I point with my chin to the wall. Hypatia's eyes follow and round as she looks at Cin. Her perfect cheeks pink. I love it when she becomes embarrassed and flustered. Even after all this time in our company, she is still woefully unaware of how alluring she is. Lately, I have made it my duty to fluster her at least once a day. I seldom fail.

Cin agrees with my request.

"I have some sketches of our dear little scribe, but not a portrait. You're right, My God, it is high time we rectify that."

"You are painting me now, Your Highness."

"You are in a portrait of the three of us," Cin counters. "I believe we need one of just you. Perhaps in the observatory or maybe the study."

She rolls her eyes in that way I've come to know means she thinks we are both idiots. We are. For her.

"Again, I say, it is a ploy to see me naked."

I rest the book in my hand on my abdomen and place both hands behind my head. "It is our constant endeavor to see you sans clothing as much as possible."

An oil cloth comes whizzing past my head. Her hands find her hips, and she playfully glares while Cin laughs.

"You both are the worst men."

"Your men," I say with a wink. She giggles and blushes again, returning to her work. Gods, this woman is the best thing to happen to Cin and me. Having her here heals parts that have been long since broken.

"What is it you are so busy calculating?" I ask, sitting up and turning the book over, so I can fold the page edge down. Cin hates this and on numerous occasions has called me a monster, but I am not a god who can be tamed by the straightness of the edge of books. I bend them with wild abandon, to hell with the consequences.

"I'm writing my report for Athena and my findings, or lack thereof." She dips the quill in the ink once more and scratches along the parchment. Frowning, she jams the quill into its holder and, placing her elbows on the desk, rests her chin atop her hands. "I don't know that I've ever seen you read, My"—she stops herself and a shy smile plays at the corners of her lips—"Apollo."

Over the last few days, she has said my name more times than I can count. And each time, it is as though a symphony plays. My pulse speeds up and those damn butterflies I have come to expect let loose inside. I long to hear her call it breathlessly, desperate for me.

"Did you think me illiterate, Asteria?" I tease, and she nods.

"Yes."

Feigning shock, I swing my legs over the settee, ready to pounce on that smart mouth. She giggles. "Madam! You insult me! I most certainly can read, you insolent woman. Would you like to know what?"

"Don't fall for it, Hypatia," Cin warns with a smile. "His books are not for the faint of heart, I assure you."

"Cin doesn't find my taste as entertaining as I do, although he benefits from it greatly. What is it you like to read, sweet Hypatia?"

With a turn of her head, trying to determine what we mean, she shrugs. "Science, of course, philosophy, anything on Euclid geometry, writings and teachings in the library. On occasion, a few warriors have brought back books from the human realm, and they have been fascinating. One warrior brought a book about the findings and study of steam engine locomotion."

Cin turns to look at her from his easel and sets his brush down. "Are the humans just now discovering the power in steam engines?"

She nods in the affirmative excitedly. "Yes, they are! It is fascinating, as we are far past that and have bullet trains to move the citizens of the empire from province to province. Steam engines are still new to them, and the technology is rudimentary at best, but I enjoy the topic. They are also looking at trying their hand at flight without wings but with gliders. Terribly fascinating."

They both nod, sharing a mutual love for science and technology.

"What about romance?" I ask.

She twists her lips, and I meet her gaze with a lift of my brow. "Pardon?"

"Do any of the warriors bring you books with romance?"

"Some, not many." She shrugs.

Tuning several pages in my book, I motion her over. "Come, perhaps you'll enjoy romance more if you read it."

She slides around the desk and sits beside me, taking the book. Her gray eyes flit across the page, absorbing the words. All of a sudden, they widen, darting to me and back. Her cheeks pink again, and she takes in a soft gasp.

"Oh!" she exclaims and shuts the book quickly. Opening it again, she continues reading, before shutting it softly this time.

"I warned you, little scribe. Apollo owns many volumes with quite the education on their pages." Cin's laughter fills the room—it's deep and robust, much like the man. I take the book from my poor, too-sweet lover and clutch it to my chest.

"You enjoy reading that—"

"Smut?" I offer. "Yes. I enjoy it. Now, my library is hardly as extensive as Aphrodite or Eros, but I do have a mountain to look after." Smirking, I open the book again. She's looking at me with such curiosity that I feel as though I'm under a microscope. "Something to say, Asteria?"

I fully expect her to tease me or even better, put color to those cheeks, and return to her desk. Instead, she frowns in thought, tilting her head.

"Are they all about . . . that?"

I'm not sure where she's leading me with this line of questioning, but I'm intrigued all the same. "About what? Sex?" It's my turn to frown. "No. Not all, although many are romance in theme and story. I read for the connections and the beauty, but I do enjoy the descriptions. Anyone would, I'd imagine." Tugging on her arm, I draw her closer. Her eyes soften when they meet mine, and I melt. "Although I'd rather try what's written more than reading it."

She doesn't gasp. Doesn't blush. Doesn't even pull back or call me a silly name. Hypatia holds my gaze for several breaths before she stuns me.

"Read it. Aloud."

It isn't a question or even a request. It's a demand. My Hypatia is making demands. The air between us electrifies, and one of her damn fingers finds the muscles of my thigh, tracing in slow, teasing strokes. Cin has stopped painting and stares at us. I'm certain everything in the room—hell our world—stops dead. The wind. The birds. The damn sun pauses in its descent. I blink several times, unsure of what I heard her say. She never takes her eyes off me. They have turned the color of stone as I fumble for words.

"I enjoy your voice. I enjoy it when you speak, when you sing, when you groan just as you . . . release." A flick of her eyes low and back up steals breath from my lungs. "I think I shall like it even more when you read."

She makes it sound as though it is as innocent a request that could be made, but her hand on my thigh and a single digit methodically tracing patterns tells me it is far from innocent.

"It's a simple request, My God. You wouldn't deny me, would you? Read the passage aloud, nice and slow." Her euphonic voice pitches lower as her features turn sultry. Wanton. She is looking at me as if she is a starving woman about to devour her prey. *Fucking Zeus*, I would enjoy being devoured by her. It adds to the charged exchange between us, and I do the unthinkable. I blush.

Clearing my throat, a half-chuckle escapes, and I'm reduced to a fumbling idiot at this change from the more demure Hypatia at the beginning of the summer. If I'm being honest, I much prefer her now. She's confident. Herself. I suddenly want her to control me, need her to lead. Her eyes glimmer—boldness, heat, and desire flashing in her irises like a storm. She's intoxicating.

"We should go to my chambers, Asteria." Leaning closer, her little tongue darts out. I caress her forearm, making my way to her wrist. "This settee isn't large enough for both of us to stretch out."

"Read," is all she says.

I dart a look to His Highness who has perched himself on the edge of the desk, his long fingers gripping the edge.

I begin to read, starting from where I left off in the chapter. This part is all emotion, a confession fireside by two lovers on the run. As I read, I fall into that familiar pattern of inflex and dips in my voice, changing as characters speak. Hypatia watches me with such intensity that I grow nervous. She doesn't move. Doesn't stop the labyrinth she draws into my skin.

When the lovers kiss, she smiles, and I stumble over the damn words. The kiss on the page turns heated, more passionate, and yet she continues, listening to the rise and fall of my voice as I take her along their journey. I have almost fallen into a rhythm when her lips find mine. For a moment, I stiffen, startled, but I melt into her. Taking my bottom lip into her teeth, she tugs as she releases, and electricity shoots through me.

"Continue." Her breathless command spurs me on, and I lean forward, sliding my hand along her jaw, aiming for her mouth.

"No"—she moves out of reach—"read. Continue to read."

The whimper I make protesting her refusal is desperate and needy.

"Hypatia," I beg, for what I'm unsure, but she pins me with a penetrative look. Her run lips along my cheekbone, until she reaches my ear.

"Read or I fuck Cin and make you watch." Her words are barely a whisper but they illicit a groan all the same. My sweet Hypatia doesn't say such things, at least not often.

Fuck any god—all of them—whatever their names are. I have no intelligent thought after hearing "fuck" fall from her lips.

My thumb grazes her jaw, tilting those lips closer. "You win, sweet Hypatia. Your god submits to you." I read one sentence. Her lips find my neck, nibbling down the side. Another sentence. Her breath mixes with mine and she kisses me in between words. Another sentence and her tongue traces my neck, skimming across my pulse.

I want you, Apollo. Now. Right now.

Her voice rings in my head, and the slight nod she gives me sends all the blood in my body right to my already rigid cock. The fire in those gray eyes lights and it takes my breath away at how beautiful, how powerful she looks. Rising, she heads for my chambers without a word. Cinthus follows first, leaving me panting after them. When I follow through the door into the chambers, they are already locked in a kiss that had I not already been fucking hard, I would have become just watching them. Cin's armor is in a pile on the floor, and he is walking her back towards the bed. For a few seconds, I fear she will make good on her threat and force me to watch but she breaks the kiss. Finding me halfway between the door and my bed, her lips are hot and demanding, bruising as she crushes them to mine. Her fingers tug at buckles and laces.

Shivers run along my spine, and I feel drunk on her kisses. Her tongue against my own evokes desperate noises out of me. One moment I'm standing, half-dressed, trying to remove clothing without breaking from her mouth, the next I am on my back on the bed and a gloriously naked Hypatia is climbing up my body ready to consume every inch.

I reach for her, and she smacks my knuckles, causing me to yelp in surprise.

"Hands above your head. Touch me again without my permission, and I'll be forced to tie you down." Her core rocks against me, fingertips graze my shoulders as she pushes me back against the mattress. She clasps my hands overhead, and I sink into the down mattress, obeying her. I am aglow with want; light playing in her stone-gray eyes, dancing with heated mischief. She leans down, and I can't suppress the noises I make as her nipples graze my chest.

"You are mine, Apollo. Mine to tease. Mine to tantalize. Mine to control."

Her mouth is so close, her breath my own. When she rolls her hips, I lose that last shred of dignity I've been clinging to.

"Fuck, Asteria. Please," I beg, raspy and desperate. "Please."

She only *tsks*. Rising, her hand slides down her neck to her breast, pinching a nipple before traveling over her stomach and finally between her parted thighs. Her head throws back as she plays, breaths coming in short gasps. I'm a willing prisoner, trapped beneath her, committing voyeurism in my own chambers.

Removing her fingers, she sucks them into her mouth, and I watch, enraptured by the woman. Lowering herself, she captures my attention.

"Do you enjoy watching me?"

I nod, gulping back a needy whimper.

"Good. If you're a very good god and do what I say, I'll let you come. But if you don't, I'll leave you with only lust pulsing through your veins until you're driven half-mad."

"Fuck." A smirk teases my lips. "Let me touch you."

"Not until I say, My God. "

I reach up playfully but retreat when she smacks my hand again, this time harder. Flushing, I imagine her smacking my ass.

Fucking Zeus!

I would let her spank me senseless if there was a chance I could touch her. My fingers burn, light radiating around the room, piercing the dark. Each pass of her hips brings her warm center dancing along my cock, silk gliding along steel, base to tip, but that's where it ends. No touch. No tasting. Just the infuriating sensation of her hips rotating and my inability to move. I'm sure I'm going to die under her with a massive hard-on if she doesn't stop teasing me. I let loose a frustrated growl.

"Such desperation, My God."

"Apollo," I grit out behind gnashed teeth as she continues the delicious torture. She brings her lips dangerously close to mine.

"I'll say your name when you've earned it."

I almost come just from those words alone. Whatever this hold she has on me is, it is both thrilling and terrifying. I am at her mercy, begging to be fucked like the damn needy god I am. Gripping the mattress edge tight enough to rip it in two, my body shudders under her delicate touch. Walking her fingers down my chest to my stomach, over my abs, she glides her hands over my thighs behind her.

I'm in agony.

"Let him taste you." Cin's voice rattles beside me. He kisses her, stroking down her neck then cupping a breast. My hips flex, clutching the mattress so hard my fingers throb.

"Yes," she rasps as he takes her nipple into his mouth. Her fingers entangle in his hair, holding him there before he releases with a pop.

"I want to see you sit on our god."

A bewildered Hypatia cocks her head. This position we haven't tried yet.

"My mouth," I groan, helping her out. "Come here, Asteria, and sit on your throne."

The cutest fucking expression runs across her features. Climbing up my body, she gets into position but pauses as if she is calculating angles. She is such a heady mixture of brilliant and innocent, goddess and seductress. I'm no longer able to do as she commands and keep my hands off her.

"Lower, Hypatia, strangle me between your thighs."

Grabbing her hips, I guide her to my mouth with an eagerness I've never experienced. Flattening my tongue, I run it from her opening to her clit, and her luscious thighs clamp around my ears. Her taste floods my senses, her moans are a melody. A hand smacks the headboard, getting her balance as I work her clit: sucking, flicking, teasing.

This is euphoria.

As I focus on my goddess, Cin strokes my cock. His tongue travels from my balls to the tip before he slips me in that hot mouth of his. Wasting no time, he takes me all the way to the back of his throat. He has mastered the art of taking me deeply without gagging and I momentarily stop my assault on Hypatia's delicious pussy. He holds my hips to the mattress and takes control. His mouth drives me to the edge of oblivion, but she won't be ignored, and grinds down, forcing me back to work.

Cin's fist tightens around my base, and he dominates me with that mouth I love. Hypatia's hand digs into my hair as her hips thrust against my tongue. I'm a man lost to the sensations both my lovers are creating.

The only sounds in the room are the three of us, reduced to panting whimpers and low moans. She is close, between her thoughts, and her erratic movements, she is seconds away from being flung off the cliff when she lifts.

"I want to watch," she groans, swinging a leg over me and readjusting. When she sits again, her nails claw my stomach, my head is gripped by her thighs.

"Deeper," she commands Cin, who moans, and I have to remind myself not to come yet.

"You look so pretty with our god's cock in your mouth," she repeats back the phrase he used the first time she sucked my dick. He moans and the vibration brings me closer. "Make him come, Cin."

As if on command, I do. Hard and fast. So hard, in fact, my hips lift far off the bed. Cin takes every last drop I give, pumping me with his fist as his tongue circles my shaft. Hypatia has fallen with me. Shaking, wild, riding my fucking face with abandon.

I barely have time to recover when she moves again. My cock is still hard as she wraps her lips around it, sliding her tongue down and then up. I'm certain she'll continue, but she straddles my hips instead. She slips me inside, taking me all the way to the hilt in one go. Sitting up on my elbows, I grab her knee.

"Pain. Pain." I pant, still catching my breath. "Is there any pain?"

She hums. "You always ask." Her head throws back on the stroke back up my cock. "No, you sweet man, no pain, only pleasure. Pleasure you are giving me."

It's enough to satisfy me, and I sit up, grabbing the back of her neck and pulling her in for a kiss. My tongue sweeps in, letting her taste the sweetness of her pussy. She quickens her pace, and I collapse back against the mattress, unable to hold myself up. Hypatia wastes no time rolling her hips, using me. Slow devotion to her lover and her god, her hips the lyrics, her sex the words. I can't take my eyes off her, helplessly under her control, until I smell the familiar scent of almonds. Cin is behind her, rubbing oil just below where she is. Two fingers circle the rim of my ass and I don't know how much more I can take. He pushes one in, then another and I shiver from the sensations. Cin lifts my knees, positioning me how he wants.

"Lean forward, little scribe," Cin instructs, "I'm going to fuck our god while you fuck him."

"Fuck, Cin." I groan and reach for my girl, steadying her, as his cock slips inside. For a moment, I don't know what to concentrate on, him or her. Setting his pace to hers, Cin pulls her back against him as he thrusts, hitting that spot inside me. Each stroke, each thrust sends me to the edge. I shake at the sheer intensity of the feeling.

"Fuck." I can only curse as they work together to bring all three of us to orgasm.

"That's my girl," Cin praises. "Ride his cock, just like that. Make a mess of our god, ruin him for anyone else but us .He reaches between her legs, playing with her clit. Her pussy clenches around me like a vise grip. I catch her staring at me.

"You love it, don't you? Being used by both of us," Hypatia coos as she slows her strokes, prolonging the inevitable and keeping me walking a tightrope. "Don't hold back. Tell us how good you feel having both at once."

Between their words and the feel of both, I surrender. I'm undone, owned entirely by them both. Groans are my only answer as speech evades me; low, deep groans, primitive and needy. Cin increases his speed, his thick cock filling me.

"Gods!" Hypatia cries, clenching from within as her legs shake. "Apollo!" It's a scream, torn from the very core of her.And I fall. Coming with such force, that the world around me shatters to pieces. Golden light radiates into the room, filling every corner. It drips from my fingertips, stretches from each toe. I am no longer a god; I am only ichor and sun and golden liquid light. I'm certain my very soul has been flung from my body and sent into orbit. Space, time, everything suspends until I return to my body.

I don't know how long I lay there, wrung out, unable to move, fucked to the point of ruin. Ruined for anyone else. The room is dark, not even a fire in the fireplace. Light touches of fingertips running rhythmically against my chest brings me back into myself. Hypatia rests beside me, her head nestled on my chest, her fingers drawing shapes. Cin lay snoring, the familiar melody soothing.

She lazily smiles and lays two kisses on my chest, looking up at me. "My Apollo."

I stroke her beautiful face, still flushed from her orgasm. "Your Apollo."

Chapter 30
The Scribe

I don't know what came over me. A hidden part of myself has roared to life, coming to the surface. I keep my eyes closed as my mind catches up to my actions a few hours ago.

I was untethered, a woman in charge of herself demanding what she wanted. From a god. A powerful one.

And I wanted to do it again.

Commanding Apollo, his compliance, fueled my arousal more than anything else could. The way he looked at me, the way Cin did. I was powerful. Belonged. Theirs.

And they are mine.

I roll over, reaching for one but find miles of smooth sheets. Opening one eye, all I see is dark. I roll to the other side, assuming one of my partners has awakened and is roaming the room. It isn't uncommon I am without one, but when my arms again find nothing but smooth sheets, I sit up, suddenly very much awake.

Soft moonlight from the open balcony doors bathes the room, but my men are nowhere to be seen. I haven't been alone in either of their chambers, ever, and the realization is unsettling. Shivering against the lack of warm male bodies, I wrap a robe around myself and go looking for them. I don't have to look long, as I hear Cin's low rumble coming from the open doors.

"Gods be damned."

It's a strained, husky whisper as if he's trying to stay quiet for my benefit, but as I step onto the balcony, I realize it isn't.

Silvery steams of light caress Apollo's body. His wings, half-open, glow with a light all their own. He's on all fours on the lounger, and Cin is behind him. I stand still on the threshold, enraptured by the beauty of the powerful union. Moonbeams highlight every line, every ripple of masculine resplendency as if the celestial body above is just as in awe of them as I am. Cin rocks forward and Apollo's deep, salacious moan sends heat straight to my core.

"Gods," Cin hisses. "Fuck, Apollo. This is what you wanted, wasn't it? Me. You needed me."

His failure to answer is met with a loud, hard slap to his ass. Apollo whimpers.

"Yes, my prince. Fuck! Yes." The settee groans as he pushes his hips back, driving Cin further into him.

Another smack.

"You're taking this cock slow, fucking needy god. You don't deserve a fast fuck. Beg for me. Beg for my cock." He reaches forward, intertwining his fingers with golden curls that glow with a brilliance only a god can produce. Apollo does just that—beg—and my knees almost buckle.

Tugging, Apollo raises to his knees, his back to Cin's front, as the prince—his prince—wraps an arm around. The soft golden glow of Apollo's skin radiates through the dark like the awakening of dawn. Sounds of kisses on skin mixed with heavy breathing leave me frozen in place, just as I was the day I walked in on them. But now, it isn't embarrassment and curiosity that keeps my feet pressed to the marble, but the lustful enjoyment of watching my men together.

Enjoyment . . . and salacious voyeurism.

I move closer, unable to keep my distance. The unencumbered male noises leave me panting for breath, my blood heating in my veins. Neither of them notice me, lost in their passion for each other, so when my fingers skim over Apollo's stomach to Cin's hand, they both gasp.

"Little scribe!" He pants, as Apollo reaches down and grips his partner's hips. "Did we wake you?"

Such an odd question given their current state. Both are breathing heavily, chests heaving in the starlight. The god returns to all fours. His gaze locks with mine from over his shoulder.

My fingers follow Apollo's side, tracing the lines along his sculpted physique. I brush his narrow hips, dancing across the muscles around his ass. In an instant, I'm desperate for them to continue. In all this time, I rarely get to watch them enjoy each other. Cin captures my chin, lifting, forcing me to look at him.

"Enjoying the sight of your men?"

I nod again. "Yes, Cin," I remember to respond, even if it's only a whisper. "I'd like to watch."

"Mmm," he mumbles as he leans over, his lips dangerously close to mine. "I should send you back to bed, force you to fantasize about us." His eyes search mine. "If you stay, I have two rules. Do you think you can be very good and listen, Hypatia?"

The way he says my name sends shocks to the ache between my legs. I rub my thighs together, wanting relief. He moves his hips slowly, and I glance down to his cock moving in and out of Apollo. The smell of the oil they use tickles my nose, filling my senses. The god's shuddered breath tells me he is steadily climbing to the desired precipice. Mesmerized, I can barely tear myself away from their beauty, but when I do, I'm met with dark brown eyes that glimmer in the moonlight.

His tongue darts out before he speaks, and I shiver, remembering exactly what that tongue can do. He thrusts his chin behind me.

"There." His strained command causes my muscles to clench low in my belly. "Sit there. You can watch but only watch. Do not touch yourself." He leans in and pecks a kiss on my lips. "I want you desperate for us when we're done. Obey and you get rewarded. Don't and you'll pay the consequences."

I nod and move to do as he says, but his hand grabs my forearm, halting my steps.

"And, Hypatia." His serious tone makes me turn to look at him over my shoulder. "No using that beautiful mind of yours to distract our god."

I can't help the smirk that grows across my lips. I bite my cheeks to hide it, but it's no use. His Highness knows me too well by now. Inclining my head like the obedient woman he wants me to be, I lower my gaze, but not before I catch Apollo looking in my direction.

"Of course, Cinthus," I say smoothly. "I'm very obedient. I wouldn't dream of disrupting."

All three of us know I'm lying. Apollo hisses, bracing himself against the arm of the furniture. When my bare feet touch the plush rug, the prince has one last direction for me.

"Kneel. Hands in your lap."

Doing as I'm told, I kneel, wiggling into a comfortable position, and placing my palms on my thighs. I meet their hungry looks with one of my own. As Cinthus moves, I watch each flex of his hips, the lascivious dance they have perfected over centuries. They don't rush, taking their time to enjoy each other. I'm consumed by their love. It floats around me in cosmic waves, and I finally understand why these two have lasted as long as they have in this hostile world. Cin strokes Apollo's back, between his wings, in that spot Apollo loves and they spread out, covering much of the balcony in white plumage. Curling inward, he pushes back, driving Cin further in and increasing his speed. His wings flutter, lightly flapping as he gets closer to falling off the edge.

"Not yet," Cin groans. "You come when I say."

They both are moaning, and the rise and fall of each dark vocalization leaves me wanting more. Clutching my thighs, I find myself rotating my hips in time with Cin's strokes. My breath comes in short bursts as I watch. I rock back, trying to find some sort of friction. I'm left wanting as they continue, Cin edging the god even closer while holding him back. Forgetting my instructions for a moment, my fingers find my clavicle. They are cool against my heated skin, and I let out a soft noise as they dance along the edge of my robe, flirting with the trim. When I look up, Apollo is watching me with such intensity that I might burst on the spot.

I'm obeying, My God. I'm being good, just as he wants.

He half-smiles and shakes his head. I glance at the prince, who is busy gripping the god's hips, keeping him walking the knife. Returning to my task, my fingertips float down the opening of my robe to the tie. In a tug, it's open, and I adjust the sides until my body is fully on display, framed in silk. Apollo groans at the sight. I trace the swell of my breast, locking eyes with the god of light.

Is this what you want, My God? To watch me as your prince dominates you?

Another groan and he pushes hard against the arm of the settee. I feel a giggle bubble up, but I press my lips together, keeping it contained. One finger rounds my nipple while the other plays with the opposite side. I don't know how much longer the god of light can hold out. Even in the moonlight, I can tell his knuckles are white as he grips the edge. Down my fingers go, over my stomach, to where I'm needing. Placing one palm on my leg, I spread my knees apart. Finding my clit, I jolt at the first touch.

I can't remember being this sensitive, this slick. Light touches, followed by increased pressure, keep me on edge with them. Cinthus increases his speed, pumping in and out of Apollo in such a demanding way I'm helpless but to ache for a time he is that way with me.

I'm soaked. My fingers glide through my arousal as I stroke down and up. The feeling is euphoric, watching them while I please myself. Tipping my hips so I can tease myself further, I can't help it when my head throws back as I circle my swollen clit.

"Fuck, Hypatia!" Cin scolds, harsh and gravelly. I hadn't realized I'd closed my eyes. Hadn't remembered making any noises to draw attention to myself, but when my eyes snap open, I see him glaring at me.

"Following directions"—he thrusts forward, shoving the god's face into the cushions—"has never been your strong suit, has it, little scribe?"

Caught, I suggestively bite my bottom lip and continue on my path to release. Cin yanks Apollo's hips, slamming into him so hard that their flesh slaps together. It is a punishable rhythm for both the god and me as I struggle to keep up with them, wanting to fall when they do.

"Come, My God. Come for me like the good god you are."

Shuddering, Apollo falls apart, splintering in pieces before me as I hungrily watch. His cries mix with Cin's moans, and I hurriedly stroke myself. I'm almost there, almost to bliss, when I'm roughly hurled to my feet. He is breathing hard; his barreled chest rises and falls in quick succession.

"The things you fucking do to me, Hypatia."

Grabbing my wrist, he slips my fingers into his mouth, rolling his eyes at the taste. His hands shake as they travel down to my ass, hoisting me up in his arms. My legs wrap around him of their own volition, and I kiss his neck as he walks us back inside the room.

I'm thrown with care onto the bed, bouncing once, before scrambling to the center.

"Kneel," Cin growls, grabbing for the cloth in a bowl beside the bed. The sounds of water sloshing come as he wrings out a white cloth, doing his ritual of cleaning between partners while keeping eye contact with me. Moving to the trunk at the end of the bed, he grabs something out. Eagerly, I obey, kneeling on the soft mattress, awaiting my prince. When he joins me, his glare is punishing. "Are you ready?"

The Prince

I am not an ignorant man. I knew as soon as I gave my girl rules, she would break them. In fact, I was anticipating it. Hypatia of Alexandria isn't one for taking orders, even if those orders mean pleasure for her as well. Watching her with Apollo, commanding him, bringing him under her control, I saw the woman she was. The one she hides for fear of retaliation and reprimand in the home of Athena. A woman like my little scribe deserves to be here, with us, where she can be who she was always meant to be. I knew that first night she would be a force to be reckoned with and tonight she proved it, in more ways than one.

She's looking up at me with those darkening eyes filled with lustful thoughts.

Such a brat. *My brat.*

"Close your eyes," I whisper, and she does. Trusting me fully now, giving herself to me to do what I will.

To a point.

I slip the silken tie over her eyes and secure the knot behind her head.

"You wanted to watch, but you wouldn't listen. Let's see how you do when you're denied sight."

A playful smile curls those mauve lips, and I have to keep myself from fucking her as hard as I want to.

Gods, this damn woman.

Apollo glances my way, and I nod. He climbs beside her, and I slip a hand to the back of her neck, pulling her to me. Her little gasp thrills me. Her pillowy lips are inches from my own.

"Gods, Hypatia. I want to punish you for what you do to me," I grit out. "I want to push you to your limits, see how far you're willing to go."

Her pink tongue darts out, wetting that bottom lip. "Then do it, Your Royal Highness."

I don't know who growls, me or Apollo or her. Tonight, I'll learn exactly how much she can take. I'm eager to. I have been waiting for her to meet me here where we can explore the parts of herself that only I can bring to the surface. Grasping her waist, I have her on her back in a flash. She lets out a nervous laugh and reaches for me. Gathering both wrists in my hand, I deny her touch. I run my nose down the side of her cheek as she turns towards me, trying to find my lips. Her heart is thumping so hard, I can feel it in her wrists. She doesn't struggle, but relaxes, letting her body sink into the downy mattress.

Wordless, I trail kisses along her jaw, down her neck. Apollo joins on the other side, and she squirms between us. Her robe falls open, silk fabric laying like colorful wings on either side of her body. She is a vision, ours for the taking. My lips softly touch the rise of her breast as the god pulls her nipple into his mouth. Her little cries are heavenly. Arching her back, her legs shift against the sheet.

"Cin."

"Yes." I drag my tongue along her nipple, teasing it into a tight peak. "Hands above your head, Hypatia. Keep them there, or I'll tie you down."

She gasps, and it sets loose a feral beast screaming to be set free. I take her nipple between my teeth. Apollo sucks the other, easing off, then returning. Her skin turns hot, flushed, as we tease. It reminds me of that first encounter in the bathhouse. But unlike before, she'll get no relief from our torture anytime soon. Kissing further down her body, my lips caress the velvety skin of her belly. Goosebumps appear as downy hairs arise at each soft press of my lips to her skin. Agonizingly slow, I draw circles around her belly button with my tongue. Her groan rumbles through her body, felt all the way down here.

"Cin."

She's becoming desperate with each call of my name, and I revel in the beauty of driving her out of her mind.

Apollo caresses down her thigh, his fingers skimming along like a skater in winter. She's opened her legs to us, inviting us to where she wants us, but I'll not detour. My tongue resumes its slow, deliberate path to her core and her hips rise slightly the closer I get. I nip one hip.

"Gods, please. Please."

"What are you begging for, sweet Hypatia?" Apollo coos, sliding his hands up her body, tracing her curves until he reaches her mouth. He leans in, close enough to kiss her, but refuses. Her whimper spurs me on. Flattening my tongue, I trace the rise of her lower belly to her opposite hip.

We work her into a maddening frenzy. Soft touches, slow caresses, never kissing, never fulfilling any of her wants, always just out of reach. Her body is shaking with need when I finally return to her mouth. I enjoy the parting of her lips.

"Cin," she whispers.

"Shhh," I whisper back. Apollo is pressing soft, feathering kisses into her neck. "You should have listened, little scribe."

Tracing her lips with my finger, I chuckle quietly when her tongue darts out, teasing my finger.

"Now, now. That's cheating," I playfully scold.

"Continue to tease me, Your Highness, and I'll have no choice but to make Apollo come again."

My eyes dart to the god, who is smiling. Touching his temple, we both know he is listening to every cry, every thought she's having. He lets out a half-laugh, and I have to admit, I'm impressed with her tenacity.

This fucking woman.

I'm watching her bloom right before my eyes. Watching her transformation unfold. Something in me snaps to life when I realize she is only submitting to me because she enjoys it. That at any second, she could rise and do as she pleases. A true switch partner who can throw our dynamic into a delicious tailspin if she wants.

At that moment, I've had enough of teasing her. I want her. Apollo leans in, kissing her passionately. Her fingers intertwine in his curls, and I move down, opening her legs, wanting nothing more than to taste her. When I dip my head between her thighs, she rocks against my lips. Licking, sucking, nipping, anything and everything to bring her to the edge as fast and hard as possible.

"Fuck. Gods. Your mouth, sweet Hypatia," Apollo hisses words, and I look over the rise of her hips to find she's taken his cock near to the balls. He has her hair in one hand as she grips his ass. Her other hand finds its way into my hair, holding me to her, refusing to allow me to tease her further. She is effectively keeping her men right where she wants us.

As she bucks against me, I know her orgasm is mounting. I'm no longer satisfied to be only tasting her. I need to feel her around me. In a moment,

I sink into her and that sweet pussy clamps around my cock so tight I fear I might not be able to withdraw. Gripping her hips, I thrust, hard and fast. The control I keep on a tight leash snaps, and I break free. Finally.

I should make her wait, teasing her until she cries with frustration. But I can't. I meant what I said, she is my undoing. I'm teetering on a narrow precipice as Apollo cries out. Untangling, he flops onto the mattress but instead of staying on her back, my scribe rips off the silken blindfold and rises, grabbing my shoulders. Her fingernails dig into my skin.

"I want to watch as you come, Cinthus." Her mouth slams into mine, and I lift her off the mattress, fucking her with such force, I'm afraid I'll bruise her, but I can't stop. I can't slow down. Tasting Apollo's seed on her tongue sends me over the edge, and I increase the already relentless pace. When her walls spasm around my cock, I am lost, screaming out as I pump, determined to release every last drop of cum into her. Her pussy pulses around my throbbing cock and we fall together into whatever bliss this is.

Collapsing still joined, she strokes the sides of my face, running her palms along the crisp hairs of my beard. Her head is on Apollo's middle and he's stroking her hair as she smoothes her hands over my shoulders and down my back.

Our breathing mingles, becoming one, and I rest my forehead on her shoulder. Her legs have wrapped themselves around me. She's cradling me as though I'm fragile.

"You're mine, Cinthus," she whispers. "Always mine."

Chapter 31

The Scribe

I have been soaking in the bathing chamber in my room for around an hour. I mentioned that I needed a soak to ease the tenderness from last night's rather exuberant activities; my men tried to convince me I should bathe in Apollo's bathing chamber. But I know better. One thing would lead to another, and no bathing would occur. I hum a tune I remember my mother singing when I was a girl as I tie my robe and head into my chambers to dress. Sitting at my dressing mirror, I notice my reflection as I unwind my hair from the ivory combs. It falls slightly longer it had at the beginning of the summer.

A smattering of soft freckles dance across my nose. My skin is sun-kissed, my cheeks have a healthy glow to them. I look . . . happier. There is a shine to my eyes, a glimmer I've never seen before. I fiddle with the objects on my dressing table. The perfume Apollo insisted I take. The jade bangles Cin surprised me with. Little trinkets and bobs from the last few months displayed lovingly by someone who cherishes them. Looking around my chambers, more evidence emerges of my time here, of my contentment. Silken robes sewn to my specifications. My once generic bedding now in colors I prefer. An easel stands proud at one end of the room. Cin left some of his brushes and papers so he could paint if the mood struck. A large wooden desk Apollo had specially made for me sits beside it. He had the carpenter make three, so I'd always have a place to work should I need it, no matter whose chamber I happened to be in.

Without my noticing, they have become entangled in my life as much as I am in theirs. My presence is also evident throughout their chambers. Reminders that they are no longer just two, but three.

And I will be leaving. Forced from the only place I have truly felt at home to return to my duties. Melancholy settles in my chest like a damp blanket. It isn't just my men that I don't want to leave. The nymphs and I have become good friends and confidants. I enjoy their daily company. Their antics and relentless gushing over one warrior or another makes me feel as though I belong, that I am a part of something bigger than myself. Even the warriors have come to respect my position and many stop to bow or ask a question. I am teaching again, alight with sharing my knowledge with others. Overcome with the thought of leaving, I let it sit, flicker with pain that cracks deep, deep enough to penetrate my soul. I want to weep, to rail, but I tamp it down, pulling logic around me like a shawl. Pushing it out of my mind, I swing around, intent on the wardrobe.

I dress for the evening meal, choosing a beautiful lavender chiton with stars embroidered along the hem that one of the nymphs gave me. Looping a himation over my shoulders, I pin it at the shoulder, securing it with a leather belt. I pull one end over my hair that I had wound back up when a gentle breeze from the open balcony doors causes something on my desk to flit. I pause mid-motion and gasp when I see it.

Settled atop a stack of scrolls I had begun packing for the library was a single eagle feather.

"No," I said to the empty chamber. "No, no, no!"

Moving fast, I pick it up, wanting it to be an apparition but knowing it isn't. Beside the feather is a small, rolled parchment tied with the signature silver band of Artemis. My hands shaking, I unroll it and try to comprehend her words. I am barely through the first sentence when a cry erupts from deep in the back of my throat. The next thing I know I am in the hallway, rushing toward the prince's chambers, my only thought is finding my men. I need them to wrap me in their collective arms and tell me I can stay. That they need me as much as I need them. I am desperate and on the verge of hysteria as I hurry along the corridor. The sting of tears pricks behind my eyes, and I try to rationalize with logic.

I knew Artemis would come.

I knew this was temporary.

I knew I couldn't stay.

None of that matters now. I am in a fury as I round a corner and run into the middle of a grouping of warriors.

"Lady Hypatia," one says, bowing, his fist to his chest.

A mournful sob releases itself then, stealing my words and liberating the tears I have fought to contain. I touch my fingertips to my lips and try to collect myself enough to speak.

"Lady Hypatia!" another warrior asks, touching my elbow. "What is it?"

Murmuring of deep male voices comes from all sides and I, succumbing to my instant grief at the idea of leaving all this, can do nothing to help my cause save gasp in between racks of sobs.

I am being overly dramatic. I knew this day was coming early in the summer. I had written Artemis not a week ago after my failed attempt at locating a new star and requested she come collect me after the closing ceremonies. It shouldn't be this much of a shock, and yet, here I am, sobbing to the point of frenzy over leaving. I am normally reasonable, and this is an entirely unreasonable reaction to something I knew was coming. Questions come at me rapid fire and two of the men draw swords, ready to fend off the foe that broke my heart open and caused me such distress.

Someone mentions the prince, and I feel the familiar beat of footfalls against the marble.

How can I leave when I know one of my loves by the vibrations of his foot striking marble?

Catching sight of him above the head of one of the warriors, I do the most dramatic thing of all. I sprint to him. To safety. To the arms I need around me. Slamming into him, my arms find themselves around his waist, and my head smacks into the leather of his breastplate. It is enough to knock him off balance, and he rocks with the force. He had drawn his sword when he heard the sobs, but his blade drops, the steel clanging against the marble, when I collide with him.

"Hypatia. Gods! Hypatia, what is it?" His hand is on the back of my head, cradling me close. "What is it?"

A warrior answers, then another, and the growl that rumbles up from his chest vibrates against my tear-soaked cheek.

"What happened? Someone tell me this instant!"

"We don't know, Your Royal Highness," someone says.

"She was crying when she came round the corner, Your Highness, already upset," another chimes in.

"Hypatia." His voice lowers as he tenderly cups my cheeks and brings my head up. I try to speak once more, but it is no use. I am reduced to a lachrymose woman, my heart pierced as though with a sword. "Did someone hurt you?"

I shake my head and shudder another tearful cry. He scoops me up into his arms and carries me down the corridor. Burying my face in the leather, I cling to him like a lifeline.

Apollo! I scream in my mind. Clutching the pendant, I remember he enchanted and call for him. *Apollo! Apollo! APOLLO!*

Cinthus is partway to his chambers when a flash of light sparks into the hall, stopping Cin in his tracks.

"Cinthus! What the hell is the matter?" the god roars.

"I found her like this."

At the sight of him, the tears, which were calming, start again. I take in a shaky breath, reaching for him, wanting him to know I can't be without either. Transferring me from one set of muscular arms to the other, my two lovers surround me, and I feel safe for the moment. Seconds later, we are in Apollo's chambers, the god having moved us from the hall. Sitting in one of the loungers, he gathers me into his lap, wrapping his arms and wings around us.

I have never been dramatic. And yet this—being told where I was to go, when I was to leave, where I was to live—having no way to voice my choice is turning my normally sensible mind to cinders. Logic has disappeared and, in its place, only desperation to be with them.

"Hypatia," Apollo tried to soothe me, removing the edge of himation from my hair and gently untwisting my bun.

"Please, my love, tell us," Cin says in Mycenaean, a language I haven't heard in centuries. Our ancient language, from our human lives. I snap my eyes to his distressed face, followed by Apollo's, who looks equally as upset. Cin has never called me by any term that could be an endearment. He has stuck strictly to little scribe or my name, but knowing I am out of time, that I will soon be without them, the thought of not hearing little scribe almost sends me into another fit. I wipe my tears with my hand. It feels as though a weight is pressing against my chest and my attempts to draw breath are met with heavy resistance. Apollo offers me water from a chalice, and I sip, letting the cool liquid slide over my tongue and down my throat.

"What is wrong, Asteria? We are both out of our minds with worry." Apollo is rubbing my back, keeping me in this soothing place where I can finally vocalize why I acted the way I did, why I lost hold of my senses. I hold out my hand and slowly open my palm.

"Artemis is coming." Fresh tears flow; my voice thickens as I hold the flood gates at bay. "I have days left and I—I don't want to go. I can't go back to the Tellus Province, to Athena's, to my duties. I want to stay. Please, please, Apollo"—I sniff and wipe the tears with the back of my hand—"I want to stay."

Chapter 32

The Scribe

Hours have passed since Cin found me sobbing hysterically in the corridor. I calmed down considerably when the god of light agreed that I could stay and would personally ensure that Artemis sees reason, especially since I now desire the same things they do. How could I want anything else? Apollonion is my home, my refuge, where I feel the most at home. We will need to find a way for me to maintain my duties at the library while remaining under the same roof as the men who hold my heart, but that can come later. Apollo refused to leave the chambers after I settled, so tonight, at least, we feast together casually—which, for my men, means sans clothing. I recline on the bed at the foot, admiring them as they once again fight over food. This time, it is lamb.

Cinthus grabs my calf as he swats at the dish Apollo holds aloft, stabbing at the air, hoping to steal a piece of meat from the god of light. Laughing at their playfulness, my heart soars, knowing Apollo will do exactly as he said and keep me.

"Now, now, it's his, Cinthus," I chide. He scowls and attacks my toes, tickling the arch and causing me to squeal, kicking as I squirm away.

"Hey!" Apollo protests, wiggling out of bed. "I am a starving man and you two almost upset my dinner." He stabs a sizable chunk of lamb and holds it out like a trophy. Cinthus swiftly rushes off the bed and bites the hunk off the end of the fork. The shocked gasp from both Apollo and me sends us into a fit of laughter. The prince preens as he chews, proud of himself and his spoils.

I love this side of them, the men they are when we are allowed to be just us. Cin rounds the edge of the bed and produces a hunk of lamb that he promptly gives up to the god.

"I wouldn't want you to starve," he says, placing the meat in the open mouth of his lover and kissing him softly on the cheek.

With the evening meal finished—or devoured—the tray of food resembles a ransacked citadel of Troy more than mere remnants of our dinner. The two men lounge in bed at the head while I settle in between them at the foot. Apollo reads aloud from one of his scandalous books, and I doodle my favorite math equations on an old scroll. How he can read such deliciously salacious material with a straight face is worthy of study. I am content to do nothing more than admire their power and beauty on display.

Sculpted chests and arms as though carved from marble. Defined abs and toned legs. They are living, breathing works of art. But my favorite parts of them are at their hips. A soft line of muscle low on their bellies forms a ridge that narrows to perfect v's, pointing toward their cocks, but it is that space between where their hips joined that holds me mesmerized.

"You're staring, little scribe," His Majesty interrupts Apollo, who glances over the edge of his book.

"Always," I say with a wry smile, unbothered by their noticing. Touching my hip, I hold their collective gaze. "Here. My favorite part of you both. What would that be called?"

Apollo grins and touches the prince at that spot. "I call it my Apollo's belt."

"You named Cin's body parts? Scandalous." Giggles bubble up.

He leans towards me and arches a brow. "I've named my favorite parts of you."

"You impertinent man!" I slap my hand to my chest. "What names?"

Cin's low chuckle warms the room with its merriment. The god leans forward, touching one of my breasts, and lets a wicked smile slide across his lips.

"Mine." He touches the other. "Mine. And"—sliding his hand to between my legs, he lightly touches me through the fabric, and I take in a sharp breath—"Mine."

He kisses my lips, falling back against the pillows.

"Poor Cin." I pout. "He didn't get an opportunity to name a part."

Lowering his chin, my other partner's eyes are dark, hooded. "Oh, little scribe, do not mourn for me. I am a man who shares with his lover. What's his is most certainly mine as well."

My jaw drops at their flirtatious nature, and I gasp as if scandalized. I shall never leave them now; my adoration for them is too strong. Smiling at them, a silly idea pops into my head, and I crawl up closer, bringing the quill and ink with me. Dipping the nib, I start at his knee, drawing up the prince's well-defined form.

The ink leaves scrolling black lines across his perfect skin. The nib catches on the tiny hills and valleys, imperfections in the otherwise unmarred golden-brown canvas of his thigh. His muscles contract the closer I bring the quill to his rather awake endowment that sits atop a finely sculpted nest of crisp hairs. It moves, and Cin grunts.

"What are you doing?" He stretches lazily as Apollo puts the book down. Months ago, the sight of the two of them would have sent a blush coloring my cheeks. But this evening, their nakedness is as familiar as my own. Although, I still feign modesty in the sheer night dress. The light fabric slips from my shoulder as I prop myself up between them. Finding the inkpot, I again dip the quill, watching the ink drip before continuing to draw on His Majesty.

"I'm marking you as Athena marks her warriors," I say, watching my hand create dark swirls along his stomach. Apollo leans over to investigate my handy work.

"If you are to claim him, Hypatia, I would grow jealous if I wasn't next."

Cin ruffles his curls, and Apollo kisses my exposed shoulder.

When did *we* become an *us*?

I can't imagine my life without these two, without their affection, without their protection, without being theirs. And yet we haven't been together long, but the ease we share is peaceful and lovely—home.

My home. Finally belonging.

My quill glides along the prince's bicep to his forearm, skipping over the prominent veins and strong fingers. Dipping the quill once more, I follow the path of Cin's hand, to Apollo. The men have entangled their hands and arms until it is hard to tell who ends and who begins. My quill pauses at Apollo's ribcage, ink dripping from the sharpened nib as I realize how in love I am with them. Equally. It's as if my heart has two chambers beating simultaneously for each of them. The ink drips again and Apollo scowls as it slides down to the bedclothes, staining the sheet with a black spot.

"My dear Asteria," he begins, intent on playfully scolding me, but he stops, as I'm sure my face is telling the truth of my thoughts. It's overwhelming, this realization, and I can do nothing but confess.

"I love you," I say softly to both. "Both of you. I love you both, desperately."

They look at each other and then at me. Seconds tick by, but I'm confident in my declaration. I don't need them to reciprocate my feelings. I don't want false expressions. I know what I'm doing, giving my heart away this way, but I'm freely doing it all the same. I have no grandiose ideas of what we are outside these chambers. I am still a scribe, a lower station than either, but it matters not. I want none of the conventions of what most women seem to want. I want them.

Simply. Together. Us.

Apollo moves first and captures my lips. His kiss burns me.

"Hypatia," he murmurs before His Majesty's lips are on my neck, my cheeks.

"You are ours, Hypatia," Cin says, cupping my face. "Can you not see? We are the ones in love with you."

He places his forehead to mine as Apollo rests his head on my shoulder.

"I am in love with you, little scribe. *My* little scribe."

Pecking his lips with a tender kiss, I grab both of their hands, running my thumb along the palm of one and my fingers caress the knuckles of the other.

"I have loved you long before you came here, Asteria. For centuries." Apollo traces his fingers along Cin's jawline. "We were a we, but you have made us an us."

My eyes fill with tears for a completely different reason, and I'm overcome with joy that swells in my heart to near bursting. They love me. *Me.* It is impossible, this love, as convention is usually very much a coupling, but these two are the equal parts of me, my other halves. My very soul must have been made of two pieces, because I feel it fall into place, finally whole.

"Can you mark me, Apollo?"

He is looking at me with love in his eyes, but it fades some, and he shakes his head as if he didn't hear me. "I beg your pardon?"

"Athena marks her warriors. Ares marks his as well. I want nothing more than this, than us. I never needed fancy palaces and lavish things. I only want you. Both. I want Olympus to know who I belong to, who has my heart. Can you mark me like other gods?"

I don't know if he has this ability or even if it's possible. All I know is if the warriors bear marks to the god they vow loyalty to, then I could can do the same with the one I love.

He sits up fully, and crooks a finger under my chin, forcing me to look at him. "Are you sure?"

I nod and smile. "I want to be yours, Apollo, in every way."

"Mark me as well," Cin says, kissing my cheek. "There isn't any doubt as to who I belong to. I am forever yours, Apollo, forever loyal. But I am also yours, my love," he says the last part in Mycenaean, and it causes tears to spill their banks. *My love.* "Mark me for both of you."

Apollo sits staring at us for several long seconds before a lopsided grin curls the edges of his perfect mouth. He kisses me first, then Cin.

"Where would you like it?" he asks the prince first.

Thinking for a moment, he looks down. "My chest, over my heart."

Apollo's hand glows gold, rays of light gathering in his palm. He splays his hand on Cin's pectoral, right over his heart. The prince hisses, letting out a little curse, breathing heavy against the pain, buying his time until his god removes his hand. Once his hand moves, golden markings stay. Tattooed into his skin is a sun intertwined with a moon, the symbol of the Cosmis Province. Surrounding the celestial bodies are stars, points of golden light etched onto the outer surface of his heart. Going through the middle, however, is a sword that looks like the one Cin carries. I sit up and begin gathering the edge of the nightdress.

"Where would you like it, sweet Hypatia?"

Fisting the fabric, I expose my thighs.

"Here," I say, touching my right. "Mark me here."

When Apollo touches me, the warmth from his hand radiates into my bones. It's gentle at first, but soon, searing pain follows, and I steady myself against it. My thigh feels as though it is on fire, and I wonder how much more I can bear. As he lifts his hand, the golden tattoo emerges. The same depiction of the stars and sword, the same moon and sun intertwined, but mine also has an arrow piercing through as if shot.

I am theirs; forever marked by our love.

Chapter 33

Three days have come and gone. Apollo said the other morning he sent word that I was staying, and I'm starting to believe Artemis will allow it. Being her right hand has been my title, scribe my job, but here is where I belong. It's well into the afternoon, and Apollo and Cin have been in a council meeting for hours. There is discord among a few of the warrior companies, minor infractions that need addressing, and then the installation of the new Epsilon warrior, all needs to take place before Apollo can close out the solstice festivities. I was surprised to hear Athena had found an elite warrior so quickly. Cinthus and I discussed this at length two nights ago after the evening meal, with Apollo giving his opinions freely.

I enjoy discussing the inner workings of the palace with them and it makes me love them all the more that they entertain my thoughts on such subjects. I am valued for more than our lustful joining. They see me as an equal. It gives me insights into how they think as well, and I'm constantly impressed with Cinthus and Apollo's diplomatic approach that leads to fair outcomes.

There is a reason the Cosmis Province is rarely involved in dramatic altercations with other provinces in the empire. Apollo and Artemis govern with their people in mind. One more reason I feel at home here: It reminds me of Alexandria. Of my time as a human—well, mortal human.

The nymphs invaded the archives earlier, chattering on about tonight's festivities. Closing ceremonies are upon us, and they're trying their best to secure a warrior or two for the evening. There will be dancing, of course, wine by the barrels, and rumor has it my god will sing and play.

After taking inventory of my gowns and determining I need something different, I find myself in one nymph's chambers decimating her wardrobe. She once lived with Ares and Aphrodite, and several of her chitons reflect it. Two such dresses catch my eye. One fits me like a glove, and I can't wait to wear it tonight. But one I currently have on has me tossing my head a little higher than usual. It is a soft blue, the color of Apollo's eyes, and falls to a respectable length. Tying it at one shoulder, I fix a brass pin to keep it secure. But it is the long slit up one side, giving glimpses of my tattooed thigh when I move, that sends a thrill through me. It is unlike any dress I've worn before, and I am sure my men will enjoy the flashes of gold ink that marks my skin.

Marks me as theirs.

Wanting to show off the garment, I seek them out. Never mind, they are in an endless meeting filled with warriors and councilmen. Never mind, I am meeting them in a few hours to enter the dining hall for the closing ceremony festivities. I am brimming with a confidence I haven't known before, one that won't wait.

Nodding to the guard outside the room, I open a side door and slip inside.

Grumblings from a company of warriors greets me.

"My God, consider your position," a council member scolds with a reproachful tone.

Apollo waves a hand, annoyed. "I am not to be swayed, councilman. He was in the right. Next."

Papers shuffle and more grumblings come up, opposition to whatever was decided upon, I assume.

Apollo and Cin sit side by side at a long marble table on the floor. The throne sits several stairs above them. A not-too-distant memory floods me of my god and I standing on those stairs and greeting villagers for the Solstice Feast, and now here we are in a last meeting. The quickness of how this is all ending is dizzying. My time on Olympus sometimes feels endless and eternal, and yet these last few months have flown by like the wings on Hermes' sandals.

His throne room is used for many things, but a large gathering room for villagers and warriors alike is its most common. Golden banners still hang on either side of the long, gold-trimmed, white runner. The atmosphere is still lively. The room is still grand.

Cin notices me and nods as I move to stand on one side. A company of warriors, smaller than the rest, gestures to one another and moves closer. Cin is first to make sharp movements with his fingers, followed by longer ones. Touching his cheek and forehead with crisp, jerking motions, he points to himself and then Apollo. The god follows, after a response from one warrior, speaking with his hands. I realize the company is without hearing and is communicating through gestures. I have heard of sign language but have never seen it used where both parties understood one another. Mainly I've seen the deaf person trying to communicate and others becoming frustrated when they couldn't communicate back.

The silence in the room is calming, several warriors nodding in agreement with what is being said. One warrior makes a flat sound and gestures again. Apollo responds and Cin writes something down. I watch, mesmerized by them, and make a mental note for the two to teach me. If I am to stay, I need to know how to communicate should I come across other such warriors.

"Agreed," Apollo says, turning to the councilmen seated on his left. "We have the wood and brass for new weapons, councilmen?"

They answer in the affirmative with nods and grunts.

"Votes?"

All hands raise unanimously and the company each salute one by one; First Apollo, then Cin.

"Next," Apollo calls out, shuffling papers.

When he looks up, he catches me staring and smiles. *Gods of the Asphodel Fields!* He is so very beautiful when he smiles. His golden curls are tossed today as if he has run his fingers through them multiple times. My fingers dance, twisting imaginary curls around the knuckles as I did last night, his head in my lap, listening to me read from one of my favorite books.

"Madam."

A member of the council I don't recognize waves at me. I don't recognize the sash he wears. It's not like the ones worn by council members that are decked out in dark blue with stars; his has waves of fading blue, like a rolling sea. He's hissing a whisper at me as his hands flail in my direction and he moves closer.

"You need to remove yourself." He waves me toward the door I came from, scowling. "These meetings don't allow nymphs."

Straightening my spine, I stand my ground. "I am not a nymph, sir," I whisper back, thinking that will be the end of it. I was wrong.

"Human, then?"

I nod, keeping my eyes on my men. They are discussing something with another company of warriors.

"Fine. You need to leave. You aren't to be in these meetings."

I eye him. "Because I am human? Or because I'm a woman?" I turn to address him, my chin rising in defiance.

"Women need to be preparing for this evening, madam. This meeting is for warriors and councilmen only, of which you are neither."

"Women belong in all rooms of the palace, councilman," I retort. I don't know if it is the dress or my relationship with my men, but the woman I was months ago would have left the room when told. Obeyed without resistance. The woman I am now will do no such thing, and I'll defy anyone who tries to make me.

"Madam." His whisper is harsher, a warning wrapped in a formal address.

"Hypatia, dear, please come before the council."

Apollo's commanding tone ripples through me like sultry waves. My feet move, and I toss the arrogant councilman a look as I make my way to the front. His lip curls as I pass. Once before them, I bow, placing a hand over my heart in salute.

"My God," I say with my head still lowered. "Your Royal Highness. Councilmen."

"I wanted the council to be aware of a change I've made to the map of Cosmis Province." He waves a hand, and a large map magically unfurls before the room. Apollo keeps his eyes on me, and I do my best to calm my nerves. I may not be trembling like the first night in the dining hall, but I would still prefer to observe from the back.

"I draw your attention to the name of the hills." His voice might carry in the room, but he is addressing me.

Looking up, I quickly find the place and stare in disbelief. Scrolled across a drawn depiction of the hilled area at the foot of the Hyperion mountain, the mountain Apollonion sits atop, are the words *Hills of Asteria*. My mouth opens, but no words come. When I finally look at the both of them, they have sat back in their chairs proudly.

"From here on, the hills will be known as the Hills of Asteria." His eyes turn soft, cloud-like. "Named for the woman who's captured my heart."

A rumble behind me should send a blush to my cheeks. Apollo has not only named a place after me, but he has, in one sentence, declared to all in the palace I am of importance. Making them bow under threat is one thing. Giving me a position is entirely another.

"A scribe cannot hold a title." The sharp cry comes from behind, and I resist the urge to turn and see if it is the councilman from earlier. When he steps beside me, I realize it isn't. "As I told you months ago, My God—"

"As I told you, councillor, I don't need your permission." Apollo's words fall heavy in the room, a warning.

"You cannot bestow a goddess' name to just anyone, particularly one who is—" Another councillor has joined the opposition but snaps his mouth shut when Apollo turns his glare down the table.

"Asteria was the goddess of the falling stars, was she not?"

More male grumblings.

"They killed her during the great war when many gods lost their lives, yes gentlemen?" Two nod, but most stay silent. "Then it stands to reason that honoring her is long overdue. Hypatia studies our heavens, maps the stars, and has single-handedly curated the library. The very one that holds all knowledge and history and furthers the advancements of our great empire." He looks down one side of the table and then the other, challenging anyone to defy him. "She is intelligent and kind and embodies the goddess of old. Naming the hills is an honor to both."

Cin glares at the room, daring them to object, and it dawns on me as it never has before, just how much power the two of them exude together. They are magnificent as individuals. A god and a prince, both willing to do what needs to be done for the part of the empire they govern. Together, they are a force driven by purpose and compassion. And both are ready to defend me at any given moment. I shouldn't want that. I should insist on defending myself. I should see their displays as overtly masculine and scold them or rebuff their attempts, but it has the opposite effect. It emboldens me.

Smiling sweetly, I turn to the councilman in question.

"My dear sir," I say, my tone thick as honey, "it is an honor, do you not agree?"

Both of them are watching me intently. Without turning, I know Apollo has a prideful, lopsided smirk plastered across his face. While Cin is studying me with dark eyes, taking in my every move, every word.

"An honor to be named for an old goddess? Hardly. A scribe who knows her place wouldn't entertain such a notion as to have her name forever tied with a goddess."

I let silence fall between us. Let the councilman believe he has me feeling remorseful. I bite my tongue, keeping the retort behind my teeth, biding my time. Softening my face, I lower my head as though shame has set in. Moving to stand between them, I place a hand on each shoulder and lift my chin. The room is watching, holding its collective breath, waiting to see how I react. Ready to write me off as hysterical if I rail and frail if I concede. I know it all too well. I am no longer the woman I was, and being here is the reason for it.

"You are right, councillor; I do know my place. It will forever be between the god of light and his prince. Immortalized now with a name Apollo bestowed upon me. I am a scribe, but I am also Asteria. The Scribe of Asteria."

"My Asteria," Apollo states, taking my hand and kissing the palm.

"And mine." His Royal Highness places an arm around my waist, and I catch a smug glimmer in his eyes when he relaxes back into his chair.

"I move for her official title to be changed." Apollo's voice rings in the quiet room.

"Second." Cin is quick to respond. "Move to vote." Five councilmen answer in the negative, and I wonder if there will be retaliation for my two men later. But seven answer in the affirmative, acknowledging me in my new position. Whatever feeling the nays have, they'll keep it to themselves now that the majority has ruled.

I feel it then, the snap of pride becoming self-assuredness. I know at that moment I have changed. With a finger slipped under the god's chin, I force him to look at me. The room around us is deadly still, waiting.

Tell them to go, Apollo.

"Dismissed," he says huskily, his eyes locked with mine.

"My God, I must insist," one councilman protests, but the god cares not. "We still have the installation of the Epsilon warrior and new business to attend to. My God, we must continue."

Rising, his lips find mine, kissing me as if we are alone. I don't know how long it takes for the room to clear. Or even when it does. I just know when I come up for air after kissing him back, the room is empty save my men.

Chapter 34

The Scribe

After what happened in the throne room, I fight the urge to take them both in that very room. A change has come over me, and I welcome it. No longer will I allow my life to be determined by others. I will fight for the very things I want.

I have dressed for the evening when two nymphs enter my chambers and stop dead in their tracks.

"Evening, ladies. Oh, you look beautiful."

And they did. Both in lovely chitons, decked out in their finest jewelry. I am proud to call them both friends.

"Gods damn, Hypatia," one exclaims when she sees me.

"Shit," the other says. "We had thought to ask if you wanted to borrow a dress, but it looks as though you have that part covered."

I glance down at the chiton I'm wearing. It is a deep blue at the top that fades to a soft purple at the bottom, like a deepening night sky—embroidered with stars and pearls that run along the hem. A series of knots tied in fabric form a ladder from the bottom of my spine, below my hips, to my shoulders. The fabric then twists to form two straps that holds the bodice in place, allowing a line from my clavicle to below my breastbone to be bare. Lower than any dress I have ever worn, the bodice accentuates my breasts perfectly and my skin glows rosy from the oil I used after my bath.

I applied color to my cheeks and lips and tied half my hair back with the ivory combs, with the rest flowing below my shoulders. I even went so far as to adorn myself with the jewelry of my lovers. The crown on my head, the necklace around my neck, bracelets made of jade on one wrist, the golden cuff on the upper portion of my opposite arm; I look regal.

Like a goddess.

They admire me for several more seconds before I feel the familiar sting of a blush on my cheeks.

"It's borrowed. I didn't have it made, if that's what you're wondering," I quickly explain, as if I need to. I don't, but I am suddenly very self-conscious of my choice. "Perhaps I was too bold and should change."

The first shakes her head. "Nonsense. You look—we should go. You wouldn't want to be late."

I move and they both gasp.

"You're marked!" one exclaims.

I forgot this dress has splits in the fabric on both sides, so every move exposes one thigh or the other. My tattoo glimmers in the light, shining as it peeks out from the garment. Reaching down, I run my hand over the marking.

"Yes," I say with a smile, "I'm marked."

"No wonder he calls you Asteria."

Sighing loudly, I say, "I suppose everyone in the palace knows what happened this afternoon, then?"

"Of course," the other says with a shrug, looping her arm through mine and leading me into the corridor. "News like Apollo renaming the hills and honoring you stayed in the hall only as long as the men were also in the hall. The palace buzzed with the news the moment the men were dismissed.

"The men are terrible gossips," the first chimes in, and we all laugh. It is true, of course. People always accuse women of spreading gossip, but in my experience, men talk just as much, or even more in some cases. They can't wait to chatter on about how Apollo had kicked everyone out while kissing me and then speculate as to what happened after the last of them left. Of course, only the three of us know the truth. I gently scolded him for doing such a thing such as renaming a whole portion of the province without first approval of the council, and he and Cin held their ground, insisting I was being too cautious. Then I excused myself to dress for dinner.

The rumor mills will have us in tawdry positions, but the truth is much more boring. I am beginning to see the merit in the tawdry positions.

Rounding the corner, we come to a grouping of warriors who part to let us pass. I can feel my cheeks burn as they eye us. By the time we turn down the next corridor, I decide to worry less about the stares of random men and more about the stares of just two.

We part ways, and the nymphs enter the dining hall, each on the arm of rather handsome warriors, while I continue to the private dining room of the god of light. A guard bows as I enter, but not before his gaze travels the length of me stopping at my thigh. Upon my entrance, my men are arguing with the councillor.

"Fine, councillor, you win," huffs an exasperated Apollo as he takes a large gulp of wine. "We shall install the Epsilon warrior tomorrow morning after the morning meal."

"It was supposed to be done today, My God. Putting it off any longer would be an affront to Athena and our province."

"I already declared you the winner, councillor. No reason to continue beating this dead horse." His voice trails off as he turns and catches sight of me. Suddenly unsure, I clasp my hands in front.

I've never seen a god speechless. He stares for several pregnant seconds, then, in an unrefined manner, turns Cin bodily around to face me, all while keeping his eyes locked with mine. The prince's jaw drops, literally.

He stands gaping, his dark eyes wide, and staring. Even the councillor has grown quiet.

"Evening, gentlemen," I mumble as I bow and salute. "Are you ready to go in?"

"Dismissed," Apollo says out the side of his mouth. "Fuck—everyone. Hypatia, the gods be damned."

I can't tell if it is approval or shock that holds him to the marble and, not knowing causes my fingers to twist in my opposite palm.

"I can go change if—if—"

"If you take the dress off, we shall not make it to the evening meal," Cin rumbles darkly. I let out a little half-laugh and run my hand down the softly flowing fabric. Someone hisses, sucking in air through their teeth.

"Oh, yes. My mark." Parting the dress, I show off my golden tattoo. "I thought you'd approve, My God."

Cin grips the leather chair at the end of the table, his knuckles turning white. "We can't allow her to enter the hall," he says without blinking, and Apollo sharply nods.

"Agreed."

"Excuse me?" I snap and march towards them. "I've taken care choosing my ensemble, and I'm quite proud of it. You won't dictate where I can and cannot go. Because I am marked, I'm now property?"

"It'll be a bloodbath." Cin's expression is so dark that it gives me pause.

Apollo bites into his bottom lip. "Many will have to die."

I press a finger into both their chests. "What are you two going on about?"

Cin caresses my arm, his fingers gliding over my soft skin to my hand, where he laces those fingers through mine. "You are a vision, little scribe. If you enter that dining hall, I will be forced to reduce our numbers."

The god nods as he reaches for my waist. "I can't take my eyes off you. Any man who merely looks at you this evening runs the risk of invoking my jealousy."

They are staring at me as if any minute I will find myself on my back being devoured.

Oh! A blush colors my cheeks. "So, you like the dress then?"

They continue touching me, running their hands over my arms, my shoulders, my waist, as if at any moment I'll vanish before their eyes. It is quite exhilarating. Trying my best to ignore the flush that travels down my body at each stroke of their hands, I clear my throat.

"Gentlemen, we shouldn't keep our guests waiting."

One of them groans in protest. When Cin's fingers find their way to my back, I believe for a moment he will come apart at the seams. He steps closer, his hand shaking as it stalls. He caresses several knots one at a time, following the line down my spine.

"I borrowed this from a nymph who was employed under Aphrodite for a time." Apollo stops listening and presses kisses into my bare shoulder. "It's a bit more daring than what I usually wear, but I thought I'd like to be more daring this evening."

"Are you aware of what you're doing to us? I don't know that either of us will be able to perform any duties tonight with you in this." Apollo trails kisses up my neck, and I briefly wonder if a meal is even necessary.

"She knows exactly what she's doing, don't you little scribe? Driving us to the point of insanity is her specialty," he responds, still mesmerized by the series of knots at my back.

"I believe she called the knots and ties shibari," I say over my shoulder to Cin.

"I'm well aware of what they're called, Hypatia. I just never imagined you in something designed with them."

Boldness, from either the dress itself or the power I feel when I'm with them, comes over me, and I grab Cin's chin. "Be good, Your Royal Highness, and maybe I will let you show me the extent of your knowledge on the subject."

He groans deep within his chest when I kiss his lips. Breaking from them, I step forward. We will never enter the hall at this rate, and I can't let the god and his prince not appear on the last night of the celebration. It is their duty, and if I'm to stay, mine as well.

"Come along, gentlemen, we must go in."

Hours later, the meal is eaten, and my men have quite possibly been driven mad like they said, because every move I make has them responding with hands that roam. Cin is sitting back in his chair, his one glass of wine drank.

"I have to ask, Cinthus," I begin. He lifts an eyebrow and runs a knuckle over the arm of his chair. "I've been awfully curious about something."

"I have no answers, I'm afraid." He leans in. "All I can think about is slipping you out of that dress, little scribe."

I take the opportunity to tease. "That was the plan, Your Royal Highness," winking for good measure. I toss my chin at his abandoned chalice. "Why only one glass of wine in the evening?"

He sighs, long and heavy, and picks up the glass in question, studying it before setting it back on the table. "My father was a drunk, little scribe. A destructive alcoholic who let his love of the drink rule his judgment. He was a tyrant and fueled by alcohol made him nothing more than cruel to my mother, myself, and my siblings. He was a rotten hearted man and I hated him. But I was the favored son, the firstborn, the prince meant to carry on the family legacy." He turns to look at me and the far-off gaze that shades his expression squeezes my heart. I place my hand over his.

"I was betrothed before Apollo stole me. A marriage to benefit two kingdoms, the union decided when I was six years of age. But when I fell in love with Apollo, they cast me out and whipped me for daring to reject my destiny. Daring to go against my father's wishes."

I glance at the god and then at my prince, squeezing his hand, lending my support in the only way I know how.

"I was to carry on the family line. Marriage and children were my only worth, according to my father. Loving Apollo wasn't something he could abide, because loving the god meant I was no longer a son who could give him heirs. He didn't care who I fucked, so long as it was occasionally a woman. All he wanted was to ensure the lineage of our monarchy, and I failed him when I fell in love. I was a stud horse, Hypatia, and that was all. Worth nothing if I couldn't fulfill that role." He sighs again and I thread my fingers through his. "But here, I am Apollo's. I'm free and without the guilt my father put upon me. I am respected by the court and loved"—he kisses my knuckles—"by two strong individuals."

"Do you want children, Cin?" I have given little thought to the idea of children. My duties in the library keep me busy and, with only one other experience outside of these two, the notion was abstract at best. I don't want any for years yet, if ever. I am content to be just us. Until now, I hadn't considered the idea, but even so, I'm not ready.

He shakes his head. "I can't sire them, Hypatia. After my punishment for falling in love with Apollo, my father gave me wine laced with an herb that made me sterile. If I couldn't give him a secure line, I was denied any ability at all. It was then Apollo stole me away to here, to Apollonion. He was afraid my father would try to kill me, given the chance. He may have if I had stayed."

His story pricks my soul. How anyone could be so cruel to such a loving, wonderful man makes me ache. I want to pull him into my arms, surround him with my love, and tell him I am here. That I care for him. Love him. He touches my cheek.

"Do you want children, Hypatia?"

I shake my head. "Not now. Not anytime soon. I'm content with how we are, Cin. How we love. I love us. Just us."

His smile is so heartbreaking that I give in and pull him to me, kissing his cheeks, then his lips. He sighs again, but this time it isn't heavy; it's lighter, as though, by telling me, a weight has lifted from his chest.

"And that's why you only have one glass."

He nods and stabs the last of the meat on a silver tray. "I refuse to be like him." He puts the hunk in his mouth, chewing slowly.

"You're better than he ever was, Cinthus." His eyes meet mine and they soften. "You are the better man."

He kisses my lips again and sits back in his chair, a warm smile across his bearded face. Resting my head on his shoulder, I let the moment sink into our bones. Lively dancers twirl around the room in a rousing commotion while Cin and I sit in comfortable silence.

I am sitting in my chair at the high table as Apollo takes his position with other musicians. The lyre rests comfortably in his hands, and he relaxes into the seat, content with the instrument he is proficient at.

The first note plucked from the strings hums through me in a wave of intense, captivating pleasure. I can't tell if Apollo is using magic to direct the notes, but each one seems to bend and float around every cell in my body until I feel as though I am the one plucked and not the lyre. I cross my legs, the tattoo glimmering in the candlelight overhead, and clutch my thighs together. When his voice rings out, clear and achingly beautiful, I grip the edges of the table. My fingernails bite into the wood.

The music swells and his voice dances across the room on ethereal wings. Airy and gentle, ebbing and flowing around all in the hall. His velvet notes caress my skin, and I'm weightless, caught between each rise and fall without an anchor. Closing my eyes, I let the song envelop me in warmth and light. The hum of the strings moves through his words, pointed and direct. I lose myself to the music, forgetting the hall is full to the brim with warriors and villagers. Warmth spreads through me and the waves of melody and notes mix within my blood, heating it and making my heart ache. The last note is still vibrating along my spine when Apollo touches my hand.

"Dance with me."

The tempo increases, and other dancers take to the floor. My hands shake, and I know he can tell how overcome I am, even though I try to hide it. Apollo stands smiling, hand outstretched, and that moment steals my heart. Forever his.

"I'm terrible at—"

"I care not. Dance with me." Undeterred, he grabs my hand. "Please, my sweet Hypatia."

I melt, dissolving into a puddle of silly feelings that tumble around inside me. Placing my hand in his, I allow him to lead me to the center of the floor. It is a rarity to see pairs, as most festivities lead to rounds of group dancing, but as I move into his arms, I realize Apollo has orchestrated all this on his own. He signals the musicians, who then begin a song unbound by this realm, a song suspended in the air, carried on a breeze of melody. Apollo places his arms around me, and we move as one, gliding across the marble floor that glitters at our feet as though we glide on glass.

As we move, the dress parts, revealing one thigh, then the other. The god of light shuffles me closer, his hand at my back, just under my shoulder blade, holding me to him, steady and sure. We are one, effortless in the haunting beauty of our movements. The room spins around us, and I can do nothing more than keep my eyes locked with his. There is nothing I want at this moment. No one else but my men.

Rhythms and notes push us along, melodic approval of our symbiotic movements. His lips find my neck as he dips me back, my body parallel to the floor. His firm hands bring me upright and pull me close.

I am light. Air. Wind.

When the music reaches its crescendo, he twirls me round and pulls me close again. Ending with my body pressed to his, the god of light leans down and captures my lips as my heart flutters wildly against my ribs.

"Apollo," I breathe against his lips.

He smiles knowingly, for no words need to be spoken.

Chapter 35

The Prince

She is a vision of pure sensuality and damn Artemis for keeping her locked away for so long. The way she carried herself into the receiving room this evening had both Apollo and I rethinking our last night's festivities. This is my favorite feast of the year, but one look at Hypatia makes me want to lay her out on the table and have my own celebration. Fuck her until all three of us can't walk.

She walked in as though she owned us, and she did, in a way. We were completely hers. Hers to command. Hers to love. Helpless men and happy to be in such a position. Her head was tossed high, and I couldn't help the pride that filled my chest at the knowledge that Apollo and I were privy to her newfound confidence. One that has always been there, just under the surface.

But that dress. I should be arrested and flogged for the thoughts that danced in my head most of the evening. The unique positions. The audience. *Fuck*. Having to sit next to her, watching her mark peek out from the split with each movement, turned me into a desperate man. I couldn't keep my hands off her, nor my eyes. I was happy when she wanted to retire early.

Happy and eager.

On our way to Apollo's series of chambers, she stops at the throne room and slips inside with that wry smile of hers. The two of us follow, weak to her charms. Hypatia is a siren, calling us to our demise, and fuck, if I'm not excited about it.

The room is dark and cold, but with a flick of his wrist, Apollo lights the candles on the chandeliers. Our footsteps fall soft against the marble as we walk the length of the cavernous room. The golden accents scatter about glitter under the candlelight. Hypatia twirls once, then twice, coming up on her tiptoes and returning to the floor. I've counted her cups, and I know she isn't drunk. It's happiness. Filled to the brim, it seems, so much she can no longer contain it.

She is like a dryad, delicate and wistful. It's a side she rarely shows, but it's a side I want to see more of. I want her happiness to overflow like a well-dug spring. She hums as she moves, and I realize I've never heard her sing. It's sweet and soft and surprisingly in tune, mellifluous like her laugh.

"What is that you're humming?" Apollo asks, curiosity getting the better of him.

"Something my mother used to sing to me." Stopping just at the end where the steps rise to meet the dais the throne sits upon, she turns to face us. "I'll admit, I'll be sad tomorrow morning when the villagers and warriors begin making their way back to their homes. It will feel empty when the palace isn't teeming with life, will it not?"

"Mmm," Apollo mumbles, pulling her to him. She giggles and my heart lights in my chest. "But you get to stay. Ours, Hypatia."

Placing her hand on his chest, she pushes back just before the god's mouth claims hers. His wicked smile gives his thoughts away as her teeth sink into that bottom lip, and it's all I can do to keep my whine at bay. Her laugh turns husky, deeper.

"Now, now, My God. What kind of lady do you take me for?"

"One that's mine." He growls playfully, pulling as she pushes against his onslaught of kisses. Her squeal of delight is adorable, and when she breaks free, she takes off in a run toward the throne.

"Come here!" Apollo shouts, chasing after her.

Their laughter and mine blend, and this memory will forever be seared into my mind. They are winded and laughing when I gain the steps to join them. Hypatia's cheeks are a warm rosy color, her eyes shining like stars as she meets my gaze. Apollo caught her easily and has taken it upon himself to keep her contained within his embrace.

"Impertinent, willful woman," he scolds, peppering the back of her neck and behind her ear with kisses.

My two loves.

They soften me, challenge me in ways I never believed anyone could. When love is conditional, a man learns to guard his heart, but they have shown me what unconditional love looks like. I made sure iron ran in my veins, steeling myself against the cruelty I knew and the duty I was expected to uphold.

But then Apollo loved me. Saved me. Trusts me. Relies on me. And I was content with him until her. Until a field of daisies surrounded my heart. My equal. Until them, I had buried my feelings under the misconception I was hard to love. That I was meant for only two things: breeding and succession. But they love me, not for what I was but for who I am. Chipping at my armor until I am bare, then wrapping me in tenderness. It was effortless, this falling for them. As if I was always meant to.

"Cinthus." Her giggled call pulls me out of my thoughts.

I smile despite my best efforts to remain forever their stoic counterpart.

"Are you not going to come to my aid?"

"I wouldn't want to intrude on any lesson My God might be trying to teach." I wiggle my eyebrows at her, and she swats at Apollo.

"Brute."

"Your brute, little scribe. Yours."

He stops his halfhearted attack on her tender neck. She looks up at me through short, dark eyelashes that frame those beautiful gray eyes. I can't contain my need for her any longer. Reaching behind her head, I pull her to me and kiss her until she breaks away, panting. Her tongue sweeps along her bottom lip, and she slams that plump, mauve mouth into mine, grasping at me, tugging me to her. Running my hands down her back sends heat racing to my cock as I follow the line of intricate knots to the lowest point. When she steps back, I almost shiver from the loss of her warmth.

"I have a rather wicked idea." The spark in her eyes burns me. "Up for the challenge, gentlemen?" She shifts her gaze over her shoulder to Apollo, and the coy grin that tugs at the corners of that mouth leaves me feeling exhilarated. I'm ready to give her the reins and watch what she'll do with them. She's a temptress in a crown made for a goddess and a dress made for sin.

Both of us nod. Words are useless. I can almost hear Apollo's thoughts when she sits on his throne and leans back, crossing one leg over the other, her tattoo on full display.

"Are you wishing to be worshipped?" I tease. "I believe we have proven to be quite the devotees in the past, little scribe."

A clench in Apollo's jaw, the muscle bouncing in my peripheral, tells me he is just as curious about what she has in mind as I am.

"If you're asking for a throne, Hypatia, I'll build one," he coos at her, shooting me a look. "For I am willing to do the bidding of our goddess. She need only ask."

"Kneel." She points to the marble with one graceful finger. Apollo hits his knees, submitting to her and her whims. I remain standing, smirking; it will take more than a one-word command for me. When our eyes meet, heat flashes between us, sparking in the candlelight. She arches a brow questioningly.

"I'll not be dominated, Hypatia, even by one as alluring as you. It's my boundary, if you recall."

Shifting her weight, she relaxes into the chair. A test of wills has begun. "I think you'll want to obey this time."

Obey. The word rattles in my mind. I use it, freely commanding my lovers what I want. If I give in, will she use my willingness against me? An uneasy feeling creeps over me, and I try my best to keep it at bay. I give commands, not take them—not for a very long time. But if we are to do this, be this triad of sorts, I want to give some of myself over to her. My mind swirls.

Unsure when I closed my eyes, they fling open when her warm palms slide into place on either side of my cheeks, her face inches from my own. I gasp in surprise, not having heard her move from the throne.

"I have no intention of dominating you, Cinthus. I'm merely thinking of you, of your pleasure. So often you are on the fringes of Apollo and I. Tonight, I want that to change. But this only works if you trust me."

I nod because she's right. My inclination is to resist, to remain in control at all times, but having Hypatia so easily switch from submitting to me to commanding Apollo means there has to be a level of trust between us.

"I want to watch you kiss him."

She's telling me the order, letting me see it's okay to let her lead us. I slide to my knees, and Apollo immediately has his mouth on mine. Gods! This damn man. He kisses me with such intimacy, such sensuality, that any lasting resistance vanishes. His tongue dances with mine, entangling together, his hands in my hair, I sink into all of it. The way I need him leaves me vulnerable. A moan from him or me, I'm unsure, is low and rumbles through me. When we break, we are both panting. Apollo lays softer kisses on my cheeks, his lips skimming the crisp hairs of my beard.

"His armor," she commands from the throne, where she must have returned.

I realize as Apollo undoes the breastplate and tosses it aside just how much she enjoys watching us. Several nights ago, she was wild and unencumbered watching us, and tonight is the same. We are her aphrodisiac. Knowing this, seeing how she tracks our every movement, I use it to my advantage.

"Chiton," she pants.

Swiftly, I set to work removing Apollo's armor as well. My fingers are to the ptergues belted around his waist when mine hits the floor. A pile is growing of fabric and leather, and all I can think of is getting my hands on her. My chiton goes over my head, followed by Apollo's, and we are finally bare before her. The god of light doesn't wait for further instruction and instead begins kissing my neck and chest, where he stops, tracing the new mark with his fingertips. Love softens his beautiful face, crinkling the corners of his eyes. He bends and lays a kiss on the tattoo that binds me to him. Placing one palm against his cheek, I let my gaze capture his.

"Love you," I whisper, and Apollo nods, agreeing.

His hands travel down to my cock, that is standing up on its own. When he reaches for it, she scolds.

"Ahh, not so fast. Apollo, come to me." He's on his feet, leaving me on my knees before her. She touches him, and he jolts. Sliding her hand down and then up, keeping her eyes on me, she strokes our god. With each movement of her fist against his cock, she brings him close then backs off, over and over, bringing him to the brink, then denying him release.

Fucking Zeus!

I am breathless, painfully hard, and unable to move, even if I wanted to defy her. It's as though I'm tethered to the ground waiting to be told what to do next. She directs our god to stand beside her. When she turns to me, she crooks a finger, and I almost come at the anticipation she is causing. I rise to stand, and she shakes her head.

"Crawl to me, Cinthus."

All those months ago, I admitted to myself how much I wanted to test her, push her to her limits. Tonight, she is going to push me to mine.

She lounges back on the throne, her tattooed thigh on full display. "You want to worship me? I want to watch you crawl."

I can choose to obey; she isn't commanding me the way I do her. I can rise to my feet and refuse to comply. The way she keeps adjusting in the seat, I know she wants me to. She wants me to defy her.

Gods damn, I want to punish her.

I curl my fingers into a tight fist, then relax, my palm burning. My gaze flicks to the marble table, and I wonder how fast she'd orgasm if I scooped her up, bent her over that table, and spanked her ass until it turned bright red. Apollo is watching me. He knows exactly what I want, what I'm aching to do.

I choose to surprise us all. I crawl. The marble is cool under my palms as I stalk towards her. Both Apollo and my girl have widened eyes when I reach the throne. Rising, I cage her in, my hands gripping the arms of the throne, and I bring my mouth dangerously close to hers. She doesn't flinch, doesn't back away. Her eyes flick to my mouth and back up.

"That's all you want, little scribe? To see me on my hands and knees before you?" Her breath stalls as she looks up at me. I reach between us and uncross her legs, opening her up. Grabbing both her thighs, I yank her to the edge of the throne and revel in her sharp gasp. "What's next?"

"I want—want," she stammers, her pupils swallowing the silver color as she tries to regain her composure.

"Yes." My breath caresses her lips, and she whimpers.

"I want to watch Apollo suck your cock."

I don't know who makes the primal noise that bubbles from deep inside one of us. Possibly both. Either way, we lose our finely held composure hearing her talk like that. Scooping down, I lift her, trading positions. As soon as I'm seated on the throne, she scrambles off the side, giving Apollo room. His mouth hungrily finds my dick, and he does what he does best, taking all of me to my damn balls. Hypatia watches us, licking her lips and panting. Apollo releases, licking up my shaft when she hits her knees and joins him. Her tongue swirls with his, dancing across the steel rod that is my cock until I'm sure I'm going to explode.

"Fuck. Oh fuck, Hypatia."

"Don't you dare come, Your Highness. Not until you use your words and tell me which mouth you want on your shaft and which on your balls."

Both the god and I cuss. Apollo kisses that filthy mouth of hers, and I fist my painfully hard cock, willing myself not to release and scoot to the edge of the seat. When she looks up at me from her knees, I lose myself.

"You," I rasp, gripping my dick like it's a fucking lifeline. "I want your pretty lips around my cock and my balls in Apollo's greedy fucking mouth."

Keeping eye contact with me, she does what she's told. Apollo's warm tongue runs the width of my sack as she slides her tongue down my length. They work in tandem, tongues and mouths pushing me towards the edge. I do my best to last, but as her head slowly bobs down, I fist her hair in my palm and thrust deep.

"I'm so close. You'll take all my cum. All of it. Every last fucking drop."

My cock fills her mouth, making it hard to respond. She pulls off and flattening her tongue, licks the bead of cum off the tip, nodding.

"Answer. Fuck, Hypatia, answer."

"Yes, Cin."

"That's my good fucking girl."

When her lips surround me, I watch as Apollo moves behind her, slipping his hands over her curves.

"Spread your knees," he rasps while looking at me. When she does, he dips a hand between her legs, and she stops taking me to the back of her throat long enough to groan. Her head falls back against his shoulder.

"That's right. Gods, you're so wet." He locks eyes with me as he continues his delicious torture. "I need to watch you make Cin submit. He has wanted you all evening." His lips travel down her slender neck. "His thoughts have been loud in my head. Make our prince come with this pretty mouth of yours."

Her hips rotate at his words, her chest heaving as she brings herself under control enough to take me once more between her lips.

I'm undone. I don't last. I can't help the erratic thrusting, my hand going to her head to steady myself, not wanting to cover her face in my seed. Some leaks out the edge of her mouth, but she does as she's told, taking every last drop. Reaching forward, I wipe her mouth with my thumb. Apollo halts my hand and sucks the remaining drop off my thumb.

"Come here," I command, pulling her to her feet.

We move to Apollo's chambers, and I'm unsure exactly how. I care not. I need to fuck her. Punish her. Then fuck her again. Over and over until there is nothing left for us to do but collapse. As soon as I locate the mattress, I roughly toss her over the edge of the bed, face down, bunching up her dress that has somehow remained on, to expose that nicely shaped ass I love. I admire it, smoothing a hand, tracing the roundness, feeling her soft skin against my shaking fingers. She looks over her shoulder at me.

"Hands above my head like before? Or would you like to tie them behind my back, Your Royal Highness?"

Fuck me. The growl that comes with that loaded question is not of this realm. It's a beast clawing to be freed. I have lost control of myself and her. There is no domination here, only reaction to her every word.

"Fucking Zeus, sweet Hypatia," Apollo murmurs as he watches, fisting his cock. "That mouth of yours." He hisses air between his teeth.

"As I recall, you quite like this mouth of mine," she retorts.

"Grab the damn mattress, Hypatia," I grunt out.

My hand comes down, smacking her ass, and she fucking moans. *Moans*! Gods! I'm certain she'll orgasm in two more swats. I test the theory.

Smack.

Moan.

Her hips flex, and she squeezes her thighs together, trying to get any type of friction between her legs.

Smack.

"Oh gods, Cinthus." A low whine is my response.

"Fuck! You're going to come, and I haven't even touched you yet," I tease. For good measure, I dip a finger into her and find her soaked, glistening in the firelight. She rocks against me, wanting more. I deny her any release.

Smack.

Moan.

As much as I want to redden this ass, I want her more. Flipping her over, I drag her hips to the edge and open her wide to my hungry gaze. Burying my face between her thighs, I keep her spread open as wide as she'll let me. It takes maybe two licks and a flick to her clit before she explodes. Hard and fast, her body shaking.

Everything about tonight will be hard and fast.

I lap up everything she gives and continue. I want to make her orgasm repeatedly until she is hoarse from screaming out my name. Licking, sucking, playing with her clit, she is close again on the heels of the first. Stopping, I smack the inside of her tender thigh, and she cries out. I nip the pink mark and return to her sweet pussy.

Bringing her to the edge again, I turn to the other thigh, laying a smack on her skin before soothing it with a love bite. She squirms under me.

"Either let me come or fuck me, Cin," she growls.

"I don't believe you are in any position to make demands." Another smack to the opposite thigh and she cries out. We are both fighting for control. Both showing our teeth. It's fucking addictive. She reaches between her legs and rubs her clit, making sure to make eye contact as she does.

"I've never needed a man to make me come, Your Highness."

"Fuck!" Apollo cries out as he comes watching us.

I let her win. *Damn it.* I'd let her win any round we go, if I'm honest with myself. Grabbing her once more like a rag doll, I toss her to the center of the bed.

"Fine. You want to watch? So do I. Watch us. Apollo fucks me while I watch you play." It's not a request, and she knows it. I grab her chin. "Say, 'Yes, Cin.' "

There is no denying now who is in control. She's panting hard as she lays back. "Dress on?"

Chapter 36

The God

It has been weeks since I sent word to Artemis that Hypatia was staying. Weeks since the Summer Solstice Festival ended. This morning, I awoke with Hypatia just finishing her bathing and pouted most of the morning that I didn't get to join. Having her in my home, in my bed, is healing my weary soul. Her contentment is infectious. As my time is less overrun with meetings now that the palace is almost back to its routine, I have more time to spend with just her. Some afternoons I find her in one of the libraries reading books on any number of subjects, from crystal mining operations that are said to improve the empire and its magic, to the conduction of electricity throughout every province, not just where The King resides. With the heat refusing to give up its grip on the mountain and finally turning to autumn, I curl up like a cat with my head in her lap and listen to her read from one such book as she twists the curls on my head.

But watching Cinthus and Hypatia is a joy I didn't know I needed. The two frequently launch into lively debates on the good of our province, and Cin listens intently to her ideas, agreeing with some and arguing with others. She's made several improvements to his painting setup, including a metal container for his brushes, and introducing three fresh paints made from chemical reactions. Science and art, technology and math, dance in synchronized choreography in the minds of two of the most brilliant humans in the realms.

Night is her time to shine. She has become fixated on the rotation of the planets and is back to calculating how to determine the number of moons one planet has in our solar system. Her mumblings of numbers and drawings of constellations endear her to me even more. The three of us have fallen into a routine, a rotation around each other that is easy and light. Like gravity, we are held together, pulled towards one another.

Even in our happiest of days, there, in the pit of my stomach, gnaws the sense that Artemis won't let her go easily. That she'll take the one person that makes Cin and I complete, the missing piece we didn't know was missing until she came.

Hypatia and her knowledge as well as her hand in the keeping of history, artifacts, and scientific advancement is incredibly important to our empire. More important, I fear, than our love. My sister hasn't sent word or a feather or one of her nymphs to collect her right hand. Radio silence from my ever-opinionated twin is chilling in the light of the fact I haven't exactly told her *why* Hypatia is choosing to stay. In my petition, I simply stated she wanted to conduct further research, assuming it would pique her interest enough that Artemis would come, and I could explain our situation calmly.

The sense of dread I feel tears at my stomach and this afternoon it colors my attitude. That is until my sweet Hypatia enters an empty throne room, my smaller one used for special guests—that usually involves my sister, a few council members, warriors, Cinthus, and her. She's wearing a wild crown of purple flowers on her head that matches the soft purple of the peplos she's donned. Her feet are bare, and she has on limited adornments, choosing simple over fussy, flower crown aside. If I didn't know better, I'd say she has spent the day with Persephone, as she's ethereal and delicate looking. I rise from my work at the marble table and greet her.

"Afternoon, my dear sweet Hypatia."

She grins wider at my welcome. Her warmth radiates around us and despite my sour mood, I find myself smiling back. The fear that's gripping my heart lessens.

"I have something for you both," she says with a nod to one of the centurion guards I have assigned to follow her around. The palace may be empty save for the ones who live here year-round, but I'll not take chances with those I love. The gods are ruthless and will not hesitate to take out anger on each other. Or jealousy. Or any other emotion. The ones dear to me get extra protection for this reason.

Cin sets down his goblet and folds his arms, pretending to be formidable, but I know he'll roll like a scroll the second Hypatia does anything. Their love is beautiful to watch, so pure and full of respect. It makes me love them both all the more.

How in this empire did I get so lucky as to be favored by the fates?

Reaching into a leather bag the guard holds, she gingerly pulls out a wild mess of flowers—a stunning color of purple I don't recall coming across before. Separating the bouquets, I quickly realize the bunch are crowns. She gains a few steps to his wide desk and rounds it to sit along the edge. Cin was standing, looking over something, when she came in. He's now frozen, his eyes darting to mine, knowing if he tries to escape, she'll follow and force him to comply with whatever she wants. I've followed behind her, curiosity and all that.

"Bend down here, Your Royal Highness." She tugs on his breastplate, pulling him to her. Cin has the widest grin I have ever seen plastered across his face.

"Madam, I implore you," he protests as she places the crown of flowers on his head.

Like any good fairy creature, she ignores his pleas. "I was with the nymphs this morning, by where the Delphi priestesses worship." Placing her hands on either side of his face, she rubs her nose against his. Turning, she crooks her finger at me, and I shoot a helpless look to my prince, who shrugs and adjusts his crown, sitting down at his desk regally. "Just behind their temple is a field of purple flowers as far as I could see."

The crown is placed, and she smiles up at me as I straighten.

"When I saw the field, I had the most intense urge to weave crowns for all of us." Her hands find her hips, and she narrows her eyes at us. "Now, I went to all this trouble and spent hours making these. I expect them to stay on the rest of the day."

Bewildered, I glance at Cin, who frowns.

"The rest of the day, you say?" He smirks. "Even after the evening meal?"

"Of course." She pulls him by his breastplate once more, kissing him. "Now, don't you look formidable and handsome?"

"Or rather, ready for the festival of Dionysus," I chide. Turning to her, I capture her fingers, threading them with my own. "You're in a good mood."

"I am," she says with a sigh, sitting down on the desk and crossing her ankles. "I'm happy. So incredibly, incandescently happy. I was thinking of you both while I made these ridiculously silly crowns, and all I could think about was how happy I am."

Cin scoots close, touching her knee as she softly hums. Then, suddenly, she smacks her thighs.

"What else do you gentleman need to accomplish this afternoon? I have decided to break from my calculations and could use a distraction."

314

Taking her hand again, I pull her to me, off the desk, and twirl her. I don't know why; I just know I want to be in her orbit. Stopping with a light giggle, she comes up on her tiptoes and flings her arms around my neck.

"Dancing? I'm still a terrible dancer, Apollo," she breathes against my lips.

"I don't care." slipping my hands around her waist, I pull her closer. "You are quite proficient at other things more important than dancing."

"Is that so?" She raises both eyebrows, and I nod, our noses rubbing together. Capturing my lips, she murmurs something against them as I press my tongue against the seam, beckoning her to deepen our kiss. Her response is a tangle of tongues and soft sighs, and my hand finds her hair, holding her in place. She stops kissing first and I, in a moment of ridiculous lovesick impulsion, start raining kisses down on her face. Her eyes, her nose, her cheeks. She squeals, playfully pushing against me.

"Apollo!" she protests between shrieks and giggles.

Air moves on tight vibrations around us as if the very molecules have become angry all at once, and I have just enough time to twist both of us as a silver arrow goes whizzing dangerously close to my ear.

"REMOVE YOUR HANDS FROM HER!"

Neither of us move. Confusion crosses her delicate features as Hypatia tries to grasp what's happening. I shove her towards Cin and duck at another silver arrow that narrowly misses it's target. This one embeds in Cin's chair. Wide-eyed, I meet the pissed-off outline of my twin from across the room. Artemis is stalking towards us, the next arrow loaded, and an expression to rival Medusa darkens her face.

"Apollo." Her tone is deadly. I know she missed my head on purpose. It was a warning. Artemis is deadly accurate and she won't hesitate to embed one in my chest. Magic whines around us, tugging, calling to mine.. Our connection keeps us linked, and our magic plays off each other when we need it to. It's been that way since we were young but at this moment, I wish it wasn't so. Together, our magic is powerful, but it can also be the very thing that brings the opposite sibling to their knees.

Cin is standing in front of Hypatia, his sword drawn and a shield in hand—one we keep close, just in case. He's ready for battle and I worry she'll attack him before she listens to reason. Resisting the call of Apollon takes effort. I know if I transform into him, this altercation could turn into a bloodbath, and I can't risk it. So I fight to remain calm.

"I send my right hand to conduct research, ensuring her protection by sending a guard, and this is how I find her? Assaulted by the very sibling I was trying to protect her from!!"

"Artemis," I begin, but she whips around and aims her arrow at Cin.

"And you! I hold you to a higher standard. You just stood there, watching the attack." The bowstring hums and an arrow flies across the dais. Cin expertly deflects the deadly aim with his shield. Shoving our mutual love behind him, he places himself in harms way and I move to react.

"Artemis!" This time it's Hypatia that shouts. "It isn't what you think."

"Don't defend his actions. I know what I saw."

"You saw him kissing me." She steps around Cin, who grabs her and tries to push her behind his protection once more. "I wasn't being attacked, Artemis. He was kissing me and I was kissing him back."

She glances at Hypatia, then at me and back, trying to determine if what she's saying is the truth.

"You're jumping to conclusions again, Artemis."

Fuck, that was the wrong fucking thing to say.

The bow disappears and my sister rushes me, sending bolts of magic racing across the marble. They strike me square in the breastplate and I fly off my feet. I don't have time to react before she is above me. Her delicate silver wings flutter wildly, and she hits me with another direct blow of intense magic. Struggling to keep Apollon at bay, I refuse to fight back. From the corner of my eye, I watch as Cinthus, ever my protector, rushes to my aid. His steps fly and he twists, sending his shield like a discus flying through the air into the middle of the fray. Artemis throws a hand out, sending him flying backward off the dais and onto the marble below. He hits with a sickening crack, crying out, before he comes to a stop in a heap at the bottom of the stairs. I only get a few bursts of magic in as retaliation before she turns her full force to me again. Guards from every corner of the room swarm in, coming to stop her. I don't want to hurt her, even if she's wrong.

Hypatia screams her name and rushes forward as Artemis raises her arms to send another burst of magic. Hypatia steps between us and the magic that has left my twins' fingers screams towards my love. Doing the only thing I can, I throw up a shield of protection in front of us. Hypatia doesn't blink when the bolt slams into the shield, sending magic like electric currents splintering in every direction.

"Kill me instead," she yells, her hands up defensively. Cin and I both shout, our cries mixing with hers.

Artemis pauses her aggression. "Move," she orders, but Hypatia shakes her head.

"Hypatia!" Cin yells from the ground, holding his shoulder and scrambling to his feet.

"No." My beautiful, intelligent Asteria lifts her head and straightens her shoulders. She looks every bit the goddess I named her for. Unyielding. Unafraid. "If you're going to get pissed and throw magic around, then aim for me. Kill me. I am the one who went against my position. I haven't been conducting myself as your right hand, as an extension of your court. I've been inappropriate with a god, and his prince and have enjoyed every single moment. All rules I am to follow I broke. I'm the one that deserves your anger, Artemis, not them."

Artemis raises one eyebrow. "Them?"

"Yes. Both of them. Apollo and Cinthus. Both, Artemis."

I can't tell if what I feel is pride or fear. My sister looks at her as if she has lost her mind but lowers her hands all the same. It is then I notice the state of my throne room. Several guards have drawn weapons. Behind them, several more warriors. There are scorch marks on the marble, and my heavy throne has been moved several feet to the side. Purple flowers lay in disarray all around me, flowing down the stairs to where Cin stands. Artemis looks around my formidable protector.

"You've put her under some sort of damn spell, haven't you? Drugged her and used her for your own amusement."

"No," Hypatia snaps. "I chose them. I willingly and freely chose both. To give my heart to both. To love both."

Rising to stand, I place a hand on her shoulder. "It's no spell, Artemis. It's true. I wanted to tell you. We are in love—"

"No."

No one moves. No one breathes. The quiet of the room rings within my ears.

"You may not like it, Arte, but it's true."

She's glaring at me as though at any minute she'll return to blasting me with enough magic to leave me bedbound for days. I've been polite, considering, but her adamant refusal to accept that Hypatia is mine pisses me off.

"Despite your best efforts, it seems," I add because Cinthus is right, and I am an ass. Hypatia turns slightly and glares at me.

"I—"

"You refused to tell me where you hid her, *Artemis*." I spit out her name and let anger guide my words. "You knew I was searching for her, and you kept her hidden away in a palace where she isn't appreciated. Where her rank means more than anything else. You hid her out of spite and nothing more. So, if anything, you should be mad at yourself for sending her here knowing full well who she was to me. I would have had her in my bed much sooner had you only told me where she was."

At that, Hypatia whips around and gapes at me. "Apollo!"

It isn't the usual scolding tone she takes when she's playful. This is the tone from her early days. The one where I have to question if she isn't magical, because I swear she could kill me with the look that is burning in her eyes.

Fuck.

"Is that all she is to you? A body in your bed." Artemis asks, her voice cold and measured. I can answer one of two ways, and both, I fear, will bring her anger down upon me. I deserve her it, truthfully. Once I learned who Hypatia was, I should have stayed far away, but love rarely makes sense.

"No," my prince says. His arm is dangling oddly, and he's clinching it to his body. "No, she isn't, she is important to us. We are both in love with her."

"I asked him." Artemis tosses her chin at me but I notice the prince isn't looking at her as he speaks. His deep eyes are locked with Hypatia's.

"Cinthus is right, she is important to us.," I answer between gritted teeth. "I'm in love with her Arte. I'm hopelessly in love with both of them. Maybe if you weren't so blinded by being right, you'd see that."

Hypatia is still glaring at me and, by the thoughts she is drilling in my head, yelling a string of unladylike words, I deserve it. Artemis stares at us as she speaks.

"This ends now. You're coming back with me, Hypatia. Back where you belong."

The woman opens her mouth to argue.

"Now!" Turning her gaze to her friend, my sister tilts her head. "The library needs you; you belong there, not here with *them*."

"But Apollo petitioned for me to stay. I want to stay, Artemis."

She's shaking her head. "That isn't possible. You have work you need to attend to. Important work. Much more important than whatever it is you've been doing here. You should have returned when you failed to determine the new star. I should have collected you weeks ago. It is clear I was lapse in allowing you time to make certain you had failed."

Each time Artemis says 'failed,' Hypatia flinches, and a red-hot flame of anger begins to grow inside me.

"She didn't fail, Artemis. It isn't failure when she determined there wasn't anything new to discover, it was simply a theory. One she tested. One she worked for. How dare she be made to feel like her time here has been wasted," I counter, stepping beside my love. "She has made plenty of other discoveries here, advanced our empire, been brilliant. She has learned more from the transcription of the scrolls of the Oracle, information that is pertinent to our world.. Hypatia hasn't just been—"

"Fucking you," Artemis interjects. This causes the woman we are talking about to lower her head.

"Fuck you," I spit, and Cin shoots me a look. He's leaning against the desk as though at any minute he'll collapse. "You have no right to become so angry about anything that has happened between us when you refuse to listen to the entire story."

"Like hell, I don't," Artemis spits back. "Hypatia is needed. Her work in the library, her discoveries keep us advancing. Her position as my right hand elevates her and earns her respect amongst her peers. To stay here with you, reduced to nothing but what she can do for you is an insult to her intelligence and her station. I can't allow that. She can't have both, Apollo, and you know it. She deserves a better existence than you can offer her."

It hits me then, the truth I don't want to admit. All this time, I have been fooling myself into believing that if I only found her, if I knew her, I could keep her. That Hypatia was mine. That loving her would be enough to have her stay. But it isn't. She is much more a pretty face from a dinner. Much more than an infatuation, a dream I've conjured. Her duties mean far more to this realm. Olympus is ripe with power, magic, gods, monsters, warriors and yet it is her, my love, that rises to importance above all of us. She can't stay here and continue the work in the new Library of Alexandria simultaneously. She can't live in both worlds, can't be in both places. I meet Cin's eyes over the top of her head, and I realize he is coming to the same conclusion. And it's at that moment my heart breaks. Breaks in a way I didn't know gods could break. Turning her to face me, I wrap my arms around her, placing my forehead against hers.

"She's right," I whisper. Hypatia protests, but I continue. "You are needed more outside these walls than within. Gods how I want you to stay. I finally found you and you're slipping through my fingers. But you were never meant to be mine. Or Cin's. You've always belonged somewhere far more important than Apollonion." Shaking her head, she clutches at me as if that alone is all that is needed "Artemis is right, you are needed there."

"But—I made the choice, Apollo. I'm choosing you. I need you both. I want to stay." She sniffs, and I wipe tears that flow from those gorgeous gray eyes. "Please, let me stay."

Her whispered plea tears at my shatters heart, cutting the wound deeper, leaving me bleeding. "I love you, but I can't be selfish with you, Asteria."

"But I love you. Both. I can't go back without you. Without either of you."

"I know." Kissing her brow, I look over the top of her head at Cin, who is shaking his head. "We have to let her go," I say to him and almost crumble when I see his lips tremble before he tucks his emotions behind his steely demeanor. She's still shaking her head when I kiss her. She's still pleading when Cin comes up, and with one hand, thumbs tears over her cheek.

"You're hurt," she exclaims and wraps her arms around him.

"I'll heal, little scribe."

"I love—" her voice cracks.

He nods. "I'm aware."

"I'm not choosing to leave, Artemis. I don't want to go."

But my sister doesn't argue. She merely takes Hypatia's hand.

And then she's gone.

The Prince

It's been a month. Or more. I'm unsure how long, since Artemis came to claim Hypatia. Fall has taken over the mountain and turned our days colder. Colors burst with golds and reds, oranges and yellows along the hillsides and orchards. The harvest is in full swing, and it's been days since the autumn equinox.

It's fitting, now that she is gone, that most mornings are gray and lonely. It mirrors how I've felt. How we both have. My arm is still in a sling. When Artemis flung me across the room, I broke my clavicle and, even though I might be immortal, I'm not invincible. For a moment—lying on the ground, watching blow after blow rain down on Apollo, helpless to do anything about it—I thought I might die. The pain was so great, so excruciating, I did everything in my power not to pass out. I wouldn't have gotten to say goodbye if I had.

Apollo has returned to the moody, self-righteous bastard he was when I first came here, and I don't blame him. I have been of the same mind. We have been short with staff and councilmen alike. Apollo has reverted back to his old ways, from centuries before. The nightmares have returned with a vengeance and I'm not sure how long they'll last this time. We have each other, seek comfort with each other, but we are both painfully aware something is missing. Exhaustion has settled in my bones and my heartache in my chest, coloring my temper. I threw out a damn councilman the other afternoon from a meeting. Not figuratively, no, I picked him up and tossed his ass. I'm on edge and short tempered and so is my lover. We are a pair, him and I. Where I am usually the one who can talk some sense into him or clam him down, I have let him rage unchecked because truthfully, I want to rage. I want to storm Athena's home and bring back our love. I have sent missive after missive, feather after feather to Artemis begging she reconsider. All have been met with deafening silence.

I find myself in Hypatia's chambers this evening after Apollo awoke to yet another nightmare. Moving about her empty room is a metaphor of sorts for my hollow heart: empty, cold, and melancholy. Running my hand over her desk, I can't help the flood of memories that rush in. Ones where she is murmuring to herself a string of numbers. One where she perched herself on top of this very desk and lectured me about my insistence on the crops for the next year. Ones where she fastens metal to metal and creates something useful.

Opinionated. Bold. Alluring. Mine.

She is all of that, and so much more. Hypatia breathed life into us. She helped me see sides of myself I thought no longer existed. Different from Apollo. I miss her with an ache I can't shake.

She is my equal.

My equal and she's gone.

Chapter 37

The Scribe

"Y ou wanted to see me, My Goddess?" I bow as I always do, saluting Athena, defining her position over me. Months have passed, and I have fallen into a routine again, trying to fill my days as best I can. Athena looks up from her task. Beside the goddess, Aro, her owl, sits preening her feathers and looking unusually bored.

"Yes, Hypatia." Her greeting is warm, and I instantly bristle. Athena isn't known for anything that would be akin to friendship, so a companionable greeting sets me on edge. "I was wondering how the categorization of the scrolls you transcribed were coming along."

Sighing, I clasp my hands in front of me. She has asked similar questions as of late, and I am tired of being summoned to her chambers for daily reports. "Has my work been unsatisfactory in some way, My Goddess?"

The woman I was before—before them—would have nervously answered and tried her best to be as accommodating as possible. The woman I am now wants to be left alone. I hadn't ever thought of myself as imprisoned in the palace of Athena, but after tasting freedom and agency and choice, I reject anything less.

She jerks her head and motions for me to sit. I refuse. "No. In fact, from what I've been told, you have been dutiful. The library project is coming along, and I hear you are collaborating with Hephaestus with an invention of sorts."

"A prototype for now, yes. We have been discussing stronger and lighter weapons, shields, and things. It's still in the development phases, but I believe in time we will be able to present our designs."

She eyes me. "Excellent."

"Is that all?"

Drumming her fingers against the table, she fidgets for a moment, then sits back in the large wooden chair, folding her hands in her lap.

"If that's all, I'll return to—"

"You aren't sleeping." She lowers her chin and gives me a pointed look.

"I wasn't aware my sleep habits were of any concern of yours." I should learn to bite my tongue, but wounded as I am, I care not if I offend her. When I first arrived, I begged Artemis to send me back. I even came up with a solution to where I could live in both worlds, where all of us could thrive, but Artemis stubbornly dug her heels in. Alone once again. I hadn't realized all those centuries I lived in solitude how alive I could be. But one summer has shown me exactly who I am. I am Hypatia of Alexandria. I am the Scribe of Asteria. Because a powerful god and wonderful prince love me, I refuse to be anything less. Athena smacks the table, and I flinch.

"It has been months, Hypatia. When are you going to snap out of this?" She motions to me. "Whatever this is?"

I straighten my spine. "If my work is satisfactory and you have no complaints, I ask to be dismissed so I can return to the archives and finish my calculations."

She shakes her head. "I summoned you here to tell you I am sending you to the Cosmis Province."

My heart stalls in my chest.

"You need some time away. Some contemplation, perhaps. Artemis requested you be sent to her home through the winter solstice. Maybe if you take a few weeks, you'll come back in better spirits. I want to send you to the Phorcys Province on a diplomatic mission of sorts to greet the new ambassador Poseidon has installed, but I'm reluctant to do so given your current state. It's a matter that can wait a few more weeks until you are in a better temperament."

Of course, it would be to Artemis' home. She'd not allow me to go back where I belong. I scowl. "I am never asked to go anywhere, My Goddess. Why would you send me now?"

"The new ambassador has requested I send someone, and I thought it might do you good. You've never left Tellus before this summer, and I felt if you were more traveled—"

"I might just get over the fact I am not allowed to be where I want. That I'm forced to stay here, is that it?" Her eyes flash and for a split second, I worry I may have pushed too hard. Annoyed and angry, I give a sharp nod. "Fine, My Goddess, if you think it best, I shall go to Artemis first then to Poseidon to meet the new ambassador. If that is all, I'll return to my chambers to pack."

Turning, I don't wait for her dismissal.

"They are just men, Hypatia," Athena calls out as I march away. It stops me in my tracks. "You are intelligent enough to see that, aren't you? Your worth isn't tied to men, and the sooner you believe that, the better this empire will be."

"My worth," I say over my shoulder, "has always been my own, Athena. I have never needed someone to see value in me before I saw it in myself. But my heart—my heart belongs to them. They are just men, but they are *my* men." I leave the chamber without a backward glance.

Weeks have passed since Athena sent me to spend the winter solstice here in the Cosmis Province. Festivities filled my days, healing my heart, but my evenings remain barren and cold. Donning a heavy wool chiton, sturdy and simple, I wrap a wool himation around my shoulders, pulling the end over my hair and letting the rest of the fabric drape over me, keeping me warm. I hug my arms around myself, breathing mist into the frosty night air.

My balcony is one of only a few that face out into the woods that surround Artemis' home. The low light tonight obscures the moon, but I can still make out the peaks of the Hyperion mountains. My thoughts wander to them. I picture Apollo, dressed in his finest for the evening meal, his white cape wrapped around him to ward off the cold. Cin and his blue wrap come into sight in my mind. His beard is longer, I bet, keeping his chin warm in the winter. My men. The better halves of my soul. I play with the necklace, running it through the chain, feeling the stones between my fingers. Lost in a world I've created in my mind; I don't hear her enter my chambers until she clears her throat behind me.

Whipping around, I find Artemis leaning against the stone archway.

"You've missed four evening meals in a row," she says accusingly, pushing off the stone. "I was beginning to think you'd sequestered yourself in here as some form of protest."

"I'm not in the mood to join the others to eat."

"You haven't been in the mood for months."

"And your point?"

She flops into one chair and tents her fingers over her abdomen. "Don't you think all this moping is enough, Hypatia?"

I shrug. There is nothing I can say now that I haven't already said before. She grumbles low in the back of her throat and turns her face to the night sky as if pleading with Zeus himself to give her strength. If I wasn't so heartbroken, I might have called her dramatic.

"I'm not moping."

"You are. Gods, Hypatia, it's just Apollo and his prince."

"And when Orion died," I challenge, "how long did you, as you say, mope? How long did you grieve?"

She shoots me a cold look, and I say a small prayer she won't kill me where I stand for bringing him up.

"No one has died."

"Maybe not, but you silenced me in this matter. You forced me back to Athena's and into the library without allowing any counterpoints. You refused any suggestions I gave. Because of you, Artemis, my choice was taken from me. So, excuse me if I mope," I snap. In public, I wouldn't dare talk to her this way, but here, in my chambers, Artemis is not a goddess. Here we are on equal ground.

"Fine." Her annoyed answer puffs out like smoke from her mouth and floats in the chilled air.

"Fine, what?"

"You win. You win, Hypatia."

Creases form on my forehead as I pinch my eyebrows together in confusion. Pointing her finger at me, Artemis rolls her eyes.

"You win."

"I don't understand."

"You can return to my asshole brother's palace if that is where you want to be."

Still confused, I find myself shaking my head. "I beg your pardon?"

"You came to me with a plan for how all of this could work. How you could continue your work in the library and still be part of Apollonion."

I nod.

"Okay. You win," she repeats. "I'm allowing you to go. Go to Cinthus and Apollo."

Stunned, I try to grasp what she's saying, but my mind won't believe it. "What?"

Artemis stands and takes one of my hands. "I'm not a bitch, Hypatia. I hate seeing you like this. By throwing yourself into your work, I thought you would get over them. But you haven't. I thought bringing you here would ease your heartache but it hasn't. I'm still not completely convinced he hasn't put you under a spell." She squints as she speaks, turning her head as though looking for any sign I'm under the influence of magic. "Even so, I'd rather you be happy and content than whatever the hell this is."

I'm still not sure I've heard her correctly.

"Go. I don't know what you see in Apollo," she says, a half-smile pricking the corners of her mouth. "He's so arrogant. And that prince of his . . ."

"But Athena?"

She shrugs one shoulder and tosses her flaming red hair and it shimmers copper in the sliver of moonlight. "I already sent word you were going. Athena might rule over you when you are working in the library, but I have the final say, seeing as you're my right hand. You'll spend half your time there, from spring equinox to autumn but once the north winds blow, you'll return to Athena's." Wrinkling her nose, Artemis sniffs. "Will that be sufficient for you, Asteria?"

Apollonion is crowded as I push past several warriors. The feasts of winter solstice are over, but in true god of light fashion, he has invited the villagers into the dining hall. Music drifts around me and the marble under my feet vibrates with the heavy thumping of the dancers in the middle. I weave in and out of groups of men and Olympians half in their cups. Passing a long wooden table piled high with food and drink, I grab a glass off the table and take a swig.

Threading through the rambunctious crowd, anxiety gnaws at my insides. I didn't send word I was coming, choosing to surprise my men instead. But I can't help but wonder if they have missed me as much as I missed them. Taking a rather large swig that finishes the glass, I turn towards the high table. I arrived later than I wanted tonight, as I insisted on taking one of the bullet trains to the mountain. A slight delay unfortunately foiled my plan to surprise them both privately. I hadn't even had time to put my belongings in my chambers when I decided I would greet them in the dining hall.

"Lady Hypatia!" a warrior exclaims, greeting me with a wide smile. "We hadn't expected you to return."

"I have," I say. "I think."

"Cinthus will be so pleased," he replies, throwing back the last mouthful of wine in his glass.

Cinthus. My heart squeezes. *But not Apollo?*

This is beginning to feel like a terrible idea. I had made the god promise me there would be no one else while I was at the palace, but for months I haven't been. If he has found someone else, my time here will be very short indeed. I don't want one without the other, and I won't stay if I have to choose. My heart beats wildly in my chest, thumping against my rib cage. As the dancers part, I catch sight of the high table, but it is short-lived. I go up on my tiptoes, briefly thinking I can see over the crowd. The music crescendos and then fades, signaling the end of one of the dances. As people return to their seats in the momentary lull between songs, I catch sight of the table again. Cinthus sits, wineglass in hand, staring out over the crowd in his usual frowning manner. He slumps in his seat, his aloof posture when bored and wanting to leave. He looks burly and handsome, and I can't help the smile that comes the instant I see him.

My feet hurry towards them, towards home, weaving in and out of groups of people. The musicians play several notes and dancers move to the center, giving me an unobstructed view of the high table. Rounding the end of the row, I freeze in place. Cinthus sits in his chair and Apollo in his, but between them sits a pretty, dark-haired woman. Her cheeks are flushed as she laughs heartily at something Apollo says. He tosses her a cheeky grin and takes a swig of wine--the way he used to be with me.

I want to run. I want to turn around quickly so they can't see the disappointment on my face. So, I can disappear, return to Artemis, and put this whole thing behind me. I want to, but I can't.

"Hypatia!"

My name carries above the crowd, above the music and the laughter and dancers. Apollo snaps his head around, his eyes searching the crowd. Cin stood when he called. He is rounding the edge of the table, coming towards me with such purpose that I remain where I am, as though I am now stitched to the marble.

"Hypatia."

He calls again, and I wonder if he thinks I am a figment of his imagination. I am a damn fool. Apollo can only commit to a relationship with Cin. Logic told me this, but my damn silly heart believed he could choose me too. When Cin reaches me, his face explodes with pure joy.

"Damn the gods!" His arms go around me, and I am helpless again, lost to the feel of him. I throw my arms around his shoulders as he lifts me in what could only be described as a bear hugging a human. On instinct, I bury my face in his shoulder and breathe him in.

Laurel soap.

Setting me back down, he smooths hairs out of my face. "How are you here?"

"I see you've recovered from being thrown." It was the dumbest thing I have ever said to anyone.

Confusion and joy mix as his dark brown eyes with blue in the corners searched mine.

"How," he repeats. "How are you here? I sent letter after letter begging Artemis—" He hugs me again, kissing my brow, sliding his hands on either side of my face. "How?"

"Hypatia?"

Looking over Cin's shoulder, my heart drops to my stomach. Apollo stares at me, his head shaking in disbelief. His beautiful face contorts as his sky-blue eyes turn watery. I open my mouth to ask who the woman is. To explain that I understand he couldn't wait for me. That I will return to Artemis in the morning so as not to upset his newest lover. But the words die on my tongue. I don't know what to say or how to approach the subject. So, I twist my fingers in my palm and stare back.

Apollo is to me in two strides, his arms sliding around my waist, his wings cocooning us in downy privacy for a few seconds. When he pulls his head back, his face explodes into pure elation. His lower lip trembles as he continues to stare.

"Asteria," he whispers pulling me tighter to him.

"I didn't tell you I was coming," I begin, the words tumbling out of me while he presses his forehead to mine. "I should have, but I wanted to surprise you. But if this isn't what you want. If you have someone else, I—I can leave. I mean, I won't stay—if this isn't—"

He looks at Cin and then back to me. "What?"

I push out of his arms, straightening the chiton I wore, and trying to regain some semblance of dignity. I wanted to see them, and I have, so if that is all I am allowed, I have to be content with it.

"If you have someone else, Apollo, I understand. My boundary with you was clear and I haven't been in the palace for months, so I understand if you've changed you're mind. I want us. Just us, but if that's not what you want—. Cin is your forever love and I—I . . ."

He slides his hands on either side of my face and scowls. "You belong here with us, Asteria." He kisses my cheek. "How could we want anyone else?"

Tossing my chin at the high table, I do my best impression of a reasonable woman. "The woman at your table."

"Is one of the priestesses." He smirks. "She had just sat down not a few moments before. Jealousy looks good on you, Hypatia."

"I rather like it," Cin says with a wink in Apollo's direction.

"I'm not jealous," I retort, indignant at their insinuation.

"Of course not," he teases.

"Not in the slightest," Cin chimes in, and I huff.

"Brute."

Cin smiles as he grumbles low in the back of his throat. "I have missed you calling me a brute, little scribe."

"I have a name," I snap playfully back. Snorting in annoyance, Apollo takes my hand, kissing my knuckles before he begins pulling me through the crowd. "Where are you taking me?"

Pulling up short on the edge of the crowd, Apollo turns and pulls me in his arms. We stand in the open archway that leads out to the gardens as frigid air twists around our legs. The three of us bathed in soft moonlight.

Apollo bends and captures my lips, and despite the chill in the air, I melt. Next, Cin pulls me into his arms and kisses me as if I am air and he has been waiting to breathe.

"We have missed you."

Chapter 38

The Scribe

On the next Summer Solstice . . .

I curse in my native tongue and then look around to see if anyone noticed. One ever-present guard yawns at the far end of my study. No matter how long I've lived amongst the gods, I will forever be my father's daughter. And therefore, a sharp wit is better than a coarse tongue, or at least my father would have said. I grab a fresh roll of papyrus and sniff the edge. It is my favorite smell next to ink. Well, and Cin. A lightness settles in me the longer I'm here with Apollo and Cin. They make me happier than I have any right to be.

"Excuse me, madam."

A rich accent I haven't heard before cuts into my reverie. Peaking around the enormous rack of scrolls, I am treated to his back. His wings are white like all the men in Apollo's court, but the centurion cape is missing. He turns, and the sun plays amongst his flaxen strands.

"I apologize for the intrusion, madam, but I was told I was summoned." He inclines his head, and I briefly look around to see if Apollo had entered while I was preoccupied. Only me and my less-than-enthused guard.

"Summoned?"

"Yes. I was told one of Apollo's scribes summoned me." He tucks a hand into the leather strap that crosses his chest. That's when I see the wooden prosthetic hanging from under his tunic and remember I am the scribe.

"Oh yes! Me. I summoned you." I scurry over and lay the two new parchments on the table, scooting several scrolls to the side in an unorganized heap. He watches my actions with a scrutinizing gaze.

"Remind me," I say as I move to the opposite side of the table. The warrior steps back, giving me ample room to rush by. The action is a little odd, given most warriors tend to crowd my space. "You're Evander?"

He nods as he follows. "Evander Crossfield, Duke of Bradford." He shifts his wooden arm awkwardly and straightens himself—so incredibly stiff and formal. I tilt my head at his introduction. Most of the warriors merely grunt, some give me their name when I ask. I've never had any give me their human title.

"Am I supposed to be impressed?" The tick in his jaw tells me my joke isn't appreciated. "Never mind." I wave a hand and stop at the next table. "This is why I called you in."

Reaching under, I lift the heavy object onto the table, and it smacks the wood with a thump. He eyes the case with unease and stands even more rigid, if that were possible.

"I had hoped to have a better example ready, but you came more swiftly than most of the warriors. It isn't quite done."

"I obey all summons," he says simply.

I glance up and shrug. "Yes, well. So do other warriors. But they usually take their sweet time first." I grunt as I move the case and unlatch the buckles. "Hephaestus was rather helpful in making the metal parts, and I tried my best with the calculations. Since I didn't have a true measurement to go off of, I used my best judgment."

He furrows his brow and frowns.

"It was at Maximus' request, I assure you."

His scowl deepens into confusion. "Maximus' request for what, exactly?"

"Your arm," I say, spinning the case around to show him. He glances down at the shiny metalwork and back at me.

"Maximus thought you might like a new prosthetic."

"The one I have serves me well."

I eye the wooden arm hanging from its position. It was the best they could do in his time, I'm sure. In my days in the human realm, wounded warriors lived without their appendages. Technology has made advancements since then, but humans can only do so much without proper calculations. I, however, have access to crystals, and magic, and advancements mortals do not.

I smile reassuringly. "It may, but this one will allow full range of movement, grasping of your fingers, and such. And touch."

He looks at me with eyes filled with questions and I ponder where on earth Maximus picked up this warrior. England, obviously, from the accent. But he seems so young and so guarded all at once. He is coiffed and put together, if stoic. His hair is combed just so, held in place by propriety and good manners, if I had to guess.

"I assure you, it is well made. Shall I help you try it on?" I offer and watch as his face pales.

"I...um...try it on?" he stutters, and I snort at his uncomfortableness. I am used to walking out to the training yard and seeing men stripped naked, fighting each other in practice. Something tells me this particular warrior would never participate in that part of Olympic life.

"Yes," I say, picking up the arm. "Take off your tunic so I can properly fit it to you. I need to make sure this fits into the leather garter that holds your current one in place."

Looking around, he glances at the guard at the far end and seems to relax some. As if having someone else in here is better than just the two of us. I bite my lip, holding in a grin at his expense as he unlaces the front and back of his linen garment. Unlike the other men who wear a chiton, he's opted for a tunic and a kilted fabric under his pteruges. Another odd distinction amongst the warriors.

"Don't worry about Apollo." I wink, trying to reassure him. "He is well aware I have half-naked men in my personal study all day long."

The warrior clears his throat and blushes. Pink colors his sun-kissed skin and his cheeks heat. I give in to the laugh bubbling up.

"I wasn't aware you and Apollo. That is—I wasn't aware that Apollo—" He stumbles around for words, and I can't help another giggle as his tunic comes off. I don't dare tell him that my arrangement also includes Cinthus. The poor young man may faint at that admission.

"That I am Apollo's lover? Or that he liked women as well? Well"—I wrinkle my nose—"he does, and I am and proud to be."

He doesn't know what to say to that and chooses instead to stare straight ahead. That's when I notice his mark. The tattoo scrawled into his pectoral is that of Athena like all the warriors, but he has the telltale Greek E. *Circle of Epsilon.* A group of elite warriors that take vows to obey Athena in all her fickle endeavors. And all are celibate. I now understand his hesitation. Warriors can be ruthless to each other, especially if they want to climb the social ladder to get closer to Athena. One incident wrongly perceived could cost the poor man his life. He must be the one Apollo installed some time ago during the last solstice festivities. I make sure to keep my interactions respectful. I wouldn't be the reason any warrior met the wrath of Athena.

He quickly works the leather straps and unhooks his arm.

"Oh." I let slip as his wooden prosthetic comes off. "I was under the impression your amputation was total. To the shoulder, I mean. I made a space, but it might not be large enough."

Evander shakes his head. "No, madam. I prefer to wear a full prosthetic, but my nub is only to here." He points to his bicep.

"Well, now. This is only a prototype," I say as I fit his arm into the socket and attach the leather to the hooks, "so it may not fit exactly. Once we get everything sorted, your new arm will be to your specifications."

He buckles the leather expertly and his arm hangs into place. I make quick work of adjusting dials and knobs, making sure movement will be smooth. Those won't be part of the final product, but for now, are necessary. Tilting my head, I study him. I can't help but notice his handsome profile. Briefly, I wonder what made him choose this life as he tightens straps. He seems lost, a piercing sadness mars his expression. I can't explain why, but I feel like he carries a great weight. He's staring straight ahead, pulling himself back from engaging with me. I choose to ignore this.

"How long have you been a warrior?"

One of his striking blue-green eyes glances at me from the corner, but he answers. "I haven't been keeping track. Time moves so strangely here."

I agree with a twist of the last nob. "That's true. Decades in the human realm feel like only months on Olympus. I don't have the opportunity to go as often to that realm as you warriors. It's a blessing, really. I can toil away on machines and instruments to my heart's delight, unaware of the passage of time."

His turn to nod.

"I myself sometimes forget how long I've been here. It's been centuries, but it doesn't feel like it."

He turns to face me. "Centuries?"

I smile. "Yes. Immortality and all that. I was thirty when I came to Olympus. And I've been a scribe for almost"—I squint one eye against the sun as I look towards the ceiling—"a thousand years."

He furrows his brow and acts as though he's about to say something but doesn't.

"How does that feel?" I ask and he studies the arm. It moves and his face is so full of genuine surprise that I smile widely. With a loud compression of air, the entire arm shifts as he turns his hand over. He smiles, and a dimple appears on his young cheek, his eyes wide. His arm moves again and swings out. Evander laughs, and I can't help but laugh with him.

"It is the oddest sensation," he says and bends his arm, completely in awe. Light seems to radiate from his wide smile, and I find myself grinning at his innocent reaction.

"With practice, you should be able to move it as fully as your other arm. Now, like I said, it's a work in progress, so you'll need to report back to me every couple of weeks for a while until we get it fitted and working exactly as you need."

He stares at his arm, and I'm not sure he hears anything I'm saying as he opens and closes his hand several times.

"Now, it is made with crystals, so it should last for a long time without requiring charging. However, the case features a crystal lining." I show him and he glances up from his hand long enough to mumble something to the case before he goes back to rotating his wrist. "The crystals charge the arm, so it's best to take it off every night."

I'm lost in the innocent wonder on his face.

"Try your sword," I urge, and he snaps his head up.

"My sword?"

"Yes. Try to wield your sword."

Sliding his weapon out of the sheath with his left hand, he grasps it with his new prosthetic. The metal tip clanks to the ground, and he grunts. Evander tries again to pick it up, but it's like watching a new warrior learn to fight for the first time. He's awkward and clumsy.

"You'll need lots of practice with that arm if you want to be able to use weapons in combat."

"Yes. I do believe I will." He sheathes his weapon and touches his metal arm softly with his other hand.

"Can you feel that?"

His light-colored eyebrows draw together.

"Hold out your hand." Obediently, he opens the jointed metal, and I run my index finger from the palm down to the tip of his middle finger. He laughs and stares in wonder at his hand.

"Do it again," he says, and I resist the urge to ruffle his hair as if he is my son. His delight is endearing. I run my finger palm to pad, and he laughs again.

"By the gods! The strangest of sensations. I haven't felt anything but phantom pains since I was a lad."

He spends the next several minutes moving his arm with joy and wonder as I watch, enthralled in his childlike delight. After a half hour, he begins to dress himself, lacing with one hand before he realizes he has two. Another flash of excitement moves across his face and gently he uses both hands to lace his tunic. It's so innocent and wholesome that I soak up the moment. It's rare in the place I have grown accustomed to; it feels almost intimate to watch this young warrior discover a new world. The doors at the end of my study open suddenly.

"I thought you died!" An Irish brogue rumbles towards us. He's dressed as a warrior, but swathed in a saffron fabric, kilted and belted around his waist with a sash pinned to his shoulder. I now understand Evander's leaning toward tunic and kilt.

"I've been waiting nigh on an hour. All the food will be gone from the hall, *dearthair*."

Evander turns to greet the intruder with a half-snort. "If you thought I died, why wait? Why didn't you go to the hall yourself and eat?"

"I wanted to make sure I got your portion if you did die."

The man clapped him on the back.

"Oh! Look at your fancy arm! So, this is why you were summoned." He slaps the metal shoulder, and Evander flinches.

"Be careful." I scold and march between them. "It's only a prototype. It's not as sturdy as the one I will make once I get your feedback and adjust my calculations."

"My apologies for my idiot brother," Evander says, and jabs his metal elbow into the man's stomach.

"Liam," the other warrior says with a smile. His eyes are kind. "His idiot brother is named Liam."

They push each other and toss words back-and-forth. I am so absorbed in the show of genuine comradery that I don't hear them come in. When two strong arms skim around my waist, pulling back against a muscled chest, I jump. Looking up, it's my prince I see first. Cinthus offers a slow seductive smile, and I flush.

"So, this is where you've been hiding," Apollo says into the sensitive skin on my neck. I shiver and tilt my head. The two warriors stiffen, stopping their good-natured insults. Their warmth is gone in the sight of the god that is ignoring them.

"I apologize, My God. I was helping young Evander here with his new arm." I pat his arm and try to pull away, reminding him we are in public, but Apollo doesn't care and nuzzles my shoulder. "You remember, don't you? He's your Epsilon warrior."

"Yes," he says without looking up. "And are you finished? Are they dismissed?"

I keep forgetting that while I may not be anything in the way of a wife of Apollo, there is still respect for my position as his lover.

"Yes. Dismissed, the lot of you. Go enjoy the evening meal." They begin to walk off when I call, "Evander."

He turns on his heel.

"The case."

He comes back, and in seconds the two are out of my study, loudly tossing halfhearted insults back-and-forth. I thread my fingers through Apollo's curls as his lips make their way down my neck, grazing my shoulder. My gaze meets Cin's, whose eyes have turned that dark lust-filled brown I so enjoy.

"Are you hungry, little scribe?" The deepness of his timbre rolls over me, and I pull him closer, wanting both of them. My appetite for them hasn't wavered, it has only grown more intense the longer I stay with my men.

Cupping my breast, Apollo murmurs into my skin, "I believe dinner is served in our chambers, Hypatia."

"I believe neither of you intends to eat."

"Oh, but we do," Apollo mumbles.

I stall for a second and catch both sets of eyes. Running my fingers over Cin's rough chin and burying my others deeper in Apollo's hair, I sigh contentedly. "I love us."

And I do. They are my sun and moon, the light and dark of my world and I am delighted to be part of them. My two men pull me through the corridor and to our chamber.

About the author

E.M. Meyers lives in Florida with her husband, two children, and a
menagerie of animals
ranging from several chickens she calls her ladies, to two horses named
Coty and Dudley.
E.M. is a Texas girl at heart and has been known to kick up her boots....and
flop down on
the couch to read a good book. Preferably something from the romance
genre.
E.M. writes spicy fantasy romance that usually takes place on Olympus.
When she isn't
dreaming up wild plots involving gods and goddesses, you can usually find
her at her
favorite bookstore, handing out treats to the store cats and purchasing
books. E.M. enjoys
quiet evenings in her backyard oasis, time spent at the beach, and an
obscene amount of
coffee.

You can find her books on KU Amazon, Barnes & Noble, and many indie
bookstores across the US.

Join her newsletter and get updates on pre-orders, new works in progress, snippets, follower her on socials and much more.

Scan the code

Acknowledgements

Finishing my second book in under a year has been a surreal experience. It has been so many late nights and self-doubt. When you finish your first book, you think the hardest part is over, but I quickly found out how naïve that was. Even so, I would have never had the courage to write this book, let alone publish it, if it weren't for the support and love of the special people in my life.

I always start with my husband. That man loves me so damn much and is so proud of me. Thank you, babe, for once again being my sugar daddy and working hard for our family, then coming home and taking over so that I may have hours of uninterrupted time with my imaginary friends.

To my kiddos. My daughter, for being absolutely amazing. I am forever inspired by you. And it has to be said, since acknowledgments are tiny time capsules of the life of the author at that moment, you kicked ass this year and graduated high school AND your dual enrollment program with honors. You are going to go out and awe us all at university. To my son, you are the light of life. My sweet boy that keeps trying with a wild imagination that I am always inspired by. I love being y'all's mom.

waves HI MOM & DAD Y'all went to a book signing, talked me up, and are incredibly proud. But please, please, for the love of god, DO NOT read this book. No, I'm begging you. I love you both, but I will never be able to make eye contact again if you do.

To Beckie. You are my inspiration. My ride or die. My person. I can talk to at 3 am when I am doubting myself. The one who has helped me become more confident. And who will absolutely help me hide a body if I ever need to.

To my alpha readers: Ana, Andrea, and Sabine. Y'all read the earliest version of this book and encouraged me with your comments and your suggestions. You helped *Scribe of Asteria* better. You fell in love with Hypatia, Apollo, and Cinthus from the get-go, when I was still worried this book was going to be too spicy. You all read the passages and asked for more.

To my friend who read through Cinthus and Apollo's parts and made sure I was depicting them in a loving and healthy way. You are an inspiration to me. I adore you and your husband, but mostly, I appreciate you helping me make their love shine.

Thank you to my street team for supporting me and finding the words I write worthy of suggesting to other readers. I am always in awe that y'all wanna talk up my books. Your support means everything to me.

Thank you to the readers and fans who find Olympus so much more enjoyable than the human realm. Thank you for your emails and DMs. It is because of you, I continue to do this.

Thank you to Kim Cavrak at Spirit of Ebullience for the amazing cover. You, once again, knocked it out of the park. Your artwork is exquisite, and you are so damn talented. I will always sing your praises

To Heather, my editor. My dear friend and loudest cheerleader. I'm convinced you and I will be in our 90s, little old ladies sitting on our respective front porches, separated by an entire country, and I will send you another smutty retelling and you will get ridiculously excited. You, my dear friend, are my person. No matter the absolute emotional roller coaster this author life puts me through, you are right there with me. If we lived closer...

Being an author is magical. Taking twenty-six letters and turning them into moments that make reads giggle, sweat, laugh, and cry is truly magic. I can't wait to do it again.